PENGUIN BOOKS

A KNIGHT BEFORE CHRISTMAS

A Knight Before Christmas

CARA STOUT

PENGUIN BOOKS

PENGUIN BOOKS

UK | USA | Canada | Ireland | Australia
India | New Zealand | South Africa

Penguin Books is part of the Penguin Random House group of companies whose addresses can be found at global.penguinrandomhouse.com.

www.penguin.co.uk   www.puffin.co.uk   www.ladybird.co.uk

First published by Penguin Books 2025

002

Text copyright © Cara Stout, 2025
Chapter head artwork © Adobe Stock

The moral right of the author has been asserted

Penguin Random House values and supports copyright. Copyright fuels creativity, encourages diverse voices, promotes freedom of expression and supports a vibrant culture. Thank you for purchasing an authorized edition of this book and for respecting intellectual property laws by not reproducing, scanning or distributing any part of it by any means without permission. You are supporting authors and enabling Penguin Random House to continue to publish books for everyone. No part of this book may be used or reproduced in any manner for the purpose of training artificial intelligence technologies or systems. In accordance with Article 4(3) of the DSM Directive 2019/790, Penguin Random House expressly reserves this work from the text and data mining exception.

Set in 10.75/15.5pt Adobe Caslon Pro by Six Red Marbles UK, Thetford, Norfolk
Printed and bound in Great Britain by Clays Ltd, Elcograf S.p.A.

The authorized representative in the EEA is Penguin Random House Ireland,
Morrison Chambers, 32 Nassau Street, Dublin D02 YH68

A CIP catalogue record for this book is available from the British Library

ISBN: 978–0–241–69118–2

All correspondence to:
Penguin Books
Penguin Random House Children's
One Embassy Gardens, 8 Viaduct Gardens, London SW11 7BW

Penguin Random House is committed to a sustainable future for our business, our readers and our planet. This book is made from Forest Stewardship Council® certified paper.

To Dad, I love you
To Santa, for always making Christmas morning magical
Still waiting on the puppy though

1

GARRICK

The key to a successful break-in – own the place. I glance over my shoulder, and wink when I meet the wide-eyed stare of my date. Well, if we want to get technical, she was someone else's date when the night started. What can I say? The lady has excellent taste.

'I don't know about this, Bill.' She twists her phone in her hand, the light she's providing me to 'break' the lock fluttering to the side.

When my buddy Tyrone Boakye and I decided to crash a Halloween party a couple of cities over, we needed adequate alter egos. In my defense, I did actually say my name was Garrick, but there was a huge crowd, and she misheard, so I went with it. I'm used to playing a character. Usually, it's easier just to continue the charade in the off-hours.

'Look at me. Do I look like the type of guy who'd get you into trouble?' I flash my signature grin. The one splashed all over the poster of the theme park I am currently picking the lock of.

OK, truth? I don't have the slightest clue how to pick a lock. But it's not necessary when I have the key. Let's be honest: if she did happen to see me slip it from my jacket, she'd probably be relieved I wasn't *actually* committing a crime. It's the thrill that she's after – we both are.

That's the reason people love theme parks. Why Fairytale Gardens has been shuffling guests through these rusty turnstiles into a magical fantasy land for twenty-five years. All the thrills of danger, but none of the consequences that come with the real thing.

'You look a lot like trouble.' Her eyes sparkle, and I know I'm in. I push the side gate open with a dramatic swing. The scraping of metal on cement might scare off the average thief, but I'm not worried. 'Milady.'

I touch the small of her back, leading her into Fairytale Gardens' dark, frosty interior. The usually bright pink, blue and sandy-colored Arthurian-style architecture is merely shadows in the background of our evening. I almost prefer FTG (our nickname for the park) in the off-season. The dark rides glisten in the late-October frost. Wait, it's past midnight now – guess it's November.

The park will open next week for the first Christmas season ever. A few catering gigs and events won't keep us afloat, so it's time for some actual revenue. It'll save us. At least that's the spiel Dad and my brother Ivor gave.

Last summer, FTG had a bit of, well, let's just say, *negative* press. Dad was accused of creating fake charities and taking donated money for himself – it blew up online. Imogen, my brother Tristian's girlfriend, was responsible for the whole thing. Seeing the error of her ways, she helped us clear his name, but the damage was already done. People didn't trust us.

We've spent the last five months building it back. We've just about gotten there, but we're still only as steady as a newborn giraffe.

My throat tightens at the idea of the park going under. But I quickly shove that all aside.

'What if we get caught?' Jen wraps her arms around mine, leaning further into me.

Wait, was it Jen? Or Jem?

'Maybe you'll get to see my sword work.' I *might* have forgotten to mention my family owns this park and that everyone is gone for the night. But again, it's all a pretend thrill.

I flip a switch on the carousel – the poor old guy takes a few minutes to get going, but then he's up and running. I shudder to think that one day I might say the same about myself. But I'm only seventeen, lots of years ahead of me. Course, I know from experience that all the years you think you're entitled to aren't always guaranteed.

I help Jen on to the wooden horse, stepping off to click 'start', when a voice pierces through the merry music.

'Garrick, what are you doing?' My twin brother, Tristian, being the absolute buzzkill that he is, walks toward us. Luckily, we're fraternal, so the looks won't be a dead giveaway we're related. I got bright blonde hair from our mom, and he got light brown from our dad.

'Bill?' Jen – I'm going with Jen – calls from the ride.

I shake my head slowly at Tristian, sliding a hand across my throat in a slashing motion, telling him, without words, to *kindly, screw off.*

'Really?' He doesn't understand or care that he's blowing

my cover right now. 'Do you know what time it is?' He sounds so much like our older brother.

'I don't know, *Ivor*, what time is it?' I push a hand through my hair, leaning against the railing. I shoot Jen a quick smile. 'No worries. I'll sort it out.' I turn back to Tristian, lowering my voice. 'Scram or I'll tell Imogen you wet the bed until you were ten.'

He scoffs. 'That was Aldrich.'

'Who's to say? Either way, I'll tell her it was you. Now, go. I'm clearly busy.'

But it's too late: Jen – dang, actually, I think it was Jem – is off her horse and twisting through the others back to us. 'Do you know each other?'

'No,' I say, as Tristian says, 'Yes.'

I suppress a growl. I cherish my little bro – by five minutes – love the guy. But right now, I wish he was anywhere but here. He's killing my chance at a distraction for the night.

'I'm Tristian, Garrick's brother.' He puts his hand out to shake hers, but she keeps them folded in front of her.

'*Garrick*, is it?' Her voice is edged with annoyance.

'Middle name.' I sigh, already giving up on this night ending with anything other than a bag of Halloween candy pilfered from my youngest brother, Aldrich. I have to get them while I still can – at fifteen, this is probably his last year going out trick-or-treating.

'So, you like work here or something?'

'Or something. Come on, Jen.' I mumble the name, in case I'm wrong. 'Does it really matter that I might have told a *little* white lie? It's all for fun.'

My hopes rise momentarily when it looks like she's about to change her mind, but then logic takes over, and I can't blame her. I lied and brought her to a theme park in the middle of the night. Even with all my privilege of being a guy, I know that's not a good look.

I scratch the nape of my neck. 'I'll take you back to the party.' I push myself off the railing.

'No, thanks. I drove. I'll see myself out.' She shoves between us and heads back the way we came.

'Does that usually work?' Tristian asks as I flip the ride to 'start'. We both got revved up, so there's no use in wasting the old boy's time for nothing.

'Quite often, actually.' I jump on as it starts moving, sliding on to my favorite horse – the one with the blue sash and the black mane. The familiar shape of the worn-down seat feels like I'm where I'm supposed to be. I carved my initials into the underbelly when I was six. Every time it gets a paint touch-up, I have to go back and retag it.

'Why are you here, T? I thought you and Imogen were going to a party. Or handing out candy? What do boring couples do these days?' I make the joke with ease. They always come that way. But there's an annoying little twinge in my chest this time. Tristian and Imogen have been dating since last summer – when she tried to destroy our theme park by accusing Dad of the previously mentioned charity fraud. They managed to sort out the drama. While I don't subscribe to the love thing, they seem happy.

Tristian is on his horse a few feet away. 'We did hand out candy, but all the kids are asleep by now.'

'Not if they did trick-or-treating right. They should be on a straight sugar high.'

'This little stunt doesn't have anything to do with Dad rejecting your idea about the fencing camp, does it?' Tristian's voice is carried away on the wind.

Licking my lips, I shrug – a move I'm pretty sure I perfected in the womb. 'It was just an idea. I come up with great ones all the time, so it's no biggie.' This is my second white lie of the night. The fencing camp *was* a brilliant idea, and it did sting when Dad turned it down. I wanted to use my skills to teach kids who needed a place to go when things got tough, somewhere they could escape their own brain for an hour or two. I floated the idea of having it at Knight School and offering it free of charge.

Dad said he didn't have the money or time to fund a non-profit of this scale at the moment. So, like not a 'No, never going to happen', but I've been around long enough to know that it might as well have been.

'So, who was she?' Tristian pesters after a few rounds of merry music.

As we spin, I can just make out the Christmas decorations we've been setting up around the park over the last few weeks. The colorful light bulbs are dark as the festive ribbon blows in the breeze, along with the bells and baubles lining the massive garland strands and oversized wreaths. 'Jen?'

'I thought last week it was Tamara?'

I grip the restraint wrapped around my hand. 'That was last week.'

Tristian lets out a low whistle, and I roll my eyes before he even talks. I don't know if it's the twin thing giving me a telepathic preview of what he's about to say, or it's just that he's so freaking predictable.

'At this rate, you'll be alone forever.'

'Nah, I'll just pick a new dating app. They have a few for eighteen and under. I heard about one launching in the new year I can't wait to try.'

'I'm serious, G. Don't you want to find love?' He doesn't sound judgy, but I grind my teeth all the same.

The carousel stops, and I leap off like it's on fire. 'Dude, you're such an old man. We're seventeen. Live a little.'

Tristian from last year never would've talked like this. But ever since Imogen, he's all starry-eyed and love-drunk. And look, I'm happy for him. After Mom died two years ago, everything was crappy for a long time – some things still are, probably always will be. I doubt we'll ever truly get over losing a parent, especially one as great as my mom. I was her little buddy. I used to stand by her in the kitchen and watch everything she did, absorbing it like a sponge. When I'm at the stove now, sometimes I swear I can still feel her beside me, guiding my hands.

So, it's great to have the old Tristian back, but just because love and happily-ever-after are what he wants, it doesn't mean the rest of us are on board.

'You ready for next week?' I ask him as I shut off the ride and we head home, pushing aside the heavier thoughts so they don't drag me down.

'Actually, yeah. I think it'll be good for the park. Don't you?'

A hand grips my gut, and I nod. 'Freaking hope so.' I need this place to get back on solid ground because it's the only plan I have. I've never been the guy to have grand visions for the future. Not like Tristian. He wants to see the world and make his own way. I live moment to moment, and I hope when I leap there's something to catch me. FTG was always supposed to be here. I'm going to play a knight till I die, and I couldn't be happier.

So, it can't fail.

It doesn't take long to get home since our house is on the edge of the property. Dad and Aldrich are already asleep. I snag a few pieces of chocolate from his Halloween candy stash. The kid tried to hide it, but I'm like a bloodhound – I always find it. I head upstairs and crash into bed, ignoring the pile of clothes on the beanbag chair I was supposed to put away and the mountain of homework I've been avoiding like the plague.

My bed is shoved against the wall, with a few posters from the park taped to the ceiling. They're older ones I saved from the trash pile. I like the retro designs. Mom used to help make them: I don't know if she did these exact ones, but I like to think so.

This was Ivor's room, but I commandeered it as the new oldest when he got married and moved out. Sometimes, I find myself missing the sounds of Tristian in the bottom bunk. We'd shared a room forever. But, more or less, I'm used to my alone time now. This room does have a great view of the castle spires and doesn't smell like Tristian's farts. I was planning on moving into the FTG apartments when I graduated high school, but then freaking Dad dropped the bomb that they're tearing them all down next year to build an addition to the park. Apparently, we were wasting valuable real estate – Dad's words.

It's fine. I'll pivot. I'm the guy who never lets anything bother him. *Garrick, it'll just roll off his back – no worries.* And sure, usually that's true. But when I lie here in the dark, just me with my thoughts as company, those worries aren't so easy to let slide off. I need Fairytale Gardens. I don't know who I'll be if I'm not the dashing knight in this dusty old theme park.

Tristian is making college plans, and while campus life does have its appeal, the actual classes do not. Everything is changing, and I just want it to stay the same. Ever since Mom died, it's been hard to keep my footing. Everywhere I step is a pile of quicksand. My body is constantly on high alert so I don't fall through a trapdoor.

I just need to make sure this holiday season is freaking amazing. Then at least one thing can stay the same.

2

RIPLEY

I'm eating baby food for breakfast. Technically, it's toddler food – little puff cereal balls in pastel colors because they're made with natural ingredients. And also, it's not really *my* breakfast. It's my niece Molly's, which she refuses to eat, so I'm trying to show her it's not that bad.

Spoiler: it's gag-worthy.

'No.' Molly crosses her arms in her chair. Her purple bow clings precariously to her brown curls as she shakes her head.

I glance down at my watch, nerves flaring when I see time slipping away. She's supposed to be at preschool in ten minutes. I volunteered to drop her off before I head to school. 'Molly –' I lean down and whisper so my *very* pregnant sister, Anna, won't hear – 'if you eat this for me, we can get ice cream later. Deal?'

She breaks into a grin that makes her look so much like her mom. 'Deal.' She shoves a handful of cereal into her mouth. I remind her to chew before swallowing as I get up to help Anna, who's spilled her purse contents all over the floor.

'I got it.' I squat, grabbing the runaway items. Anna's house is cozy, with a rustic fireplace in the center of the living room, accented by wood trim and paneling on most walls. It's a few steps away from being a full-blown cabin. I'm not a nature person, but this kind I can get behind. It's like being hugged by a tree.

Huffing, she pushes hair out of her face, the same ink-black color as mine. 'Thanks, Ripley. Seriously.' She leans against the couch, hands coming around her *huge* belly – something I would never voice out loud, obviously. 'I don't know what I'd do without you. With Mike traveling for work, I'm burning the candle at both ends.'

Mike. I curse silently, grinding my molars. Anna's no-good husband is never around, even when he is home. If Anna hadn't got pregnant with Molly, I wonder if they'd still be together. They never seemed like they were in love. Then again, most people who say they are usually aren't. It's best to avoid the whole thing, if you ask me.

'Molly,' I call, rechecking the clock. I loathe being late. Watching time get away from me is like a woodpecker *tick, tick, ticking* against my skull. 'Time to scoot. Anna, maybe you need to use Mom's app to find a husband who'll be a real partner.'

Again, I don't believe in that crap. True love, happily ever after, blah, blah, but Anna does, and so does our mom. That's why Mom runs a dating app and has been married four times – the latest ending a year ago. I haven't bothered to form a relationship with any of the husbands – my birth father included.

'Juliet, stop.' I know my sister is serious when she uses my first name. No one calls me Juliet except Mom and teachers on the first day of school. I hate it. I refuse to share a name with a tragic chump from a centuries-old play who was so conned by love that it ended up killing several people. If that isn't a life lesson that infatuation is dangerous, I don't know what is.

'Just a suggestion.' I keep the rest of my opinion to myself. Secretly, I think Anna only stays with Mike because she doesn't want to end up collecting as many divorces as Mom – got to love generational trauma. It's like she's trying to prove that the apple did fall very far from the tree.

I shoulder on my backpack, spine aching from the weight. I'm trying to graduate early, but so far, junior year has been the toughest yet.

My phone rings as I strap Molly into her car seat. 'Ugh,' I mutter.

'Ugh!' Molly copies me. I need to be careful what I say and do around her. She's in the mimicking stage.

I bite my thumbnail – a nasty habit I can cope without most times. I debate not answering as Mom's face stares up at me. But if I don't, she'll just call back and then call the police if I don't pick up that time.

'Hello?' I put the phone on speaker as I slip into the driver's seat. My car is relatively new, a gift from my father on my sixteenth. Probably hoping I'd forget that he wasn't there most of my life. I didn't forget, but I accepted the car all the same.

'Juliet, dear.' Mom's voice fills the car and I'm immediately on edge because she's using her extra-nice tone. 'I need you to come by the office.'

I pull out of the driveway, Molly singing a song from her favorite cartoon at full volume.

'Sorry, Mom, I can't hear you. I'm taking Molly to school.' I nestle my face into my knitted scarf. The air is crisp this morning, the windows dusted with a light frost. Orange leaves are scattered on the ground, the trees shuddering with their newly empty branches, all signs the winter season is nearly here.

Mom is unfazed by my attempted sidestep. 'I need you to come by the office before school.'

I use my arm to brush hair off my face where it escaped my ponytail. 'I don't have time. I'll be late.'

I love my mom, really, but she does not take no for an answer. It's her way or the highway. Apparently, stubborn runs in our family because I've been told the same about myself.

I can hear her typing on her computer – ever the multi-tasker. I remember my ballet recital when I was seven, and I looked into the audience to see Mom on her phone instead of watching me. That's one of those core memories I don't think will ever go away, no matter how much therapy I have. At least now I understand that she works tirelessly to ensure that Anna and I are always provided for. It's hard to be resentful when you think of it that way.

'I'll write you a note to skip first period.'

I hate to miss school, but I wouldn't put it past her to show up and have me pulled from class. No, it's better just to get it handled now.

I sigh, giving in.

The first thing I notice when I get to Mom's office is everyone is on their phones.

'Finally.' A twenty-something guy I've never seen before rises from his desk when I approach. 'Ms Ripley has been waiting for you.' I don't miss the undertones of annoyance.

'Sorry.' I offer the usual platitudes we have drilled into us as girls. 'I don't think we've met. I'm Ripley.'

He doesn't look at me, just keeps typing on his phone. 'I'm aware. I'm Brett, head intern. I'll be interning for the duration of the show.'

Pressing my lips together, I hold in my retort. I'm pretty sure all the interns are on an equal level, but sure, Brett, you go ahead and think that. 'Is there a problem?' I ask, noticing the tension vibrating around the room.

'Where to start?' Brett rolls his shoulders. 'First, there was the article about the top-performing dating apps and the ones that have fallen behind. Beeloved is at the bottom of the list. Couldn't ask for worse timing.'

Mom started Beeloved fourteen years ago, after her divorce from my dad. I was a 'let's-save-our-marriage' baby, which clearly didn't work because I was three when they split. It was a bitter divorce. Beeloved had wild success in its first five years, but it's taken a hit with all the new ones coming out.

I know Mom is proud of what she's created here, but I can't count how many times reporters have pointed to her divorces as the only reason she came up with the idea. Like without a man, she wouldn't have been successful. I would hate for people to think that I only made something because of someone else. That's why I have decided love, and all its ick, has no place in my plans.

My stomach twists as I glance at Mom pacing in the glass-enclosed boardroom. I know she loves me and Anna, but Beeloved is her baby too. Honestly, I think she's put more effort into raising it than she has us. Still, I don't want it to fail. Good thing I was never the jealous type.

'Then,' Brett continues, stalking toward the boardroom, 'our lead dropped out.'

'Monique?' My shoulders tense up as I analyze the situation. 'Really? But she was so excited to be the star.'

'Cold feet.' I can tell Brett doesn't actually know the reason Beeloved just lost the star of their upcoming reality dating show. But guys like him like everyone to think they're in the loop. I make a mental note to ask Mom for all the details later.

The youth version of Beeloved is launching in the new year and to create buzz they're airing a reality dating show based on its algorithm. It's all Mom has been able to talk about. She came up with the idea after she and husband number four split. When she can't find love for herself, she gets it for others. I use the word *love* generously. Everyone knows that's not what these apps are for.

Every seat in the conference room is full, along with interns standing by the windows, tablets in hand. This production isn't network TV big, but Mom and the team scored a significant investor, giving them a healthy budget to work with. The office has swelled with the addition of ten interns and the twenty production team members they hired to work alongside the Beeloved crew for the filming.

Someone offers me their seat and I slide into a chair at the back of the boardroom while Mom stands at the front. She's dressed in her usual business attire, a trouser suit in one of several varying colors. Today, it's a deep red – war mode. Her outfits are like a mood ring for everyone to see. She has the same dark hair as me, but hers is cut into a short bob.

'OK, everyone, I know we've had some hurdles to overcome this morning. But good news first: I'm happy to say we're in the final stages of contract negotiations with Fairytale Gardens, just dotting the i's and crossing the t's. This location is really going to make our show stand out. How many dating shows have you seen set at a theme park?'

She pauses, then adds, 'I know some of you voiced concerns about the negative press they received last summer, but I assure you, we did extensive market research and concluded that public opinion has shifted favorably.'

Everyone smiles and murmurs their agreement.

I frown in confusion, still unsure why I needed to be here. It certainly isn't to give my praise for a theme park. I've never even set foot in the place. Which Mom might say is a lie, but technically, when she brought me there, I was a baby in a stroller, so my feet never touched the ground.

When she told me this was the venue they chose for the show, I was shocked. Sure, at one point in time this place held a spot in her heart. It's where my parents had their first date. But that marriage ended terribly, so why would she want a daily reminder shoved in her face?

Once again, I do not get the psychosis love inflicts people with.

'Now to the less great news,' Mom continues. 'I can confirm Monique will no longer be starring in the show. I know this is extremely last minute, leaving us little time to find a replacement.' I watch the familiar lines of stress appear around Mom's lips before they disappear. 'But, as with love, sometimes serendipitous things happen.' She glances at me with a smile.

I stiffen in my seat, fingers digging into my bag. I don't like where this is going. If dating apps are fake, reality shows are on an entirely new level. Everybody knows those people just want to get famous. So, why am I here? She probably wants me to get kids from school to volunteer to be contestants.

I can't think of anything more mortifying than asking my peers if they want to be on a reality show. I already get enough crap when they find out my mom owns Beeloved.

I shrink into my seat, hoping she'll just forget about me. She's done it plenty of times before.

'Juliet . . .' My mother smiles at me. 'I want you to step in as our star.'

3

RIPLEY

Is she out of her mind? I grab my bag from my car when I arrive at school, nearly ripping off the strap when it gets caught on the doorframe.

Me, the lead of a reality dating show? Absolutely no way that's happening. I would rather walk across a thousand Legos barefoot than be anywhere near those cameras. And when I explained that to Mom, she had the audacity to guilt-trip me with logic. Thus far, the investors have only agreed to fund the show. If it goes well, they will continue to invest in the app itself for further growth after the initial launch. Which means if the show never gets off the ground – or is an utter disaster – everything Beeloved and Mom have worked for will be at risk.

Obviously, I don't want Mom to lose her livelihood, but I also know that me as the star is not the solution she thinks it is. I'm just convenient because there are less hoops to jump through.

I'm fuming, cheeks flushed as I walk into school. I hate that my body always puts on display my inner turmoil. First period is nearly over, but I should be able to get in and see what I missed. I try to take a few calming breaths. I have an app that's supposed to help, but I refuse to pay the monthly fee any more. I'm so tired of living in a subscription world.

I place the backs of my hands on my cheeks. The cold feels good. My body takes a few minutes to react, but the heat on my cheeks isn't cranberry red any more – just a soft cherub pink, or a mad Cupid.

Walking to class, I formulate an exit strategy for this whole reality show idea before Mom lets it get too far. She said they had a pool of candidates for me to choose from. They just need to narrow it down asap to prep for filming starting next month.

As my mind spirals, assessing all the ways this could go horribly wrong, I bite my thumbnail again. That's the second time this morning Mom has pushed me to the edge. I try to rein it in before I lose it completely.

This is fine. I can fix this.

All I need to do is give Mom a better star than me. Shouldn't be hard. I don't exactly scream leading lady material. That's why I can't figure out why she picked me. Maybe she's projecting her lack of love on her closest living relative.

Speaking of – my phone buzzes with a text from my dad. It's a message to pass on to Mom. They've been doing this since forever. First, Anna was the translator, but now that she's out of the house, it's my job. The messages always have a bitter undertone. All these years later, they still haven't let it go.

Is that all life is? A string of messy breakups that destroy you every time. Or worse, being stuck with someone you hate simply because you can't afford to go it alone?

As I slip into my seat in class, next to my two best friends, I'm once again thankful that I've already decided to skip the whole love thing.

'Oh no,' Nathan says as he glances up from his computer. His red hair is messy on top, where he's been fluffing it. It's barely November, but he's already counting down the days to Christmas. He's wearing his favorite Santa earrings with the bright, glittery fake snow on Santa's rosy cheeks.

'What?' I pull the neck of my camel knit sweater, worried I got Molly's breakfast all over me. The rest of the class is busy listening to the lecture, but a few near us glance back. I scoot lower into my seat. I'm not a fan of attention unless I've initiated it. Again, another reason me and a camera won't mix.

'*What?*' Melika, my other best friend, echoes. She's got her tablet up, but instead of schoolwork she's tracking her eBay bids. Melika's family owns a wildly successful chain of authentic Hawaiian bakeries – they use recipes handed down from generations, but she's not ready to join the family business. She wants to own a vintage store one day and is always hunting for unique pieces to sell via her online shop.

'You're in a state,' Nathan answers for Melika, who's furiously punching away at her screen as she does all she can not to get outbid.

'I'm not.' I don't look at them as I yank out my tablet to copy the notes up front. Next to my tablet I'm surprised to see one of Molly's favorite picture books. I pull it out, having no idea how she snuck it in there, and place it on the desk.

'OK, we'll circle back to your state in a moment, but first –' Nathan grabs the book, flipping through it – 'why do you have a Fairytale Gardens storybook? Please tell me you've finally decided to give in and try a roller coaster.' His eyes light up like Santa came early.

'I have not.' I take notes to distract from the dry mouth and heart palpitations. 'Molly must have put it in there.'

'You're really missing out, Rip,' Melika says, re-entering her chilled state now that she's won her bid. She is usually the tame cat, but her lioness emerges when she's determined.

I don't do theme parks. Nathan and Melika go every year, but it's just not my vibe. I hate all the noise and heights and the feeling of head-spinning nausea. 'Yeah, I just don't get the appeal.' I'm feeling a little better, now that I'm back with them.

'I'll give you appeal.' Nathan grabs his phone and shows me a picture. 'This smoke show is one reason. Sir Kendrick, be still my heart.' On screen is Nathan, next to a guy our age dressed like a knight.

'Is that Garrick Walton?' I zoom in on his face. His bright-blonde hair shines in the sun; his sun-kissed skin and charming smile are almost as bright. There's a look behind his eyes that tells me he knows he's hot.

'Yeah, you know his family owns the park, right?' Melika says.

'Of course I do.' Everyone knows the Waltons. They've been wildly popular since we were kids. I've barely said a handful of words to Garrick. We don't run in the same circles. I've had a few classes with his brother Tristian, but that's about the extent of our interactions. Still, I have admired him in the hallways or across the cafeteria once or twice. He's got a way about him – people flock in his direction.

As I finish taking notes, the brief distraction of Nathan and Melika wears off and I'm back to the reality show. Mom needs a lead that isn't me. So, what if I found someone who is already good at performing and has ties to Fairytale Gardens?

I pull up Instagram and search Garrick Walton. Of course, he's got a ton of followers and plenty of likes on his thirst traps. I might not know him, but this isn't surprising, which is fine because that's exactly the energy I need for my plan.

Garrick Walton has a built-in fan base from his Fairytale Gardens persona: an audience Mom could use to boost her show and app. Nathan was drooling over Garrick, which means getting a bunch of girls to fall in love with him shouldn't be that hard.

Before I can overthink it, I send him a DM, which I *never* do. I'm not the shoot-your-shot type of girl, but I'm desperate. I could find him somewhere in school, but that feels too much. Plus, I don't know where he is. I wait for the little message to say he's seen my DM, but as class ends there is still no response.

OK, so Garrick Walton is officially ignoring me. Fine, maybe not *ignoring* me, but he hasn't even looked at my DM and it's been hours. My throat constricts as I reread the message at the dinner table for the hundredth time – the desperate tone so unlike me. Maybe I should have got the Beeloved account to send the message. It would've sounded more professional.

I know he's been on Insta. He's posted a story of his food

and a reel of him in a Santa outfit – I'm not sure what that one was about. But what he hasn't done is answer me. My foot taps loudly against the brick floor, the phone trembling under my iron grip.

'Juliet, no phones at the table,' Mom says as I look at her over my plate of take-out chicken parm. Tonight, it's Italian. Last night, it was Korean. Tomorrow, it'll be BBQ or sushi or anything from the plethora of takeout go-to's we have. I don't ever remember seeing Mom cook. Maybe if I dig back really, really far into my toddler memories, before my parents were divorced, I might scrounge one up. But I wouldn't count on it.

I try to hold back my sarcasm as I point to her phone, which is also on the table. 'Is this a "do as I say, not as I do" moment?'

Mom quirks her lip, almost like she wants to smile but doesn't. 'Yes.'

I sigh, putting my phone face down on the table, willing Garrick to respond while I wolf down my dinner.

The lighting in the dining room is moody. A large brass chandelier hanging from the vaulted ceiling casts a warm glow on the oversized, reclaimed-wood table. Despite the warm materials made to make this house, it's always felt cold. It's probably due to the sparse decor. Mom is a minimalist and doesn't like clutter. That includes pictures of her family. There is only one, on the entryway table – a picture of me and Anna at her graduation from college.

'Did you look at the email I sent with the contestant files?' Mom asks.

'No,' I say with a mouthful of pasta, red sauce coating my chin.

'Juliet, this type of eating will not do on the show.' Her lips press into a thin line.

'This is how I eat.' I mean, it kinda is. I might be playing it up *slightly* for dramatics.

'We need to get waivers signed, and the longer you wait, the tighter our deadlines get. Christmas is a busy time, and even though we are only pulling contestants from surrounding areas, it's still difficult to have enough willing to be on our show for three weeks over the holidays.'

'I'm sure the TikTok followers are a nice incentive to miss out on precious holiday memories.' I push my plate away, appetite soured. That's why I know we can find ten willing girls to be contestants in plenty of time.

Mom looks blankly at me.

I cross my arms, leaning back in my chair. 'People go on those shows to get famous. Not to find love. Especially at our age.'

Mom shakes her head. 'Don't be such a Negative Nelly, Juliet. Everyone wants love.'

All opposed, please raise your hand. I raise my hand.

'What are you doing?' Mom asks.

Oops. 'Stretching.'

'Will you read the email tonight, please?' She sips her wine.

'I promise I will get your star ready.' The almost lie tingles on my tongue.

She beams, and I leave off that it's not me.

After dinner, I'm more determined than ever. I video call Nathan and Melika as I flop on to my bed. My stomach churns from worry and undigested chicken parm. My room is the only place in the house with some personality. I have pictures of me and the people I love most in the world strung on fairy lights around the walls. I nestle into the fluffy teal blanket Anna gave me last year for my birthday.

'OK, take me to this infamous theme park you two fools love so much,' I say when their faces pop on screen.

'Really?' Nathan beams, like Christmas came early.

I told them about my mom's show at school and my idea to get Garrick involved. They annoyingly said I should be the lead, but I shut that down. I don't know what's in the air, making anyone think I want to be the star.

'Infamous is the right word,' Melika adds. 'We all heard about that charity scandal last summer.'

I might not care about Fairytale Gardens, but I literally could not escape the drama. It was all anyone talked about for like two weeks. All I thought was how bad I felt for the Waltons. Having your family drama spread across the internet for people to consume and comment on sounds like a nightmare. But they appear to have come out of it for the better, if what I've spied on social media today while waiting for Garrick to respond is any indication.

'But that was resolved, right?' Mom said they looked into it.

'Yeah,' Nathan says. 'But still a big 'ole yikes.'

Digging my fingers into my blanket, I steady myself. 'I don't care about that. I just need Garrick to agree so that I can convince my mom that he's a better choice than I am.'

All of that's easier said than done.

4

GARRICK

I need to get to Knight School, but I have a pit stop to make first. 'You're the best, dude – seriously.' I slap Tyrone on the back as he hands me the package.

'We can call it even, if you put in a good word with Layla for me.' Even behind his dark sunglasses I know he's sneaking a peek at the popcorn stand a few paces away from us in the Village Center. He's been crushing on Layla, who runs the stand, since last summer and, despite my pestering, hasn't plucked up the nerve to ask her out.

'Consider it done.' I rip open the bag and yank out the Christmas ornament I had custom-made.

I run my gloved fingers over the edge of the gold frame. Inside, sits a picture of my whole family from Christmas seven years ago, before Mom got sick. The familiar ache is there in my heart, but I still smile when I see us all together.

'C'mon.' I drag Tyrone from his gawking and toward the Christmas tree. 'I need you to play lookout.'

This is opening weekend for the Christmas season, and it's been hectic, to put it lightly. All of us Fairytalers – that's what we call FTG staff – have been earning our wages today.

In the first hour, the Christmas tree lost three ornaments after a bird flew into it. They fell off the branches and nearly hit Aldrich in the head as he did his carriage ride. Then, when they turned on Ice Shards, we blew a fuse and lost power to the Royal Fare restaurant just as they were getting Santa's meet-and-greet breakfast ready. I managed to cover and say the elves were doing repairs for the upcoming big night. Still, I thought Dad would pop a blood vessel by the look of his face, which turned brighter than Rudolph's nose.

They outdid themselves with the decorations around the park. I don't know where they found the massive tree to put in the center, but it's absolutely incredible. I might try to convince Dad to let us open our presents under it on Christmas. It's filled with a whole bunch of custom ornaments depicting different moments in FTG history.

But it needs one final touch.

There's not a back side I can sneak to and tuck this picture in, but dressed in my oversized coat, no one knows who I am right now – so I won't draw my usual crowd. Tyrone stands in front of me, and I duck under the branches and over the small barrier to keep out the guests. I nestle the ornament into a limb where it's sure to stay put, no matter the weather. No one will be able to see it, but knowing Mom's here makes me smile.

'All right,' I say when I climb out. 'Places to be, damsels to save. Karaoke later?' I shout as I'm running away.

He gives me a thumbs up.

'You're late,' Ivor says when I skid into the backstage of Knight School. I hear the eagerly waiting kids just outside the curtain.

I fling my coat at his head. 'Santa emergency.' He grumbles as I slip my sword back into my sheath. 'From now on,' I say, trying to distract him, 'I think I'm only gonna work in the winter. Not having sweaty leather stuck to my skin is much more pleasurable.'

The sun has melted most of the frost off the stage, but a glistening water shine is left. I'll have to be quick on my feet, so I don't faceplant.

I run a hand down the smooth leather of my jacket, tightening the straps around the sleeves. I sometimes wear the whole shining metal suit typical of knights – usually when I do meet-and-greets. But most of the time I wear leathers and linen undershirts. It's much easier to perform my sword skills that way.

I didn't think opening for the holiday season would be all that different. But as I move without the possibility of stripping off a few layers of skin from the leather adhesion, I got to say, this is much better.

'You're preaching to the choir, G.' Ivor is my older brother by six years. Ever since he married James and had my nephew, Bradley, it's been all about retirement funds and mortgage interest rates. But at least when we're in the park he drops the adult worries and acts like one of the boys again. 'Also, if this gets us the sales boost, I'm sure it'll be a regular thing.'

Since graduating high school, Ivor has moved into a role with more responsibility. He runs Guest Relations and Experiences – while still playing a prince. So, it makes sense that he's got more to worry about than if his sword is shined or his stage make-up is too cakey. I help around the kitchen, but no one's making me fill out budgetary reports or sales projections. Or whatever it is Ivor's complaining about.

'*Kendrick, Kendrick,*' kids chant out front.

I cup a hand behind my ear, cracking my signature grin. 'Hear that, Ivor? My adoring fans await.'

My whole family has FTG alter egos that correspond to characters in Carpathia. Carpathia is the fictional land Fairytale Gardens is based on. King Osgar (Dad) and Queen Isobel (Mom) ruled the kingdom of Carpathia peacefully. But one day, a terrible blight from the nearby lands attacked the kingdom. Lots of townsfolk died. Crops failed. All the horrible things you find in fairytale stories meant to set the scene for a heroic final act.

The king had three sons: Prince Thornton (Ivor), the oldest; the middle son and the bravest, Prince Winthrop (Tristian – not really sure how he landed the starring role when I was available, but I'm glad because my part is the best one); and Prince Eadwulf (Aldrich), the youngest.

The King sent Winthrop and Sir Kendrick the Kind (that's me – guess I look more like a knight in shining armor than Prince Charming) to fight a devastating plague. The prince defeated the blight with the help of a fairy, Princess Arden (that's the role Imogen slipped into last summer), from a neighboring forest. They fell in love, saved the day and everyone lived happily ever after.

I had that story memorized before I knew how to read. It's part of my DNA now.

My body hums with the anticipation of going on stage. It's only been a few months since the park closed after the summer season, but I've missed being able to perform – being the center of attention is always a nice bonus.

'Did Dad say you could play Santa?' Ivor asks me as I grab a candy cane from the bag to hand to the kids after the class ends. It's not really a 'class', but we let the kids swing wooden swords around and hit each other for twenty minutes while the parents take videos, and we attempt to teach them a few moves.

'No one claimed the suit, so I figured I'd give Santa a youthful upgrade. I don't think the guests will mind.'

I'm used to Sir Kendrick's meet-and-greets. But dang, being Saint Nick is a whole different experience. I get the heart-eyed teens who want a knight to sweep them off their feet, but based on my first meet this morning, Santa gets all the dirt on who's been naughty and nice.

'Just don't screw it up, OK? You have to take it seriously. We need this.'

Ivor's words touch a sensitive nerve deep under my skin. It's not a secret in our family that I'm the screw-up. Screw-up might not be the right word; I just don't care. What's the point, I say? It's easier to skate by. Still, I nod. 'You can count on me,' I say as we slip into our alter egos.

As usual, I'm all in when I step out to meet the rambunctious kids. They make me forget about everything else for twenty minutes. This is the feeling I wanted to replicate with my fencing camp. Except there, I could actually teach them the real thing. Who knows, I might train the next Olympic gold medalist – or not, since it's never going to happen.

The kids are supposed to be twelve and under, but today

there's a white girl my age with dark hair and pink fluffy earmuffs. I'm surprised because there's an age limit for participating. It's a legal thing, so no one gets too injured. I know this from experience because Tristian and I have had more than enough scrapes and splinters.

'Welcome, future knights,' Ivor says to the waiting crowd. *Crowd* might be a generous term. There's only a dozen and a half kids – plus the mystery girl. We split the group into pairs so they can spar. And, working my magic, I make sure the girl and I are left together.

'Looks like you're stuck with me.' I flash my signature grin again. I'm not sure if it's the knight's smile or mine. By this point, we've blended into the same person. Even before I was allowed to play Kendrick in the park, I pretended to be him, waiting for the day I would get my chance. I guess I don't really know who I am without it.

'Just how I planned it.' She smiles, but it's forced, her shoulders tensed and cheeks flushed.

'You wanted to spar with me?' I hand her a wooden sword from the rack and take one for myself. 'I do love a lady with initiative.' I twist the hilt in my hand, my fidgeting put to good use.

All I receive in return for my witty quip is a roll of her deep-blue eyes. Those eyes, coupled with her raven-black hair, nudge at nostalgia in my brain – a memory that I can't yet place. It's not that I know her – trust me, I'd recall if I did – but she feels familiar somehow.

'Did you want me to show you a few moves?' I ask.

'I'm a quick learner. I'm sure I can keep up.' Her hair

is pulled into a no-nonsense bun, but a few strands have managed to escape and frame her face.

I'm working all my charmer moves, but she doesn't budge. For a girl who sought me out, she doesn't seem to be in the mood to flirt.

So, guess that means I need to try harder.

'If you say so. *En garde*.' I lunge toward her at half speed, and she hops to the left, her sword swinging up to catch the tip of mine. We do a little dance in a circle, each of us eyeing down our opponent. My lips curve when she glides toward me, feet nimble on the frozen ground.

A solid strike sounds when our swords collide. She's not bad – clumsy with her hand movements, but she's got the gist. I spin past her, our hands quickly grazing as we circle around in my favorite type of dance. Her cheeks are flushed even darker, and a tiny line between her brows appears as she huffs in frustration at being unable to catch me.

'I can slow down, if you like. Walk you through the basics. This is a full-service class.' I don't fight my grin as I fling my sword from one hand to the other in a move I like to bust out to impress. But this girl isn't batting an eye.

She wipes the back of her hand across her forehead, looking anywhere but at me. 'A generous offer, but not needed,' she says, clearly flustered. A chorus of screams echoes in the distance from the Triple Crown roller coaster.

I try a different move. 'Do you have a name?'

'Everyone has a name.' She deflects my advance with the sword. To be fair, I'm not trying very hard. I've trained to be a fencer since I was three. Can't bring out all those moves here. But I'm giving her more of a show than the kids get. Something about her tells me she can handle it.

'Want to share it with me?' My blood pumps in my ears, and I doubt it's the cardio. I'm working harder to crack her than I am at the sword work.

She bites her bottom lip, and my stomach gives a tug. She's got a line of freckles across her nose and cheeks. Her bun has fallen out into a loose ponytail that she flips to the side, still fighting that smile I know she wants to give me.

'Ripley.'

'*Ripley*.' I repeat the name and like how it feels. 'Do we go to school together?' Now that I've gotten a moment to look at her, I've definitely seen her. I'm not sure how I haven't talked to her sooner.

'Yes. And I have a question for you.'

I lean in close, pushing my sword against hers. The wood bites into my skin, but I ignore it. 'I'm all ears.'

She clears her throat. I conceal my smile because I have a feeling she wouldn't like it.

'First, do you have a girlfriend?'

I can't stop my smile now or the chuckle that follows. 'Talk about getting right to the point.'

Her flushed skin turns deep crimson as she quickly shakes her head, taking a moment to study the castle beside us before continuing. 'I wasn't asking for me. I just ... I need to be sure you don't before I ask my second question.'

'Well, now you've got me intrigued,' I say, twirling the wooden sword in my hand. 'No, I don't.'

'All right, I was wondering ...' She looks around like she's waiting for backup, but no one comes to her rescue. 'My mom runs this dating app, Beeloved, and they're launching a teen version, so they're doing a reality dating show for promo and it's going to be filmed here. I'm assuming you already know all about it?'

Actually, this is my first time hearing the news. I make a mental note to interrogate Ivor later. How dare he keep such intriguing information from me.

'And the original star had to back out, which means they need a new one,' she adds.

I'm unsure where this is going, but I already like it. Ivor waves from across the group, motioning for me to come help with a rowdy pairing, but I ignore him.

'The lead gets moderate compensation for their time. So, I was wondering if you'd want to do it?' she finishes.

'Absolutely.' I don't wait for further explanation.

'Don't you want some more details?' A little frown appears on her face, a deep line between her eyebrows.

'I've heard of Beeloved. I'm actually pretty excited about a teen version. What more do I need to know?'

Her flush dissipates as the determined tone reappears. 'Where? When? How? Who? The basics.'

I twirl my sword, flipping it into the air and catching it. This trick usually gets me some applause – Ripley gives me nothing. 'You said it's a dating show where I'm the star, so I presume I'll have a bunch of girls fighting for my attention. That's all the detail I need.'

'You know what –' Ripley holds her sword to me – 'never mind.'

'Wait, wait, wait.' I step in front of her to keep her from walking away, steering us clear of two kids who are definitely pushing the constraints of our safety standards. 'You can't just drop this on a guy and then change your mind. You got me all excited.'

'I need someone who's going to take this seriously.' She folds her arms across her chest, which is hard to do in her puffy coat. 'Don't you have a brother? Or a couple? Maybe I'll ask one of them.'

'One, I am the best brother. Ask anyone. Second, if you want a star, trust me, that's me.'

She doesn't respond, and I know she knows I'm right. That's why she came to me to begin with.

I plaster on my best puppy-dog smile. 'Doesn't this look like the face of a reality dating show?'

She bounces up and down, trying to keep warm as a gust of frigid air blows through. 'Yeah. It's exactly the type.'

I'm pretty sure she's being sarcastic, but her face is so straight I can't tell. She is an enigma, and I need to know more.

'Kendrick, get over here – *now*!' Ivor bellows. From that tone, I know I only have a few precious seconds before he drags me away.

'So, do we have a deal?' I place out my hand to her.

She waits an excruciating amount of time before taking my hand. Her hand is warm in the cool winter air, and I shake it a moment longer than I need to.

'Deal.'

I know I should have asked more questions. But it's a reality dating show. It's not like anyone's really expecting me to find love. Plus, it'll be great promotion for FTG, and maybe I can get Tristian off my back about finding a girlfriend. Also, depending how much they'll pay me, I might be able to start the fencing camp myself and not pester Dad about it any more.

This sounds like the perfect way to spend my Christmas season.

5

GARRICK

'You can never go wrong with canned cranberry,' I say, feet propped on the table as I lean back in my chair in the kitchen under the Royal Fare restaurant.

Upstairs has a classic, vaguely Victorian Christmas aesthetic, with all the deep greens and reds accented with silver and gold – the perfect decorations to match the wood beams and cathedral ceilings of a restaurant built into a castle. But in the belly of the beast, I made sure we put *Whoville* to shame. I threw up every over-the-top Christmas decor item I found over the last few months at garage sales and thrift stores – I'm working on a budget. The color scheme is rainbow: anything goes.

I'm meeting with Jin, the head of food and beverage, to review the menu for the charity Thanksgiving dinner we're hosting at the end of the month. It might seem like we're doing this just to score some good publicity – and yeah, sure, we are – but it's also something Mom would've loved.

We used to volunteer at the local soup kitchen every holiday. I actually got the idea to do it here from her. I'd been organizing the kitchen office – Jin took over after Mom ... Anyhoo, no one had bothered to clean it. So, I was doing it.

Mostly because Ivor told me to, but it turned out OK because I found one of her old notebooks. She loved to doodle and scribble notes, just like Aldrich does. One of the notes, tucked into the back pages, was an idea to host a Thanksgiving at FTG for those who couldn't afford their own.

My throat is thick at the memory of holding her words in my hands. I could hear her voice as I read each line. I shake my head to clear it so I can focus.

'Plus –' back to the cranberries – 'it's cheaper than making it. We can load up on the giant cans at Costco.'

Jin is old-school. He loves making everything from scratch. But even as someone who hates math, I know we should probably keep to a budget. Thanks to our Christmas season experiment, our staff is full, but I'm not taking any chances at overspending. People here have families to provide for or college tuition to pay. Fairytale Gardens means the world to me; it's my whole life, and I know for a lot of folks who've worked here for years it is for them too. I don't want to play a part in stripping that away.

'You're going to put me out of a job one day, kid.' He skims the to-do list.

I let that idea float around in my brain for a moment. I'd be a fantastic boss, but taking on that much responsibility makes my skin itch. 'Nah. Too much work.'

OK, I'll admit that, on occasion, I have thought about eventually taking the job. But then I'd be in charge of a whole set of people, and they'd look to me for answers. Which I think we can all agree would be a terrible idea.

'Garrick!' I hear Imogen before I see her. The melodic trills of her voice echo into the kitchen. Imogen may have only started last summer, but she's been coming to FTG all her life. I dare say she loves it *almost* as much as I do. 'Oh hey, Tristian was looking for you.' Imogen is wearing her princess costume, but her blonde wig is slung over her arm, allowing her short red hair to fly freely as she shakes the waves with her fingers.

I glance at my phone. I have a few texts from him and my other brothers. 'Sorry,' I say to Jin. 'I'm a very in-demand guy. You'll have to finish without me.'

Jin waves me off in response, and I follow Imogen upstairs to a waiting Yvette, who is typing away on her tablet, as per usual. Yvette Ortiz is only older than us by a few years, but she packs all the punch of a linebacker. I can see why Aunt Maria hired her to be in charge of keeping us characters in line. 'You need to get to your meeting, and then you have a Santa meet-and-greet scheduled in an hour. So, let's go.'

I give her a salute. 'Aye, aye, captain.'

We're careful to avoid the eyes of the guests eating their delicious meal in the main dining room. Peeking through the swinging door, I can just spy the bushy Christmas tree with its navy blue velvet ribbons and gold baubles. What I like best about the decorations is that every land has its own theme – you can experience four different Christmases in one day.

'I still can't believe they're letting you play Santa.' Imogen snaps a picture of the Christmas tree as we head outside. It's not snowing, but the air is icy, the sky a threatening gray. The walk between the apartments and the main office is the least festive. I wanted to install a Santa sleigh on the roof, but I was told we didn't have the budget for decor outside the park.

'More like I can't believe it took this long for someone to think of a Christmas at FTG.' I blow hot air into my hands to keep them moving. I didn't grab my coat from the kitchen.

'Thank you. It really was a brilliant idea on my part.' Imogen beams. She is the sunshine to Tristian's cloudy day. Even when all seems hopeless, Imogen manages to find the best in every situation. Which is helpful, since there are still those awkward moments with her and the fam when we all remember the drama she caused us. I'm cool with her, but Ivor and Dad still need some ice chipped off their shoulders.

'We have a meet-and-greet,' Yvette says to Imogen. They head toward Pixie Forest as I venture to Dad's office. I might bust Tristian's balls about his lovesick ways, but I do really like Imogen. She's the lifeblood FTG needed to keep its heart pumping when it seemed like we might be dead on the table.

'Is there something you'd like to tell me?' Dad asks when I step into his office. He sits at his throne – I mean *desk*. The oversized portrait of us dressed like the Carpathia royal family hanging behind him only adds to his overbearing presence. He's working on it, but he still thinks he's the king of the realm.

All my brothers are there in various states of prince dress. Aldrich looks back and forth between me and Dad, twiddling his phone anxiously. Ivor stands by Dad's side, arms crossed. I guess, being a dad himself, he's used to the parental stare-down. Tristian looks like he wants to laugh. So, now I'm really confused.

I rack my brain, thinking of anything I could've done that would get me in trouble right now.

'Garrick?' Dad prompts when I haven't spoken, tapping his finger on the button of his gray suit jacket.

Scrolling down everything that might have gotten me in hot water takes a minute. Then it dawns on me. 'Oh, yeah. The dating show?' I hook my thumbs in my belt loops and lean against the sofa's armrest.

I take it back: *this office* is the least festive of anywhere on the property. I make a mental note to grab a Grinch from my collection in the kitchen and put it in here.

'Dating show?' Aldrich asks, while Tristian says, 'This should be good.'

'Yeah, Ripley – she goes to our school – her mom owns Beeloved, and they're launching a new teen dating app. I'm upset no one told me they were filming their reality show here, but I forgive the slip.' I fill them in on my part in the endeavor. 'And since the park was already the backdrop, it was a no-brainer that I step into the open lead role.'

Dad leans back in his chair, pushing a hand through his hair. The once light brown is tinged with gray. He's been better since the whole 'being accused of embezzlement by my twin' last summer. We've started to talk again, really talk, but he's still Dad. It's hard for him to loosen the reins on anything FTG-related – it's practically his fifth child. 'I know you agreed, because I received an email with a revised contract from Ms Ripley and her team this morning.'

Ms Ripley? Is that Ripley or her mom? I don't get to ponder the thought long.

'You can't just agree to things like this without consulting me,' Dad says, fingers pressed into a steeple grip under his chin. 'We had plans in place for their filming requirements but having you as part of the show is a whole different story.'

'One –' I raise a finger – 'I didn't sign anything, so I can still back out. And two –' I raise another finger – 'adding me to the mix will be killer promo for the park. And god knows we could use it.'

We're all trying not to look at Tristian, who squirms at my side. My heart aches for my twin, really. Getting used by the girl you're falling for – freaking sucks, bro. But if he'd listened to me and not bothered with the love, he wouldn't have hurt so bad.

Still, I suppose it's working out for him.

'This is the first season of the Christmas markets,' Ivor chimes in, rubbing a hand over his massive beard. He'd put a lumberjack to shame. 'We're already under enough pressure to get this right. We need you fully committed to FTG.'

I crack my knuckles. 'Most of it will happen during the week while the park is closed, so I'll be free to do it. It's mostly gonna be on me.' Just saying that makes my stomach flip. But I ignore it and continue. 'Dad, you're always saying if we have ideas, that this is our park too. So, this is mine.' I leave off that it might also help launch my fencing camp, since I don't want to fight a battle on multiple fronts.

Dad, for his part, looks a *tiny* bit proud of me. It makes me stand a little taller. I'm not the kid who's used to getting praised for my ideas. I'm the one begging for forgiveness because I didn't bother to ask permission. 'I don't know, Garrick. We're already taking a risk allowing them here at all, but making you the face of it ... Is this the kind of thing we want to be doing for our brand? A reality show?'

'It's going to be fine. We're all about love and happily-ever-afters. That's what the show is gonna be. It'll be classy, not tacky.'

I actually have no idea if that's true. But from my brief encounter with Ripley, she seems like a classy gal. So, I'll stick with that line and hope I'm right.

After a little more convincing, Dad agrees to it. I'm glad because I'm not sure Ripley would take no for an answer. The park is struggling, and I do hope that this helps. Also, if I get to enjoy the company of some lovely ladies for a couple of weeks, well, that's just a cross I'm willing to bear for the sake of Fairytale Gardens.

As I head to the break room to grab a snack before Santa's meet-and-greet, I receive an email from Ripley – I have no idea how she got my email, but it doesn't surprise me. It's a detailed itinerary – and when I say detailed, I mean planned down to the very last minute. Over the next month, I have meetings twice a week. They will cover everything from wardrobe to media prep. Ripley will be my handler – which sounds more like a babysitter, but Ripley is an enigma that intrigues me, so a little more face time might help me figure her out.

The production crew will arrive at FTG on 8th December to start pre-production and the show begins a few days later. There's also a questionnaire attached that I have to fill out so they can use the app's algorithm to pick the contestants that will be the best love matches for me.

As I skim the questions, my heart rate ticks up and my palms are so sweaty my phone nearly slips out of my hand. The word love is in here *a lot*, and every time I read it my blood pressure rises. But it's OK. It's just part of the gimmick, right? I don't really need to find love.

6

RIPLEY

'I don't know why *I* need to be there all the time.' I'm lounging on my sister's couch watching Molly dance to *The Muppet Christmas Carol*.

'Because you're a part of the production,' Anna says from the dining table as she inputs receipts on the computer. 'You told me you would use it on your college apps.'

'I did, and I am. But I'm only doing it because it was the compromise Mom made me agree to so I don't have to star.' I thought it was going to be harder to change her mind. But I guess she also saw the benefit of getting the extra boost from Fairytale Gardens fans.

Of which I am *not* one.

This is why I'm on Anna's couch, willing the hours to go slower before I have to head to Fairytale Gardens to spend the next four weeks living in their stupid apartments with Mom instead of in my own room. She wanted to be closer to production, and apparently leaving me alone at home around Christmas would be cruel. Yeah, because our sad, undecorated tree screams 'holiday spirit' every year.

'Don't you need me to stay and put up your tree?' I sit up to look at her.

'Tree, tree, tree,' Molly chants from the ground where she's sprawled.

'Mike will be back Sunday. We're doing it then.'

I turn around so she doesn't see my eye roll. That's just another reason I'm glad I'm not 'in love'. Relying on someone else seems tedious and unhelpful. I tried to have a boyfriend once. It lasted all of three weeks before I caught him kissing another girl at a pool party. I was more relieved than upset when we broke up. I'm an evidence girl – I like facts. And all the facts and evidence I've gathered lead to the same conclusion: Love = Misery.

I look at my phone and see a text from Nathan.

'Ugh. I have to go, I guess.' I convinced Mom that Nathan and Melika also needed to be part of the production and she agreed to classify us all as interns. They were both game since it gets us out of class two weeks before winter break starts.

My production duties actually started a few weeks ago. I hadn't seen Garrick more than a dozen times in the last several years, yet now I've been around him almost every day – barring weekends. For a start, I was only supposed to see him at our twice-weekly mandatory production meetings and outings. Like the time I had to go shopping with Garrick, Brett the intern and two other production members. Garrick insisted he needed to do a try-on montage like in the movies and even picked out his own music to play while he did it.

But then, as if the universe didn't think I was getting enough Garrick, the Monday after he agreed to be in the show my gym teacher went on medical leave and they combined our classes. Which meant Garrick and I were now together five days a week participating in team sports, proving that both of us have a competitive streak. That did win our team a volleyball game, allowing us a brief moment of celebration together among the never-ending Beeloved prep.

App development or television production aren't careers I'm going to pursue, but it will still look good on my college application. I want to be a lawyer. Not because I like the showboating aspect, but because I like the idea of fighting for the little guy. Also, I've been told I'm good at swaying people to my side. Which feels like a nice way of saying I'm pushy until I get what I want.

I hug Anna and promise Molly I'll sneak back to watch *Elf* with her before Christmas.

Fairytale Gardens isn't any more appealing than it was last month. After convincing Garrick to do the show, I immediately peaced out, to Nathan and Melika's horror. They were hoping to get me on a roller coaster.

Absolutely. Not. Happening.

I plan on being so busy these next four weeks that no one will be fast enough to catch me and force me on to a ride.

'I am so hyped to see the park after hours,' Nathan says, once again in full Christmas attire with his vintage bell-and-holly sweater Melika gifted him last year.

'Me too. Do you think we can go ghost hunting?' Melika asks. Her hair is braided partway down on the side. The remaining curls cascade over her shoulder.

I'm in the back seat of Nathan's car, working on my stats homework. 'I'm sorry, *what*?' My eyes flick between them. This won't come as a shock, but I don't believe in ghosts. I'm not opposed to the idea of them existing; I've just never seen any evidence.

Nathan turns to look at me, the car swerving slightly. Melika grabs the wheel with practiced ease. 'I heard a story that there are ghosts on the pirate ride.'

I scoff, raising an eyebrow. 'Was someone murdered there?'

'Maybe a grieving person dumped their loved one's ashes in the water. I hear it happens a lot.' Melika gives the wheel back to Nathan.

Shuttering, I focus on my schoolwork. 'Another reason you won't catch me on those death traps. Both for the living and the dead, apparently.'

'Come on, Ripley. You can't live at a theme park for a month and not go on at least one ride.' Nathan catches my eye in the rearview mirror.

Melika pulls an FTG map from her bag, twists back in her seat to face me and spreads it over my homework. 'I've marked down the rides I think you'll like and numbered them in order of intensity. I thought you'd appreciate that.'

I do, actually. The organization makes my heart flutter in the best way possible. Who needs love when you can have an itemized list? 'Your thoroughness is always appreciated. But I already memorized the map.' I fold the paper up and hand it back to her. 'And I'm still not doing it.'

When we arrive, a bubbly white girl around our age with red hair greets us. She's wearing a bright-blue sweatshirt with the Fairytale Gardens logo on the front in pink. 'Hi! Welcome! I'm Imogen, and yes, before you ask, the apartments smell exactly how they look.' Her mega-watt smile doesn't falter.

I glare at the brown, stucco buildings and imagine I've entered a nineties sitcom. 'Lovely.' I squeeze my fingers around my thumbs to keep myself from biting them. We're in the back lot of the park – it consists of the apartments, parking and an office building. It looks exactly like any other business complex. The fairytale magic and whimsy are reserved for the paying customers.

'You get used to it. Which one of you is Juliet?' Imogen glances between us.

I cringe. 'It's Ripley, actually. Only my mom calls me Juliet.'

Imogen gives a knowing smile. 'Noted. Well, I'm here to show you to your rooms. Melika, I have you staying with me. I promise I don't snore, and I make a stunning mocha with whipped cream and chocolate shavings. Ripley, you're with your mom. And Nathan, I have you bunking with Garrick.'

'Garrick's staying here?' Nathan perks up.

'Sort of. I guess he wanted a place to crash if he doesn't want to go home. Which is literally just around the corner. But that's Garrick.' Imogen shrugs, leading us up the stairs and down a creaky outdoor hallway. 'Sorry about the noise. Honestly, you'll barely notice it. They just didn't want to repair anything since these are getting torn down next year.'

'Do you go to our school?' Melika asks.

'No, but I worked here last summer. And then Tristian and I started dating.' Her face softens at the mention of his name.

Nathan and Melika share a knowing look – Nathan mouths '*scandal*' to me.

Imogen doesn't notice and keeps going. 'The rest of the crew arrived an hour ago and are settling in. We have a dinner planned for everyone at the Royal Fare tonight. I'll see you there.'

'If the food is free, count me in,' I say as I take the key and open the door to an apartment that smells like day-old hot dogs and baked beans. Yum.

Dragging my stuff along the hall, I see Mom has already dropped her things in the bedroom on the left. I take the other, carefully sorting out my clothes into the drawers and closet.

After I finish, I head to the living room, checking Instagram on the way. The moment I open the app, I'm greeted with a picture of my dad and his wife. They're smiling, with an older couple who I think must be her parents. But how would I know? I've never even met her. Swiping out of the app, I throw my phone on the couch and settle down to solve complex math equations – a much more enjoyable sight.

The sun has long since set when I hear knocking at the door. When I don't immediately answer, Nathan presses his face against the window, causing it to fog. 'Oh, Juuullieettt!' He pulls out every syllable of my name.

I've been working on my homework at the dining table so I won't fall behind in the classes I'm missing. I untangle my legs from the wooden chair, and let Melika and Nathan inside.

'It's freezing out there.' Melika pulls her wool coat tighter. 'You ready to go?'

'Go?' I frown, trying to shut the door, but Nathan stops me.

'Yeah, free food at the Royal Fare. Everyone's going.'

I sigh, remembering the alert on my phone thirty minutes ago. I hate being late. I quickly slip on my short boots and blue, puffy winter coat. 'I'm ready.'

'That's what you're wearing?' Nathan gives my leggings and baggy sweater a once-over.

I pull at my ponytail to tighten it. 'Why? What are you wearing?' I thought this was just theme park food. 'I didn't realize there was a dress code.'

Nathan opens his plaid coat to reveal a striped candy cane button-down and red slacks. 'You know, you always dress for a moment.'

I laugh. '*You* do, but that's not really my thing.' Nathan's closet is like Willy Wonka meets Ken, with a dash of David Rose from *Schitt's Creek*.

'Seriously, Nathan. Ripley is fine. Let's go, I'm starving.' Melika takes my arm as we leave the apartment and go down the rickety stairs. Salt to melt the ice crunches under our shoes.

'How are your places?' I ask, wishing I'd grabbed my scarf as the wind cuts through my bones.

'Smells,' Melika says, nose wrinkling with the memory. 'But Imogen seems cool.'

Nathan beams. 'A dream. Like, I will tell my grandkids one day how I shared a house with a knight one Christmas.'

'A fake knight,' I correct.

'They don't need to know that.'

We exit backstage through a glittering gold fake apple tree and into the land of Carpathia. I haven't explored the park personally, but I researched by watching videos online and studying the map. It's an easy enough layout to memorize.

It has a Village Center and four distinct areas branching off from it. As the namesake of the fictional country where the Fairytale Gardens story takes place, Carpathia holds the castle. Then we have the Perilous Sea – a water-themed land that I imagine smells like fish. Glacier Peaks – ice-themed, which might as well be the whole place, given the current temp.

Last is Pixie Forest. I won't say this out loud, but it seems the most magical, with its fairy influence. If I were to venture out on my own, I'd start there.

But tonight, we are headed to the large castle in the center of the park and the restaurant it houses within. The castle is imposing, considering this is just a family-owned operation and not a major conglomerate like other theme parks. I have to crane my neck to see the top of the medieval-inspired turrets and spires. It's a dusty sand color with copper accents. Since it's the holidays, it's covered in lavish Christmas decorations and bright-colored lights.

And while the castle looks ancient and weathered, the Royal Fare looks straight off a movie set crafted to perfection, with its large wooden beams and arched ceilings. The place is adorned with the most regal-looking decor I've ever seen. Large velvet-ribbon bows are affixed to every wall, while garlands surround the windows with twinkling lights. The room could feel overwhelming, but the lush red carpet and faux fireplaces create a coziness despite the ample space.

Rich smells of gravy, berry sauce, potatoes and roasted meats fight for my attention. An extensive buffet set-up calls my name, with buttery rolls and enough desserts to feed a kingdom.

'Juliet ...' I hear my name before I can reach the food.

'Come here. I want you to meet someone.' Mom stands near the giant Christmas tree, gesturing me over.

'Save me a seat,' I whisper to my friends as I leave.

Even if I weren't familiar with the entire Walton family after deep-diving into the park's history, I would've easily guessed this was Garrick's dad. The perfect posture and elegant suit give all the vibes of a man assured of his place. The fictional king come to life. He wears a well-practiced smile and holds his hand to me when I approach. 'I'm Barth Walton. Nice to finally meet you, Juliet.'

'Ripley,' I correct, shaking his hand. 'Thank you again for letting us use the park.'

He nods, lines tight around his lips. 'I hope it's as beneficial as Garrick has promised.'

'It will be,' Mom answers before I can.

I smile, giving the correct response. 'Beeloved is dedicated to making it successful for both of us.'

He twists a gold band around his ring finger, the only sign of discomfort. 'Ms Ripley says you'll be sure to keep Garrick in line. I must warn you, he's the hardest one to wrangle of my four sons.'

That I have already surmised.

'Are my ears burning?' Garrick materializes out of nowhere. 'Ms Ripley, great to see you again, and of course my trusty sidekick,' he adds to me.

I roll my eyes, ignoring his lines as I've practiced doing the last month.

Mom is not easily impressed, but Garrick's welcoming nature seems to do the trick. 'Garrick, we are so happy the time has finally arrived to start filming. But go, eat. Enjoy the last night before we kick into full gear.'

I've already committed to memory the production schedule and know she's not lying. It's going to be tight.

As Garrick and I walk away, Barth and Mom keep talking, discussing the final details for the show.

'We've got plenty of space at our table.' Garrick motions near the front window, overlooking the park. I recognize his three brothers right away. Sitting with them is a Black man around Ivor's age, who I assume must be his husband, James – their son, Bradley, who is the spitting image of James, sits between them. 'Your friends are more than welcome to join, too.'

I smile politely, but my anxiety makes my stomach turn at the idea of having to small talk with strangers. 'Thanks for the offer, but we already have seats.' Nathan and Melika are waving at me from the opposite side of the room. 'See you tomorrow.' I walk away, but when I reach my seat, I glance back to find Garrick staring at me with a puzzled look.

7

RIPLEY

This is not going to work. I sit beside Mom and the newly hired camera crew, watching Garrick utterly fail. We're in an old office set into the fake mountains at Glacier Peaks. Before our arrival, storage boxes filled most of the floor, but they are now shoved to one side to make way for the camera and lights. A series of square windows overlooking the empty park below serves as the background to our shot.

Garrick is supposed to be filling out the app with information about a dream girl he would like to date. It's a series of questions meant to find you a true match.

All right – *fail* is a strong word, but he's certainly not taking this seriously.

'I already did this, didn't I?' Garrick leans in his chair, rocking back and forth on the back two legs. He's wearing a Fairytale Gardens T-shirt and soft-blue jeans.

'I think he should stand.' I jump up and yank Garrick to standing. He's a good six inches taller than me, and when he stares down at me through his thick eyelashes I have to look away. A weird thumping fills my ears. Maybe I need a doctor?

'What's wrong with sitting?' Garrick asks.

'I think standing looks better.' Really, I'm just giving him one less prop to play with.

I step away quickly, returning to Mom's side.

'Ms Ripley, what do you think?' *head intern* Brett says. I can't get away from his incessant ass-kissing since he's been trailing Mom for the last month.

When I glance over at Mom, she's biting her cheek. Never a good sign. It means she's stopping herself from saying something, and that only lasts so long.

'I repeat my question: didn't I already do this?' Garrick skims down the screen. 'Yes, I told you I like piña coladas and taking walks in the rain.'

'You did,' Mom says, rearranging her fitted blue blazer – power suit day. 'But we need it on camera so the audience know what to expect when they download the app.'

The questionnaire he filled out a month ago was to get the contestants here. We couldn't have coordinated all the release forms from their guardians within three days of when they were supposed to arrive, even if they aren't coming from that far away.

'Jul—' Mom starts, but I cut her off.

'Garrick, pretend you're answering the questions to me.' If I've learned anything about him the last few weeks, it's that he's better when he has a single person to focus on to keep him on track. 'What is the top thing you're looking for in your Beeloved?'

Garrick's lips quirk up. I might only be getting to know him, but I've already guessed the answer will not be screen-worthy.

I blow out hot air, gripping the tablet tighter while he takes way too long to respond.

He taps his chin. 'I'd say someone who can keep up.'

'Care to elaborate?' I ignore the popping in my jaw when I grind my molars as Mom stares me down. Part of getting intern credit means I actually have to participate in the show. Mom seemed pleased at the idea of me taking an interest in her company, but that doesn't mean she's ready to loosen her control over everything.

'I'm never great at sitting still. So, my *Beeloved* . . .' He draws out the word. I close my eyes, shaking my head. He continues, '. . . needs to be able to go with the flow. Something I'm sure you're good at, right, Ripley?'

I level him with a glare. 'Let's keep all the answers open for whatever contestant might win your heart.' I pull up the next question. I feel Brett chomping at the bit beside me, ready to step in, but I keep going. 'How would your best friend describe you?'

'Trouble.' He doesn't even hesitate.

'If you could time travel, where would you go and why?' I continue to the next question.

'Wait!' Garrick holds up his hand. 'No follow-up comment on the last answer?'

I smile sweetly. 'No, sounds about right. So, time travel?'

'Anywhere?' he asks. When I nod, I notice the slightest dip in his smile – the barest hint at something deeper than his on-stage persona. 'Five years ago. Summer.'

'Why is that?' Mom asks. I knew she wouldn't let me run it for long.

He stumbles on his words, and that deeper something looks painful on his usually handsome, carefree face.

'Please be detailed,' Brett adds.

'What's your weirdest talent?' I pipe up. I don't know why he chose summer five years ago, but it's clear he doesn't want to say. I didn't want to do this show for many reasons and baring my vulnerability on a public stage was one of them. If Garrick has secrets he wants to keep, I won't be the one to yank them out.

The beaming smile is back, and he gives me the slightest nod. A tiny bit of annoyance dislodges in my chest, a warmth replacing it.

Melika and Nathan arrive at the tail end of it all, their footsteps up the old stairs just outside the door forcing us to stop and restart for noise issues. Brett is asking a few final questions they can pepper in throughout the show when needed. I kept Garrick on track, and I feel myself standing straighter at the feat. Another item to cross off the to-do list for the day gives me a sense of control.

Nathan is wearing a holiday FTG sweater screen-printed with the castle replica decked out in holiday cheer. I have no idea where he got this, but I'm unsurprised he already found the gift shop. 'You have to admit –' Nathan nudges me – 'Garrick is kind of cute.'

'Even I'm into him, and he's not usually my cup of tea,' Melika adds. We are both wearing matching 'Beeloved Crew' T-shirts. They have a mix of the FTG and Beeloved logos on them. It's hot under the filming lights, but the rest of the place is freezing with an upcoming storm.

I suppose I can see Garrick's appeal as I watch the single dimple appear on his right cheek. He does have that charming something that other girls are into. All I see is red flashing danger signs.

It's the ones who make you feel special that trick your brain into thinking everything is perfect – and that only burns you in the end. If I had a dollar for every time Mom went on and on about how this husband was *the one* ... Well, I'd have three dollars, but still, I learned.

'As long as he does his job and my mom is happy, that's all I care about.' After I convinced Mom to hire Garrick, she had to bring it to the investor. Like me, they also saw the strength in having a built-in fan base from Garrick's knight persona. Since the hiccups with losing the star, and the article stating Beeloved was on a downward trajectory, things seem to be taking a smoother course. So, as long as we don't totally screw up this reality show, the investment for the app should be a guarantee.

'Well, dears,' Nathan says, patting Melika and me on the cheek. 'I'm headed to FTG's hair and make-up department to further bolster my already impressive list of skills under the tutelage of a man named Pierre. I'll see my best gals later and we can ride a roller coaster. Sound good, Rip?'

I use my shoulder to push him toward the door. 'Byeeeee.'

Melika goes with Yvette, who is helping coordinate the locations we'll use for the dates. 'This is going to be so helpful for my future shop set-ups,' Melika whispers giddily as she walks away. At least someone is having fun.

'Will you take Garrick around with the team and get some B-roll?' Mom asks as they remove Garrick's microphone.

'Do I have to? I have some homework I wanted to work on.'

Mom huffs. 'Juliet, this is what interning looks like. I can't mark off that you've done your job if you don't help.'

Holding in my groan, I nod. 'Garrick, let's go.'

Garrick leaps over the cables on the floor and slides toward me on the wood. This cramped room was getting musty; it will be nice to breathe in some fresh air.

'Just the person I wanted to get some more face time with.' He flashes me a grin.

This time I don't bother suppressing my groan. We walk around the park and ensure everything we need for Friday is set up. That's when the girls arrive. At that stage, we'll do our interviews and prep for the first date, which is on Saturday. Most of the show will be filmed when FTG is closed during the day, but we want a little bit with the park open, so it looks like there's some interest in this place.

'Garrick,' the producer says when we get outside. It's sunny, and if you were looking out a window, you might mistake it for being warm – it's not, however, and I slip on my mittens hoping to stave off the frostbite. 'Why don't you walk us through the layout of Fairytale Gardens, for the audience.'

There are six of us out here. Garrick, myself, the producer, Garrick's aunt Maria, who's in charge of HR, a camera person and Brett.

Not one to miss out on showboating, Garrick slips on his million-dollar charm as the camera starts rolling and begins rattling off a script with ease.

'Now, if it's young kids you've got, or you simply like to take things a bit slower, Pixie Forest is your main hub. It's got all the best fairy-themed rides – Mushroom Spin being a general crowd-pleaser. But, if you're like me and seek a bit of a thrill –' Garrick winks at the camera, but since I'm right behind it, it feels directed at me – 'I'd highly suggest you give Ogre Escape a go. While still located in this land, it might scare the little ones, or set them up as a lifelong roller-coaster lover like myself. But discretion is advised.'

'You couldn't ask for a better star,' Maria whispers to me.

'That's exactly what I was hoping for.' I breathe easier the more people who agree with my choice of Garrick. If it goes great, Mom can take the credit, but if it fails, I'm on the hook for bad casting.

'He's never one to shy away from the spotlight. But ...' Maria glances over at Garrick, who is scaling the side of the train for a photo. 'He might seem like he's handling it all without a care in the world, but this family has been through a lot the last few years. A charming smile and quick jokes don't always tell the whole story. Be gentle on him, will you?'

'It's not really up to me,' I say, but add when she still looks melancholy, 'I'll do my best.'

We head out of Pixie Forest and show off a few market booths in the Village Center, sampling delicious caramel popcorn and spicy hot chocolate on our way. Then it's off to Carpathia.

'I do my best work at Knight School.' Garrick waves his hands dramatically at the wooden stage behind him. On either side, it has those life-size display pictures with the faces cut out that you can put yours into, to make it look like you're a knight jousting. 'You won't find anyone in all the lands more adept at sword fighting.' He doesn't wink, but I feel like his eye twitches out of habit.

We wander through the backstage passageway and past the horse stables back to Glacier Peaks. I glance at my watch, wondering how much longer this will take. I didn't realize I was signing up for a guided tour this afternoon.

'Am I not entertaining enough for you, Ripley?' Garrick pops up beside me, nearly making me drop my tablet.

I clutch it against my chest, taking a step away. 'It doesn't matter if *I'm* entertained. It's the audience that counts.'

He frowns, overly exaggerating it with a shake of his head. 'Ripley, if there's one thing you should know about me, it's that I will not rest until everyone leaves satisfied.'

I level him with an uninterested stare. 'I guess you'll be really tired these next few weeks.'

He counters, 'If there's another thing you should know about me, it's that I never back down from a challenge.' He walks away with the last word.

We capture key places in Glacier Peaks, like the ice cream parlor and the log flume ride, White Out. Then it's just the Perilous Sea that's left.

I've mostly tuned out Garrick by repeating my to-do list in my head. A calming trait I'm developing as I learn to stop biting my nails. But I dial back into his voice when he starts to talk about the pirate ride.

'Fairytale Gardens isn't known for scary rides, but if you pay close attention on Pirate Adventure, you might just get a few chills.'

I might not care about behind-the-scenes at FTG, but

I know Melika and Nathan do. And since I'm the best friend ever, I'm going to surprise them with a little treat.

Once we stop filming, I grab Garrick and pull him to the side.

'Here to admit you were wrong about my lack of entertainment skills?' Garrick asks.

Oh, geez, this boy is going to be the death of me. 'Nope. But I do have another question. Do you believe in ghosts?'

8

GARRICK

'You should just text her,' I tell Aldrich while we wait near the castle for my nighttime adventure to begin. It's past ten, and all the lights are turned off, except a strategic few.

Aldrich shrugs, staring at the ground while he makes doodles with the rain-wet toe of his shoe on the cement. He can't help himself – art is in his blood. He's been accenting our walls with finger paintings since he was a toddler. 'It's not that easy for me. I'm not like you and Tristian.'

Fastening on my big brother mantle, I say, 'You're not like me, sure – but who is?' I nudge him with my shoulder to make him look up. 'But Tristian? Please. He's not at all smooth, and look at him – he got an amazing girlfriend. Just slide into this girl's DMs and ask her to come by for some rides or snacks.'

'Fine, I can send a message, sure, but what happens when she's here in person?' His cheeks are pink, and I don't think it's from the cold. 'Like, what do I say? Every time I *think* about it, I get all tongue-tied and sweaty.'

'Well, luckily it's winter and you'll be outside, so she won't notice the sweat stains on your pits.'

'Not helpful, dude.'

'That was very helpful, actually. But since I'm such a kind and generous soul, how about I come along? We can do a double date or something.'

'Aren't you going to be a little busy with your *reality show*?' He's playing it off as a joke, but his lips dip a little.

'Never too busy to help my little bro learn the finer points of courtship,' I say, but he still looks skeptical. 'Ivor and Tristian can have the true love. You and me –' I fling my arm around his shoulders – 'we're just here for a good time.'

'Love doesn't sound that bad.' He looks over at me with those big round eyes, his artist soul peeking out.

Great, I think. *I've lost my last brother to the love boat.*

'Slow your roll, dude. Let's get you a first date before you go drawing your future wife a wedding announcement.'

'Thanks, G.'

My chest warms as his goofy smile clicks back into place.

'Any time. But right now, I've got an adoring audience to entertain,' I say as our group exits from the Fairytalers' section and heads toward us.

'So,' I say, when we've all gathered, clapping my hands together so hard they sting – the frigid night air isn't helping things, but it's needed to set the mood. 'Who's ready for a ghost hunt?' When Ripley asked me if I believed in ghosts, it took me about half a second to tell her that of course I did. But I didn't expect her to ask me to help her find one.

Melika jumps excitedly. 'This is so cool.' Frozen breath escapes from her wide grin, bright white teeth on full display.

'I don't know ... I'm not really into tempting the spirit world,' Nathan says, hand tucked into his plaid peacoat, shoulders pulled up to his ears to keep warm.

'I give you my promise that all the ghosts here are friendly,' I reassure them. I glance over to Ripley, wearing her puffy jacket. She must feel she's being wrapped in a blanket. Her face is unreadable – a look I'm realizing is her signature. I can't tell if she's unhappy or excited. I can never tell how she feels, which throws me off because I pride myself on being able to read people with ease.

I decide that my focus needs to be on the tour rather than deciphering the enigma that is Ripley. I invited Tristian and Imogen along, as well as Aldrich and Tyrone – a nice size test group – thinking that maybe if I did a good job, Tristian and I could convince Ivor to host a Halloween ghost tour next year. That'd be an awesome way to drum up more sales.

'Dang, I was hoping for some vengeful spirits.' Tyrone cracks a grin. 'I brought my salt and everything.'

'You watch too much *Supernatural*,' Imogen counters. 'FTG is more like chill spirits who just needed an eternal vacation. Right, Tristian?'

Tristian looks skeptical. 'Or, you know, just an illusion brought on by mass hysteria.'

I slap him hard on the back. 'Every show needs a naysayer. Glad you knew which part you were playing, brother. Speaking of, Aldrich, I need you to be my cameraman.'

He holds up his phone. 'If there are ghosts, G, I'll catch them.'

'I knew I could count on you.' With the roles set and the dark not getting any darker – it's showtime.

'To start our tour, we head down to the Village Center.' I use a deep, low voice, adding a spooky rumble to my words. The spookiness is offset by the cheerful Christmas decorations, but I'll just pretend the vibe is *A Christmas Carol*, and I'm calling forth the ghosts of Christmas past, present and future.

They hang on my every word as I spin the scene. I walk backwards so I can adjust my performance should I see them losing interest. Luckily, I know this park better than anyone, so I could walk backwards with my eyes closed and never run into anything.

'So, legend has it that many, many years ago, long before Fairytale Gardens was ever built, there was a *murder* on this very spot.' Tristian tries to cover a laugh with a cough, but I take the high road and ignore him. This isn't a true story. But neither is the Fairytale Gardens epic and we pretend like it is all day. All good narratives need a little embellishment.

'Two men robbed a bank, and they were here trying to hide their loot, but one of them got greedy – let's call him Simon – and decided he wanted the gold all for himself. But the other man – Yanis – was no fool. He sensed his partner was up to something, and before Simon could act, Yanis shot him in the chest and buried him, along with all the evidence of the crime, right here beneath these very cobbles you walk on. Sadly, he never got to come back for the gold, for he died the next day in a freak carriage accident. Some say the money from the bank was cursed, and that anyone who touches it will suffer the same fate.'

Ripley gives a little scoff, and I look back at her. 'Did you have something to add?'

She tugs on the ends of her ponytail. 'No. Well, it's just you might want to work on your story. Seems like you're mixing a few too many cliches. I'd just streamline for believability.'

People might find this annoying. But I believe it shows engagement, which is essential. 'You make some interesting points. We should brainstorm later, you and I.' I wink.

I don't wait for her response, knowing it's probably a blank face. I lead us toward the Perilous Sea. It's a cloudy night, and I've purposely left all the lights off to add to the eerie atmosphere.

'Now, I know this is what y'all really came for. Because this is where the real ghost lives.' I spin around, opening my hands wide as we reach Pirate Adventure. 'It's not just me who knows this story. If you search Fairytale Gardens online, you see lots of people talking about how they've seen a ghost among the pirates.'

Aldrich chimes in, almost like we planned it — we did. 'I've totally seen one.'

'Tristian, get your camera ready. You'll want to put this on the socials. If everyone wants to head inside, we'll start the ride and I'll point out the different places the ghost has been spotted.'

Everyone shuffles in, and Tristian gets the ride up and running, but I notice Ripley hanging back near the entrance.

'Don't wanna be stuck out here by yourself with the ghost, do you?'

Ripley holds herself tight as the wind cuts through. 'I'm not that worried about it. I'll wait at the exit for you.'

'Ripley, I didn't picture you as someone who was afraid.'

There's a cute little uptick in her lips, and I'm going to say that it's a smile. Her nose is pink from the cold. 'I'm not scared of ghosts. I just don't like theme park rides.'

My jaw drops as my eyes widen. I hold my hands up in retreat. 'What? You don't like theme parks?'

She plays with the zipper on her coat. 'Technically, I said theme park *rides*. But also, you're right, I don't like theme parks either.'

'That's shocking, considering you approached me *at* a theme park.'

'I don't have to like the place to know it's a good idea. So, go on with your ghost tour. I'll wait out here.' She slips her phone out of her pocket. 'But if I see a ghost, I'll make sure to send you a picture.' She hops up to sit on the cement planter decorating the exterior.

I nod to Tristian and use our twin telepathy to tell him to go on the ride without me. I saddle up beside Ripley, spying a picture on her screen of her and a woman who must be her sister.

She looks over at me. 'What are you doing?'

I shrug, kicking my legs out as I lean against the cement on one elbow, so I'm turned toward her. 'I decided I don't wanna go on the tour either. I've seen the ghost plenty of times. Me and Jeb are buds.'

'Jeb?' Her blue eyes are dark, like the deepest parts of the ocean.

'Yeah, the ghost. You didn't think his name was just *ghost*, did you?'

I watch the wheels turning behind Ripley's eyes. 'Good to know you and *Jeb* are on such good terms. We wouldn't want him interfering with the filming.'

'Ugh. I almost forgot about that.' I scrub my hand across my face.

'I thought you were excited?'

'I am excited. I'm just ready to get started.' Tilting my head back, I count the stars visible between the clouds. 'All this prep is so much work. I'm usually "jump in and start" guy. I don't like to plan.'

'Good thing I'm here. Because this show won't be successful without a lot of planning.'

I bump her shoulder. 'Looks like we make a good team. But don't worry, I won't make you admit that. It can be our little secret.'

'How chivalrous of you.' She looks down, kicking her feet against the planter.

'What?' I ask as I study the change in her demeanor – tension in her shoulders and hands as she grips the cement.

'I just – this is really important to my mom. I want this to go well for her. Beeloved needs this show to be a hit.'

'You're a great daughter. I can tell. I'm sure your mom knows you're doing all you can to make this successful.' My throat tightens, and it has nothing to do with the cold closing my airways. I like to think my mom knew I would help her with anything, but I was still so young when she got sick. And I've done a lot of growing up in these last two years. I just hope the kid I was then showed Mom how much she meant to me.

It's a stupid thing to dwell on. I know there is nothing I can do about it now. But that doesn't stop the thoughts from coming in uninvited.

'But it's not on me to make this a hit,' Ripley adds, taking me out of my head. 'You're the star. There's only so much I can do behind the scenes.'

'We might have only just become friends,' I say, and she scoffs. 'But as I'm sure you can tell, I'm more than capable of carrying a show. I mean, look at my amazing ghost story.'

She turns her head, and I swear she's hiding a smile. 'Oh, trust me, I won't be forgetting.'

'Is that your sister?' I nod to her phone.

'Yeah, Anna.'

'Older?' I blow air into my hands to keep the feeling in them.

'Yeah. She's married.' There's a weird dip in her voice on the word *married*. 'She has a little girl, Molly, the freaking cutest child ever. But Anna is set to have another baby soon – a boy – so, I guess I'll have to amend that title.'

I can see the sadness in her eyes when she talks about them. It's how I'd feel if my family wasn't around during the holidays. 'You should tell them to come by the park. I'll give them a private tour.'

Ripley isn't looking at me – her gaze is far away, like she really is seeing spirits from Christmas past. 'The ghosts might be a bit much for Molly.'

'All Christmas-themed, I promise.'

She bites her nail, before pulling away and shoving her hands into her pockets again. 'I'll consider it.'

9

GARRICK

The next few days are a blur of cameras, tinsel and interviews. The production crew has taken over the apartments and the main office, setting up their hubs for the show. Dad was strict about ensuring they didn't interfere with the park during guest hours, so we've struck a happy medium.

I'm thrilled this pre-stuff is almost over because it is *tedious*. I've been asked more questions in the last few days than in my entire life. I think I blacked out on the previous round and have no idea what I said. I'm ready for the girls to show up so we can get to the fun stuff I was promised.

'So ...' I say, pinning my letter to Santa on the paper Christmas tree hung on the wall in the break room. 'What hints are you giving me today about my potential true loves?' I slide into a chair.

'The same as I have every day,' Ripley says, not looking up from her breakfast. 'None.' She's sitting with Melika and Nathan, discussing their top Christmas songs. Which I would totally engage in any other time, but I've got another mission.

'Come on, Ripley.' Nathan nudges her in the shoulder. 'Just

one. Because I also would like a preview.' He glances at me conspiratorially. 'She won't let me see the pictures either.'

'Yeah, because I know you can keep a secret as well as a strainer holds water.' Ripley sips her orange juice, daring Nathan to argue.

I raise my hand. 'I'm actually great at keeping secrets.'

'You two are terrible influences.'

I lean closer, sneaking a piece of bacon off her plate. 'Just like three hints. That's all I'm asking for.'

Ripley watches me eat her breakfast before saying, 'Blonde, brunette and seventeen.'

'That's the hint?' My brows knit together in a frown. 'I could have guessed those things.'

She shrugs, pushing her chair away and grabbing her now empty plate. 'You said just three hints. This is a good lesson in being specific. I'll see you guys on set,' she says to the table before tossing her trash.

But I'm not done yet, so I follow her out the door.

'Ripley, I have to say, you're one tough cookie,' I say as we flow into the hallway.

'Thank you. Tough women get things done.' She scrolls through an itemized list on her phone.

I smile to myself. 'Of that I have no doubts.' I've seen her in action over the last few weeks and she is a machine. 'But seriously, help a fella out. I'm about to meet ten strangers.'

She spins around. Her hair is down today, framing her face in raven waves. 'My condolences.'

I start listing things off on my fingers. 'Are they easily queasy on a roller coaster? Do they like to eat turkey legs?

What's their favorite ice cream flavor? These are all important things a guy needs to know.'

She frowns, bringing her nail to her mouth like she's going to bite it before quickly dropping it. 'You didn't ask if they were pretty.' It's not a question, but she seems stumped by it all the same.

My body flushes with heat, and I shuffle back and forth. 'Well, I mean ...' I stumble on my words. 'Pretty is nice, but there are more important things.'

Ripley's face softens, but confusion clouds her eyes.

'What?' I lick my lips.

She shakes her head. 'I'm just surprised, I guess.'

'Oh, Ripley, stick around and you'll see I'm full of them.'

I hate that I can't read her. It's seriously my best skill. It's what makes me a great performer. I don't know why figuring her out is such a struggle – or why I kinda like it.

'Wait, so the girls aren't here yet?' Tyrone is sprawled across the sofa in my living room later that evening. Nathan, my new roomie, is peeling a boiled egg at the counter.

I came in the other day and Nathan had decorated the entire place for Christmas. There's garlands and lights, little Christmas houses on the bookcase, even a tree. I have no idea where he got the time to work that magic, but I'm impressed.

'They're being picked up tomorrow,' Nathan says.

I recline with my feet on the kitchen table. Aldrich sits across from me, doodling on a napkin.

'Bro, I only came here to see the girls.' Tyrone bends back over the sofa to look at me upside down.

'I thought you came for the free food and theme park rides?' I ask, playing with a nutcracker dressed like a pirate.

'OK, that too. But I've gotten neither. Where's my peppermint popcorn and roasted chestnuts?'

I toss him a half-eaten protein bar I snagged after my meet-and-greet. Dad is letting me take it easy on the knight duties since I'm starring in this thing, but I still make a few appearances – mostly because I love it. Summer is always the greatest time of year. People fawning over me, and me getting to show off my moves with a sword. Nothing better. It's usually too quiet the rest of the year. It gives my brain unwanted time to think. And trust me, nobody wants that.

'Let's go.' I stand up to stop my previously mentioned brain. I'm dressed in regular clothes, so we can walk around the park without much fuss. A few dedicated fans will recognize me, but we should be fine. I live for the hustle and bustle of the people crammed into every nook and cranny of the park. I feed off their excitement, letting it take me to another place.

A stroll down the Christmas market is the first priority. I love it here all the time, but after dark is freaking magical. The twinkling lights and festive music really scratch that holiday itch. I grab a cone of spiced nuts, warm and sugary, for Tyrone, and one jumbo gingerbread castle cookie keeps my little brother satisfied. I'm in the mood for something savory and opt for the Christmas dinner mac and cheese from one of the more popular booths – luckily, with a little sweet-talking the woman who runs it gets me a bypass on the line.

Stomachs full, we hit up two rides in Glacier Peaks – the roller coaster, Ice Shards, and the dark ride, Mystical Caverns – but skip White Out because I'm not about to get soaked and have my clothes freeze to my skin. While the momentary distraction is nice, it only lasts for so long before talk returns to the reality show.

'So, you just get to date these girls and then pick one in the end?' Aldrich says, nibbling on a slice of pizza he picked up from Glacier Eats.

'That is typically how a dating show works.'

'What if she doesn't like you?' he asks.

I chuckle, grabbing him by the neck and ruffling his hair. 'Little bro, you should know by now, everyone likes me.'

'Isn't this supposed to be about love?' Tyrone sneaks a handful of popcorn as we pass the cart. He smiles cheekily at Layla. After some subtle hints hyping him up the last several weeks, things are finally starting to happen with them. Baby steps at least. Maybe a little Christmas magic will move things along into the new year.

As I watch a banner with the Beeloved logo going up near the castle, a panicked hand squeezes my insides. This might be a terrible idea. Do I really want a camera shoved in my face asking me questions about love on a national scale? Heck, no. I only thought about how fun it would be having ten girls to date. Plus, getting promo for FTG and some inflow of cash to launch my fencing camp next year. The rest of the details didn't exactly seem important.

I dodged a question yesterday in an interview, when they asked about Mom. It felt like my throat was closing up and I couldn't breathe. How many more times will I have to create a clever way of getting around answering things like that?

'Dude, are you listening?' Tyrone elbows me in the rib.

'Yeah, sorry. Just thinking about my best pickup lines.' I shrug it off.

'Are you really going to find love?' Aldrich prompts, and I look around to see if there's a hidden camera. It feels like I'm being interviewed again.

'Love is for chumps. But I'm willing to fake it if it helps FTG.' That's the most honest answer I've given. Not that I'd say that on camera. I suspect Ripley knows it, but she doesn't seem to care. In fact, I don't think she wants to be here at all. She's only doing this because of her mom. And Nathan gave me a little insider info that Ripley was supposed to star but switched me in instead. I made a note to tease her about that later.

I only briefly saw her this morning at breakfast and I've missed the witty banter that's been getting me through the day. She's been too busy with the final arrangements for me to get much face time. But as we head into the backstage area, I spot her mom and my dad. They're standing in front of the apartments, both moving their arms animatedly.

'I changed my mind. I want to ride White Out,' I say, yanking Aldrich and Tyrone to a stop. The last thing I need is to be roped into a conversation with those two. They both love to be in control.

'Garrick,' Dad calls before I can sneak back through the apple tree. He waves me over.

'I got somewhere to be,' Tyrone, the coward, says, scurrying away.

'I need to finish my homework.' Aldrich heads off too, leaving me to walk the plank alone.

'Hey, Dad, Ms Ripley. What's up?'

'We need you for a fitting,' Ms Ripley says, no-nonsense.

Dad's jaw tightens. 'I told you, the current costumes are an FTG staple. He needs to be in those if you want him as a knight. They're iconic.'

'I need to be in costume?' I raise an eyebrow.

'We considered having you dressed as a knight when the girls arrive. Play into the fairytale theme. But your current costume doesn't fit the color scheme we are going for with Christmas.'

'He's not a Christmas nutcracker,' Dad interrupts. 'The original costume will do just fine. I have to put my foot down regarding maintaining brand purity. Right, Garrick?'

Usually, Dad wouldn't ask my opinion, but he needs a second.

I open my mouth, but Dad continues, 'Per your contract, we get equal say as regards Fairytale Gardens-related business.'

'I agree,' I quickly add, so I can bail. 'They need me in … uh … Ripley needs me.' I say the first name I can think of before dashing away. I'll leave them to argue. I need to clear my head before I meet my new love interests.

10

RIPLEY

It feels like everything has led up to this. We've got the rooms ready, the production team is here, Garrick is as wrangled as he's going to be and, finally, the girls are arriving. Garrick won't see them until tomorrow, when we do the welcome shoot. But these are his top ten matches. That's the new gimmick for this app. You're supposed to be able to find your match in ten clicks or less. And OK, sure, these girls aren't *exactly* his perfect matches. There were only so many candidates to choose from. It's not like most parents let their kids leave for three weeks over Christmas.

Plus, this is first and foremost a reality show. And the intentions of the type of people who apply for these kinda things are usually the same. I'm not saying that every girl here is looking for their five minutes of fame, but I'm not *not* saying it. We live in an influencer-obsessed social media world, and there's a lot to gain from upping those follower counts.

Hell, that's really all Beeloved is after, too. We want the views, so people in turn will download the app, which increases revenue. This is nothing more than a business transaction – as much as Mom, deep in her heart, would like to think it's about true love.

For such a smart, accomplished woman, I don't know how she let love hoodwink her so deeply. Someone in this family needs to have their eyes open to see the truth, and since Anna and Mom aren't up for the task, it has to be me.

So, the girls arriving today are the best we could get. But does it matter? I doubt anyone's actually watching this show for that; they're just tuning in for the drama. Why else do people watch reality shows? Still, if it gets Mom's app downloads when it launches, that's all I care about.

The van arrives from the hotel a few miles away, where the girls were dropped off by their parents. I see the shadows of people moving in the back. On board are the contestants, interns acting as handlers, and production and camera crew. We want the show to seem as natural as possible, so we will have set dates and interviews mixed in with scenes of the girls just relaxing and chatting. Those less scripted scenes are where they're hoping the drama happens.

They picked girls from different schools so they wouldn't already know each other, but given social media and multi-school sports events, I wouldn't be surprised if a few of them have had some contact.

While the girls are free to visit each other whenever they want, and have monitored access to their phones and the internet, we did want to limit the time Garrick spends with the girls off camera, just in case the magic moment happens. I might think love is a sham, but even I know that doesn't seem like the best way to produce natural chemistry.

My stomach somersaults – *why am I nervous?*

Maybe because I need this to go well, and also I want it

to be over. All this true love crap is giving me a headache. I glance at my tablet and scroll through the dossier with the contestants' pictures and bios.

Licking my lips, I square my shoulders and put on my fakest smile. To be fair, I've been told it's my only smile, but sometimes I don't think there's much to smile about. The girls clamber out of the van, with lots of chatter and squeals as they look past me to the castle beyond the backstage entrance.

I'm not sure where Garrick is – he's supposed to be somewhere out of sight. We want the first time he sees them to be a grand reveal on camera. He pitched having a life-size cut-out of himself here to welcome them, and I've never seen Mom veto something so fast. It really made my day.

'OK, ladies,' I yell, motioning for them to come toward me. 'If you'll line up and give me your names, we'll get you to your assigned rooms.'

With a list in hand, I'm in my element as the first girl approaches, and then Mom shows up.

'Make sure you're checking them off,' she says, like that wasn't what I was already going to do.

'I know.' I push my hair behind my ears. Trying my best to ignore her, I look up at the girl standing before me with an eager grin. 'Name?' I recognize her because I've memorized them all, but just to be sure, I let her say it out loud.

'Harmony Kim. This is so freaking cool.' Her black hair is twisted into cute spirals on top, secured with pastel butterfly clips.

'Totally.' I knew they'd be excited, but their enthusiasm is drowning me in stimulation. My head feels like it's swimming and, despite the cool air, I'm sweating under my Beeloved sweatshirt. I find Harmony Kim and check her off.

Harmony Kim (she's allergic to gluten! Remind food staff!)
Age: 16
Career Aspiration: CEO

The next contestant is a girl with a half ponytail of voluminous curls and a neon green scrunchie. 'This place is bigger than it looks on videos.' Her brown eyes drift to the roller coaster visible past the apartments and bare trees.

Kahoa Finau (has an adorable ginger-colored dog — also named Nathan lolol)
Age: 17
Career Aspiration: Mechanical Engineer

'Don't worry, everyone gets a map in their welcome pack,' I assure her. I spent last night finalizing them with Melika, so they were ready to hand to the girls when they arrived. Along with maps and filming schedules, it tells them their room assignments and where the hangout lounge is. It's a converted apartment the team fitted with cameras so they could record group chats more easily, without a production person having to be in the room. Melika helped deck it out with games, comfy seating and Christmas decor – they even have a hot chocolate machine with all the toppings.

'Do we get our own rooms?' the next in line asks before I can say anything. She's got on a red silk shirt and green corduroy pants. Red and green glitter dots the pale skin of her neck and clavicle. Apparently, she got the Christmas memo.

'If you read your welcome pack, you'll see there are four girls to an apartment.' I mark her name off without asking for it.

Desiree Sinclair (wants a green juice shot delivered fresh every morning to 'perform well' — assign job to Brett)
Age: 17
Career Aspiration: Life Coach/Actress

'You must be Ms Ripley.' Desiree's attention slips from me to Mom. 'I just want to say what an honor it is to meet such an accomplished woman like yourself.'

Mom smiles politely. 'Thank you, you're too kind.'

Desiree places her hand over her heart. 'I, too, am a woman with a plan. I've studied acting since I was three and really pride myself in my craft. So, if you need someone with a thespian background to take the lead, just know I am more than up to the task.'

I press my lips together to stay quiet as Mom says, 'I will take that into consideration.'

Looking a little distraught by the dismissal, Desiree moves along.

'I brought some treats for the crew,' says a girl with deep-set eyes and pronounced dimples. 'I hope that's OK.' She holds out a gift box wrapped with a bow.

'What a lovely gesture.' Mom takes it and hands it to Brett, her shadow. She raises her eyebrows at me and gives a subtle nod of approval. I guess we already have a front-runner.

> *Arianna Stefanopoulos (watch 1st name spelling. Crew keeps forgetting an 'n')*
> *Age: 17*
> *Career Aspiration: Pastry Chef*

The following two girls are polar opposites of each other. A tall girl with a killer embroidered denim jacket and velvet boots – which seem impractical if it snows, but I appreciate the commitment to a look. And a very petite white girl with the most extensive bangle collection I have ever seen on someone's arm. It goes to her elbow – she must be able to lift a ton after all that.

> *Zoya Gupta (show her the horses! She'll love it)*
> *Age: 17*
> *Career Aspiration: Vet*

> *Sophia Hume (Sophia no.1. Sophia H for the show)*
> *Age: 16*
> *Career Aspiration: Influencer*

The next girl is a model and is working the short distance from the bus like she's on a catwalk. Tyra Banks would be proud. Despite the cold weather, she's wearing a short dress, showing off her long, tanned legs. She even adds a hair flip at the end, her blowout nearly hitting me in the face.

> *Sofia Lima Alverez (Sofia no.2! With an 'f'. Call her Sofia A)*
> *Age: 16*
> *Career Aspiration: Model or Miss Universe*

A Black girl with round yellow glasses gives me a high five as she approaches, before taking my hand and offering a gentle squeeze. Her purple nail polish sparkles in the sun as she whispers, 'So, when do we meet the prince?'

'He's a knight, actually. And soon, I promise.'

Maya Hall
Age: 17
Career Aspiration: FBI Profiler (dying to hear more about this!)

The second to last girl is lugging three giant suitcases. She's also wearing a crossbody bag and a backpack. I do love a lady who comes prepared for any situation. But I'm worried she might pass out, all flushed cheeks and panting breaths.

Riya Fong (has CPR training — good to know just in case!)
Age: 16
Career Aspiration: Pediatrician

And *thank god*, we've reached the final contestant. She hands me a travel-size tinted lip gloss from her bag. 'I never come without gifts. This color will look stunning on you. Trust me.' She's wearing a *Black Girl Magic* T-shirt I recognize from the collab she did with a major beauty brand a few months ago.

I take the tube with a surprised, 'Thank you.'

Ellie Burton
Age: 17

Career Aspiration: Beauty YouTuber (she's already one and has a massive following. Will bring a much-needed boost to the episodes!)

'Let me just make sure you got it all in there,' Brett says, taking the tablet.

I let out a steadying breath through my nose. 'Shouldn't we get them inside, just in case Garrick is peeking?' Knowing him, he most likely will be.

After the girls get to their assigned rooms, we drop off their luggage and shuffle them into the Royal Fare. We have a super-tight schedule, so there is no time for relaxing this evening.

When we arrive, Nathan is dressed as an elf, standing in front of a table of ten preassembled gingerbread houses. On another table is an absurd amount of candy and treats, ready to decorate the houses: glass jars filled with peppermint candies and brightly colored gummies coated in sugar. And bowls of salty offerings, along with chocolate and marshmallows galore, adorn every available space.

'Did you buy out the whole store?' I whisper to Melika, who is leaning against the wall.

It's muggy with all the lights and camera crew. Plus, they can't turn on any air because it screws with the sound. I can't wait to see what a drippy mess the royal icing turns into on these creations!

'No, just mildly raided several. I didn't want to take *all* the stuff and leave some poor kid crying in a shopping cart.'

I smile as she hands me a pack of Hot Tamales. I pop one in my mouth, motioning to Nathan as they set the girls up for the shot to begin. 'Since when is Nathan on camera?' I ask through a mouth of spicy candy.

Melika grins, snapping a picture of Nathan. 'Since your mother dragged him over – we needed an elf to present.'

Nathan has exaggerated rosy cheeks, pointed ears and a striped green-and-white costume with red pointed shoes. He does a spin when he notices us watching him.

The cameras start rolling, and the girls are instructed to decorate their houses the best they can, because tomorrow Garrick will be judging. The winner will get the first one-on-one date.

Knowing this will take a while, I settle into a chair near the back, hoping Mom will be too preoccupied to find something for me to do. The girls laugh and chat as they make their gingerbread houses, and I find myself a little jealous. I can't remember the last time I did anything festive like that, or if I ever did. I didn't think I cared much about Christmas, but being surrounded by it, I wonder if I just pretend to make myself feel better.

Twenty minutes in and I am getting a little antsy, wondering if I can get away to do homework while they finish. Then I look out the window and spot a pair of binoculars.

'I'll be right back,' I whisper to Melika. Slipping out unnoticed, I weave around the side of the castle until I see the culprit behind the spyware.

'Absolutely not.' I yank the binoculars out of Garrick's hand and step in front of him to block his view.

'Hey,' he says, trying to take them back from me, but I whirl around so he has to do a spin with me. 'Those are mine.'

He attempts another grab, but I shove them behind me. His hand skims my waist, and my breath hitches as our cheeks brush. I nearly drop the binoculars, but manage to step away.

Taking a calming breath only does so much when I have to deal with him constantly doing the opposite of what he's told. 'You're supposed to be anywhere but here!' Annoyance drips from every word. Why must I babysit him? But I know Mom will freak out if she finds him. She's so dramatic, she'll think it's the end of the world.

'But here's where all the excitement is.' He grins.

'Save it for the showmance. Come on.' I grab the front of his shirt and drag him away from the windows. We're up in one of the towers off-limits to guests. 'How do we get out of here?' I huff after a minute, not knowing which way to go so he won't pass the girls.

He wraps his hand around mine, and my chest does this weird skipping thing. Maybe it's something I ate.

'Why should I tell you? Maybe I like being up here.'

'Look, can we both agree this thing needs to succeed?' I try to look over his shoulder, so I don't have to stare directly into his handsome face. Over the last few weeks, I've discovered that as much as he annoys me, his storybook hero-worthy face does not.

'I don't know. Can we agree on anything?' I don't like how his eyes follow the lines of my face, studying me, trying to figure me out like I'm a gift-wrapped present and he wants to know what's hidden underneath.

I don't want him to know me. I just want to get this over with.

'Garrick.'

'Ripley.' He steps closer, and I stand my ground.

'Do you want to ...' I glance over the edge to the theme park down below. Ugh, I don't want to go on any rides, but maybe there's something else. 'I don't know, play like Ring Toss or something?'

'I suck at those games.'

'Great, let's do that then.'

He chuckles, and it's a lovely, soft rumble. 'You want to see me fail?'

'I think it might be fun to watch you struggle, actually. Yes.' I smile slightly, so he knows I'm joking. Sort of. It does seem like everything comes easy for him. It might be nice to see what happens when it doesn't.

'Now, when I say I *suck*, I actually mean I'm way better than the average person. Just not as good as my brothers.'

'Of course you are.' I roll my eyes, returning to find him studying me. 'Better save some of that humbleness for your lovely dates.'

'Want to give me any more hints about them?' He kicks his leg up on the railing on my other side. He's always leaning on something. It can't be good for his posture.

'No. It's a surprise.'

'But if I'm supposed to find true love, I might want a little foresight.'

I scoff, and his eyes light up.

'Are you surprised I know such a big word?' he jokes.

I laugh despite myself. 'I mean, yes, but it's the true love line I can't take seriously. No offense. I know you work at a fairytale park.'

His blue eyes are bright in the afternoon light, and I stare longer than I should before I snap out of it.

'Shocking as it may seem, you and I have something in common. I also think true love is a ploy.'

'Don't let my mom hear you say that.' But I relax at the idea that at least on this we can agree.

'Wouldn't dream of it.'

'Juliet?' Mom's voice carries up the stairs.

'Who's Juliet?' Garrick says, a dangerous glint in his eyes.

'I don't know.' I try to play it cool. I've gotten lucky she hasn't called me that in front of him until now.

'Juliet Ripley!' I know that tone. If I don't get down there asap, it'll be trouble.

'Wait –' Garrick's fingers skim my wrist as I try to slip past him – 'your name's Juliet?'

I sigh, hot breath creating a puff of mist in front of me. 'Yes.'

His eyes have a mischievous glisten, and I know this will come back to bite me. 'You know, people often say I'm a Romeo. Maybe I've just been waiting for my Juliet.'

This is precisely why I don't go by Juliet. I don't need cheesy pick-up lines or references to damsels in distress. 'Hilarious ... I've never heard that one before.'

I tell him to return to his room and stay there until it's time to meet the girls. I'm not sure if he'll listen to me, but I'm also not sure it's my problem.

11

RIPLEY

Fairytale Gardens is alive with bustling energy as the evening crowds pour into the park. All the magic and splendor of the holidays, backdropped by a fairytale castle, has brought the people in droves. I hope this atmosphere also directs viewers to the show.

Is this typically how I would choose to spend my evening? No way. But Anna is coming with Molly, and I couldn't miss a chance to see them.

I grab a box of popcorn from the stand as Mom and I head to the entrance to greet them. I've enjoyed this little treat the past few days, and I guess I can see why people might like theme parks. There really is a difference in the popcorn – or maybe there's a secret FTG recipe.

'Juliet, we start filming with Garrick and the girls tomorrow. I don't have time to be out here,' Mom says as I steer her from running into a couple taking a selfie. Her eyes are glued to her screen, so she doesn't even notice.

Pushing her phone away, I offer her my salty treat. 'Here.'

'Thank you. I forgot to eat dinner.' She pops a few kernels in her mouth, then adds, 'Did you eat?'

She's never forgotten to feed me intentionally, but I did have to remind her plenty of times. Still, as I've gotten older, it's more like me being in charge of feeding her. 'I did. There was pizza in the break room.'

'I should probably ask if you had any vegetables.' Despite her need to return to the office and micromanage, she's happy. She believes this is all going to work out.

'Do the green peppers on the pizza count?' I smile.

She returns it as we reach the turnstiles that release guests into the park. 'I suppose it'll have to do. We'll make sure you get some veg at Christmas.'

I'm honestly shocked she remembered it's almost Christmas, but I won't hold my breath on that big feast.

'Aunt Ripley!' Molly yells, running into my arms and disrupting my thoughts of the sad Christmas that awaits me. Her sparkling shoes shimmer in the lights as we spin before I place her back on the ground.

'Close your eyes.' I crouch to her height. She promptly does, and I withdraw a plastic crown from my pocket, arranging it in her curls. 'Done. You're officially a princess now.'

Her eyes burst open. 'Take a picture. I wanna see.'

Snapping a shot, I turn the screen to show her. 'Perfection.'

Molly grabs Mom's hand and drags her away. 'Daddy! Daddy, look!' Molly runs to Mike, who's scrolling on his phone a few paces behind Anna.

Anna helps me up and pulls me into a hug. 'I never thought I'd see you participating in theme park culture, Rip.'

'I'm not. It's a plastic crown. I didn't buy stock in the place.'

My eyes drift to Mike, and my cheerful mood sours. 'I thought it was just going to be you and Molly?'

When Anna said she was coming, I agreed to hang out immediately, despite all the schoolwork and production stuff I should be doing. Would I have said no if I knew Mike was tagging along? OK, my answer would always be yes, but I could have mentally prepared myself to see his stupid, smug face.

He acts like he doesn't just abandon them without warning all the time. He probably thinks he's freaking father and husband of the year. How am I the only one seeing how terrible he is?

'He just got back in town and wanted to see the Christmas markets.' Anna rubs her belly, currently growing my newest favorite person. 'Gosh, he's doing somersaults tonight.'

'I'm shocked Mike had the time to spare for you.' I grip the edges of my sleeves.

'Juliet, can you not?' Anna looks so tired.

I squeeze Anna's hand with a nod before calling to Molly. 'Molls, what ride do you want to go on first?'

Molly jumps into Mike's arms. 'I think we should take her on the carousel,' he answers for her. He's always doing this for her and Anna.

I bite the inside of my cheek. 'Well, *Mike*, last I checked, your name wasn't Molly, so let's see what she says.'

Molly's little feet kick with glee. 'The train.'

My grin widens. 'The train it is.'

Pixie Forest is crowded with families, and the screams of delight from the roller coasters in the far corners echo around us.

The rides more suited for younger kids are located in the heart of the land.

'Anna said you don't do rides,' Mike comments as we reach the line for the Pixie Train.

'I don't, and I'm not going on the ride. But you and my mom can take Molly. Anna can't ride because she's pregnant – wouldn't want the baby shook up. So, I'll wait with her.'

Leaving the three of them, Anna and I head to a bench to wait where we can still watch.

'Ugh, yes, I love this bench. It's my new favorite place to be.' Anna groans with relief as she sits. 'So, how's it been going here with Mom?' She takes a handful of the popcorn I'm still holding.

'Interesting. I don't think I've ever spent this much consistent time with her. It's weird. But everything seems to be going off without a hitch. We'll just have to see what happens, now that all the contestants are here.' A lady selling light-up Christmas- and winter-themed balloons walks by, a trail of kids following behind her.

'She said you're doing really well, Rip.' Anna eats the kernels one at a time. Once, when we were younger, she shoved a whole handful in her mouth and cracked a tooth on an unpopped piece. She's more cautious now.

'She said that?'

'Yup. She's sent me pictures from set. Garrick, is it? He's a cutie, right?'

I frown. 'Ew, Anna. He's too young for you.'

She responds by taking my box away and holding the popcorn for herself. 'I meant to someone his age. Such as you, *little* sister.'

'I hadn't noticed.' I bury my face into the collar of my coat. 'Why?'

I turn to see her staring at me. 'Because I've been a little busy.'

'It just seems like you two are always together in the pics I see, so I assumed you would've glanced over at some point and noticed.'

'Nope. Maybe I'll add it to my to-do list and see if I can work it in.'

Anna just shakes her head, laughing.

Opening my phone, I check if Nathan or Melika has messaged. I told them to let me know if there was an issue with the girls and that I'd come back. They're shooting scenes with the contestants in the lounge tonight, getting their initial thoughts and excitement.

I spot a message to my dad from Thanksgiving. The response, an emoji of a turkey and a thumbs up. I didn't even warrant a heart emoji too?

'Did you see the pics of our little half brother with Santa?' Anna asks when she spies me staring at the screen.

'Who?' I close my phone, shoving it into my pocket. 'The only family members I recognize are you, Mom and Molly.'

Anna loops her arm through mine. 'I love you, Rip. So does Dad. He just doesn't know how to show it.'

I don't think that either of those things is true. I'm saved from having to respond by a notification that Garrick posted a reel on Instagram. I open the app and Garrick's mega-watt smile greets me. He's wearing a Santa hat and standing in a kitchen I don't recognize.

I click the volume up to hear him over the park noise. 'It's the day you've all been waiting for!' Garrick does a little shimmy with his shoulders. 'Well, tomorrow actually, but I'm building the suspense.'

'Is that him?' Anna asks. I nod. 'See, he's cute.'

'Shh.' I nudge her with my shoulder.

Garrick is still talking. '... for the next two weeks-ish, you'll get a video every day celebrating the Twelve Days of Christmas Cookies Countdown.' He pulls a string on a popper that releases confetti into the air. He is nothing if not committed.

'That's right, get ready for a whole bunch of mouthwatering cookies you will be able to wow and impress your loved ones with. These are a few family favorites that I've added my own twist to. Be sure to tag me and Fairytale Gardens if you make any at home!' Garrick bows and the video stops.

'I can see why you picked him as the star,' Anna says when I slide my phone back into my pocket. 'He's very charming.'

'He sure thinks so.'

'Do you think you can score me some of those cookies?' she asks as we watch Molly board the train, waving wildly to us.

'I'll see what I can do.'

Garrick Walton proudly presents
The Twelve Days of Christmas Cookies Countdown
13 December
Day 1
Chewy Molasses-Spice Cookies

Servings: 36 cookies

INGREDIENTS:

- 240g plain flour
- 1 ½ teaspoons baking soda
- 1 teaspoon ground cinnamon
- ½ teaspoon ground nutmeg
- ½ teaspoon salt
- 300g sugar
- 180g unsalted butter, softened
- 1 large egg
- 80g molasses (can use treacle – will make cookies sweeter)

INSTRUCTIONS:

1. Preheat oven to 350°F (180°C). In a medium bowl, whisk together flour, baking soda, cinnamon, nutmeg and salt. Add 100g sugar to a shallow bowl.
2. Using a mixer, beat butter and most of the remaining sugar (reserve a few tablespoons)

until combined. Beat in egg and then molasses until combined. Reduce speed to low; slowly mix in dry ingredients, just until a dough forms.

3. Roll dough into tablespoon-sized balls. Coat balls in reserved sugar.
4. Arrange cookies on baking sheets, about 3 inches apart. Bake, one sheet at a time, until edges of cookies are just firm, 10 to 15 minutes (cookies can be baked two sheets at a time, but they will not crackle uniformly). Cool for 1 minute on baking sheets, then transfer to racks to cool completely.

12

GARRICK

My costume is trying to kill me. I pull at the neck of my undershirt as it bunches in my leathers. While the fabric is usually soft, today it's like wearing a sack of hay. We're in a private room at the Royal Fare. It's a Saturday, so we couldn't close off the entire space. They put up soundproofing barriers between us and the downstairs, but I can still hear the chatter of the kids and parents eating their Christmas feast.

'Why are you fidgeting?' Ripley asks from beside me. She's not supposed to be in the shot, but we haven't started filming yet. 'Stop it. You need to look like you're happy to be here.'

'I am,' I say unconvincingly. Did someone turn up the heat? I'm sweating like it's the middle of July.

'Seriously –' she drops her voice so only I can hear – 'I thought you couldn't wait for this?'

I couldn't. *Right?* That's what I've been telling myself and everyone else since I signed up. But *freaking A*, now that these girls are about to walk through the door I feel like someone put itching powder in my costume.

I shoot a glare at my brothers standing by the door. But they don't appear to be holding in a laugh, so I'm guessing they didn't do that. Not that they would. This is too big of a deal to screw up. Great, so I guess it's all me. Being in the knight's skin has always made me feel like a million bucks. But that was in the context of the Carpathia story. What if under the judging eye of a camera lens it's not as dashing and heroic as I pictured?

Rolling my shoulders, I crack a sly grin to cover for these invasive thoughts. 'Don't worry, *Juliet*.' I emphasize her name, and her scowl loosens my tension. 'I got this.'

'For both our sakes, I really do hope so.' With that nugget of encouragement, Ripley heads behind the camera, where she prefers to be. I ignore the coldness I'm left with now I'm alone. It was nice having her there. Ripley is perfect company because she doesn't count. I mean, she counts as a person – but she's a safe zone. She's not a girl vying for my attention, and sure I like to flirt, but that's just me. Nothing is going to happen between us, so I can relax around her without worrying about my every action being caught for the show.

This 'dinner' is at noon, but they need to get it in early so I can have a one-on-one date tonight. I try to focus on that. I'll get to share the company of some lovely girl and do what I do best: charm.

Time to put on a show, Garrick.

I'm told there will be a voice-over when the show airs, explaining who the girls are as they walk in. Shoulders back, chin high, I roll out my hero smile and welcome each girl individually. I did manage a quick peek yesterday before Ripley stopped me, but not enough to recall much. I had no doubts these girls would be pretty, and I'm correct. They all come dressed in their princess best – gowns glitter and shine under the hot studio lights.

'Ellie, I love the matching gold eyeshadow to your dress,' I comment when I meet the first girl. 'Top marks for coordination.'

'A guy who notices that already gets an A in my book.' She smiles, batting her thick lashes.

This would be the first time I got an A in anything, but I'll save that info for the second date.

I meet several more girls and try my best to remember their names. But just as I think I'm going to mess up royally, Ripley holds up a giant whiteboard with the girl's name. I need to thank her later. Maybe by buying her a jumbo pack of markers – it seems like the type of thing she'd like based on the color-coded notes I've noticed.

The last girl I greet is named Sophia, just like the one before, and I'm glad there is one less name I'll have to remember. When I turn around, all the girls are staring at me, and I realize I'm the entertainment they came for. I might be a twin, but I've always been a one-act show – time to make good use of that skill.

'So, ladies, who's ready to eat?' I clap, attempting to make eye contact with each of them. I imagine they're the cheering crowd at Knight School, and it comes easier. It's all pretend – just the way I like it.

The food is good as always, but I barely taste any of it. It's buffet style, so I can talk to the girls while we eat.

'Wait …' I sit backwards on a chair at a table with three girls. 'You're going to be a FBI profiler? Like on TV shows?' I ask Maya.

She tucks a tight curl behind her ear. She's wearing a light-blue dress, simple in form, but the showstopper is the shimmery glitter all over her skin and nails. It makes her look like a moonbeam. She'd fit right in at the Starlight Ball the park holds every summer. 'Well, not exactly like that, but yeah.'

'That's freaking awesome. You also must have a stomach of steel and be incredibly smart.'

'I can handle myself on a roller coaster, if that's what you want to know.' Her soft laugh is demure – just like the princess I'm sure Beeloved would want me to choose.

'I played a dead body in an episode of *Law and Order* once,' Desiree chimes in, casually laying a spray-tanned arm over the back of my chair. Her fire-engine red dress is all the indication I need that she's going to be a scene stealer.

I crack a smile. 'You're far too pretty to play a dead body.' The smooth charm comes easy. The girls at the table swoon accordingly, but out of the corner of my vision I spot Ripley rolling her eyes.

I say my goodbyes and walk past Ripley on my way to the next group. 'Juliet, are you having a laugh at my expense?'

She glances over my shoulder to her mom across the room. 'You aren't supposed to be talking to me.'

'But you're so fun to talk to – that effortless way you laugh and fawn at my every word.'

Her brows pinch together. 'I definitely don't do that,' she whispers.

'*No*, but you're going to.' I've leaned into her without realizing it.

'Go,' she hisses before shoving me toward my next table.

I didn't think I'd be intimidated. I don't mean to sound cocky, I just don't get nervous at this kind of thing. But then again, I've never been the center of attention for ten girls simultaneously. And they're all so bright and pretty. I put on an extra layer of charm to compensate for my shakiness. When I feel myself slipping, I look at Ripley. Her unimpressed face should annoy me, but it weirdly makes me calmer. She feels like the only real thing in the room.

'Now, I don't want to scare you, but this is a very important question.' I slide into the empty seat at the last table. Riya, Sophia and Zoya are gathered in, like I'm the best present at the party. 'You're theming your Christmas tree decor – what do you call it?'

Riya wears a look I'm all too familiar with on my own face – mischief. 'You first.'

I match her stare. 'Riya, obviously I only have one option: The Knight Before Christmas. Complete with full armor and a sword.' The girls laugh, leaning in toward me. Riya even adds a hair flip for good measure, so I offer her a wink.

'Mine is Christmas in July,' Sophia says, twisting her napkin into the shape of a rose. 'Filled with flowers and sunshine, because I love summer.'

'We have that in common.' I place my hand over hers. 'Also, you have to show me how to make this, OK?' She nods eagerly.

Zoya taps her chin, eyes roaming the room before she says. 'Menagerie. It's covered head to toe in those cute felt animals.'

'Remind me to show you the stables. I think the horses will love you.' OK, I'm getting the hang of this. My shoulders relax and my costume finally feels like home again. 'All right, Riya, did you buy yourself enough time?'

She sticks out her tongue. 'Around the World in Twelve Days. So, instead of the traditional stuff, each day represents a different country and its culture.'

'You and my brother will get along nicely.'

She raises an eyebrow. 'I think I prefer this twin.'

I lean in conspiratorially. 'Me too.' I know it's only night one, but someone has just pulled into the lead.

After dinner, we move on to the gingerbread competition.

'I don't know how I'm going to pick.' I whistle as they roll out the gingerbread houses. 'You all did an amazing job.' I'm not exaggerating. These houses look like they could be on display in a museum. These girls came to play, and I respect that. I love a little healthy competition.

Attempting a bit of mystery, I keep my face neutral as I walk along the table filled with sugary creations. Some have chosen a colorful Hansel and Gretel aesthetic, while others have kept to a basic white, red and green combo. The sweet scent of frosting and spicy ginger cookies wafts toward me as I do my third pass.

Ultimately, I choose a house that looks Victorian, with lots of intricate lace detail and latticework on the roof. It's not my typical style, but the amount of work they put into the icing is out of this world.

'So, who's the lucky lady I get to go on a date with first?' I scan the line of girls after I make my pick.

There's a dramatic pause. The girls look at each other like they're unsure who it is. I'm guessing this was pre-planned because, after a few minutes, Arianna steps forward.

I give a shy half-smile – and while I'm not looking at her, I swear Ripley is rolling her eyes right now. 'I should have guessed the pastry queen would be the winner.' I hold out my hand to her. 'Shall we see what this date has in store?'

The first date was planned to give FTG its best exposure. We walk the park, drinking hot chocolate and eating snickerdoodle cookies while getting to know each other. They stop us at strategic places to work in the perfect shot of the rides and assembled holiday booths. As we stop and start for the fifth time because of noise and lighting issues, I'm really hoping the editors are good because this feels very manufactured.

While the show hasn't aired yet, we have been promoting it like crazy, and it seems a few guests here tonight are aware that's what we are up to. The Beeloved interns are working the crowd to keep them from intruding on the shots but without disturbing their theme park experience. Dad was very clear that the show was not to mess with operations and guests' experiences.

'You good?' I ask Arianna when Pierre jumps in to fix her make-up between shots.

'It's all a little weird, right?' She glances over at the camera. 'I've never done this kind of thing before.'

'Don't worry, you're doing great.' I hand her a candy cane from my pocket. I nabbed a few extra from my Santa meet-and-greet.

'So are you.' She lingers a little as our hands touch when she takes the sweet treat.

I'm not surprised that the date goes well. I'm fantastic at making conversation. Some people say I never shut up. We talk about our love of food and how we learned to cook when we were young – her from her Greek grandmother and me from my mom. I skate around talking about Mom too much. I don't know how much these girls know about FTG and my family. I'm sure they had some sort of briefing. But I don't feel like bringing up my mom's death on a first date. And I *really* don't want to talk about it on camera.

I'm used to an audience, so it doesn't bother me to have the cameras and the crew behind the scenes. But every once in a while I catch Ripley's gaze, and I stumble. My charm seems to be working on Arianna, but I wonder what would happen if it was Ripley sitting in her spot.

I imagine there would be many more puzzling looks, and I'd have to fight for that smile. Arianna gives me a smile about every three seconds. Don't get me wrong, I'm eating it up. But, I don't know, it feels like it would be more rewarding if I had to work for it.

Which I know is shocking to hear from my mouth because working for it is about the last thing I ever want to do. Easy going and unbothered is my preferred speed. So, why do I keep looking at Ripley when Arianna is sitting in front of me?

13

RIPLEY

'I think this might actually work,' Mom says as Arianna laughs for what must be the hundredth time at something Garrick has said. We're in an alcove of Pixie Forest, the warm glow of lights speckled in the trees and shrubbery.

As much as I want to, I haven't been able to take my eyes off Garrick. Because, *ugh*, he really is charming. A little too much sometimes. I don't know how anyone else doesn't see that he's clearly performing. I want to run over and shake him to see if the real Garrick falls out. If I hadn't spent nearly every day with him for the last several weeks, I'd probably be fooled too, but I've seen enough peeks at the boy beneath the armor to know the difference. Still, the girls seem to be eating it up, and the cameras too. That's all that matters.

I rub my thumbnail over my bottom lip, trying not to bite it as I look back at Mom. 'So, does that translate to "Well done, Ripley, I should listen to you more often"?'

She pulls me into a side hug and kisses the top of my head. I relish the gesture – the warmth of her against the cool evening. Lately, she's always too busy for me. 'Like mother, like daughter.'

'That feels more like you're complimenting yourself.'

'Shh, we don't want to ruin the shot,' Mom says before walking away – moment over.

Whether Garrick's putting on a show or not, I'm just happy that the first day went off without a hitch. I was worried Garrick wouldn't take it seriously, but he's great. He really was made to be on stage.

I wonder what that's like? Feeling so confident in your own skin. It's not that I'm not confident. It's just that I don't always know how to do it in a way that doesn't feel like I'm trying to prove myself. Garrick makes it look effortless.

Garrick says goodbye to Arianna and the cameras shut off for the night. Everyone goes their separate ways to finish post production or to get some sleep before tomorrow's early shoot.

'So, how did I do?' Garrick says, walking up beside me as I finish an email. Mom wanted me to send her daily updates for accountability and progress reports to the investor.

'Satisfactory.' I don't want to inflate his ego any more than necessary.

His nose and ears are pink on the tips. 'Really? I don't even get a "Good job, Garrick" or a "Thank you for saving my butt, Garrick"?'

I level him with an impassive stare. 'Nope.' I spin away, but he takes my elbow, sending sparks flying up my arm, despite the fact I'm wearing a heavy coat and can't even feel his skin against mine.

'Fine. Will you at least indulge me in letting off some steam? I'm too wired to go to bed.' He scrubs a hand through his blonde locks, messing up the perfect swoop they created for the show.

I raise an eyebrow. 'What did you have in mind?' I shouldn't engage. Still, I'm curious to know what Garrick does to unwind.

His gaze sweeps the park before settling back on me. 'Want to go do a ride?'

I should have guessed that would be his go-to activity. 'Ugh, no. I don't like theme parks, remember?'

He recoils like I punched him. 'Oh, I recall you tearing down my livelihood, yes.'

I shrug, ignoring how his undivided attention makes my cheeks warm and my heart beat faster. 'They're loud, and I don't trust the safety standards.' I leave Pixie Forest behind, heading toward the apartments via Carpathia. I've been running on coffee and fumes this last week, getting everything ready. I'm already exhausted and filming has only just started. I should nab whatever sleep I can get and leave Garrick to his nonsense.

'Then why did you wanna film here?' He jogs to catch up.

'One: it wasn't my decision. And two: I don't actually have to ride anything.'

He rubs a hand across his forehead, leaving a red mark. 'OK, that is a sentiment we'll have to deal with later. But for now –' he taps his fingers against his chin – 'what do you say to some karaoke?'

'You have a whole day of filming tomorrow.' We step through the hidden exit in a sparkling apple tree. 'You should get your rest.'

He slings an arm around my shoulders and my heart skips

a beat. 'I told you, Ripley, I won't be able to sleep.' He is just so effortless. It makes it easy to like him.

So, I relent, slightly. Call it professional curiosity. 'Karaoke? Let me guess, you have a whole set-up in your apartment?' Totally seems like something he would do.

'No – great idea for the future, though. Remind me to ask Santa. But for now, I know a place.'

I decide, if I'm going to let Garrick drag me around, I need backup. Nathan and Melika are more than happy to tag along when I message them. They were helping in the lounge where the girls had been hanging out and debriefing about meeting Garrick while they waited for Arianna to come back from her date.

Garrick and I are waiting by his car for them when a voice rings in the darkness. 'Hi!' Imogen bounds across the parking lot. 'Tristian is a party pooper and decided sleep was more important than singing.' Her sparkling dress is peeking out from her coat. 'But I have no such responsible bone in my body, so let's do this.'

'Happy to have you as my surrogate twin for the night, Imogen.' Garrick grins.

We pile into Garrick's car a few minutes later when Nathan and Melika arrive. He takes us to a building a few miles away. The faint glow of stars is visible in the ink-black sky. A neon sign blinks in yellow letters, reading Wayward Bar. Cars fill the tiny parking lot, but that doesn't faze Garrick as he pulls around the back, stopping next to a dumpster.

'A bar?' I say when he turns off the engine.

He grins in the shadowed light. 'Yes.'

'Oh, Rip.' Nathan conceals a laugh in the backseat.

I ignore my friends. 'Let me guess, you have a fake ID?'

Garrick gets out of the car. 'Juliet, I would never.' He grabs his chest. 'Besides, I don't need one. I have a hookup.' I follow him reluctantly to a side entrance.

Garrick sends a quick text. I huddle against Melika as we bounce up and down to stay warm. I'm about to tell Garrick to take us back when the door opens. A tall Black guy around our age with a T-shirt sporting the bar's name gives Garrick a toothy grin.

'Tyrone, you already know Nathan. And this is Melika and Juliet.' Garrick motions to me.

'It's Ripley,' I correct. Garrick is getting way too much enjoyment out of that.

Garrick has the audacity to wink at me before turning to Tyrone. 'Tristian needed his beauty sleep, but Imogen is here in his stead. We wanted to do some karaoke.'

'Sure thing. We had a cancelation, so we got an open slot.' Tyrone pushes the door open and we head through.

The packed bar is in front, the music blaring and the crowd rowdy. It smells like fried food and malty beer. As we head toward the rooms in the back, the faint sound of music spilling out, the scent lessens.

'We have several private rooms you can rent for parties and karaoke,' Tyrone explains as he unlocks a door, swinging it open to reveal a moderately sized space with a large TV on one wall and a brown leather sectional attached to the other, with a coffee table in front of it. In the center of the room is a karaoke machine and several microphones.

'I'll go first.' Garrick takes a minute to scan the karaoke options from the tablet.

'I must warn everyone,' Imogen says, yanking off her jacket. 'While I may have dressed like a pop star, I do not have the vocal cords to back it up. So, I'm just apologizing in advance. But what I lack in talent, I make up for in enthusiasm.'

'Don't worry, babe.' Nathan pats her arm. 'I've got enough talent for the both of us.'

'Bless you.' Imogen does a little spin before running up and stealing the tablet from Garrick.

'So, is this a date?' Nathan asks, digging into the loaded fries Tyrone brings us.

'Between me and you?' I deflect. 'Nathan, I didn't think I was your type.'

'Ten points for the dodge,' Nathan says, the cheese pull catching on his chin. 'But no. With our star over there.' He nods to Garrick, who has wrestled the tablet back from Imogen and is studying the songs like a manual to deactivate a bomb.

'Nathan, duh. Of course not.' I pop a fry in my mouth, the delicious salty bacon coating my tongue. 'He's got plenty of girls to choose from.'

'But if he didn't?' Melika chimes in.

'If he didn't, nothing. Garrick just wanted out, and I figured he needed a babysitter.'

'Mm-hmm, sure.' Nathan smiles. 'I just see the way you two spar. Seems like it has some electricity.'

'Whatever electricity you're imagining between us is to power the success of this show.' But even as I say the words, my eyes drift to Garrick. Maybe another life. In this one, I've seen the way love holds you captive and next thing you know, you're raising a (very awesome) kid, but with a person who is killing you slowly each day in a million different ways. Full autonomy of the heart is the only way to go.

Garrick finally makes his selection, and I recognize the music before the words start. It's 'Juliet' by LMNT. I groan, fingers covering my face.

'This one goes out to a special someone,' Garrick says, winking at me.

What have I got myself into?

The second the song ends, I jump out of my seat and grab Garrick's microphone.

'Hey, I have another song in my set.'

I push him toward the couch. 'Sharing is caring, Garrick. Let someone else have a turn.'

'Well, then ...' He smiles. 'Please grace us with your lovely pipes.'

As he walks away, I realize I'm holding the microphone and am now expected to sing. But I have another idea, since I don't want to wake every dog in the neighborhood with my terrible voice. 'Nathan, Melika, Imogen, get up here. Time to spread some Christmas cheer.'

Nathan bounds out of his seat. 'I know the perfect song!' He taps the tablet a few times to get to his selection and the bright notes of 'Jingle Bell Rock' start.

With the colorful flashing lights and overwhelming beat of the song, I forget for a second that Garrick is even here. I'm lost in the music, laughing through the lyrics Melika and I don't know by heart, unlike Nathan, who is word perfect.

Unable to sit still, Garrick joins us on stage and finishes the song.

'Encore, encore,' Nathan yells, spilling water down his front as he chugs from his glass.

This is the first time all week I've felt relaxed. It's been non-stop with the show and Mom's stress levels hitting the max. But here, it feels like none of that matters – it's like my brain let out a huge exhale. 'You can't encore yourself!' I laugh.

Nathan ignores me, picking three more songs for us all to sing. 'Wannabe' by the Spice Girls – obviously. 'Shake It Off' by Taylor Swift. And one more Christmas hit, 'All I Want for Christmas Is You', because it's not Christmas without Mariah. When those end, Garrick adds a few more, and then Melika takes her turn, with Imogen acting as backup vocals and improv dancing.

The hours blur by. I don't know how long we've been in this muggy room, but, for once, my logical brain isn't worried about calculating the time left on the clock until my next to-do-list item needs to be checked off.

Nathan spins Melika round as Garrick takes the lead on the final chorus. Not to be outdone, Imogen grabs my hand and we twirl around the stage, stumbling into each other as our sides ache from laughing. Usually, I wouldn't be keen on this, but it feels like the exact right thing to do. There is no show, no knight in shining armor ready to pick his beloved. We're just five friends letting off steam on a Saturday night.

I giggle as I stumble into Garrick belting out the last chord – ever the professional, he doesn't miss a beat.

'Admit it.' Garrick grins when the song ends. 'This was a good idea.'

I bite the inside of my cheek, glancing around the room. 'Ask again in the morning.'

'One for the road?' Garrick hands me the microphone. 'You didn't pick any yet.'

I know we should go home, it's past midnight, but one more song won't hurt. I pick a classic One Direction song and let the world slip away. Not admitting to Garrick that this is the most fun I've had in a long time.

The Twelve Days of Christmas Cookies Countdown
14 December
Day 2
Candy Cane Cookies

Servings: About 42-48 cookies

INGREDIENTS:

- 240g butter
- 200g caster sugar
- 25g icing sugar
- 1 teaspoon vanilla extract
- 1 teaspoon peppermint extract
- 1 egg
- 300g plain flour
- 1 teaspoon baking powder
- ½ teaspoon salt
- Red gel food coloring
- 2 tablespoons finely crushed peppermint candies
- 2 tablespoons granulated sugar

INSTRUCTIONS:

1. In a large bowl, beat together butter, the caster and icing sugars, the extracts and the egg on low, just until combined. Stir in flour, baking powder and salt.

2. Divide dough into two equal portions. Add red food coloring to half of the dough until the desired color. Wrap each portion of dough in plastic wrap and refrigerate for 3–4 hours.
3. In a small bowl, combine peppermint candies and granulated sugar. Set aside.
4. Preheat oven to 350°F (180°C).
5. Take one teaspoon of each dough. Roll each teaspoon into a rope. Place one red and one white rope next to each other and twist them together. Press ends together to prevent unraveling.
6. Place on an ungreased baking sheet, curving one end to form a candy cane shape. Bake for 8–10 minutes or until lightly browned. Immediately sprinkle cookies with the sugar/peppermint mixture. Place cookies on wire rack to cool completely.

14

GARRICK

I don't remember requesting a wake-up call, and if I did, it wouldn't be for obnoxious knocking at seven a.m.

'Go away.' I bury my head under my pillow, one hundred per cent sure that it's Sunday and the park doesn't open till ten. But then everything comes flooding back. I'm starring in a reality show and have actual responsibilities beyond the walls of this theme park. And apparently, being the star doesn't mean you get to sleep in.

The intruder banging at the door doesn't wait for my permission before they open it and barge on in. 'Get up, sunshine,' Tristian says, kicking my bed, then kicking me for good measure. 'You know they've been calling you for like thirty minutes?'

The vibration rattles my already fuzzy brain. 'I should've never shared the womb with you.' I was having a really good dream, and I do not appreciate Tristian's mug interrupting.

Tristian is fully dressed and empty-handed. If he's going to pry me from my sweet dreams, the least he could do is come bearing coffee. 'You're the wise guy who decided to spend your night singing karaoke. So, forgive me if I'm not sympathetic to your suffering.'

I fumble for my phone, my hand hitting the wooden nightstand, and I curse under my breath as I tap the screen to see a dozen missed calls.

'Garrick, come on, you can't be doing this.' Tristian pulls the blanket off and me with it.

I barely catch myself before my head hits the ground. 'It's a little early in the morning for character assassination, no?'

I wasn't trying to screw it up. I just may have made an error in judgment last night, going out to karaoke – only because I'm tired. Not because the karaoke itself was a bad idea. Honestly, the crap I'm going to get for being late is all worth it for seeing Ripley's face when I sang 'Juliet' to her. I'm going to have to do it again. I've made it my side quest during this show to get her to smile – *really* smile – for me, even if it's just one more time.

Tristian doesn't leave my side until I'm inside the main building and on my way to get ready.

As I sit in hair and make-up, I tune out Ms Ripley and Dad lecturing me about the responsibility of being on time. I offer an apologetic smile, giving them an affirming 'yes, sir' and 'yes, ma'am'. By the time we're headed to the park for a group date, I've smoothed things over.

'Hey there, Sleeping Beauty,' Ripley says as the fresh cold air hits my face as we get outside. Her cheeks are rosy, and she's wearing fluffy pink earmuffs. They're very whimsical for her, and it makes me smile. Also makes up for the long lecture I got before this.

I don't have to wear my costume right now, so I'm in a thick flannel and jeans, topped with a gilet and dark brown boots. 'How do you think I keep looking this good?' I give her a nudge with my shoulder. 'Let me guess, *you* woke up at the crack of dawn, ready to conquer the day?'

'I'm on my third coffee, and it's barely seven-thirty. How do you think I'm doing?'

She might feel tired, but I'd say she looks beautiful. Her oversized coat is zipped to her chin and she keeps burrowing deeper inside. Her blue eyes, just peeking over the collar, give me a shot of caffeine right to my veins when she glances at me.

'Remind me never to listen to you again.' There she goes, always pretending she doesn't like me. But if I annoyed her as much as she plays at, I doubt she would've gone out last night. She's warming up to me, even if she doesn't know it yet.

'Oh, Juliet, you can just tell me you had a good time.'

She doesn't deign to respond and skips ahead to where the girls are waiting at the ice-skating rink.

'I like the earmuffs,' I call after her.

She flashes me a narrowed gaze over her shoulders. 'You can borrow them later.'

'Don't think I won't hold you to that!'

She smirks before turning away, and I press a hand into my chest. It's all warm and fluttering.

Today's the first group date – if you don't count the welcome dinner. We're going for a full winter wonderland. The ice-skating rink in the Perilous Sea is ready with stage lighting and cameras. The 'sea' in the center of the land usually smells like chlorine, but any hint of that's gone and a fresh, glassy ice rink stands in its place. All around us are the various sea-themed rides.

The Mermaid Grotto, with its stage set up, is the production hub. I've never been on an actual set, but I'm guessing this is a scaled down version. Most cameras are small, and sometimes they film on their phones. But it is legit because I met the investor and everything. He was a bit high on his horse for my taste, but I guess when you've got money multiplying while you sleep, it comes with the territory. Perhaps he could give Dad a few pointers.

We have to do this early because the park opens at ten. We don't want to give away anything that will be in the show. They're really hyping this up. I'm committed to doing social posts for it daily – I've worked it into my Cookies Countdown videos. It's been nice to revisit Mom's family recipes; it's almost like she's here celebrating with me.

I can already tell from my growing follower count that the show will be a hit or a disaster. It's a good thing people will watch for both.

Everyone's bundled in their winter best, and we've got the castle and holiday lights on. Dang, it does look pretty magical. All we need is a little snow. The forecast doesn't show any, but I hope we get a white Christmas.

Riya spins around like a pro on her skates the second they touch the ice. 'We should have a race,' she suggests, and I'm very into her competitive side. 'Winner gets the first one-on-one time with Garrick. That cool?' She turns to me for approval.

'Oh, I'm never one to stop a bet. By all means.' I dig my blades into the ice with a blur of shavings. Whoever I pick to stick around until the end needs to be able to grab the audience's attention. Love isn't my endgame, but I do want a good time – and I think Riya will be more than up for the challenge.

We just started, though, so I don't want to count the other girls out yet. 'Still, to keep everything fair, I'll make sure I get a chance to talk to everyone. So, no worries if you aren't a world-class figure skater . . .'

The girls line up at one edge of the rink, and I'm on the other. 'On your marks,' I yell. 'Get set, skate!' They take off in a flurry of arms and ice. No surprise, Riya is in the early lead – proving her front-runner status once again – her skills on skates unmatched. If she wins, I know what I'll be asking her about.

But just as I think the game's over, Ellie comes out of nowhere with a burst of speed and skids past Riya and right into my arms. She's panting and can barely see me past the curls in her face.

'Remind me to always bet on you in the future.' I brush the hair from her eyes. 'Seriously, all of you can join my skating team any day. But –' I place out my hand for Ellie – 'you won fair and square, so let's chat.'

First, I talk with Ellie about her successful beauty YouTube career – she has enough discipline and productivity for both of us. Next up is Riya, who got second place. She attempts to teach me some Cantonese but says if I want to learn more, I'll have to keep her around. *Well played.*

I'm thriving, showing off my skating skills and watching the girls. Some of them are seriously talented figure skaters.

This is fun. I'm having a good time. The girls all seem great, and I'm definitely enjoying the flirting. Riya, with her outgoing, up-for-anything nature, and Arianna, with our baking connection, have stepped into the early leads, yet ... I don't think I'm feeling what I'm supposed to be feeling. We just started, and no one expects me to fall in love immediately. And I don't expect myself to fall in love at all. But I just thought I'd feel different. Instead, it's the same I always feel when I go out with a girl.

Perhaps all that no-love talk has already sealed up my heart with a 'no vacancy' sign. I'm good with that, right?

Yeah. Totally. It'll make this all that much smoother. FTG's future is all that matters. I don't need my heart jumping in and messing things up – I'm more than capable of doing that on my own, thank you very much.

I overheard Dad on the phone yesterday, talking to the banks. I didn't catch the whole conversation, but from the dire look on his face I'm guessing it wasn't great. But we can fix it. We always do. I need to make this work and look as authentic as possible – no matter what I feel.

So, I do what I do best when I don't know what to do: I lean into the persona created for me by FTG. Kendrick the Kind, the stalwart knight, never lets me down.

I'm skating around with Desiree, and she's trying to show off a spin when her heel gets caught and she slips. I grab her to keep her from slamming into the ice. Her nails dig into my shirt, and I struggle to keep on my handsome smile through the stinging pain.

'Don't worry, I'm used to girls falling at my feet.' I do

understand that that could come off cocky, but it seems to work for me.

'*Omg*, I'm so embarrassed.' Desiree glances down, brushing hair off her face.

I lift her chin. 'Don't be. I'm just glad you're OK.' The words sound right. But they don't mean as much as she must think they do, by the doe eyes she's fluttering at me. I mean, I'm glad she's OK, but in like a general sense. I hope everyone is OK after a fall – unless it's my brothers, in which case it's freaking hilarious.

Before I know what's happening, she wraps her arms around my neck, giving me a huge hug. I wipe some ice off her cheek when she pulls away, my hand lingering there for a moment. Batting those long lashes framing her doe eyes, she leans in and kisses me. Out of instinct, I smile cheekily when we break apart.

It's not a bad kiss per se – other than a little wet. But the first thing that pops into my head is: I hope Ripley isn't looking.

15

RIPLEY

'Did you get that?' Brett whispers to the camera operator. 'That first kiss is gold. Desiree is a perfect co-star.' Everyone gives nods of approval.

If they were asking me, I wouldn't say Garrick looked like he enjoyed it very much. But maybe that's just because I'm starting to see a crack in the facade. That opaqueness of his persona is wearing away to show the real Garrick underneath. Or maybe he did like it, and I'm just hoping he didn't. That cheesy grin he's sporting might not be the mask I think it is. Perhaps Desiree's boldness is exactly the type of thing he's into.

Which is absolutely, completely ludicrous. I want him to like it. He needs to enjoy it for this to work. I shove my hands into my pockets, squeezing them into fists to keep warm. My brain is still foggy from last night. I opened the door and let Garrick slide past the barrier I should have made more solid between us. I'm letting him seep into my everyday life; my hormones or whatever are trying to trick me. Garrick is a flirt with everyone. I just need to remind my brain that none of it means anything and he's just trying to get a rise out of me.

I picture Mom crying after her last divorce and throwing out everything in the house that reminded her of him. Or the times Anna was left waiting at the movies when Mike said he'd be there, but canceled last minute – or worse, showed up and made the Anna I know shrink into herself as he controlled every aspect of the night.

OK, feeling better. I'm centered now.

Nathan is once again presenting as an elf. I hope Mom is paying him for this – I should double-check to make sure he's getting a fair deal. Nathan is living his best life, becoming the figure skating commentator of his dreams by giving a play-by-play. I haven't seen Melika this morning. She's off with Yvette, getting set up for the elimination tomorrow.

'Go check on the oldest.' Mom startles me with a nudge, and I yelp. I'd been so absorbed in the aftermath of the kiss, studying the reactions of the other girls and Garrick, that I didn't notice her coming up alongside me.

'What?' I push my earmuffs back to hear better. They're almost as good as noise-canceling headphones.

She nods to Ivor, standing a few feet away from the rest of production, arms crossed as he judges the scene. 'These Waltons are very hands-on. Go put the fire out before it starts. I'm sure Barth sent him here to report back.'

'I mean, it is their park,' I say cautiously.

'And it's our show, Juliet. Will you please do as I say?'

I lick my chapped lips. Then I remember that the lip gloss Ellie gave me is still in my pocket. I slip it out and apply a thick layer. 'Yes, Mother.' I give her a salute before walking to Ivor.

'Hey.' I offer a polite smile. I haven't spoken to him much other than when we first arrived with the crew.

'Hello.' He's brisk but polite, barely glancing at me before returning his attention to the rink. Out of all the Waltons, he comes off the most reserved, probably because he's six years older than Garrick and Tristian.

'It's really exciting, don't you think?' I ask, then add when he frowns in confusion, 'That we're finally shooting.'

'Oh, yes.' He nods.

'Garrick is a natural.' How long do I have to stand here for Mom to be satisfied?

Ivor's jaw muscles clench.

'OK, so just let me know if there are any concerns. I'm happy to help.'

Ivor looks over at me for the first time. 'Fairytale Gardens has been a part of my family for the last twenty-five years since my dad designed every aspect of it, from the turnstiles to the castle's stained-glass windows. I hope you and your mother understand we have a legacy to maintain.' His tone is firm, but I can see the worry in his eyes.

'You're aware of the incident last summer?' His words are measured.

'I read up on it, yes.'

He twists his hands in front of him. 'Well, as I'm sure you also read, it had a ripple effect on our attendance and investors.'

A business magazine did a whole spread on the rise and fall of the park. Despite the smiling face Fairytale Gardens presents to the public, it seems like behind the scenes it's been a different experience.

'I can't go into details, for obvious reasons,' he continues. 'But just know that this whole endeavor isn't just a gimmick for good press. Its success will heavily affect the future of FTG, and my family.'

The heaviness in his voice makes me worry, too. This park is their whole lives. The last thing Mom needs is a forlorn Walton walking around making her even more anxious. I offer him some much-needed reassurance. 'We'd never do anything to compromise the park's integrity.' I might not have a theme park to protect, but I want to ensure Beeloved succeeds.

'Or my brother's.' He nods toward Garrick, who is seeing how many marshmallows he can shove into his mouth at once. He and the girls are at the hot chocolate booth next to the rink while they take a break from skating.

'He seems like he can handle himself.'

'Garrick's the life of the party,' he says dully, making it sound like the worst thing someone could be. 'If it's up to him, he'll make sure it never stops.'

'OK, well, um ...' I have no idea how to follow that up. 'Like I said, let me know if you have any concerns and I'll address them right away.' I offer a quick wave before heading back to Mom.

Nathan grabs my arm before I reach her and pulls me toward the ice. 'Come on, Ripley, let's use it while they're busy.'

Riya offers to show us a few moves and I'm stunned by her skills. She's doing jumps and twists I could never even attempt. But she is nice enough to offer us newbs some pointers.

I haven't ice-skated in years. I went with Anna when she was in high school because she was in love with one of the hockey players who trained at the rink. All I remember is falling on my butt and having a massive bruise for the next two weeks. But I'm so cold, maybe a little ice-skating will warm my body.

'First rule,' Riya says, gliding backwards in front of us. 'Don't be afraid to fall. It's going to hurt, and you will for sure have bruises, but it's going to happen. So, you can't let it stop you.'

Never the worrier, Nathan takes off and promptly falls, nearly doing the splits in the process. I cringe, inhaling sharply, worried we've lost our elf, but his shocked face transforms into laughter and I breathe a sigh of relief.

'See, the first one is out of the way.' Riya takes his hands as they practice going in large circles. 'That's it. Great job. Try not to look at your skates. Keep your chin high.'

'Ripley, hurry up!' Nathan calls as they move further away.

I'm like a shaky newborn giraffe as I try not to faceplant in front of everyone. 'If we're going to keep doing this,' I say to Nathan, who is already spinning circles around me, 'I'm going to need to watch about a thousand TikTok tutorials.'

I'm the kind of person who always wants to have my best foot forward. So, I do all the research I can about the situation before it arrives.

'Ahhh,' I scream as my feet slip out from under me. Luckily, I was next to the wall, so I slide down the side of it and plop on to the ice rather than slam down. But it still stings. It's good my coat is so fluffy because it caught some of the impact.

'Juliet!' Mom yells from the side. 'We don't have time to take you to the hospital. Stop messing around.'

I wave my hand in the air from my spot on the ground. 'I'm fine, thanks for asking.' A hand reaches down to help me. I grab it before I realize whose it is.

'Milady, are you OK?' Garrick yanks me up, his voice light, but I see a worry line between his brows. I don't know how he got over here so fast.

I clear my throat, wiping excess shards of ice and snow off my coat. 'Don't you have enough ladies to play knight in shining armor with? Do you really need to be over here?' Embarrassment colors my cheeks, the flush creeping down my neck.

We're still holding hands, and I quickly yank mine away, heading off the rink.

'Ripley, I will always be where I'm needed.'

I keep my gaze down as I unlace my skates. Why does my stomach feel like butterflies are slamming into every available space? He's just a boy. He's not a knight. He's occasionally charming, if a bit over-the-top. But that doesn't mean anything.

When I finally look back up, Garrick has moved on to talking to Zoya and those butterflies suddenly fall still.

16

GARRICK

Rule One: Do not sneak out to see a contestant when all cameras have been switched off for the night.

Of course it was only a matter of time before I broke it.

It's not like they can keep us from each other 24/7. The backstage area is only so large, and the sort of people with performing genes who applied for this show could only be restricted for so long.

So, there have been random meets where we nod and smile. But my little after-hours excursion is anything but random. If I'm going to make my performance on the show look authentic, I need a little time where there's no cameras or production members staring at me. Because I don't know how long flirting without substance will work. I'm happy to play a character, but I need some background information to do it justice.

I'm going to Riya's apartment with several games in my backpack. I figured that would be the best way to get to know her – you can tell a lot about a person by their Monopoly strategy.

Arriving on the apartment's second floor, I skid to a halt when a voice rings into the silent night. As a precaution, should any production members be nearby – or god forbid, Brett – I hesitate near the stairs so I can make a quick exit.

'No, I promise, nothing is going on.' I don't know the contestants' voices well enough to tell who it is. Peeking around the corner, I spot Riya pacing in front of her door, hand over the phone to muffle her conversation.

'Babe, babe, it's *fine*.' She's attempting to soothe the person on the other end. I'm not in the habit of eavesdropping, but if the situation presents itself, who am I to deny it?

'I told you, it's all an act. Whatever you're seeing on TikTok is for show. I need this to help boost my followers. I really want to get that brand deal.'

Babe? Who is she talking to? A lead ball drops into the pit of my gut, my fingers turning white as I grip the straps of my backpack.

Riya continues, unaware she's being overheard. 'You know I love you. And I promise, as soon as this is over, I'll make it up to you.' She giggles, responding to whatever the person says. 'You know I'm not into blondes. I love your whole tall, dark and handsome thing.'

If there was any question about who she might be talking to, that answers it. Gotta be her boyfriend. So much for my front-runner.

Finding love was never on the table for me. I was looking for someone to have a good time with and maybe do a little kissing – I'm in no way opposed to that. But I guess I never thought about what the girls might be here for. I did this to get FTG promo and cash for my fencing club. Perhaps none of them are here for me either.

Does that make this easier? The bruising to my ego tells me otherwise. But it's not like I can even be mad at Riya. She's got things she wants and is taking the opportunities when she can.

Quietly, I head down the stairs and back to my house.

The Twelve Days of Christmas Cookies Countdown
15 December
Day 3
Grinch Crinkle Cookies

Servings: 18-24 cookies

INGREDIENTS:
- 300g plain flour
- 1 tablespoon baking powder
- ½ teaspoon salt
- 100g granulated sugar for rolling
- 300g caster sugar
- 2 large eggs
- 80g softened butter
- 2 teaspoons vanilla extract
- ½ teaspoon peppermint extract
- Green gel food coloring
- Large heart-shaped sprinkles

INSTRUCTIONS:
1. Preheat oven to 375°F (190°C) and line a baking sheet with parchment paper.
2. In a medium bowl, mix flour, baking powder and salt.
3. Place 100g of granulated sugar in a shallow dish and set aside.
4. In a large bowl, cream together butter and caster sugar with an electric mixer.
5. Add vanilla and peppermint extracts and then add eggs one at a time, mixing after each.
6. Slowly add in the dry ingredients until incorporated.
7. Add a few drops of green food coloring and knead the dough until the color is evenly distributed.
8. Divide the cookie dough into tablespoon-sized balls and roll in the granulated sugar to coat.
9. Place on prepared baking sheet and flatten slightly.
10. Press a heart-shaped sprinkle into the center of each dough ball.
11. Bake for 8–10 minutes or until set.
12. Allow to cool on the baking sheet for a few minutes before moving to a wire cooling rack to cool completely.

The first episode is set to air tonight, so we're up early again to film the first elimination. Before I can break some girl's heart (their words, not mine) I have to do an on-camera interview where they ask me about my thoughts and feelings – the worst part – and look like I'm struggling to send a girl home.

I actually *am* struggling, but not because I have feelings for all of them and it's impossible to choose. It's more like I don't have strong inclinations toward any of them. Especially after last night's revelation by Riya.

So, how did I pick?

I won't say this out loud, but I put all their names into a hat and drew out which one I was sending home. If we're all here for our own agendas, it felt like the fairest way to do it. Fate can decide.

'How are you feeling, Garrick?' the director, Hassan, asks me. We're nestled into Dad's old office overlooking the Village Center. They've made this area the command hub for the entire Beeloved team. Dad insisted they didn't mess with the park's operations, so Ivor suggested they use these old rooms. I hope they don't figure out this is where the evidence was found that 'incriminated' Dad in charity fraud and later cleared him. I still have a little trouble trusting journalists – and sure, that's not the production company's job, but they are here for a story.

I was bummed not to see Ripley when I walked in. At least with her I know where I stand. I doubt she's sleeping in, so she must be prepping the elimination.

Shaking my head, I dip my brows into a frown and stare into the camera like it's an old friend. The producers said that was the best way to think about it. 'It comes and it goes, you know? I'm excited to move forward with the girls who are staying, but I hate to let one of them go when we've only just started.'

Hassan nods like he understands. At least one person is buying my performance. 'Why did you choose to send this girl home?'

I had to tell them ahead of time who I was eliminating. They pretty much let me choose on my own, but there are a few girls they strongly requested I keep around because they make good content.

I scratch the back of my neck, forcing myself not to tell the truth. 'Like I said, it was tough, but I didn't feel like she and I were meant to be. She's awesome, and I know her Beeloved is waiting out there.' I almost choke on the last words, the lovey-dovey crap getting stuck in my windpipe. Everyone else is eating it up. I wish Ripley were here to roll her eyes for me.

After a few more questions, I'm ushered to the elimination. Since it's a Monday, the park is closed until early afternoon, so we're filming in front of the tree and castle. It's a lovely background to break some hearts.

The process is relatively straightforward. I stand on my mark, and the girls are in a semi-circle in front of me. They all look killer dressed up in their best fits, and I'm in a version of my knight costume Dad and Ms Ripley finally agreed on. As I say the name of each girl staying, they come up and I place a bee bracelet on their wrist.

Then I have to say a line that I hope gets easier with time: 'Will you be my Beeloved?' It's so cheesy, even for me. The first time I say it, to Maya, and she accepts with an enthusiastic hug, my gaze automatically seeks out Ripley over Maya's shoulder.

Ripley isn't rolling her eyes, but she is biting her thumbnail, face molded into a shape I'm assuming is fighting the previously mentioned roll. A laugh bubbles in my chest as I watch her struggle to contain it. I have to bite my tongue to stop myself.

Some might find the dramatic pauses I sprinkle into the elimination overkill, but I enjoy the drama. Until I catch the looks on the two girls who are left and just want to put them out of their misery. In the end, it's Sophia H I send home. Despite her being an influencer, production didn't mind letting her go since she wasn't as comfortable on camera as some of the other girls.

As we wrap up, everyone keeps saying how hard it must be and that they don't envy me. But the thing is, I don't feel anything. I mean, I feel bad hurting anyone, but it doesn't make me sad I could be losing a potential girlfriend. I learned the hard way that all letting someone get close to you does is devastate you. At least I discovered that before I got too old. I won't spend my whole life on a roller coaster of lovesick heartbreak.

Keeping people at arm's length is the only way to protect yourself.

With the first elimination done, I have the day off from filming. All the post-production editing is taking place, and I was told I could relax. But Dad has other ideas.

'Ms Ripley!' Desiree calls as Ms Ripley is walking away.

'Yes?' Ms Ripley's response is polite, but curt.

'I just wanted to follow up about that scene idea I emailed you.'

'Right...'

Their conversation fades away as I put distance between us, lest I be drawn into extra filming. I'm due out for a show at Knight School this afternoon, but I want to be somewhere else right now.

'Do you have any cookies?' I ask when Ripley opens the door to her apartment.

'By all means, come in.' Ripley steps to the side as I am already making my way in.

All the apartments look the same, so I feel like I'm stepping into my own. Only this one smells slightly better. But it does kind of remind me of a 7-Eleven. Maybe I should've asked for nachos and a hot dog instead.

'Was that a yes or no on the cookies?' I would just start opening cupboards, but my mother did raise me right.

'I think Mom bought some pumpkin chocolate chip cookies?' Ripley rifles through the cupboard and pulls out a plastic container. 'Aren't you getting enough sugar from your daily baking videos?'

'When it comes to sugar, Ripley, there is never enough.' I take the treat and start eating. They are soft and chocolatey, not as good as homemade but they hit the spot. I would ask for milk, but I don't want to push my luck. 'Plus, I've been giving most of them to Aldrich to share at school.'

'So, what's up?' Ripley asks, leaning against the counter. I notice she's got a few notebooks out with lists on them.

'What makes you say something's up?' I mumble through a mouthful of cookie, catching the crumbs before they land on the carpet and are lost to oblivion.

'I've never seen you eat a cookie so fast.' Ripley has a pen stuck in the bun on top of her head. I wonder how long it's been there. She's so organized. She probably just keeps one handy should she need to make a graph.

'Have you seen me eat a lot of cookies?' I flash a grin, brushing crumbs off the table and tossing them in the trash. 'Have you been stalking me?' This is what I need. A conversation that isn't being recorded, or that doesn't have the weight of futures relying on it going smoothly, and doesn't have to lead anywhere.

'Change the subject much?' Ripley's got this little hidden smile that tugs at something in my gut.

I should find it frustrating that she doesn't fall for any of my tricks. People tend to like me right away, and being able to get in their good graces with ease has always been a saving grace. It means I don't have to think too hard. And people don't have to think too hard about me. But working for her attention is kind of doing it for me.

'Was it hard to do an elimination?' Ripley says this a little quieter.

I take my time chewing, fishing around in my chest for any sadness that might be there from sending Sophia home. But I come up empty. It's just a rattling chasm. 'I don't wanna sound like a jerk and say it wasn't hard. I guess it was just different.'

'You didn't feel like you were sending your princess home? Still a chance for true love?'

I chuckle, popping the last bit of cookie in my mouth. 'I think that title is still up for grabs. Guess your mom will be happy about that.' I almost tell her about Riya, but what good would that do? I don't want to get Riya in trouble or force Ripley to keep this secret from her mom.

Ripley picks at a spot on the counter. 'As long as she's happy about something. This whole thing has literally been her only concern the last six months.' Her voice dips at the end.

'Not you?' No matter what my mom had to deal with, whether it was the park or when she got sick, her boys were always her primary concern. Even when it should've been herself. It's something I didn't think about until after the fact. When that person who cares about you more than anything is no longer there to do it, it is like this big gaping hole. I didn't have anyone to care any more. I know I have the rest of my family, but I don't have my mom. Tears sting my eyes and I blink quickly to make them stop.

'Crap, I'm sorry I didn't ...' Ripley trails off, not knowing what to say. 'I know your mom ...'

I shake my head, waving her off. 'Nah, don't worry about it.'

'I know we're not, like, friends or anything. But I've been told I'm a good listener, so if you need to talk.'

'You're a good listener?'

She throws a towel at me. I've deflected well enough, and I could just leave it at that, but I decide to add, 'I want to make sure this thing works. Plus, my mom probably would've loved it too.'

'I'll make sure we do it right. Your mom will be proud.'

I'm often praised for how well I can make those around me

feel at ease. It's something I actually really pride myself on. It comes from some place deeper than charm and the witty comments. Mom was like that too. Everyone always flocked to her because she made them feel special and included. I spy that exact nature in Ripley – even if she hides it behind spreadsheets and time management. She just wants to ensure everything goes smoothly and that no one has to worry about the little things. She and I would make a good team. I'll make everyone laugh while she makes sure we don't end up missing our exit.

I nod toward the kitchen island. 'You making an escape plan?'

She looks over her shoulder, twisting her bottom lip in that deep-thought way she does. 'It's Nathan's birthday, so I was trying to throw together a quick thing for him tonight.'

I perk up, coming over to examine what she's got so far. 'You're having it at *Olive Garden*?'

Ripley shrugs. 'Nathan likes Italian food.'

'You know we have Italian food here, right?'

Ripley raises an eyebrow. 'You mean at the seafood restaurant?'

I blink in shock. 'I'm surprised you knew that.'

'I read up on the food locations as research. I watched a vlog of someone trying all the menu items.' She says it like her dedication to information isn't a true marvel of brain power. 'But I wouldn't exactly call that Italian just because they serve pasta.'

I gather up her lists in a single sweep.

'What are you doing?' She tries to take them from me, but I hold them in the air, out of reach. She jumps closer, body sliding down mine. My mouth goes dry as our eyes meet, hers widening. She backs away quickly, cheeks flushing pink. 'Please, give those back.'

I clear my throat, navigating my plan back on track, but I'm distracted by the peach scent lingering between us. It suddenly feels like it's a hundred degrees. 'You have to know how to order. Plus, they make an amazing strawberries and cream cake, which I know Nathan will love.'

'It's kinda last minute.' Ripley bites her thumbnail.

'I'm the *king* of last minute. Let me handle all the details with the restaurant and we can surprise Nathan.' I return the precious lists to her. 'What do you say?'

She still looks dubious but nods. 'OK, if you promise you can handle it.'

My face breaks into a wide grin. I might have a lot on my plate at the minute, but I will never pass up a chance to surprise someone.

'Should we invite the girls? I don't think Nathan would mind.'

'No,' I say way too quickly.

'Why?' Ripley's eyes run over my face.

'Because, it's Nathan's night and I don't want to steal his spotlight.' For once in my life, I'm looking forward to being a background character.

17

RIPLEY

I cup my hand around the phone so Anna can hear me. 'No, I don't want to watch it.' I hold my arms in tight as I squeeze through the crowds gathered in the Perilous Sea to view the ice-skating show they put on at night.

'Why not? It's the first episode. Don't you want to see all your hard work?' Anna is trying to convince me to watch the show's premiere on YouTube with her later.

Seeing our futures crash or succeed in real time is just not a torment I'm willing to put myself through.

'Sure, but I don't want to see the live chat, and plus – sorry, excuse me,' I say when I nearly collide with a guy who's trying to carry three plates of funnel cakes. It would have been a million times less busy at Olive Garden.

'Ripley...' Anna prompts.

'Right. Plus, I have Nathan's party, so I can't anyway.' I finally breathe as I approach the restaurant, leaving the figure skater crowds behind.

'Is this the one you let your karaoke buddy plan?' I hear the teasing in her voice. 'You two really make a great team.'

'Bye, I have to go.'

'Wait, Rip, I was just kidding.'

'*Loveyoubye.*' I hang up before she can say more.

When I walk into the restaurant, Garrick greets me in his knight getup – the chocolate-brown leather adorned with his cape and sword makes for a rather impressive display.

'I didn't realize it was a costume party.' I run my hand over the loose, white button-down tucked into my faded high-rise jeans.

Garrick straightens his leathers. 'I didn't get Nathan a present, so I figured a night with a knight was a decent substitute.'

'Hope you trademarked that line.' I hold in my laugh, still worried about giving him too much. I wouldn't want to be mistaken for one of the adoring contestants he gets praised by all day. 'It's perfect, though. He'll love it. Is everything set up?' I glance around the crowded restaurant, adjusting the gift bag looped around my wrist. Unsurprisingly, the place smells like fish, but not as bad as I assumed it would, masked somewhat by the garlicky fried undernotes.

'Yup. We're in the back.' Garrick grabs my hand and leads me through the restaurant. I'm so taken aback by the sudden jolt of electricity from his touch that it takes me a second to remember that guests in this restaurant are watching us.

Quickly, I pull my hand away, squeezing mine together instead. Garrick glances back, a tiny frown appearing before he turns forward.

The restaurant is divided into sections to represent different parts of seafaring life. The largest area resembles the docks, with wooden crates and painted ships on the walls. To the right, we have an under-the-sea theme, with deep-blue walls and sea creatures decorating the space – it feels a little macabre to be chowing down on popcorn shrimp while their smiling cartoon counterparts stare at you. The left is decorated like you're on a great sailing vessel, complete with creaking ship noises as an accompaniment to your dinner.

'Garrick? Oh my god, it is him.' We pass a table with a family of five. The parents and little brother look confused, but the two girls have gone all doe-eyed.

My body tenses, ready to turn on intern Ripley mode, but Garrick swoops in with ease. 'Ladies, how's dinner?' He leans against the backs of their chairs.

They giggle, looking at each other. 'Good, yeah … uh.' The younger stops, deferring to her older sister.

'We follow you on TikTok and are so excited for the show tonight.' She's clutching her phone so tight I'm worried she'll break it.

'Well –' Garrick crouches between them – 'how about a picture real quick to make all your friends jealous?'

They blush and nod. Their mom quickly snaps a picture and thanks us before we leave.

'That was really nice.'

Garrick shrugs like it's no biggie. But he's always taking time to make sure everyone feels included. It's not at all how I expected him to be before we met. In fact, he's far less conceited.

Garrick leads us to the back, where French frosted-glass doors read 'Captain's Quarters'.

'After you.' Garrick opens the door and lets me through, hand grazing the small of my back. I swallow, mouth dry as his touch disappears, almost like I imagined it.

'Oh, Garrick.' My heart leaps, and I lay my hand over it to ease the fluttering. Dozens of balloons and streamers, and a celebratory banner over the back window, decorate the room. The center table is adorned with nautical-themed place settings like I saw in the other dining rooms, but each seat here has a party hat and horn. In the middle is a cake with 'Happy Birthday Nathan' on top in bright-yellow frosting.

'How did you have time to do all this?' My chest expands, filled with gratitude. This is way more than I was anticipating.

I expect the cocky grin I'm familiar with, but instead it's just a soft uptilt of his lips. 'Magic. If you stick around, maybe I'll tell you my secrets.'

'Thank you,' I whisper, tears prickling my eyes. I'm not used to someone putting so much effort into something for me. I'm usually the one doing it for others.

'Any time, Ripley.' We stare at each other in silence, eyes locked like we're trying to communicate words neither of us can speak.

The moment is broken by my buzzing phone. Melika is keeping Nathan distracted until everyone gets here.

It's another twenty minutes before all the guests arrive. The room is filled with noise and excitement as we dim the lights and wait for Nathan to walk in. I stand beside Garrick in the dark, hands brushing as we're jostled around among the excited group.

'They're here,' I tell the room, and we go silent.

The door opens, and we flip on the lights. 'Surprise!' we all yell, not precisely in unison, but close enough.

Nathan's face glows with shock as he takes in the scene, the biggest smile I've ever seen exploding from him.

When I look over at Garrick, he's not watching Nathan, he's studying me.

'You know how to bring a boy to tears.' Nathan pulls me into a hug. 'Thanks, Rip.'

I nuzzle my face into his sweater. 'Anything for you, always. You smell amazing, by the way.'

'Don't I?' Nathan puts his wrist to his nose. 'Melika got it for me.'

'It's very manly. Like you've been in the forest chopping wood and wearing flannel while holding fresh linen.' I take his arm, leading us to the head of the table.

'*Soooo*, you know how for my present you said we could see whatever movie I wanted?' Nathan puts his party hat on, then grabs mine and places it on my head.

'Yes ...' When he elongates the *soooo* at the start of a sentence, I know to prepare myself.

'I was thinking maybe we could see an improv show instead?'

'Improv? I didn't know you were into that.' We've been friends for years and he's never mentioned it before.

He blows into his horn, which sets the rest of the table off to using theirs. 'After dipping my toes into this elf presenter game ... I don't know, I think I might like to try out for the spring play. But I need to see a few more actors first.'

I smile, heart warming. Nathan wanted to come here to get out of class and spend weeks at a theme park. I didn't realize he might actually get something even more meaningful out of it.

'I will look into the best ones.' I squeeze his wrist.

'I love you, Ripley.' He kisses the back of my hand.

The dinner is delicious. I know Garrick said they had Italian, but I wasn't holding out high hopes, but just like all the food I've had in FTG, it's spectacular. Heaping portions of garlic bread, meatballs, chicken parm, and every type of pasta/sauce combo you could think of. Despite all those carbs, we manage to save room for the strawberries and cream dessert.

I grab two plates with cake and ice cream, heading over to Garrick, who sits at the far end of the long table, staring intently at the other end.

'Practicing your X-ray vision?' I ask, placing the plate in front of him and taking a seat.

'Monitoring my protégé.' He pokes his fork into the cake and shovels a huge bite into his mouth without breaking his gaze.

'Aldrich?' I ask. His younger brother and a Black girl his age in a cute baby doll-style blue dress are chatting.

'Mm-hmm.'

'Are they on a date?' Aldrich's cheeks are tinged pink as he draws something on a notepad. The girl tucks a strand of hair behind her ear, a sweet smile gracing her features.

'Yup. It's his first one.' I've never seen Garrick focus this much on anything.

They share a laugh as Aldrich points to the drawing.

'It seems to be going well.'

'The kid's super shaky when it comes to talking to girls, so I figured I'd help him out. This seemed less stressful than a one-on-one.'

'Speaking from experience?' I run my fork through the frosting, then lick it off slowly. Frosting is the best part of a cake.

Garrick finally looks over at me. 'Nah, I'm a natural when it comes to talking.'

'You do seem to like the sound of your own voice.' I bite my fork to stop from smiling, but freaking Garrick spies it anyway.

He cracks a grin. 'Guess that makes two of us.' He really does have an answer for everything.

I force my eyes from his and back to Aldrich, who, at that exact moment, spills soda down the front of him. 'Yikes, your protégé is in jeopardy.'

'I wouldn't count a Walton out so quickly. Look.' He points as Aldrich's date helps to clean up the mess. Despite the red flush on Aldrich, they're each smiling. They say something I can't hear over the noise, both laughing after.

'You're a good brother.'

'The world throws a lot of punches. I just want my family to know I'll always be there to have their back.'

Those inconvenient butterflies are back, zooming in my stomach. Which barely has room for them after all the food. 'I feel the same way about my sister, Anna. When we were little, it felt like us against the world sometimes.'

He drags his gaze from Aldrich and back to me. 'I always loved having brothers because it's like having a ready-made best friend.' He resumes eating his cake. Doing that thing he's so good at – making you feel like the only person in the room.

'Someone you can share all your secrets with.'

'Yeah.' He plays with his ice cream.

'I miss having her at home.' My chest tightens as I smooth the frosting over the plate.

Garrick nudges me with his shoulder as if he can sense my dipping mood. 'You can share some of those secrets with me, if you want.'

I open my mouth to say – what, I'm not sure – but Nathan saves me from having to work it out. 'Ripley! Come here, we're doing a photoshoot.'

'Duty calls.' I stand, but Garrick grabs my hand before I can walk away.

'To be continued?'

I only offer a shrug, leaving him to keep a watchful eye over his brother. I run my fingers over the place where his hand just was, wondering what I've got myself into.

The Twelve Days of Christmas Cookies Countdown
16 December
Day 4
Terry's Chocolate Orange Cookies

Servings: 12 cookies

INGREDIENTS:

- 90g brown sugar
- 65g caster sugar
- 150g plain flour
- ½ teaspoon baking soda
- ½ teaspoon baking powder
- ¾ teaspoon salt
- 120g salted butter, softened
- 2 teaspoons vanilla extract or vanilla bean paste
- 1 large egg
- 150g semi-sweet chocolate chips
- ½ Terry's Chocolate Orange chopped roughly (save the other half for topping)

INSTRUCTIONS:

1. Preheat the oven to 350°F (180°C) and line a baking sheet with parchment paper.
2. Combine the dry ingredients in a bowl and set aside.

3. In a larger bowl, beat the butter and sugars until they form a paste-like texture.
4. Incorporate the egg and vanilla until the mixture is smooth.
5. Gently fold in the dry ingredients, chocolate chips and chopped Terry's using a spatula until fully integrated, making sure not to over-blend.
6. Scoop out 3 tablespoon-sized balls of dough on to your cookie sheet.
7. Bake for 10–12 minutes.
8. Once out of the oven, add extra Terry's Chocolate Orange slices on top.
9. Allow to cool on a wire rack.

18

RIPLEY

The first thing I do on Tuesday morning as I head to hair and make-up is check social media. The show premiered last night, and I was such a nervous wreck I couldn't look at the internet to see what they were saying. Luckily, we had Nathan's birthday party to distract us – Garrick did a great job, and Nathan was so happy. It's all I could have asked for, and so much that I didn't.

If the premiere had gone wrong, I would've woken up to Mom telling me this was a failure. So when I get up and she is already gone – which I'm used to – I guess it's business as usual.

I open TikTok and start searching for Beeloved. A ton of people are reacting to the show and it's actually super positive. They love the setting of a fairytale theme park and – no shocker – they're loving Garrick. They talk about how easy he is on the eyes – fair enough – and how charming he is.

My shoulders sag with relief. *Maybe this is actually going to work.* Because as much as I tried to pretend it would, I wasn't truly sure. But with the hype we've been doing the last month alongside the FTG team, I should have guessed it would get a ton of attention.

'Imogen, hey,' I say when I see her lounging at a table in the break room, eating a candy cane. Her hair is arranged into two buns on either side of her head and tinsel is twisted into it. It's incredible how different the place feels when the park is closed.

'Hey there, Superstar.' She smiles cheerfully. 'Did you see we're a breakout success? I'm quoting *People*.' She laughs. 'I promise I don't normally talk like that.'

Her brightness makes me chipper by association. 'I did. Seriously, thanks again for your help with the FTG side of things on social. You guys are killing it.'

She plays with her gold necklace. 'I've trained Tristian well.'

'Maybe you can show me how to do that with Garrick,' I mutter.

She laughs again. 'Good luck. That one's a wild stallion.'

I say goodbye and head upstairs to see if the show pony, Garrick, is ready for his morning date. Everything might be off to a good start in the public eye, but we can't let off the gas. The next episode airs tomorrow, and we've got to keep up the momentum.

When I walk in, 'Shut Up and Dance' is playing, and it's the line about Juliet. Garrick, with his phone out, the culprit of the music.

'Hilarious,' I yell over the sound. 'Did you have that cued up and waiting for me to walk in?'

He cuts the music, a broad grin on his cheeky face. 'I did.'

'He's been waiting for twenty minutes with his finger on that button,' Pierre says, putting the finishing touches on Garrick's look.

'Just to annoy me? That's some intense dedication,' I tell him.

Garrick stands, his body inches from mine in the small space. I ignore my dry throat, swallowing to loosen it.

'Ripley, you call it annoy, I call it admiration.'

'OK.' I keep my lips tight, so I don't accidentally smile and let him think he's winning this battle of wills. 'I'm here to escort you.'

Garrick claps Pierre on the back. 'Pleasure as always,' he says before turning to me. 'Juliet, I am at your service.'

Pierre looks between us, amusement shifting his features, and I grab Garrick's sleeve to yank him from the room.

'You ready to find love?' Melika asks, following us to the park.

'Keeping my eyes peeled as we speak,' Garrick says. My cheeks flush when I glance over to find him already looking at me. His eyes widen like I caught him, and he quickly turns away, stumbling over his feet.

What was that about? He wasn't referring to me, right? Because that would be weird. It must just be Garrick being Garrick.

Yes. That's it.

'You're an expert at sword fighting, so this should be easy for you to teach the girls,' I tell him when we reach this morning's filming location. We're trying to mix it up, so all the areas of the park are shown and viewers don't get bored.

'I don't feel like I gave you a proper lesson the first time we met,' Garrick says. 'We should have a do-over.'

The memory of our first encounter flashes in my mind. I thought his cocky, cool-guy persona was going to be unbelievably tedious to interact with on a regularly basis, but now I actually find myself looking forward to our stolen moments.

Not that I'd admit that to him.

'Let's get through today and we can circle back on that.'

Garrick stands in front of the Knight School stage while the girls wait around back to come out on cue.

'Tell us a little about your experience almost going to the Youth Olympics,' the producer says.

Garrick's eyebrows raise, pale skin tingling a little pink with embarrassment. This is what I like to see.

'Do you have a story there?' I ask. Embarrassing Garrick is not something that happens very often. He's the type who can brush anything off, so I enjoy watching him squirm.

'Not much to talk about. I was really great, *obviously*. And I thought about showing it off to the world.' He shifts, twirling his sword, stance casual as ever. 'But I didn't think it would be fair to all the other kids to realize there was no way they'd ever beat me. I wanted to do the world a favor and let them have a chance at winning.'

That's not the real story. From the little version I heard, Garrick ended up not going to the Olympics because his mom got sick. But as fun as it is to make Garrick squirm, that's not a line I'm willing to cross.

I decide to go easier despite my better judgment. 'Is there a lady you think will excel at this?'

'Why? You want to try your hand, Ripley?'

'Focus, Garrick. I know those are words you're probably used to hearing, so why don't you try to follow them this time.'

A shudder runs down my spine as I sound exactly like my mother.

'Yes, ma'am.' He gives me a salute.

The team created a plan for the date, but Garrick slips into training mode with practiced ease, so they're letting him roll with it. The girls laugh and enjoy whacking each other with sticks, so it's all working out. I can already see the show version playing out in my head, with the music and B-roll interviews.

'His sword work is pretty good,' Melika whispers.

'Think we can bother him for a private lesson?' Nathan asks – not dressed as an elf today.

Watching Garrick stand behind the girls and instruct them how to use the sword, I have this weird feeling deep in my stomach. Perhaps a seed of jealousy? I want him to show *me* how to do that. He has this look of focus on his face when he's teaching them. This feels like the most realistic Garrick. He's good at it too – both the teaching and the sword fighting. It's too bad he never got to go to the Olympics. I think he might've liked it beyond the obvious showing off.

It makes me warm to him, which is a dangerous thought. I shouldn't be thinking anything about him. But I find myself studying him the whole time we do the shoot. Which is why I see him examining himself in a sword reflection and realize that he's just as big of an idiot as I thought he was. But even that makes me smile.

'Hey, Sofia,' I call over as she waits by the stage while Garrick has a one-on-one with Kahoa. 'Come here a sec.'

'What's up?' She greets me with a dazzling smile of straight white teeth. She is wearing an outfit more suited to a horse-riding lesson than a sword fight, but she looks super cute.

'We need to take some promo shots for this episode. Do you mind doing some modeling?'

'Of course.' One moment to the next, she slips from casual mood to full model Barbie.

'Awesome. Imogen and Tristian are near the castle if you want to go with your sword. Shouldn't take too long.'

'Good.' She sighs with relief. 'I don't want to miss my time with Garrick. Any insider tips that might score me some bonus points with him?'

My smile stiffens. I swallow hard as a tightness squeezes my ribs. 'I don't think that'd be fair. Sorry,' I add as I notice my cold tone.

'No worries.' She shrugs before bouncing off to Imogen and Tristian.

I follow her progress before turning back to Melika and Nathan. 'What?' I frown when I notice they're both staring at me. I rub my face in case I've got food on it from breakfast and no one mentioned it.

'Nothing,' Nathan says, but his voice is too high to be normal.

'Shut up,' I respond, tightening my hands around my tablet.

'I didn't say anything.' But I know that look. It means he's getting ready to give me some advice he thinks is wise and sage.

'Great, because there is nothing to say about anything.'

Melika snorts. 'I think a lot is being said without words.'

I purposefully try to look anywhere but at Garrick for the remainder of the shoot, which is very hard since he is the center of everything. I don't want anyone else besides Melika and Nathan thinking there is something worth talking about – especially my erratic heart.

'If you want more background on that case, you should check out *Morbid*. Their podcast does great coverage of it,' Maya tells me as we walk through the Fairytalers' entrance and into the backstage area. We just wrapped filming a scene where a few girls spent time with Garrick doing rides.

'Oh, I've listened to their spooky eps. They're so fun.' Nathan slurps the last dregs of his warm apple cider. 'Ripley doesn't do ghosts, though.'

Maya has been chatting about some of the true crime cases she's studied. 'I'm with you, girl. I need some hard evidence before I make my decision.'

'Thank you!' A big puff of white breath exits my mouth. The night air is chilly and the tiniest snowflakes flicker through it. 'Finally, someone who shares my love of logic.' We've hung out with a few girls, and Maya is one of them we clicked with instantly.

'Stop! You know you love my whimsy and childlike curiosity.' Nathan boops my nose. 'Maya, I need your professional opinion on Jack the Ripper.'

Her face lights up. 'First off, I don't think he named himself that. Some of those letters were clearly copy-cats ...'

'You need to check out this museum,' Kahoa says to Melika. The two have been deep in conversation since the cameras shut off. It's almost like they forgot the rest of us were here. 'They have this amazing display of clothes from the turn of the century to the present.'

If I didn't know better, I might think they have a little something going on. I tried to explain to Melika and Nathan plenty of times that they should jump on the no-love train with me, but they didn't seem interested. And while this little flirty thing probably isn't a good idea, given our current circumstances – I know Melika won't do anything to risk the show.

I nudge Nathan with my elbow, nodding toward Melika. He wiggles both eyebrows to signal his agreement with my assessment.

'Do we have to be heartbreaks and tell them to chill?' Nathan whispers in my ear.

I'm about to say, let's give them the night, when yelling from the second floor drags all our attention upwards.

'What the hell do you think you're doing?' The girl is screaming and sounds pissed.

Maya and Kahoa exchange glances. 'That's Riya,' Maya says.

'Just admit it.' The other voice is loud, but calmer.

'Desiree,' Kahoa adds. The four of them share an apartment. 'I knew it was only a matter of time before those two finally exploded.'

Before I know what I'm doing I'm bounding up the stairs, the others clattering behind me. In front of their door, Riya is wide-legged, hands clenched into fists, while Desiree's arms are folded across her chest, a satisfied smile on her face.

'What is going on?' I raise my hands and step between them.

Anger flushes Riya's face, highlighted by the fluorescent bulb overhead. 'What's going *on*, is that *she* is trying to ruin the show.' She jabs a finger at Desiree.

Desiree looks aghast. 'I'm not trying to ruin anything. I just wanted the truth to be told.' Her voice is steady, and her acting skills must be on full display because I can't read any other emotions.

'You are such a liar,' Riya huffs. 'You've always been like this, ever since we were kids.'

I glance at the others still huddled by the stairs. Nathan is the only one who looks like he wishes he had a bucket of popcorn. He did always love a reality TV drama moment. Luckily, there aren't any cameras in sight. But if I don't keep the yelling down, one might show up.

'Wait, you two know each other?' I keep my voice level. It was bound to happen, but none acted like they did.

Riya takes a deep breath, pushing her hair behind her ears. 'Yeah, we went to dance class together and she never got over the fact that I was always the lead. So, now she's trying to get me kicked off the show.'

I muster all the authority of being a Ripley and turn to Desiree. 'Explain.'

Desiree offers a knowing smile. 'Riya has a secret boyfriend. I caught her talking to him on her *contraband* phone.'

Oh crap.

'Riya, is that true?' I ask.

Riya stares at me, mouth gaping wide, glancing around like

the others might offer her assistance. 'What? No, of course not. It wasn't allowed.'

'Then show her your phone.' Desiree stokes the fire. 'I've seen him all over social media. Did you think that no one would notice you deleted those pictures?'

'I did have a boyfriend.' Riya's talking faster now. 'But we broke up before I came on the show. Nothing is going on with us. Nothing. I swear.'

I don't necessarily want to believe Desiree over Riya, but I have to ask the question. 'Do you have a phone?' The girls can use their phones occasionally, but they're locked up with production otherwise.

Riya bites her lip. 'I didn't know about it. He must've slipped it into my bag because he was jealous. And then he kept calling and texting, so I had to answer it. That's it. Desiree is trying to blackmail me into leaving, or she said she was going to release it to the media.'

This getting out would be disastrous. The investor may not mind because it will get viewers to watch all the drama, but Mom will be upset. She wants this to be meaningful, and to show that her app can lead you to love, not that they're harboring cheaters. Plus, I can't imagine that would be a good look for the FTG brand either.

'Desiree, you can't blackmail her. And you definitely can't release it to the press. It would be really bad for the show.' Somehow, I don't think Desiree runs on logic.

'I don't care about the show. I care about *integrity*.' Desiree isn't as good an actress as she thinks. She's here for herself, which is why she's always asking for extra time, and now she thinks this info will get her more publicity. She's not wrong. But I can't let that happen.

'Desiree, as a member of production —' I stand to my full height — 'I will take care of this. And remember, the contract you signed said that you weren't allowed to talk to the media. I'd hate to have you removed from the show.'

'But she —'

I cut her off. 'I will take care of Riya. Now, go inside.'

Desiree looks like she wants to argue but just gives Riya a sneering glare before stomping into the apartment.

'I'd like to talk to Riya alone,' I tell the others.

Once they've gone their own ways, I turn to Riya, holding out my hand. 'Give me the phone.'

'Are you going to kick me off the show?'

There were rules in the contract saying they weren't allowed to be dating anyone else right now. But kicking Riya out would have the same effect Desiree wants.

'I'll keep this between you and me. But you need to be careful.' Desiree doesn't seem the type to just back down. She'll lick her chops and return with a new agenda.

Riya pulls the phone from her pocket and hands it to me. 'Thanks, Ripley. I owe you one.'

'You don't owe me anything. But you do owe it to Garrick to give him a real chance. He doesn't deserve to be played.'

That's another reason I don't want this to get out — true or not. I know that he's not here to find the love of his life, but even the brightest stars would be a bit dimmed knowing they were being lied to.

The Twelve Days of Christmas Cookies Countdown
17 December
Day 5
Brown Butter Toffee Chocolate Chip Cookies

Servings: 20 cookies

INGREDIENTS:
- 225g unsalted butter, cut into 1-inch cubes
- 250g plain flour
- 1 teaspoon baking soda
- ¾ teaspoon salt
- 210g dark brown sugar
- 65g caster sugar
- 2 large eggs
- 2 teaspoons pure vanilla extract
- 240g milk chocolate chips
- 40g toffee
- flaky salt, for garnish

INSTRUCTIONS:
Brown butter
1. In a saucepan, melt the butter over medium–low heat, swirling the pan occasionally, until it starts to foam. Scrape the bottom and sides of the pan with a rubber spatula occasionally to prevent the butter from burning.

2. Cook for 5 minutes, or until the butter smells nutty and is amber with dark flecks at the bottom of the pan. Remove from the heat. Set it aside to cool.

Cookies

3. In a medium bowl, whisk together the flour, baking soda and salt.
4. Combine the caster sugar and brown sugar in a bowl, then pour the cooled brown butter over them and beat on medium speed until light and fluffy, 2-3 minutes, scraping the bowl as needed.
5. Reduce the mixer to low and add the eggs and vanilla and beat until just combined.
6. Still on low, gradually add the dry ingredients and beat until combined. Scrape down the bowl once more and beat on low for an additional 30 seconds.
7. Increase the mixer to medium–low, add the chocolate and toffee, and beat until the chocolate is evenly distributed.
8. Portion the dough into balls and place on the pan lined with parchment paper. Cover with cling film and refrigerate for at least 30 minutes.
9. Preheat the oven to 375°F (190°C). Line two sheet pans with parchment paper. Place the

chilled cookies at least 3 inches apart on the prepared sheet pans.
10. Bake one pan at a time for 10 minutes, or until the edges have set but the centers are still gooey. Cool the cookies for 20 minutes, or until the edges and bottoms of the cookies have set and feel firm to the touch.
11. Sprinkle salt over the cookies to garnish

19

GARRICK

'I'm sorry about all this,' I say to Kahoa as the cameras shut off and the mics are removed. The second elimination was done against the backdrop of the Sea Monsters' Swing and it was as easy as the first. Still, I don't like making anyone feel bad. I'm the guy who makes sure everyone is comfortable and having a good time. 'I know it's cheesy to say, but it really wasn't you – it's all me.'

She leans in close, so the nearby crew doesn't hear. 'Can I tell you a secret?'

I nod – I do love a good secret.

'I didn't even want to do this. It was my older sister's idea. She would've *loved* to be on the show but is too old. I'm just grateful you didn't keep me longer.' She cringes. 'Sorry, that sounds harsh. I'm just happy to be getting home early for Christmas.'

I shake my head. 'Not harsh at all. I like to think that my job as Santa made one Christmas wish come true.'

She's been quiet this whole time, and now I know why. Elimination has made her suddenly lighter. 'You're a good guy, Garrick. I do hope you find your Beeloved.'

Production whisks her away for final interviews, and I'm down to eight contestants. My eyes track Riya and Desiree as they head off to their post-elimination interviews. I'm not supposed to know about the little screaming match they had last night, but Nathan is terrible at keeping secrets. He didn't give specifics, but said Desiree and Riya know each other from before and got into it. I have a sneaking suspicious it's about Riya's boyfriend. A tidbit I've kept to myself because I actually am a great secret keeper.

When this whole thing started, I thought it would be a breeze, but dating so many girls and dealing with the politics of the show and the internet is draining. I've stopped replying to the comments on my posts. Who knew I could get tired of all the attention? But if I have to answer one more person asking who I'm falling for, or if I'll take them on a date after the show, I might start acting a lot more like Mr Grumpy Tristian.

'Hey there, Stranger.' I bump Ripley with my shoulder.

'Nope,' she says, not looking up from her tablet.

'Nope? I didn't ask a question.' My body sags in relief at not having a camera shoved in my face.

'I could just hear it brewing in your brain and decided to nip it in the bud before it completely formed.'

At first Ripley's indifference to my charm was irksome, but now it's a welcome reprieve. 'OK, what if –'

'I got to go.' Those blue eyes meet mine for the briefest of seconds – just long enough to make my heart skip a beat – before she's walking away.

Even with the elimination done, my job is not. Ever since Dad decided we needed to have a bigger part in the park – we can thank Tristian for that – we've been included in more meetings, even Aldrich. And that kid is barely out of diapers. OK, he's definitely been out of diapers for like a solid ten years, but he'll always be a little kid to me, even if he's only two years younger.

I'm ten minutes late to the meeting because I'm me. However, I've brought a tray of peppermint mochas to smooth it over. I could have whipped them up at home, but I decided to take the drive to the coffee shop down the road. Waiting in line with the caffeine-starved hordes made me feel invisible for a few minutes. It's not my usual preference, but since starting the show, everything has been about me and required more responsibility than expected. A brief interlude was needed so I can turn back on the star power later.

'You're late,' Dad says as I stroll into his office wearing my Santa hat.

'Sorry, filming duties.' This is a lie. But it's a great excuse. I like to play one against the other when I want to get out of something. So far, only Ripley's called me out on it.

'Is this supposed to be a bribe?' Ivor says, grabbing a coffee from me. His normally perfect waves are covered with a gray beanie.

I plop down on to the couch, careful not to spill. 'Would I do such a thing?'

'Yes,' Aldrich says, swiping the other drink. He's got paint on his hands. We had a debrief after his date. There had been plenty of awkward silences, but all things considered, I gave him a passing grade.

I hand a coffee to Tristian and keep quiet as Dad starts,

or continues, the meeting – not really sure since, again, I was late.

It's stuffy in here, the sun bright through the windows. I pull at the collar of my sweater, trying not to fidget. But I can't help it. These types of meetings make me feel strange. Like, I don't want to know the budgetary numbers or the attendance decline. Just put me in my leathers and hand me a sword. This makes the park less a fairytale dream and more like the business it is.

'Sons, I'm not going to lie. We're not doing as good as I would've liked. Thanks to Garrick, we've had a boost with Christmas and the reality show. But it looks like we're still going to have some layoffs.' In his defense, he does look devastated by the idea.

My heart plummets like a six-ton stone swirling around in the sludge of my peppermint mocha. 'Fire people?' I choke. 'I thought the whole point of me doing the show was so we wouldn't have to do that?' FTG is a family; firing someone will feel like losing one of our own. My chest tightens and my fingers start to go numb.

'I know, Garrick. It's not the news any of us wanted. But we're all going to have to make hard decisions. You and Jin must pick who we let go of from food and beverage. When the new year comes, I'm afraid we'll have some more hard decisions to make.' Dad hasn't drunk any coffee, but he swirls the cup around as he speaks.

'There has to be another way,' Tristian argues. He still feels guilty about last summer's scandal – even though we all know it wasn't his fault. But that's my brother for you, constantly feeling like he has to carry the weight of it all.

'Can we stay open all year?' Aldrich suggests. 'Or maybe we could sell more merch. I have some drawings I've been messing with.'

Dad's face remains solemn. 'This park will survive, sons. It just might look a little different.'

I won't let anyone be fired. The rest of my brothers look like they're feeling the same. But I can do something about it. This reality show was my idea to save FTG from having to make any terrible choices. So, I just need to drum up more business.

That'll be easy, *right*?

I find Ripley huddled on a lounger by the closed pool, which is shrouded in frost. 'Isn't it a little chilly?' I ask, sitting down beside her on the squeaky plastic. She's got a blanket over her lap and her coat on. Her nose is bright red from the cold. I miss the fuzzy earmuffs.

'A little.' She shivers as if just realizing it. 'But it was quiet because no one was here.'

'Yeah, because it's freezing.' The sun is bright, but it's weak this time of year, not strong enough to warm through the breeze that's picked up and dances with the free strands of Ripley's dark hair. That trusty pen that's usually in her bun is tucked behind her ear.

She looks up from her laptop, giving me a stare-down over her glasses. I've only seen her wear them when she's on a computer. They're cute.

'Then why are you out here?'

'Because you are.' The charm falls off my lips but doesn't faze either of us. I clear my throat, shaking my head and running a hand through my hair so it doesn't freeze in place with all the gel they lathered in for the shoot. 'I'm going to be straight with you.'

'I didn't realize you were capable of that,' she half jokes. But she's not wrong. Keeping people from the real me is my default.

'You're about the only person I *am* straight with.' It could be a line, but it's not. I guess because Ripley doesn't fall for my charm, the only thing I *can* be is real. The thought sends a spark down my skin, leaving a comforting warmth in its wake. 'I need more promotion for FTG in the show. Why don't we do something with catering? We can show how good the food is.' The desperation oozes out of me, and I find myself speaking so fast I'm not even sure if she understands.

'That's not really in the plan.' She taps at the computer's trackpad.

'Juliet, *please*.' This is the first time I've said her real name and I haven't been trying to get a rise out of her. It just slipped out.

A thin line folds between her brow as she frowns. 'Is everything OK?'

I would normally brush off a question like this – throw out a witty retort and an 'aw, shucks' smile to stop further closeness in its tracks. But it doesn't feel right.

My chin drops to my chest. 'No. FTG is in trouble, and if I don't find a way to fix it, people I care about will lose their jobs.' I lick my lips, looking up at her through watery eyes.

I hate being seen as anything other than carefree and chill. That's the Garrick I make sure the world knows, but Ripley isn't going to judge me. She already knows that the other guy is partly an act. 'I would really love it if we could help FTG together.'

Her eyes roam over my face, mapping the emotions I'm not trying to cover up now. It feels like I've ripped open and laid bare everything inside me. It's scary, but I don't back away.

'So, we're in this together, huh?' she finally says.

I take her freezing hand in mine, squeezing it tight. 'From the very beginning.'

Glancing at our hands, she returns the squeeze. 'OK, I'll see what I can do.' She pulls away, snuggling into her blanket. 'The second episode airs tonight, so we can get a feel for how audiences are responding. Then we can create a plan to work in some extra promo.'

'Maybe we could do a bonus episode?'

Her eyes narrow, but I recognize this as her thinking face. 'The production team is already running on super-tight deadlines. I don't think we can ask them to add another episode.'

'We can do it. Maybe a cooking segment.' I shake my hands, vibrating with the idea formulating. 'I can make one of FTG's signature items, and then we can edit and post the video on Beeloved's YouTube channel.'

'I don't know how to edit.'

'No worries, Tyrone does. I'm sure he'd love to help.'

She bites her bottom lip. 'OK, but we need a plan.'

I grin. If there is one thing I know about Juliet Ripley, she knows how to execute a plan.

'I need a favor.' I slide into the spot between Imogen and Tristian right as they're about to take off on Flight in the Clouds from the Perilous Sea.

'Garrick – what the heck? This ride is too small for all of us.' Tristian tries to push me off, but the lap bar comes down and we glide up and into the air on the gondola suspension cable strung above the park.

'Too late now.' I raise my arms and place them around their shoulders. 'But since I have your undivided attention for the next five minutes, we need to chat.' The wind is colder up here as it blows into my open coat.

Tristian crosses his arms and closes his eyes, probably trying to pretend I'm not next to him. You'd think he'd have learned after seventeen years that I'm impossible to ignore.

'Garrick, did you just leave poor Ripley on the platform?' Imogen leans over the front safety bar to spy Ripley getting smaller as we move away.

'Rude. Of course not. We're still working on her aversion to theme park rides, but I'm making headway. Anyhow, I need your guys' help.'

'With?' Tristian opens his eyes. Imogen smiles at him, and he melts.

'Right, before this gets too awkward.' I watch Village Center bustle below us as we head to Pixie Forest. 'Ripley and I want to do a bonus episode to showcase what FTG can offer.'

Tristian stiffens beside me. 'Is this because of the layoffs?'

Imogen inhales sharply but doesn't speak. Tristian probably already filled her in.

'Of course. You know we can't let that happen.' Acid churns in my stomach, my chest burning.

'I know. So, what do you need from us?' Tristian dons that Walton determination.

'Can you two run interference with production? Keep them away from my apartment for the rest of the day? Tell them I'm sick – whatever you need to do so they don't interrupt us?'

I was technically supposed to do some interview or B-roll later, I don't know. I wasn't listening to Brett rattle on.

'Oh, Garrick.' Imogen beams. 'Distraction is my middle name.'

'More like *Distracted*.' Tristian laughs.

She attempts to kick his foot but hits my shin instead. 'Sorry. Either way, we got you. Go make your magic with Ripley.'

20

RIPLEY

We bring this whole thing together pretty quickly. Garrick definitely likes to go with the flow, but when he puts his mind to something, he can make it happen. I shouldn't be that surprised after his 'last-minute birthday party extravaganza' – his words.

'This looks great,' Garrick says when he enters his apartment later that afternoon. It's already getting dark outside – which isn't ideal for filming, but it took us a little while to get everything we needed.

Melika worked wonders with this outdated kitchen, stringing fairy lights and using spare wood, fabric and tiles to create a cute filming background. We would've preferred to film somewhere in the park, but it wasn't feasible with the Royal Fare being used for dinner service this evening.

Any time I've gone into the park while it's been open, the place feels alive with guests, but the way Garrick talked, I'm worried it's not enough. He loves this place; it holds so much of his life and memories inside. I don't know what that's like. My house never really felt like a home. It did its job, sure, keeping us safe and providing a place to sleep. While I'm not totally sold on this endeavor tonight, if in a small way I can help ease some of the worry clouding Garrick's otherwise chipper brain, and Fairytale Gardens at the same time, then I'm happy to go rogue just once.

'And it barely smells like a 7-Eleven,' Tyrone says, slinging his backpack off his shoulders. 'Where can I set up my computer? I want to see what we're filming and how the audio is as we go.'

'Why don't you put it on the dining table? Melika can help you with the camera and microphone.' They waste no time getting to it.

Melika and Tyrone seem like a well-oiled machine, which is good because Garrick and I have some final details to review. Imogen and Tristian are on distraction duty, making sure no one has a reason to look for Garrick. Nathan is taking an acting lesson from Desiree – I'm still unclear how or why that's happening, but OK. Garrick decided it was better just to make a quick episode and put it up rather than asking for permission beforehand.

'Do you have everything you need?' My job was to oversee the location while Garrick's was to get the supplies for whatever he decided to make. I tried to get him to nail down the recipe, but he said he had a few in mind he was *oscillating* between.

He holds up two paper bags filled to the brim with groceries. 'I got extras in case we mess it up.'

'That's very efficient of you.' I'm shocked at the foresight.

'From you, Ripley, that's the best compliment I could get.' Garrick takes items out of the bags and I can finally deduce what he's making. It looks like a classic black forest chocolate cake.

'This was my mom's recipe,' Garrick says more to the table than to me. 'I thought it would be perfect since it was one of the first things she taught me.'

I bite my lip, deciding whether or not I should say what I'm thinking. 'You know ... if you feel like it, you could mention that. It might be nice for the audience to see your family's connection to the park – how much it means to you.'

I've never seen him move anything with such precision. He's lining up and rearranging each ingredient perfectly. 'I don't want it to feel like I'm using my mother's memory to gain favor.'

I quickly backtrack. 'No, of course not. I would never want that. Trust me. I just think that your mom is a really lovely part of this story that you've written at Fairytale Gardens, and I wouldn't want people to miss out on that. But we don't have to do anything you're uncomfortable with.'

He glances up at me this time and gives me a genuine smile. My chest feels like it's going to explode. 'I know you wouldn't, Ripley.'

'All set over here,' Melika calls from the table. 'We just need to get Garrick in costume and mic'd up.'

I grab a bag off the couch. 'I didn't think we wanted anything overly produced. So I thought we could keep it casual?' I pull out a green Fairytale Garden sweatshirt with orange print I found in the costume department.

'Retro. I like it. Where did you get it?'

'I asked the costume department what kind of merch they had lying around, and they found this.'

'Do you have one for yourself?'

I raise an eyebrow. 'Why would I need one?'

'What if I need an assistant?'

The idea of saying yes surfaces in my brain, and I'm surprised by it. I kind of want to be taught how to make a chocolate cake by Garrick. But I know that's not a good idea. This show is about him and the contestants. Of which I'm not one. I wouldn't want to muddy the narrative by people thinking there's some other girl off-screen. Not that there's anything between Garrick and me. Obviously. But the internet is the internet, and I'm not giving them any fuel.

I toss the sweatshirt at him, careful not to get it in any of the ingredients. 'Sorry, you're a one-man show today. But I know you can handle that just fine.'

Garrick rips off his sweater and I spin around as I spy his bare chest. I press the back of my hand to my cheek as my body broadcasts my embarrassment across my skin. *It's just a shirtless guy, Ripley. You've been swimming before.*

But this feels *very* different.

'Help me with the mic?' Garrick says, and I keep my eyes downcast as I help to secure it. Focusing on the task at hand, my flaming cheeks cool slightly. If Garrick notices, he stays blissfully quiet.

I turn on the lights and hit record on my phone.

'Today, I'm gonna show you how to make the world-famous Fairytale Gardens black forest chocolate cake.' Garrick mixes the ingredients into the batter and fills the silence masterfully. I'm not sure how we're going to edit this down.

'Garrick, you don't need to talk the whole time. We can't make an hour-long video,' Tyrone says from his computer.

'I just have so much wisdom to impart to the audience. I don't want them missing out.' He smirks at me.

By the time the cake goes into the oven, my mouth is watering. We stop recording for it to bake and take a break on the couch. Tyrone stays at the table to edit what we've got so far.

'Do you make videos all the time?' Melika asks Tyrone, peeking over his shoulder.

'I do a few promos for my parents' bar.' He intensely focuses on the screen.

'When I open my vintage shop, I might need to hit you up.'

Tyrone's face lights up. 'A vintage shop?' The two of them start talking in depth about Melika's plans.

'We should watch a Christmas movie,' Garrick says, reaching across me and grabbing the remote. I inhale sharply when he settles in, his arm resting against mine. I think about moving away, but when he doesn't, I don't either. Instead, I do the opposite of what I'm supposed to and snuggle deeper into the couch. Garrick's soft sweatshirt is warm against me. Despite the butterflies trying to escape out of me, it feels ... right. Sitting next to Garrick and just relaxing sends a calming effect over my body. All my tense muscles forget what they're supposed to be stressed about.

Garrick looks over, a lazy smile offered just for me. 'You good, Ripley?'

I don't trust my voice and only nod.

'Good.' He rests his head on top of mine. Our hands lay beside each other, barely touching but feeling more intimate than ever before.

We spend the time with the cake baking watching part of *The Santa Clause*. And before I know it, it's coming out of the oven. I don't want to leave the couch and disrupt this moment with Garrick, but it's the right thing to do.

'Now, I didn't give away all my secrets,' Garrick tells the camera. 'I left some of the key ingredients out. Mostly because I want you to experience it for yourself. Come to Fairytale Gardens and eat at the Royal Fare, or if you would like a more private affair, we cater. And who knows, maybe a knight in shining armor will show up.' He grins.

There's a pause, and I think he will end there, but then he keeps going. 'This was my mom's recipe. She was in charge of food and beverage here at Fairytale Gardens, and she always wanted to make sure that even though you were in a theme park, you weren't missing out on quality cuisine. My mom is no longer with us.' He stops, his voice hitching before he clears it and keeps going. 'But I like to think that every time we put a meal out, it's like she's still with us. Not as a ghost –' his face brightens into a smile – 'those are just on the Pirate Adventure. Ghost tours coming soon.'

'Cut,' Tyrone yells. 'OK, this will take me a little while to edit, but I think it will turn out pretty good.'

I come over and start taking off Garrick's mic. 'You've got something, right here.' Garrick takes his frosting-covered finger and plops some on my nose.

'You're the worst.' I shake my head, dipping my chin so he doesn't spot my smile.

'Sureeeee.' Garrick licks frosting off his finger. 'Well, who wants cake while we wait?'

'I wouldn't mind a slice,' Nathan says from the open doorway. I hadn't even heard him come in – which is why when I turn around and see Desiree standing behind him my body goes rigid. My hand is lying against Garrick's chest, while I'm unthreading the cord from his sweatshirt.

'Roomie, just in time.' Garrick flashes a grin, not a care in the world. 'Ouch. You OK, Juliet?' Garrick rubs at his neck where I just ripped the mic away.

I clear my throat, taking four giant steps away from him. 'Nathan, I thought you two were practicing your acting?'

Nathan offers me a guilty smile. 'Sorry, I didn't know we'd still have a full house. Come on, Desiree, let's go to the lounge.'

Desiree skirts past him and walks in like she owns the place. 'What did you make?' She slides alongside Garrick, dipping her finger into the top of the frosting.

'How about I cut a slice and you guess?' His smile never falters. It's the same brilliant one he wore seconds ago when he was looking at me. Everything about him is the same: the tone of voice, the casual air.

'I'm like a super taster.' Desiree closes her eyes. 'Feed it to me?'

I turn away when Garrick grabs a fork. My chest pounds against my ribs as I busy myself putting away the mic. What is happening to me? Why is seeing Garrick flirt with Desiree making my body react like this?

Through the buzzing in my ears, I don't hear Desiree's guess or Nathan approach me. I jump when he puts his hand on my arm. 'I thought you said you were filming at Melika's. I wouldn't have brought Desiree if I'd known.' Nathan has a tendency to not read texts completely.

I shake my head. 'It's fine. She's not supposed to see him off camera, but oh well.' I take the hair tie from my wrist and wrap my hair into a bun.

Nathan's brows dip, a serious look casting across his features. 'Are you OK?'

Desiree giggles again. 'Stop, Garrick!'

'You better get some cake before it all ends up in Desiree's hair,' I say, forcing myself to watch Garrick and Desiree together.

This is good. I want this. The show needs this.

One demolished cake and a few hours later, Tyrone has finished editing the video. He tells us several times that he's no pro, but he hopes he's done well enough.

I pull it up on the TV for us to watch. It's good – really good. I watched the previous episode and a few shots from the one airing tonight. But this is better. It's not that Garrick looks like he's faking it during the reality show, but he's more alive in this off-the-cuff video – more real. Suddenly, a flush runs up my cheeks, panic seizing my chest.

What if the audience can tell the difference? What if this real Garrick and the one he's putting on for the dating show are brought into question? Will people know that he thinks this whole thing is fake?

Garrick looks over at me, and I try to cover my face. 'What's up, Ripley?' He's been teaching Desiree and Nathan how to play his video game. He tried to get me to play, but I was busy working on my phone. Mostly so I could keep myself from looking at them. I'm confused by the reaction I'm having. Logically, I should be thrilled he's showing interest in one of the contestants, but some primal – unwanted – portion of my brain is doing uncharacteristic things.

Melika eyes me down from her seat in the chair across from us. I clear my throat. 'It's good – brilliant even. It's just maybe this is a bad idea? Could we wait until after the show's done airing? This might muddle the narrative.'

'No way. We need people to come to the Royal Fare, especially during Christmas,' Garrick argues. 'That's what this is all about.'

I don't know how to get out of this, so I nod and agree. I do want to help FTG. I wouldn't have done this otherwise. I'm just overthinking things like usual.

'Great. Tyrone, drop it to me and I'll upload it tomorrow morning.' Garrick grins from ear to ear, and I hope this all works out.

The Twelve Days of Christmas Cookies Countdown
18 December
Day 6
Chocolate Dulce de Leche Cookies

Servings: 24 cookies

INGREDIENTS:
- 375g plain flour
- 45g cocoa powder
- ½ teaspoon salt
- ½ teaspoon baking powder
- 250g unsalted butter, softened
- 300g sugar
- 2 large eggs
- 2 teaspoons vanilla extract
- 397g tin of dulche de leche

INSTRUCTIONS:
1. Whisk together the dry ingredients in a bowl and set aside.
2. Place butter and sugar in a bowl and beat together for 5 minutes until light and fluffy. Beat in eggs one at a time, scraping the sides of the bowl between each. Then add vanilla.

3. With the mixer on the lowest speed or with a whisk, add the dry ingredients to the wet and beat until incorporated.
4. Divide the dough into two and press into two flat discs. Wrap each disc in cling film and refrigerate for 1 hour.
5. Preheat oven to 340°F (170°C) and line two baking sheets with baking paper. Lightly flour work surface and roll one of the chilled dough discs out to 1/4-inch thickness. Using a 2 1/2-inch round cookie cutter, cut out 24 rounds. Repeat with the second batch of dough, making sure to re-roll any scraps of dough until you have 48 rounds.
6. Using a smaller cookie cutter in any shape, cut out the centers of 24 rounds.
7. Place rounds on baking sheets and bake for 10–12 minutes. Cool for 3 minutes on the baking sheets, then transfer to a wire rack to cool completely.
8. Place 1 tablespoon of dulce de leche into the center of each of the whole cookies, spread it out slightly and top with the cut-out cookie and repeat until finished.
9. Dust with a little icing sugar for a festive flurry.

21

GARRICK

'Hey.' I bump into Ripley with my shoulder when we run into each other in the hallway after uploading the baking video to Beeloved's channel. I hope to ride that wave of excitement from last night's episode and get people watching the bonus video and bringing in more business for FTG. 'Any hints on the upcoming dates?' They thought it was better to keep me in the dark about most of what's next.

She glances at her tablet, quickly pressing it against her chest to hide what she was looking at. 'I bet you were the worst little kid at Christmas. Always trying to sneak a peek at your presents.'

I grab my chest as if I'm in pain. 'You wound me. I didn't *try* anything – I succeeded.'

'My mistake.' Her face remains impassive, and it scrapes at my pride.

I was my usual self yesterday, but after Desiree got there and I was flirting with her – which I really do without thinking – things got weird. Ripley carried on with business as she always does, but I sensed her closing down. The walls I typically skate past rose around her. Then I did something I never do: I overthought every move I made. The looks I gave Desiree, or how she laughed in response. Suddenly, flirting as my natural default felt wrong.

But why, though? Ripley shouldn't even be the receiver of my flirtations – yet how she might be perceiving my actions toward someone else was a blaring foghorn in my brain telling me to back down.

'Did you post the video?' she asks, oblivious to this out-of-character inner turmoil I'm coming down with.

I shake my head to descramble my brain to its preferred setting. 'Just went up. I posted about it on TikTok and Insta too. Thanks again.'

'You're welcome. I hope it works.' She has this nervous habit of biting her nails and I enjoy the struggle when she tries to contain it. It makes these little lines form between her brows. It's cute – I'd tell her as much, but I doubt I'd get the reaction I'm hoping for.

We're due on set in ten minutes, but I wish it were longer. It was fun hanging out with Ripley yesterday – working as a team.

As we reach the stairs leading to the break room, I notice someone has hung mistletoe. I'd be the first suspect, but for once I had no part in this entrapment. The inconspicuous decor is the perfect wingman, but should I take the bait? This is Ripley I'm standing with, my no-fly friend-zone reprieve from the love machine that is Beeloved. Yet I am Garrick Walton, so I say, 'Look at that, we seem to have stumbled under the mistletoe.'

Ripley glances up, unimpressed. 'Don't tell me you subscribe to the whims of weeds?'

It's got glitter on the fake leaves, sparkling in the fluorescent lights. 'I think it's pretty.'

'Weeds can be pretty. That's not the point.' She has her hair down, curls framing her face, softening the tough exterior she always puts on for me. I'd tell her she reminds me of my favorite carousel horse, but I'm not sure she'd see it as the compliment I mean it as.

I lean against the wall, crossing my arms. 'I subscribe to anything that leads to kissing.'

She rolls her eyes, but, I swear, the teeny, tiniest smile might be hiding there. Or maybe it's just wishful thinking.

'So, what do you say?' I whisper. 'I'm a big tradition guy. But I also wait for consent.'

She studies the mistletoe, hesitating before moving closer. She's a few inches away now, and I can smell a hint of peach and coffee. My breath hitches, and I'm suddenly clammy. I wasn't expecting that to work.

Dang, I'm good.

But before she is close enough to kiss, she reaches up and yanks the mistletoe down, flinging it to the opposite end of the hall as she jogs down the stairs.

The idea for the scavenger hunt around the park was one I'd thrown out there early on in the planning stages. I was pleasantly surprised when they chose it. We used to do a version of this every year between park openings, but nothing's been the same in the last couple of years, so bringing it back has me jazzed. And you know I'm excited because I'm using words like *jazzed*.

The production team has set up specific tasks throughout the park, giving each girl a list of clues. Technically, I'm supposed to just go along with the girls during the date and help each of them find something. But that sounded too stiff for me.

Also, I wanted to find the treasures too.

'C'mon, Nathan.' I've dragged him to the sidelines. 'I haven't done a scavenger hunt in ages. I want to see if my skills are still there.'

Nathan gives Ms Ripley, who's talking to a camera guy, a quick glance. 'Are you trying to get me fired?'

'Dude, you know Ripley would never let that happen.'

He nods, then his eyes light up. 'Speaking of our mutual friend...'

The hairs on my arms stick up at his tone – it's like when I know I'm about to get in trouble from Dad or Ivor.

'What's up with you and Ripley?'

I frown. 'I'm afraid I don't know of what you speak.'

'Melika said you two were rather cozy at your recording yesterday before I arrived.'

'Sure, we were watching a Christmas movie. Cozy is a prerequisite.'

He's in his elf costume again, and with his mischievous smirk I feel like I'm getting grilled by Santa's little helper. 'Oh, Garrick, you truly are the gift that keeps on giving.'

I flash a smile. 'Too kind. So, the scavenger list?'

'Places, everyone!' the director, Hassan, calls.

'And the mistletoe this morning?' Nathan continues, undeterred.

'How did you see that?' Something tightens in my gut.

He motions to his outfit. 'You know the whole *he sees you when you're sleeping* thing?'

I lick my lips. 'Ripley and I just like to mess with each other. That's all.'

'Fine.' Nathan reaches into the satchel at his waist and pulls out a list. 'Here. But just don't get Ripley in trouble, OK? She's not like us. She doesn't enjoy the thrill.'

I want to tell him I don't like getting in trouble – but that would be a lie. And I might be a troublemaker – but a liar I am not.

Even if what I told him about me and Ripley feels like the barest hint of a fib.

This is a date, so I'm supposed to get to know the girls, but my competitive nature is getting in the way. Ms Ripley was going on about how this will help with learning how to problem-solve in a relationship. I tuned out a few words into her explanation.

I'm hiding behind a tree in Pixie Forest – which is much harder to do in the winter when there are no leaves. Good thing I know all the secret passages.

'What are you doing?' Ripley rests her hands on her hips, coming out of nowhere like a ninja.

'Shhh.' I yank her into my narrow hiding space. My breath hitches when I turn and see her bright-blue eyes staring at me.

This close to her, I can see the freckles on her nose in perfect detail. I wonder if, in the summertime, they cover her entire cheeks. But they're hiding in the winter, just like her genuine smile. Maybe one day I'll get to see them both.

She hasn't pulled away yet. 'Garrick, aren't you supposed to be with the girls?'

I am. But I am very competitive. And while I get this is a date too, I still want to win. Yes, it's a personality flaw. I was bound to have *one*. 'Juliet, I plan on winning. And if you screw this up for me ... well, I'll be really mad.'

'I think that's something I can live with.' She starts to walk away, and I twirl her back toward me.

'What's it gonna take for you to help me win this?'

She drums two fingers on her lips. And I find myself wondering if I should kiss her. It would be easy to lean in and wait for her to say yes. Which I know is very unlikely. I shake my head to make these stubborn thoughts fly away.

'You can't call me Juliet any more.'

I frown. 'What? That's our thing.'

She rolls her eyes. Which I'm finding is my new favorite part of her. 'That is not our thing. It's not a *thing* at all.'

I glance around to make sure no one is nearby. I managed to lose the camera guy a few minutes into the hunt. 'It is a thing. It's your name.'

'Only legally.'

'Juliet Ripley,' I beg. '*Please?*'

'Ugh. Fine. If you stop making that face.'

I loosen up my puppy-dog face and give her a goofy smile. 'Perfect.' A warmth spreads across my chest, my body relaxing with her near me, but also my heart is ticking faster the longer she looks at me.

This is . . . this is *what*? It feels like what Tristian described when he was falling for Imogen. That desire to be with this person, no matter the time or place – especially when it's really inconvenient, like the set of the dating show I'm starring in.

Oh, crap. Do I like Ripley? Like, *like* her.

Sure, I enjoy making her roll her eyes and working with her to make our little schemes happen – and how my skin tingles when we brush against each other. Or how she's the only person I feel comfortable enough around to show the genuine parts of me. But even still, I have kept a barrier between me and the rest of the world. I don't know if I'm ready to let someone pass that shield.

But luckily, I'm in the middle of a highly competitive game at the moment, and I don't need to focus on things like *feelings*.

'Where are you going?' I call as she starts walking away. 'We had a deal!'

'Stay there. I need to get something.'

Five minutes pass, and I'm wondering if she ditched me when she strides back with Arianna, Maya and two camera crew. My heart sinks, my face following suit before I arrange it into a leading man-worthy position.

'Ripley, you found us some teammates.'

Glancing to the rolling cameras, Ripley's face stays neutral. '*You* needed some assistance.'

I needed you.

She's right, my little maneuver to get some time alone with her was never going to work. This is a recorded date for the show. One Ripley isn't a part of.

'You ladies don't mind Ripley staying behind the camera to help us out, do you?' I maintain eye contact with Maya and Arianna, even as my vision tries to slip back to Ripley.

'Not at all,' Maya wholeheartedly agrees. 'She'll be our secret weapon.'

For a brief second, I let Juliet be the only thing I see. 'What d' you say?'

'OK.' Ripley nods.

Having Ripley on the team was a stroke of genius. I knew she was brilliant, but her problem-solving skills are next level. While Maya, Arianna and myself are decent enough, Ripley is able to uncover the clues with ease. Even if she has to do it from behind the scenes and feed the answers to us.

We crack the first two with no problem.

First, we have to take a video on top of a spinning mushroom while singing a Christmas song. We started at the back of the list, hoping to avoid the rush.

I jump on the ride vehicle, stumbling a little, even with it going in super-slow mode.

'Is this safe?' Arianna worries her bottom lip as I help Maya up with me.

'Probably not.' Maya laughs as she grabs my shirt to stop herself from falling when it spins in the opposite direction. Arianna glances at Ripley, who gives her an encouraging smile.

'Are you sure you don't want to come up here with us?' I ask Ripley when Arianna is safely on board.

'No.' She holds my phone to record me.

'Should we make the ride faster? I feel like that'll give us extra points.' It's foggy today, giving the park a soft haze.

She shakes her head. 'I think that'll send you three to the hospital. But I might get a viral video out of it. So, ball's in your court.'

'Why, Ripley, that almost sounded like a joke.' I crack a smile before singing 'Santa Baby' to the camera, the girls joining in. The fairytale music from the ride plays behind me, but we manage to sing the right notes to my song most of the time.

Jumping down, Ripley hands me the phone. 'You guys have a good lead. Maybe I should go?' she asks as we head to the next spot. Arianna and Maya are reading the clue to the camera. I stay back a few paces with Ripley, covering the mic so the camera won't pick up our conversation. 'I feel kind of bad taking your time.'

I wrap my mittens tighter around the mic. 'I choose who I want to spend time with. And I think I picked my partner wisely.'

'You've got an answer for everything, don't you?' The way she studies me always makes me feel like she can see past my shell and into the depths of my soul. Sometimes it's just a cavernous hole, but it feels a bit cozier with her.

'Usually. But not when it comes to you.' I grab her hand, pulling her toward the Perilous Sea.

It's been over an hour, and we've nearly completed the list.

'Here, I want to show you something.' As the girls and cameras head toward Glacier Peaks, I pull Ripley the opposite way toward Carpathia through a secret path, unhooking my mic to give us real privacy.

'What about the show?' Ripley looks like she wants to bite through her glove.

'They've got enough of me, they can spare a few minutes.' We both wear a guilty look when we come upon Yvette and Ivor exiting from the Fairytalers' castle side door.

'What are you two doing?' Ivor asks, eyes snagging on how close we're standing together.

Ripley must clock it too, because she takes several side steps to separate us. 'I was helping Garrick with ...' Ripley glances over at me.

'Look, I'll be honest. Ripley got lost.' She shoots me a glare, but I keep going. 'And then she got stuck in the Pixie train and, while hilarious, I felt it was my knightly duty to help her.'

Staring at her, I dare her to come up with something else. She bites her lip but stays quiet.

Ivor shares a look with Yvette, who raises her eyebrow.

'Just a heads-up, G, a few people have mentioned how often you two are seen together. Which I quickly shot down as nothing more than production-related business.' Ivor says the words slowly.

I want to make another joke, but the concern on his face sobers me right up.

'But after this little stunt, maybe I need to reiterate that we wouldn't want you two to do anything that might compromise the show or the park's integrity. Right?' The tone is softer than it might have been a few months ago, but the message is clear.

You promised you wouldn't screw this up, Garrick, I can hear him adding, if Ripley wasn't here. Normally, I just ignore it when my brothers tell me to do something, but after Nathan's little interrogation earlier I can't deny I might have let whatever Ripley and I are doing get – *slightly* – out of hand.

Ripley looks like someone threw a bucket of ice water over her. 'Of course not. We'll be better.'

Being better was never my strong suit.

The Twelve Days of Christmas Cookies Countdown
19 December
Day 7
Thai Tea Mochi Crinkle Cookies

Servings: 12 cookies

INGREDIENTS:
Mochi
60g glutinous rice flour
20g granulated sugar
125g milk
7g coconut oil
cornstarch for coating

Thai tea cookies
2 ½ tablespoons Thai tea, ground
35g milk
240g plain flour
1 ½ teaspoons baking powder
1 teaspoon salt
90g unsalted butter, melted
160g granulated sugar
2 eggs
1 teaspoon vanilla extract
granulated sugar for coating
icing sugar for coating

INSTRUCTIONS:
Mochi
1. Mix the flour, sugar and milk in a microwaveable bowl. Cover and microwave for 1 minute.
2. Remove bowl and stir mochi mix. Cover and microwave for another 1 minute.
3. Remove bowl and add the coconut oil to the hot mochi and mix. Cover and set aside to cool for at least 10 minutes.
4. Lightly flour a surface with cornstarch, knead and stretch the dough on to the surface, then separate into 12 equal portions. Coat each piece with a little cornstarch and set aside.

Thai tea cookies
1. Grind the loose-leaf Thai tea into a fine powder using a spice grinder, food processor or a pestle and mortar. Put the powder through a sieve to remove larger pieces. Make sure you have a total of 2 ½ tablespoons of ground Thai tea.
2. In a small bowl, combine the sifted tea with milk and mix thoroughly. Let it sit for at least 5 minutes.
3. In a medium bowl, combine the flour, baking powder and salt. Set aside.

4. In a large bowl, beat together the melted butter and sugar. Then add in the eggs, vanilla and Thai tea mixture until well combined.
5. Fold in the flour mixture and mix just until combined. Cover and chill for at least 2 hours or overnight.
6. When ready to bake, preheat the oven to 350°F (180°C). Line a cookie sheet with parchment paper.
7. Add the granulated sugar to one small bowl and the icing sugar to another. Set aside.
8. Divided into 12 equal balls. Flatten each ball out, add a piece of mochi to the middle, then carefully pinch in the edges to completely cover the mochi and form back into a ball.
9. Coat each ball with granulated sugar, followed by a layer of icing sugar, and place them approximately 1–1.5 inches apart on a lined baking sheet. If you're baking multiple batches, keep the remaining uncoated ones in the fridge until you're ready to bake.
10. Bake for 12–15 minutes or until the tops crack and the bottom edges begin to brown. After cooling on the pan for 2 minutes, transfer the cookies to a wire rack and cool completely.

22

RIPLEY

It's time for the third elimination, and by now we're all used to it. I feel bad for the girls sent home, especially since they seem to be forming friendships. Except Riya and Desiree – that ship sailed a long time ago. But the one thing none of them appear to be doing is developing a real relationship with Garrick. There's a lot of flirting – it is Garrick, after all – however, love isn't in the air, despite what the cameras and editing might portray.

Mom sure got her money's worth with these production people. They're making this look like a romantic love story. In their interviews, Arianna and Zoya have said they have a massive crush on Garrick and think it could become more. Desiree said that too, but it seems like that was the acting classes speaking more than her genuine feelings. Guess we'll see when she and Garrick go on their date tonight.

I know that's weird, considering we haven't even had the elimination yet. But they already said he couldn't send Desiree home. She's too good on-screen.

Two girls stand before Garrick as we reach the final moments of this elimination on the magical training stage.

He's making it look like it's hard to choose – like he's about to decide in the moment.

'This is not getting any easier,' Garrick says, rubbing the back of his neck. 'But I'm sorry, Harmony. I'm going to have to send you home. That means, Riya, will you be my Beeloved?'

There's crying and hugging like there always is, and then Harmony says her goodbyes.

'Juliet,' Garrick says when the cameras turn off. The crew splits up, one group heading to edit this final scene into the episode airing tonight while the rest set up for the one-on-one date later.

'Please tell me I can take the rest of the night off?' Garrick was supposed to wear his knight costume, but the temperature dropped, and he would have been a knight popsicle. Instead, he's wearing a black peacoat and khakis, with a gray-and-red scarf.

I toss him the water bottle I was holding for him. My job varies from moment to moment: sometimes I hand out snacks; other times, when the park is open, I wrangle fans of the show away while we film. 'You know you can't. You've got a date tonight.'

He steps closer, sliding my pink earmuffs off, the ones Nathan got me last year for Christmas because he said I needed more color. 'Will you be there?' he asks, slipping the earmuffs on to his head.

My heart skips a few beats when he says it, but he doesn't mean what I wish he meant.

Wait? What do I wish that he meant? Nothing, obviously.

'Can I have those back?' I reach for the earmuffs, but he spins away.

'No, they're pre-warmed. I'm freezing!' He clamps his hands over the pink puffs.

After getting scolded by Ivor Walton yesterday, I know this little chat is probably not the wisest. All morning, I kept checking over my shoulder, worried that people were secretly spying on us. But as the day progressed, it didn't really seem like anyone was bothering to watch me.

Still, if there was chatter, I want it to be a one-time thing.

'Fine, whatever. Just go mentally prepare for your date later, please.' I shove him in the opposite direction and turn away from that dangerous smirk, only to see Nathan and Melika staring at me.

'What?' I rifle through my production bag, pretending there's something vital I need to find so they won't see me blushing.

'Since when do you let somebody call you Juliet?' Nathan says, swinging an arm around Melika as they both burn a hole into my skull.

I bite my nail before realizing that makes me look guilty. I shove my hands into my coat pocket instead. I'll blame the cold if they ask why my cheeks are red. 'I know you've learned by now that nobody tells Garrick what to do.' But I haven't been as diligent as I usually would be if anyone else were calling me Juliet. It's just when he says it, *ugh*, there's a – I don't know, flutter in my stomach, and I don't understand how to feel about it.

'Mmm, sure, Jan.' Melika purses her lips.

Luckily, I'm saved by an angel in the form of a beauty YouTuber, so I don't have to lie further.

'You ready?' Ellie bounds over.

'Yes, babe.' Nathan links arms with her and then takes mine. 'Come now, ladies. Ellie is going to show us how to do proper make-up. I need to learn this skill if I'm going to be a star of the stage.'

I grab Melika's hand and pull her along as Ellie and Nathan start walking. 'Now you're the star of the stage? Didn't you only have one acting class?' And it was from Desiree, so I have a feeling it was more about her than actual acting tips.

'Rip, you know my toxic trait is seeing something done once and assuming I'll be a pro at said thing.' Nathan weaves us through the land of Carpathia to the Fairytalers' exit.

'You do have the hobby graveyard to prove it.' Melika isn't watching, too busy texting a person I'm pretty sure is Kahoa, so I have to stop her from hitting into a fake boulder.

Nathan ignores her and continues, 'Ellie, can you also please give Ripley a makeover?'

Ellie's eyes light up. 'I've been dying to try this new palette I got. The colors will be freaking stunning with your blue eyes.'

I shake my head. 'I'm OK. We can focus on Nathan.' Make-up looks great on other people, but whenever I've tried I end up looking like a clown in training.

'My dearest, Ripley,' Nathan sings. 'It's true I am the focus, but I will always share the stage with you. And you,' he calls to Melika. 'Miss-Can't-set-her-phone-down-for-five-minutes.'

'I've got enough brain-power to do both.'

As we break apart to step into the back lot, I whisper to Melika, 'So, who ya texting?'

A little smile twists her lips up. 'Just a contact I'm making who can help with my online shipping issues.'

I raise an eyebrow. 'Shipping issues, *right*...' I elongate the last word.

'Yes, shipping issues, Juliet.' She slides her phone into her pocket. 'Now, let's go give you a makeover – nineties romcom style.'

I do end up letting Ellie try some make-up on me and, unsurprisingly, she kills it. I've never looked like this in my life. I almost don't recognize myself when I stare into the mirror. I send a pic to Anna, who gushes and then asks what Garrick thinks. I don't message her back.

But it does make me wonder if he'll notice when I see him this evening.

23

GARRICK

The crew has set up the carousel for my dinner date. Hopefully, Desiree has a stomach as strong as me because I don't want to have to clean up puke if the spinning is too much for her. The music is turned off so they can add it in post production, but they can't stop the creaks and moans of the old machinery. Ms Ripley's been making interns oil it all day, but it's not improving. I guess they gave up and are letting it live its life.

Pierre is doing final touches on my make-up. 'If you hold that brush there any longer,' I tell him, 'it might freeze to my face.'

'You should have learned by now, I can make any look work.'

He is a true magician.

The rest of the girls are back at the apartments, so Desiree and I can get some alone time while about fifteen other people watch our every move.

'No, I need the Beeloved sign behind him, otherwise no one will see it. That's the whole point,' Ms Ripley says, rubbing between her eyes.

'Can I do anything, Mom?' Ripley offers. Any stress I was feeling melts away – figuratively speaking.

Ms Ripley shakes her head. 'No, Juliet, you're doing great, though, thank you.'

'Come on, I need a huddle so I don't freeze my nips off,' Nathan says, grabbing Ripley. She wraps her arm around him and they cuddle together on a bench.

They're still doing the final set-up, so I slip away before they notice. I plop down on the other side of Ripley. 'They should have picked an inside location. It's brutal out here.'

'Garrick, you aren't supposed to be over here.' Ripley scoots her hands into her sleeves and holds them over her ears.

'I like your make-up,' I say, slipping her earmuffs out of my pocket and sliding them on to her head.

She freezes, blinking at me. 'Uh, thanks. Ellie did it.'

'You don't need it, but it's like flocking a Christmas tree, it adds a bit of flare.'

She frowns. 'Did you just compare me to a tree?'

'An extreme compliment, Juliet. Christmas is my favorite species of tree.' I fluff her pink pom-poms. 'I thought I should give them back to you.'

I notice her throat bob as my hands linger there. 'I wasn't sure I'd see them again.'

Part of me is hyper-aware of the crew around us, but the larger part is distracted by the girl in front of me. I smile, but it's different than I usually offer, softer. 'Nah, they look too cute on you not to return them.'

Nathan clears his throat. 'Um, I don't want to break up whatever this is, but they're calling you.'

Glancing to the carousel, I see that all eyes are focused on us. Crap. 'Sorry, gotta go. Keep the earmuffs warm for me,' I whisper as I run back to the waiting cameras.

They've strategically placed heaters on the carousel so we don't end up with a couple of ice statues on a date.

'I thought I'd lost my spot for the night.' Desiree's eyes wander to the park we can't see beyond the bright filming lights. 'Sure you don't want Ripley to join?'

My gut clenches, but I ignore the weird spasm. 'It's just me and you.' Even as the words slide out easily, my face donning a charming smile, a voice in my head tells me to stop – that Ripley is watching. I don't want her to see me flirt with Desiree.

Great, this date will be interesting.

A couple of cameras are set up next to us while the crew stands near the entrance, watching on the video screens. I might not be able to see her as we spin in a slow circle, but getting Ripley out of my mind is proving more difficult.

The date is going fine, pretty much how I expected. Desiree laughs at my jokes and smiles on cue as I ask her about her pets and what she's looking forward to at Christmas. Then she mentions that she was in the play *Romeo and Juliet* last summer.

Without my consent my lips quirk into a dangerous grin. 'You don't say? That's my favorite play.'

'Really?' Desiree perks up, ready to spout her lines, no doubt. 'I played Juliet, as you probably guessed.'

Through the dark, I spy her – those pink earmuffs a beacon. I hope the camera thinks the smile is for my date and not the girl waiting off-screen. '"But soft! What light through yonder window breaks? It is the east, and *Juliet* is the sun."'

While I can't see Ripley clearly, I sense the smile tugging at her lips. I'm afraid she might break a tooth if she doesn't release it soon. When I learned Juliet was her first name, I memorized the best lines from the play just in case a moment arose when I could tease her.

They were right to keep Desiree around. She doesn't need any prompting to continue talking through the evening. Between her and me, they get more than enough footage to splice into a nice package for the next episode.

When they finally call cut, I nearly jump for joy. My toes are numb in my shoes, and my fingers ache when I move them despite being wrapped in gloves.

The ends of the dates are always a little weird because, no matter who I'm with, we're always just as unsure of what to do. If it were a typical date, I'd drop her off at home, have a goodnight kiss. Here, I just say goodbye and she's ushered away.

'I guess I can return that copy of *Romeo and Juliet* I bought you for Christmas,' Ripley tells me as they remove my mic. 'Since you already seem familiar with the text.'

'Do no such thing.' I pretend to be offended. 'I want it. And I want it signed by the namesake herself. You.'

She tosses a thermos at me. 'Some fresh cocoa, as requested.'

'Hey, where are you going? Don't you want to share it?' I thank the PA and speed walk to catch her.

'Too much sugar for this late.' Just her eyes are peeking over her coat collar.

'Probably, plus you're already sweet enough.'

'Do you really mean it when you say those things? Or does it just happen automatically, like a sliding door?' She looks over at me, confused, and I'm equally as stumped.

A month ago, I'd say it was second nature and, sure, most of it was just for fun. But staring at her, with the lights reflecting off her blue eyes, it's never felt truer.

The Twelve Days of Christmas Cookies Countdown
20 December
Day 8
Peanut Butter-filled Brownie Cookies

Servings: 24 cookies

INGREDIENTS:
Peanut butter filling
- 125g creamy peanut butter
- 60g icing sugar

Cookie dough
- 225g semi-sweet chocolate, coarsely chopped
- 95g plain flour, spooned and leveled
- 20g cocoa powder
- 1 teaspoon espresso powder (can skip or use 2 teaspoons instant coffee powder)
- 1 teaspoon baking powder
- ¼ teaspoon salt
- 5 tablespoons unsalted butter, softened to room temperature
- 150g packed light or dark brown sugar
- 50g granulated sugar
- 2 large eggs, at room temperature
- 1 teaspoon pure vanilla extract

INSTRUCTIONS:
Make the peanut butter filling
1. In a small bowl, mix the peanut butter and icing sugar together until combined and smooth. Mixture should be thick, but soft. With a teaspoon, scoop out a spoonful of peanut butter mixture (about 6g), and roll into a ball.
2. Place on a parchment paper-lined baking tray. Repeat with remaining mixture until you have 24 peanut butter balls. Loosely cover and freeze for at least 1 hour and up to 1 day.

Make the brownie cookie dough
1. Melt the chocolate in a double boiler or microwave. Microwave in 20-second increments, stirring after each until completely melted. Set aside to slightly cool.
2. Meanwhile, whisk together the flour, cocoa powder, espresso powder, baking powder and salt. Set aside.
3. In a large bowl with an electric mixer, beat the butter, brown sugar and granulated sugar together on medium–high speed until smooth and creamy, about 2 minutes.
4. Add the eggs and vanilla extract, then beat on high speed for 2 minutes. Scrape down the sides and bottom of the bowl, then beat on high for 1 more minute.

5. Pour in the slightly cooled melted chocolate and mix on medium–high speed for 2 minutes. Add the dry ingredients to the wet ingredients and beat on low until combined.
6. Cover and chill the dough in the refrigerator for 1 hour.
7. After chilling, preheat oven to 350°F (180°C). Line baking trays with baking paper.

Shape the cookies
8. Only take about 6 peanut butter balls out of the freezer at a time, leaving the rest in the freezer while you're shaping the first bunch.
9. Using a sturdy tablespoon, scoop out the cookie dough and roll into a ball, about 1.5 tablespoons/30g. The dough will be quite stiff. Make an indentation with your thumb and place a frozen peanut butter ball in the indentation.
10. Pinch off a piece of the brownie cookie dough and press it on top of the peanut butter filling, then roll the whole thing together into a smooth ball with the peanut butter hidden inside. Repeat with remaining cookie dough and peanut butter balls.

11. Place dough balls 3 inches apart on the baking sheets and bake for 12–13 minutes or until the edges appear set. The centers will be quite soft, but will set up as they cool.
12. Remove from the oven and allow cookies to cool on the baking trays for 10 minutes before transferring to a wire rack to cool completely.

24

RIPLEY

This is not good. The third episode aired last night and I'm scrolling through the comments. There are a few good reviews, but also quite a few saying they aren't sure Garrick is taking it seriously. It doesn't help that some anonymous source is claiming there's drama behind the scenes – hinting at Riya's secret boyfriend, and that Garrick has wandering eyes for girls other than the contestants. It's probably Desiree, but without proof there isn't much I can do about it. Plus, it's already out there, so kicking Desiree off the show will just add fuel to the fire.

I spiral as I get sucked into the vortex of TikTok, breaking down Garrick's interactions with each girl and ranking his interest on a scale from one to ten. According to several, Beeloved and its show are a fraud.

So maybe it is. I can't honestly say I disagree with them, but Beeloved will crash and burn before it even takes flight if the reviews stay this way. The investors made it clear that they wouldn't provide funding if everyone's screaming *fraud* into the black pit of despair we call the internet.

Mom's face pops up on my screen and I panic, sending

her to voicemail. I have to see her in less than five minutes for an early morning shoot with the girls before today's date, but I need those extra five minutes to organize my thoughts. She might not be on TikTok, but if it's there, it's bound to be everywhere. My throat tightens, sweat slicking my skin as I envision the conversation I know I'll have to have with her.

Crap.

'You need to stop.'

I look up from my phone to see Brett standing in my way to the break room, where I thought I'd grab breakfast, but now I want to hurl.

'If you want a boyfriend, you should have been the lead, like your mom wanted.' I've done my best to avoid kiss-ass Brett when I can, but like a bad smell he won't go away.

I bite my nail as flushed heat coats my cheeks. 'I don't want a boyfriend.' I hide my phone in my pocket, hoping that will somehow make the comments go away. Even though I know that's not how the internet works. I push my shoulders back, refusing to let this man intimidate me. Even if my holly-red cheeks say otherwise.

'Then why are you and Garrick attached at the hip?' He stares me down, trying to make me feel small. 'I thought when I brought this up to Ivor Walton, you'd get the hint. I didn't want to be the one to have to tell Ms Ripley her daughter was putting the show at risk. But I might have to, for the *show's* sake.'

For the show's sake. Give me a freaking break.

'Maybe you should do your job and stop watching me.' Sort of a weak response since it's probably Garrick he's keeping an eye on, not me. Garrick and I just seem to keep ending up in each other's orbit.

He scoffs, and I want to scream. 'Don't flatter yourself. I'm doing my job – which is to make Beeloved a success. As Ms Ripley's daughter, you'd think you'd have the same goal.'

I open and close my mouth a few times, but arguing with this person will not help the situation. He probably just wants to feel superior, and I'm not giving him the time of day. 'Don't you have some ass-kissing to do?' I turn around and head back outside.

I don't know for sure that he'll bring this up to my mom – it might be a bluff. Snitching on me might backfire, but he seems ambitious enough to take the risk.

I suppose I could say something to her ... No, that won't work, not after the response to the last episode. It'll just make the situation a billion times worse.

When I get to the private dining room of the Royal Fare, the gift-wrapping stations have already been set up for the girls. Giant rolls of colorful paper, bright bows and shiny ribbon fill several tables along the back wall. This afternoon, we're going to a shelter to hand out presents, so they wanted a scene where the contestants wrap the gifts beforehand and talk about their best holiday memories. I did a good chunk of them yesterday with Nathan and Melika, but there are still enough presents left for the girls to do a few each.

'Juliet.' Mom grabs my arm the second I step past the threshold. I stiffen under her grip. 'Did you see the reviews of last night's episode?'

I open my mouth to respond, but she keeps going. 'An absolute train wreck. The one thing I was clear about from the start is that this should look organic and natural. Beeloved is about blossoming relationships and cultivating long-lasting love. If the public believes it is all a sham, they won't download the app. Which means I can kiss any investments goodbye.'

I could tell her that people download dating apps all the time for reasons that have nothing to do with what she just mentioned. Or that there was no way a staged reality show would ever come off as entirely natural.

Why are she and Anna so in the dark about what love actually does to a person? The evidence has been piling up since I was a kid, divorce after divorce. It tricks you, then it ruins you. Hasn't Mom nursed enough heartaches, or watched Anna tear away parts of herself to conform for a man who doesn't deserve her, to realize that the only thing she should be counting on Beeloved to do, is turn a profit if it can fool enough people into believing its promises.

But I hold those thoughts in as I see the forlorn look on her face. My shoulders sag. *Did I do this?* Has the time I've been spending with Garrick ruined the show's trajectory?

I take Mom's hand and squeeze it. 'I will handle this. We just need to talk some sense into our star.'

Mom runs a hand over my hair in a surprisingly sweet gesture. 'If anyone can, it's you, Juliet.'

While I appreciate that she believes in me, it also feels like a lot of weight to carry. But I'm a problem-solving expert. I can fix this.

I step away from her as the contestants are ushered into the room, quickly pulling my phone back out and sending a text to Garrick.

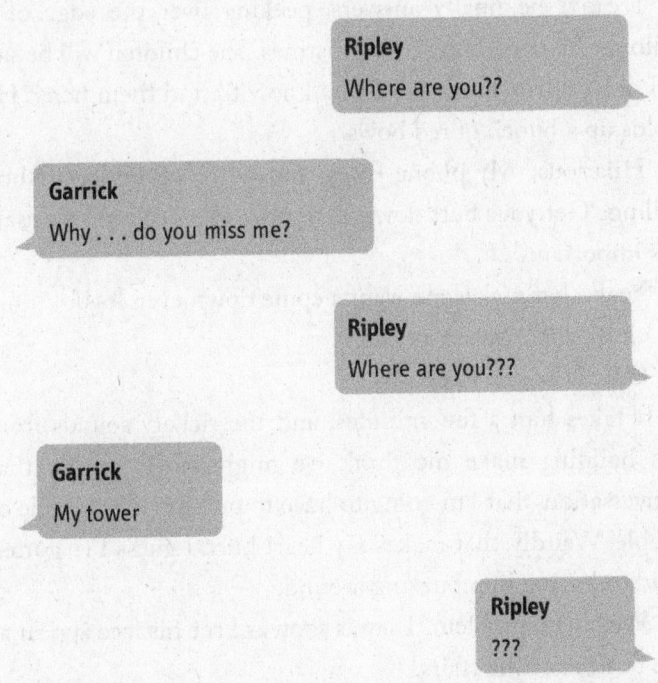

Garrick sends a picture of a very unsafe structure and describes how to get to it.

It only takes me a few minutes to find the old death trap and him waving from the top. It's a decrepit wood structure that once might have been a cool kids' playground attraction. But those days are long gone, much like my patience.

'Will you come down?' I bite my thumbnail. I'm not a fan of heights. And I'm definitely not a fan of heights when they involve dilapidated buildings. It looks like it would collapse in the slightest snowfall. My foot bounces up and down as I wait for his response.

'I can't,' he finally answers, peeking over the edge of a railing. 'I'm decorating for Christmas. The children will be sad if I don't finish. How will Santa know to find them here?' He holds up a bunch of red bows.

'Hilarious.' My phone rings, and I don't even look who's calling. 'Get your butt down here now. We need to talk asap. It's important.'

'Yeah, that makes me wanna come down even less.'

I huff, and I hear him laugh.

'OK, OK. Just a sec.'

It takes him a few minutes, and the rickety sounds from the building make me think we might never get to that conversation, that I'm going to have to pull him from a pile of rubble. Weirdly, that makes my heart hurt. I guess I've gotten used to having him buzzing around.

'We have a problem,' I say as soon as I see his face appear at the bottom of the stairs.

'Way to greet a guy first thing in the morning, Juliet.'

My annoyance for Brett is back, and Garrick is the only person around to let it out on. 'You need to take this seriously.' My words come out harsher than I mean them to.

Garrick steps back, a frown dipping his brows together. 'I'm not even sure what the conversation is about. So, how am I supposed to take what seriously?'

'Not this conversation. Well, *yes*, this conversation. I mean this whole thing in general.' I wave around at him and then at the park. 'The episode aired last night and the comments are saying you're half-assing it.' The annoyance fades away as worried notes seep in.

'Juliet, I can't believe you listen to the internet. They just like to complain. Best not to look.' He pulls a cookie from his coat pocket and offers it to me, but I ignore it.

'This whole show's on the internet, *Garrick*.' I emphasize his name. 'The whole point is to get buzz on the various platforms. Good buzz. I don't think my mom will buy the whole *there's no such thing as bad press* thing.' People think you're not taking this seriously. Can't you just for once act like you care?'

Garrick's face loses its easy charm and a hard stare replaces it. 'If I remember correctly, I'm doing *you* a favor. So, why are you coming at me?' I've never heard the sharp edge in his voice. At least I know I'm getting somewhere.

I hold in a groan, pinching the bridge of my nose. If I want this to succeed, I need him with me, not against me. 'Look, I'm not expecting you to find true love. You and I both know that that's not real. But there's got to be at least one girl you're somewhat interested in. Can you just focus on her?'

'I think something is wrong with your algorithm. Because the girl I felt something for has a boyfriend – so strike one, right off the bat.' He bites off a chunk of one of the peanut butter chocolate cookies I saw him make in his video this morning.

Riya. How long has he known about this? If I thought I saw any hurt from that revelation, it's gone in a blink of an eye.

'But did I complain? No. Maybe I'm not the problem. Maybe you have a flawed dating app, which is not my fault.' He deflects this back on me, and I feel my blood boil.

'If you hadn't been messing around while doing the survey, you might've gotten better matches.' Usually, I wouldn't be this fussed about it. I would let this guy do whatever he wanted. But I told Mom to trust me, and if I get this wrong, I will never live it down.

'Excuse me, I took that very seriously.' I'm not sure how he gets that out with a straight face.

I try another tactic. Taking a deep breath, I attempt to cool the annoyance. 'OK, it doesn't really matter whether you were screwing around and messed up the algorithm, or if there was an oversight in casting background checks. Because we're in it now, so can we just agree that we both need this to work? And maybe we can find a solution together?'

Garrick stares up at the sky, running a hand through his hair. 'You and me? I thought you were pretending you didn't like me?'

'See, if you can channel that charm for the girls, it will be all good.'

He studies me, and I try not to squirm under the intensity of his gaze. 'Did you have something in mind?'

Actually, I did. 'We need intrigue in the show. So, why don't we fake a spontaneous kiss?'

Garrick rubs his chin. 'Who did you have in mind?'

I know just the person who would be interested in this.

25

GARRICK

It is important to me that we show the good that Fairytale Gardens does for the community. After everything with the scandal last summer, people forget that FTG does a lot of legit charity work. It was another thing Mom was passionate about. She always said if you are able, you should give, even if it's just a helpful hand.

So today I'm donning my Santa suit once again and we're going to a local shelter. After my chat with Ripley this morning, I need to make sure I'm coming off genuine – not that it'll be hard here. I can almost forget the cameras, and the seven remaining contestants vying for my attention. The whole team will come with us today, including Tristian and Imogen.

Over the last few weeks, we've been collecting money and donations of toys and clothing for Christmas. We set up giving boxes around the park and encouraged guests to help. My family and the Beeloved team also chipped in. Everyone got really into it. We had to rent a truck to bring all the gifts here – the back stuffed with colored packages decked out in ribbon and bows.

The contestants spent this morning wrapping everything. Nathan showed me pictures from the shoot on the way here – I wasn't there, so the girls were free to gush about me. Even though Ripley wasn't on camera, she did wrap some gifts. I could spot hers right away because they were by far the best. She could even give me a run for my money, and I'm the best wrapper in the Walton family.

This date style will also be a great way to see how the girls react to this situation and their feelings about helping others. Many of them will put on a show – *cough*, Desiree, *cough*. I'm excited to see the kids' faces when I hand out the sweet toy cars and jousting sets I got.

After helping set up the Christmas tree with Melika's expert eye for design and the snack table – like I was going to let us visit without baked goods – the kids and adults line up to meet Santa. I'm sitting in the chair in my North Pole best, while the girls work as my elves and hand out the presents. Desiree keeps trying to inch closer to my chair to make sure the camera never loses sight of her.

'Tell me, buddy,' I say to a kid, around six, on my lap. 'Have you been a good boy this year?'

He screws up his face, and I can tell he's trying to work out how much he should spill. I know because it's a look I've worn often. 'Well, I *really* tried, but it's hard.'

Don't I know it.

'What d' ya say we make a deal?' I keep my voice low. I'm not mic'd, and the cameras are far enough away they won't be able to hear me. 'You promise to keep trying to be good, and I'll give you a present for doing the best you can so far.'

He nods enthusiastically. He reminds me so much of my nephew, Bradley. I tell Desiree to give him two gifts.

Desiree gives me a dimpled smile as the kid runs off to show off his new toys. 'You're a good Santa. Everyone seems really happy.' She runs a hand over the fur around my collar.

Ripley and I decided to plan the fake kiss for another day. We didn't feel it was appropriate here. But the way some of the girls look at me – including Desiree right this second – it might not have to be staged.

Do I want that? When I look out across the room to all the girls I should be trying to connect with, my eyes snag only on Ripley. She's in the corner with Imogen, helping a girl set up a makeshift kitchen with plastic food and dishes. Ripley's got this beautiful, soft smile. Her face is easy and happy, and those lines of stress across her forehead are gone.

Something in my heart dislodges and a warm sensation overtakes me. It's nice to see her relaxed. I've got a glimpse of it over the last few weeks, but only in sporadic moments when she forgets about all the responsibilities we're both shouldering. I yank the front of my costume back and forth to get some air.

'You good?' Tristian asks, pausing on his way to pass out some candy cane cookies Arianna made.

'Santa is a hard job.' I quickly sweep any unwanted emotions off my face. I told Ripley I'd make the audience believe I was fully invested in finding my Beeloved – thoughts about someone who is not an option need to stay far away from the prying camera lens.

'We really appreciate it,' a mom tells me as Zoya gives

her daughter a large purple box. The woman takes my hand, squeezing it. 'It's been tough this year. I didn't . . .' She tears up and can't finish.

I nod my understanding, throat thick. 'I'm happy we could help. Maybe give you a breather. Don't forget to get a little something for yourself.' The adults were given a choice of gift cards and a present because we didn't want them to miss out on opening gifts.

We're running low on toys, so I offer to slip away and grab more from my sleigh.

'You don't need to do that,' Brett says. This guy always likes to one-up everyone around him to make himself seem more important.

I wave him off as he tries to go instead. 'I insist. Santa has to make sure they're the right ones. Desiree, why don't you entertain the kids with a Christmas story while I'm away?' Her face lights up, giving me time to shimmy past the crew before anyone can stop me.

We do need more presents, but I also just want a break. Not from the kids – they're fantastic. Mainly from the girls I'm showing interest in for Ripley's sake – for the *show's sake*, I mean. I'm doing this for Beeloved and FTG, and for all those kids I'm going to help with my fencing camp . . .

But also *Juliet*, if I'm being truthful to myself. I started calling her Juliet at first just to get a rise out of her, but now the name feels so perfectly right.

When I step out back, the first thing I hear is Juliet's voice. She's talking to someone on the phone. I hadn't seen her leave the main area, which is surprising since I hadn't been able to take my eyes off her despite my better judgment. Which, in fairness, isn't the most sound judgment to start with.

'Anna, I told you, you deserve to be treated better.' There's anger in her words, but I can tell it's not directed at the person on the other end.

This definitely doesn't sound like a conversation I should be eavesdropping on. As I step back, I bump into a bunch of cleaning supplies, and if I move any more, I'll knock it over.

'No, it's not OK that he up and decided to take an extra trip on Christmas. He promised you he'd be home. Molly is looking forward to it.' Juliet lets out an exaggerated sigh. And this one's the real deal, unlike the one she gives me when she's pretending to be annoyed. Those are cute. I can tell this one comes from genuine distress.

My gut twists, and I want to make it better. I don't know what *it* is, but I don't like hearing her like this. I peek around the room divider. She's running her nail over her bottom lip, hovering so close to giving in to the bad habit of biting it.

I try to get in my head so I can't hear more of the conversation. When she finally hangs up the phone after making little progress with the person on the other line, I walk out like I just got there, creating a lot of noise. 'Hey, Juliet, are there any more presents back here?' I try not to sound like I just heard everything.

She twirls the bottom of her hair before wiping her palm across her face. 'I think there's some in the truck. I can grab them.'

'I'll come with you.' I follow her into the freezing air, the harsh sun of winter doing little to warm anything. She's not wearing a coat, and I would offer my Santa suit but it's not easy to get out of.

'Sorry I wasn't out there to see we were running low.' She opens the door to the truck and grabs a box full of brightly wrapped presents.

'You know it's not your job to carry the weight of the world.' I lean against the side, transfixed by her. Her hair is in a half ponytail, and she's wearing the most adorable holiday sweatshirt with little sausage dogs in sweaters. I love when she lets her whimsical side out. It feels like I'm getting a peek at her brain.

'Not the world, just this show.' She pulls on a ribbon curl, straightening it and releasing it to spring back. 'We already messed up with the last episode ... and then there's Brett.'

'The intern?' I raise an eyebrow. 'What about him? Was he hitting on you or something?' My heart gives an involuntary spasm at the idea of Ripley going on a date with someone.

'What?' She grimaces. 'Ew, no, gross. Apparently, he's the one who told Ivor we were getting "too friendly".' She air quotes the last words. 'He called me out on it again this morning.'

My jaw tightens at the idea of Ripley getting reprimanded. 'I'll talk to him. Set him straight.' That's not really my area of expertise, but I'm sure Tristian can give me some tips on how to be more grumpy.

She shakes her head. 'Don't. It'll just make things worse. I handled it. We just can't screw up any more – especially because I want these families to have some joy.'

'They are – don't you worry, Santa's got them covered. And as far as the negative reactions to the last episode, we'll fix that.

The masses are easily swayed. They'll be back on our side in no time.'

'Probably will, since you're such a good actor.' She climbs up the small step and further into the truck.

'I'm not sure if that was a compliment. But I'm gonna take it as one.' I grab the box she hands me, our fingers brushing as I do. An electric shock runs up my arm and I almost drop the package. I clear my throat. 'You don't seem happy about that, though.'

'I am happy about *that*,' she says. 'It's just ... life.' She shrugs, grabbing another gift.

'Tell me about it.' It sounds like a line you say just to agree with the sentiment, but I genuinely mean it. I want to know what's bothering her. *How I can make it better.*

When she looks up from collecting a handful of boxes, her eyes widen as she sees me waiting for an answer. 'Oh, was that an invitation to spill my guts?'

'I work at a theme park, I'm used to gut-spilling.'

She dips her chin to her chest, shoulders shaking in a silent laugh.

'Come on, *Juliet*, admit it, you think I'm funny.'

Her head does a giant circle, like she's trying not to look at me, but she fails and finally meets my eyes. 'Perhaps you've worn me down, and I might find *some* of the things you say worthy of a laugh or two.'

'*Or two?* Juliet, stop! The flattery is going to kill me.'

That gets a bigger giggle.

My smile is so broad it makes my cheeks hurt. *God*, her laugh is the most beautiful sound I've ever heard.

'So, the spilling of guts?' I ask when she jumps down with the final packages.

Juliet's mouth is about to open when Sofia comes outside. 'The kids might riot if Santa doesn't get back in there soon.'

'Coming,' I call over my shoulder, wishing that time would stop for just a moment so I could keep making her smile.

The Twelve Days of Christmas Cookies Countdown
21 December
Day 9
White Chocolate Cranberry Cookies

Servings: 36 cookies

INGREDIENTS:
- 170g unsalted butter, at room temperature
- 100g granulated sugar
- 110g packed light brown sugar
- 1 large egg, room temperature
- 2 teaspoons grated orange zest
- 2 teaspoons vanilla extract
- 250g plain flour
- 1 teaspoon baking powder
- ½ teaspoon fine sea salt
- 135g white chocolate chips
- 200g fresh cranberries coarsely chopped, or substitute 1 cup dried cranberries

INSTRUCTIONS:
1. Preheat the oven to 350°F (180°C). Line baking sheets with parchment paper.
2. In a large mixing bowl, with an electric mixer on medium–high speed, cream together the butter and both sugars for 2–3 minutes or until light and fluffy.

3. Add the egg and beat well to incorporate.
4. Beat in the zest and vanilla extract.
5. In a medium bowl, whisk together flour, baking powder and salt. Add to the butter mixture and beat just until combined and dough comes together.
6. Stir in the cranberries and chocolate chips just until incorporated.
7. Shape into 1-inch balls and place 2 inches apart on your prepared baking sheet.
8. Bake 12-15 minutes or until golden brown at the edges (cookies with dried cranberries will bake faster, about 11-13 minutes).
9. Cool for 5 minutes on the baking sheet then transfer to wire rack to cool completely.

26

RIPLEY

As we get closer to Christmas, I can tell the crew is getting stir-crazy. I always thought it was a kid thing, but these adults feel it too: no one wants to be at work when the smell of snow is in the air, the tinsel is twinkling and sleigh bells are ringing. Well, no one except Mom, anyway. I doubt she would have remembered what time of year it was, if it wasn't for all the festive decor.

We had an elimination this morning, and Maya went home. I'm bummed because I really enjoyed talking all things true crime with her. Garrick looked equally devastated; long pauses and dramatic eyes have been added to the new and improved on-screen Garrick. He's really stepped it up since our chat about taking this seriously.

He's so freaking charming, and with the silver bells and red poinsettias, I could mistake it for reality. He's the perfect knight in shining armor. It almost makes me wish I believed in all this stuff – *almost*.

Yesterday's phone call with Anna repeats in my mind. Her no-good husband is once again flaking out on them. Anna acts like this doesn't happen *all the time*. She deserves so much better. Why does her mind have to trick her into thinking she's in love? Despite what science says, I don't believe it has your back.

'Did you ask her?' Garrick says when I arrive at the top table he's reserved by Glacier Eats.

'Yup. Desiree is happily on board to star in our little production.'

Garrick relaxes into the tall stool, oversized puffer coat hiding his knight's costume. 'Good.' He pulls down his beanie as a group of guests walk by. I wanted to meet somewhere a little more covert, but the girls were already having lunch in the break room, and Garrick only had a short window between his FTG knight duties, since it's Sunday and the park is open all day.

'Did you have any doubts she'd be game?' I play with my pink earmuffs.

'No, that's why we chose her.' Despite his relief over the first part of our plan to prove he's falling in love on the show, he sounds nervous. 'Sit and eat, will you? I got enough food for five people.'

Burgers, fries, nuggets and pizza are nestled into ice-themed cardboard containers nearly covering the small, round table. 'I am starving.' I plop down, dipping a nugget in BBQ sauce.

He smiles sweetly and despite the cool winter day, my body warms. 'So, I picked out the perfect spot for the fake kiss.' He leans in, whispering so the guests don't hear. But they're too absorbed in their own park experience to pay much attention – other than to see if we're done with the table.

I pull out my notebook and cross his item off my to-do list for this venture. 'And I've set up a time for the shoot tonight.' That's ticked off the list next. 'Also, production agreed they could work it into the next episode, and Imogen said she'd tease it on socials beforehand. Building up hype to reveal which girl got the clandestine kiss.' The word *kiss* gets stuck in my throat and I cough to clear it.

He piles his pizza slice with fries before taking a bite. 'Sshgood,' he says through a mouthful of food. 'Please CC me on that list of yours. I want to make sure you've covered it all.'

I roll my eyes at his joke. 'Yeah, sure, I'll go make a copy right after this.'

He chuckles and then chokes on his food. 'Juliet, don't make me laugh.'

'I won't. I'd hate for you to die before we finish the show.'

He swallows before speaking this time. 'Is that the only reason you'd be sad? Or would you miss me? Even just a little?' His knee nudges mine under the table.

I take another bite of my nugget, making him wait. Also, it gives my heart a chance to chill out. 'I might miss you – like, a tiny amount.' I steal a fry from his stash. Studying it, I ask, 'So, uh, will Desiree be the only girl you've kissed during filming?'

I don't really want to know, but I should – for the show. Right?

'Do I look like a guy who kisses and tells?'

I force myself to meet his eyes. 'Is that a no?'

'Don't you think the cameras would have caught it if I did?' He deftly answers questions with questions.

'You had some off-screen time with Desiree and you knew about Riya's boyfriend. So, who knows what else you've gotten up to.' Despite the smell of lovely fried food, I'm not hungry any more.

Garrick reaches over and grabs my hand. 'I haven't kissed anyone, Juliet. Because technically Desiree kissed me the other day and I didn't kiss back.'

It really shouldn't, but that makes me smile.

As planned, later that night, after the park is closed and the only sound is the buzzing of Christmas lights, I'm standing in the underpass that leads to Glacier Peaks, waiting while they wire Garrick for the spontaneous – not at all – shot. I was bummed we couldn't manage a little bit of snow to complete the setting.

'This was your idea?' Mom startles me from behind.

'Garrick and I both.' I bite my thumbnail.

'Juliet, I thought we trained nail biting out of you.'

I hold in my sigh, shoving my hands into my pockets. I don't know why I'm nervous. This is literally just a kiss on camera. Dating shows have been doing it for decades. But as I watch them prepare, a deep ache spreads across my chest and into my ribs.

We're keeping it all PG, but the audience needs a little something to reinforce the fairytale matchmaking further. And we picked the perfect girl for the job. Desiree insisted she'd done plenty of stage kisses in her long acting career. She's seventeen, but OK, sure.

The kiss is supposed to happen in the Fairytalers'-only passageway used between lands. They'll cut this scene into a date to make it look like it happened secretly. This is more orchestrated than a Broadway play, but when their lips meet, I feel like vomiting.

Why is this bothering me? It was my idea. It didn't feel this real when it was just an item on my list.

Garrick's back is to me, so I can't see his face. I'm sure it's exactly what the audience will love. Desiree is clearly in my vision, and she's *very* into it. I doubt there's much acting involved. She's going above and beyond the call of duty.

I can't blame her. I wouldn't mind kissing Garrick either. My stomach flips as the idea settles into my brain, making itself right at home.

We've all been working our butts off, but if left to her own devices, Mom would have us continue that pace without a break. She knows we get a chunk of time off for the holidays and thinks that's more than enough. Labor laws are not her strong suit. But Nathan, Melika and I agreed we needed a breather from the grind. When Garrick caught wind, he was more than willing to throw a party. After negotiating him down from throwing an unsanctioned rager, we decided on a movie night. The minute Garrick said he'd pick the movie, I should've run for the hills.

We're having it above the Royal Fare. Its wood-clad walls make it look like we're inside a real fairytale castle. When

I glimpse these tiny details sprinkled around the park, away from the bustling crowds, I see the appeal of a fairytale-themed oasis. FTG isn't too bad when you can have it all to yourself – just the sparkling lights and whimsical music.

'Something smells divine.' Melika's eyes drift to the table bursting with delicacies. The room is bustling with excitement. I guess we weren't the only ones in need of some R&R.

Garrick stands nearby, wearing an apron that says *Kiss the chef*. 'So happy you all could join us. And thank you, I will take that compliment.'

The serving dishes are filled with what I recognize as leftovers from the Royal Fare menu, but with some new additions. Thick-cut ham with a honey glaze and mashed potatoes drowning in butter both adorn Christmas-themed plates. Piled high are small tarts with greens and cheese in some, and cream and sugared fruit in the others. The crew is large, but this table is feast-worthy – I'm not sure we'll be able to eat it all. I won't mention that to Garrick, who I'm sure would see it as a challenge.

Tristian, Imogen, Yvette, her girlfriend, Melodie, and Aldrich are also here. I spot Ivor and James loading up on popcorn with their son. Most of the crew is here too, but no contestants. Mom doesn't appear to be anywhere in sight either.

The small room would usually feel claustrophobic, but with the delectable smells and festive decorations, it feels like the inviting holiday I've always wanted. Who would have guessed I just needed to go to a theme park to get it?

'I'm sorry you couldn't invite Kahoa,' I whisper to Melika.

'What?' Her guilty face tells me everything. 'How did you guess?'

'Because I love you, and I could tell when you two were together sparks were flying.' My heart warms seeing my friend happy, even as the familiar warning bells go off in my head that she's going to end up hurt like all the rest.

Melika grins. 'We're just keeping it low-key for now – you know, because of the show.'

'I appreciate it. Maybe in the new year we can all hang out?'

She nods and hugs my side before running off to grab a drink.

I take a plate of food and snuggle into one of the beanbag chairs on the floor. Garrick plops down on the one next to me. His hair is floppy, the soft waves that come from being freshly washed and left to dry naturally. He smells clean, with a hint of spicy cinnamon and butter – probably from the sugary buns he bragged about making earlier.

I take a bite of a savory tart. Covering my mouth, I fight a moan as I taste the rich, flaky crust and cheesy filling.

'That good, huh?' Garrick grins. The Christmas lights strung up around the windows cast a multicolored glow on his features.

I fight the reaction to praise him. We don't need his ego any larger. 'Satisfactory.'

'From you, Juliet, I'll take that as a compliment.' He leans in, brushing a crumb from my lip. I freeze, all my nerves firing at once. His eyes lock with mine, and I don't know if I want to turn away or keeping watching him forever.

I'm saved from deciding as the movie starts.

It's a *Romeo and Juliet* retelling set at Christmas. Because, of course it is.

'Really?' I whisper to him.

Garrick's smile is bright, even in the dark. 'Shh.' He takes my chin and guides my face to look at the screen. 'I don't want to miss a moment. You know Juliet is my favorite.'

My heart flips, and I press my fingers into my chest to make it stop – to remind it that Garrick Walton is a no-fly zone. And even if he wasn't, that is not the route we want to take.

The movie is a loose take on the Shakespeare story, allowing it a pass in my books. The crew relaxes for the first time since we started this whole thing. It dawns on me that we're in our own little bubble here. No one will know what it was like to do this but us. Sure, there are other similar productions, but with a fairytale theme park as the background? No way.

'I'm kind of getting an idea of what it's like to be in your world,' I whisper to Garrick, who's been leaning on my shoulder for the last twenty minutes. I thought he fell asleep at one point, but he's just intensely watching the movie. 'It feels like you have a new little family when you're here.'

'As cheesy as it sounds –' he scoots up so we're eye to eye – 'FTG is like a big family. It's my home.'

'I can't relate to that.' I drop my gaze, rubbing my hand along the soft fabric of my seat. 'The only family I feel close to is my sister and Molly. I love my mom, and I know she loves me, but she's always preoccupied. Sometimes it feels like her family comes second.'

Honestly, sometimes it feels like I'm the peas someone threw on the floor because they didn't want them.

Garrick slings an arm around my shoulders, and I think he's making a move, but I don't stop him even if he is. I let myself forget about it all for just a second. I don't even care that we aren't alone here, that we've been told off for being too close. His warmth envelops me as the soft folds of his sweatshirt caress my skin. 'Well, you're part of the FTG family now. So you always have me.'

And for the first time, I really wish it could be true.

The Twelve Days of Christmas Cookies Countdown
22 December
Day 10
Cannoli Cookies with Ricotta Cream Filling

Servings: 14 cookies

INGREDIENTS:
Cookies
- 180g salted butter, softened
- 50g caster sugar
- 180g brown sugar
- 2 eggs
- 1 teaspoon vanilla
- 270g flour
- 1 teaspoon baking soda
- ½ teaspoon salt
- 100g mini chocolate chips (or regular chocolate chips)

Ricotta cream filling
- 250g whole milk ricotta
- 100g icing sugar
- ¼ teaspoon cinnamon
- 25g mini chocolate chips

INSTRUCTIONS:
Ricotta cream filling
1. Strain ricotta: place the ricotta in a cheesecloth. Twist and gently squeeze out as much liquid as possible. Discard the liquid.
2. Place the strained ricotta in a bowl and add icing sugar, cinnamon and chocolate chips. Mix until combined. Set aside.

Cookies
1. In a large bowl or stand mixer, add softened butter and beat until soft and airy. Then add white and brown sugars, beat until combined.
2. Add eggs and vanilla, beat until pale in color.
3. Add flour, baking soda and salt. Mix on low until combined.
4. Add mini chocolate chips to dough and mix until combined.
5. Line a baking sheet with baking parchment.
6. Roll cookies into 14 balls and lightly press them down.
7. Using the back of a teaspoon, press down the center of each cookie to create a well. Place about 1 tablespoon of cannoli cream mixture into the center well of each cookie.
8. Chill cookies in the fridge for 30 minutes.
9. Bake cookies at 350°F (180°C) for 14 minutes. Remove and let completely cool.
10. Dust with icing sugar.

27

RIPLEY

I'm dreaming about my bed at home, the dregs of sleep still holding tight to me in the wee hours of the dark morning, when there's a rapping at my window. I roll over, snuggling deeper into my warm bed, but the noise won't stop. Tossing the blankets off, I turn to the culprit – the window. Assuming it's one of the many trees that line the property, I get up and pull open the drapes, only to find Garrick's face staring at me, illuminated by the light of his phone.

Yelping, I yank the curtains closed.

'Juliet, "what light through yonder window breaks" . . .' His muffled voice comes through the closed panes.

Scrubbing a hand over my face, I grab my oversized sweatshirt off the dresser and slip it on. Mom keeps it blazing hot, so I'm only in a tank and shorts. I bite my thumb, frowning as I stare at the dark fabric blocking Garrick from view.

Garrick is at my window. Why is Garrick at my window?

Do I want him at my window?

My mind spirals as I study the sliver of light peeking through the drapes. The apartment is quiet. Mom is engaged in the blissful six hours of sleep she gets each night. I learned a long time ago not to interrupt her.

'Juliet!' Garrick's singsong voice flitters into my dark room. I know him well enough to know he will not just leave of his own accord.

I level him with a glare when I open the curtains again. 'What are you doing?' I hiss so Mom won't hear. My warm breath fogs up the glass, obscuring our view of each other.

'Let me in, *please*. It's cold.' He can't be *that* cold. Pulled over his ears is a gray beanie, while a striped red-and-green scarf is knotted around his neck, topped with his favorite red puffer jacket.

How do I know it's his favorite? I guess I've learned more about Garrick Walton than I realized.

I cross my arms. 'No,' I say with a sly smile. 'You made the choice to climb up a tree in the middle of the night and bother me. Time to live with the consequences.'

'It's not night. It's –' he glances at his watch – 'four a.m.'

I start to close the curtains again, knowing we have a full day of filming ahead of us and I don't want to start it with a pounding headache from lack of sleep.

'Wait.' His hand splays against the window, fogging it up with his body heat. 'I want to show you something.'

Tugging at the bottom of my sweatshirt, I ponder this predicament I never thought I'd be in. Guys showing up at my windowsill with mysterious offers is not a problem I thought I'd face. A weird buzzing covers my skin, my heart reacting with increased beats. 'Could it not wait until the sun is up?' I focus on logic to quell the stirring in my stomach – the familiar curiosity that can only lead to trouble.

In this case, trouble is spelled: G-A-R-R-I-C-K.

'Nope,' he says matter-of-factly. I bite my lip as he produces his best puppy-dog smile. 'C'mon, Juliet. I know that curious mind of yours is dying to find out what I've got up my sleeve.'

I roll my eyes. *Ugh*, I hate that he's right – that he knows me well enough to be so confident in that statement.

Pro to going outside: I get to know said something.

Con: It's dark and cold.

Pro: I'll be with Garrick, and each day I find myself wanting to do that more.

Con: Wanting to be with Garrick when I really shouldn't be.

I'm unsure where my better judgment has gone because I say, 'Fine. Meet me downstairs in five.'

I scramble to get dressed in something warm before running to the bathroom as quietly as possible. I brush my teeth while running a brush through my hair. As I head outside, I slip on my coat and Garrick's favorite pink earmuffs. The morning air is like a truck hitting me – the cold penetrating my exposed skin like a knife. I almost think about going back inside, but Garrick is standing there with two steaming red-and-green cups and a goofy grin.

'Coffee?' He holds it up, and I wrap my frigid fingers around the warm embrace.

The liquid smells of butter toffee on top of cinnamon with the bitter afternotes of espresso. After taking a few sips, I finally feel alive enough to speak. 'Where are we going?'

'This way.' He turns, having waited patiently for me to

get my caffeine hit, and heads toward the back entrance of FTG. 'Don't worry, I already told the security guy we were going to be out here when I brought him a few cannoli cookies I whipped up.'

'You were that confident I'd agree to leave my warm bed?'

He gives me a shameless smile and a shrug.

It's foggy, giving a moody vibe to the park. It hides the rest of the world from view, and as we emerge into the castle grounds I could almost believe it was real: that we find ourselves in the fictional land of Carpathia, and a valiant knight will emerge from the large wooden doors and enlist us to join him on a quest.

At least that's what happens in Molly's storybooks.

'I want to take you on a ride.' Garrick sips his coffee, looking over at me with a cautious gaze.

I stop mid-step. 'Seriously? Is that what this is?' I spin around to head back to my bed. I should have known this was a bad idea.

'Wait.' He grabs my hand, and I ignore the flutter in my chest. 'I know you said you hate theme parks, which, *ouch*, but I want to show you the park *I* see. When no one is here.' Any hint of the made-for-screen knight is gone. The boy looking at me isn't a reality star or a theme park icon – he's just Garrick.

I pick at the cardboard sleeve surrounding my cup. 'I don't like heights or being confined in a seat.' I'm exposing a part of me, chipping away at the armor I wear for the world.

He ducks so I can see his face from my downward gaze. 'No heights or seat restraints, I promise.'

And I believe him.

I look back up. 'OK, but if I hate it, I'm out of here.'

'Deal.' He puts out his hand to shake. 'But you won't.' His smile is so cocky I should roll my eyes, but I find myself returning the grin instead. I put my hand in his, and it's warmer than the coffee, sending fire into my veins.

I break away before I want to, sipping my scalding beverage as a distraction, hoping I can use it as an excuse for my racing heart.

'Mood music?' He stops at a panel near the castle and flips on the lights first. I've seen the park at night with all the Christmas lights, but with the fog and no one else here, it's a new experience. The way the swirls of mist twist and turn around the outer edges of the lights gives them a dramatic glow. Everything feels cast in a dream, like I'm in a retro film where everything is soft and clouded.

I expect Christmas music to start when he turns on the speakers, but instead, another 'Juliet' song starts playing.

'I have a playlist,' is all he offers in return. Last week, I would have made him shut it off right away, but I don't this time. The idea that he spent who knows how long finding songs with my name in them is kinda sweet – romantic, some fools might say.

We stare at each other, waiting for the other person to speak. My body feels full of caffeinated butterflies zooming around, not just in my stomach but under every inch of my skin.

I break the stare first. 'So, you often wake up at four to wander around the park?'

Garrick closes the panel, shoving his hands in his coat. 'I didn't wake up. Never went to bed.'

He starts walking and I jog to catch up. 'How are you still functioning? This shoot is wearing me out, and I'm at least getting six hours of sleep.'

He shrugs, and I see a tension in his jaw that I've never noticed. I've hit a nerve without realizing it. 'I don't sleep well these days. Not since . . .' He looks down at his feet.

I think about leaving it be, but I like seeing Garrick like this – the knightly facade cast away. 'I can't imagine what it's like to lose a parent.' My dad might not be around, but I can still call him.

Garrick clears his throat. 'Sleeping is hard because I forget.' He looks at me, cheeks pink from the cold. 'Like I'll dream about her, and when I wake up, for those first few seconds, I think she's still here, and then it all crashes down. It's easier if I stay awake. Then I don't have to remember again.'

My heart cracks in my chest. Without thinking, I reach for his hand. He slides it into mine, squeezing it. I don't know what to say to make it better. I don't think I can, but I want to try. 'I'm usually up studying, so if you ever need someone to talk to, I'm around.'

The softest smile I've seen graces his face, and my knees almost give out. 'Thanks, Juliet.'

And for the first time, I don't hate how my name sounds coming out of someone's mouth.

28

GARRICK

'Ta-da,' I say, spinning to face The Story of Carpathia. This dark ride takes guests through the adventures of Prince Winthrop, Princess Arden and Kendrick the Kind as they save Carpathia from the terrible darkness overtaking the lands. Many say this is the main attraction in the Carpathia section of the park. I beg to differ because I think Knight School is the biggest draw – but maybe I'm biased.

'Hmm.' Juliet bites her thumbnail, staring up at the mural painted across the facade that gives the rider a hint of what adventures await them. It's similar to the one in the break room – breathtaking views of the Carpathian lands and small villages, with the castle looming in the background. The mechanical horse on the front that rears on its hind legs stopped working years ago. 'I said I wasn't a fan of being locked in a tiny fake carriage.'

The brown-and-white metal carriages sit patiently on the ride track, waiting for the day to start. A dusting of frost hides their imperfections.

I grin, taking her hand. 'Well, good thing we won't be in a carriage.' It's still dark and will be for another few hours. With the fog, we might as well be the only people in the world. Well, except for all of those girls at the apartment still waiting for me to choose my true love. My stomach lurches at the idea, like I've been riding Ice Shards ten times in a row.

Juliet's voice brings me out of my wandering thoughts. 'Then what are we doing?'

The last few days, I've found myself thinking of her more as Juliet. Ripley was like an enigma who hovered on the edge of my orbit, but Juliet has found her way past all my defenses.

Letting the worries of my responsibilities fall away, I choose to focus on her. 'I knew you weren't a fan of rides. So, we won't do any riding.'

She frowns, eyebrow lifting. 'So, what *are* we doing then?'

I squeeze her hand, pulling her through the turnstile into the entrance. 'We're doing a walk.'

I flip the ride on but keep the moving carriages stationary. The fanciful music begins to play, along with the audio recording of the narrator telling the guests the story of Carpathia in a generic British accent. I tinker around with the switches, turning the volume down so I can speak over him.

Juliet pulls at the end of her hair – her go-to when trying not to bite her nails. It's fascinating watching her hands stop midway to her mouth and then quickly grab her hair as her brain catches up to what she's doing. But when she's really stressed, she gives in to her urges and the nails don't stand a chance. I blink, realizing I've started to clock all her little quirks. If you asked me what the girls in the competition do when they're nervous, I wouldn't have the slightest clue.

I've been too busy studying the Book of Juliet.

We move past the line and into the side section used to walk along should the ride break down while you're on it. 'We came here a lot when we were little. Probably not the safest place for kids to play, but it felt like we were part of the story.' The murals need a touch-up, I note now that I'm this close, but even the layer of dust doesn't diminish the memories. Some of the best ones always have a little dust over them.

'Definitely not safe for children.' She sounds serious, but I watch her eyes travel over the bright art of the Carpathia countryside and the animatronic Winthrop and Kendrick.

'Definitely. Especially because of the ghost.'

She gives me a wry look. 'Ghost? Didn't we cover this on our last tour?'

'Oh, yeah, there's at least one ghost here. I've seen it. But I don't like to divulge all my secrets to just anyone.'

Juliet shakes her head, laughing to herself, trying to hide her smile from me. But I can see it even when she dips her chin.

'When will you realize it's no use fighting it.' I give her a soft nudge. 'You know you like me. It was bound to happen.'

'Is it safe to be walking around inside a ride?' She changes the subject.

'Juliet, would I ever take you somewhere dangerous and potentially life-threatening?'

She looks at me, and *freaking A*, there it is. The bright pearly whites and those pink-tinged lips gracing me with the most beautiful smile I've ever been witness to. I suck in a breath as a ringing sounds in my ears, mouth going dry.

'I don't think you would intentionally lead me somewhere I could be maimed.' She keeps talking like she doesn't realize I've lost all feeling in my limbs when she smiles at me like that. 'But I wouldn't put it past you to go somewhere dangerous and, as a result, one of us ends up in the hospital.'

I shake my head, running a hand over my face to catch my mind and body back up to the same spot. Dropping my chin, I tilt my head. 'Will you stay by my side in the hospital bed while I recover?'

She walks ahead, entering the part of the ride that takes the guests to the first meeting of Winthrop and Arden. 'Absolutely. I will tell you I told you so the whole time.'

'As long as you're there, I'll allow it.' I follow a few paces behind, letting her experience the ride as it should be, adding my tidbits along the way. 'When I was seven, I jumped off the side of the ride vehicle on a dare from Tristian. I busted out three baby teeth.'

Juliet glances over her shoulder, eyes drifting to my lips. My stomach clenches. 'Bet you guilted the Tooth Fairy into giving you more money for the trauma of it all.'

I chuckle. *How does she know me so well already?* 'Am I that easy to read?'

When she speaks, it's totally genuine. 'No, actually. Not the real you, anyway. But I guess I've learned to see through the armor's shine. Like, I bet you took that money you bribed from the Tooth Fairy and bought something to share with your brothers.'

I still, stopping just before we reach the waterfall where the trio encounter their first battle. 'I did. I got a Lego set we'd been wanting for ages.' My heart feels like it's made of goo, melting in my chest, but in the best way possible. Filling me up with a tingling sensation.

As we walk, Juliet asks me all kinds of questions about the ride's operation and the story. Cataloging it in that big brain of hers that's filled with bullet-pointed lists and highlighted notes.

'I guess this ride isn't so bad,' Juliet says after we reach the end, where the heroes celebrate their victory.

'Can I kiss you?'

Did I say that out loud? My heartbeat thuds in my chest when I realize it *was* out loud. I was definitely thinking about it. But I knew it was stupid to say – even if I want to kiss her.

Juliet blinks at me, long eyelashes fluttering. 'OK.' She says it so quietly I think I misheard. 'But it's probably not a good idea.'

'What do you mean? It's the best idea ever.' I put my hand on her cheek, warm against me. I lean in slowly, giving her a chance to change her mind should she suddenly come to her senses. But I'm hoping her reality check waits a few more minutes.

The kiss is soft, her lips cautious against mine. We both know this shouldn't happen, but we want every minute of it. It's everything I didn't realize I'd been dreaming about this whole time. That elusive feeling everyone said I should be experiencing with the contestants – this is it. It's right here with Juliet in my arms.

'We shouldn't do this,' she says against my lips.

'Do you want me to stop?' I pull away slightly to look at her face.

'No.' Her fingers dig into my jacket, pulling me closer. This kiss is more intense because we know it won't last. We've been flirting for a good couple of weeks, but this feels like more than just a clandestine kiss in the shadows that will never happen again.

At least, that's how it feels to me. And that scares the crap out of me.

Juliet steps away before I want her to, running her hands over her pink lips. 'Well, that was just a one-time thing, right?'

It stings when she says that – something sharp invading my chest cavity. But I nod. 'We've got a week left of filming. We'll just have to stay away from each other.'

'Won't be that hard.' Juliet nods. 'Everyone's leaving for Christmas in two days. It'll be fine.'

But the whole way back to the apartment, I can't stop thinking about kissing her again.

29

RIPLEY

'Juliet!' Mom yells from the other side of my door. 'You need to wake up. We have a show to produce.'

Little does she know, I've been awake since four a.m. After Garrick walked me home, I lay in bed, replaying our kiss, analyzing every little move and wondering why my chest wouldn't stop fluttering with this weird warmth. Every time I close my eyes, all I can see is Garrick leaning in and our lips finally meeting. I felt like I'd been waiting for it my whole life. Like he was the perfect fit to a hole I didn't know I had in my heart.

This can't be good.

'I'm awake. I'll meet you there!' I call to her through the door, not wanting to look her in the eyes. I'm worried she'll see right through me and know I've messed up her show.

Have I messed it up? Maybe I'm overthinking things – again – and that kiss with Garrick was literally nothing. He probably brings lots of girls there to woo and kiss. It seems like a move Garrick Walton would have in his repertoire.

But it didn't feel like that.

Ugh!

When I hear Mom shut the door, I quickly grab my phone and call Anna. She picks up after several rings. 'I have a problem,' I say immediately.

'What happened? Are you hurt?' The panic in her voice makes me cringe. I didn't mean to worry her.

'Sorry, no, not like a life-threatening problem.' However, it does feel that way to my aching stomach. I bite my nails. 'I just... I kissed Garrick.' It feels real now that I said it out loud. Let another person in on it. I could tell Nathan and Melika, but they have terrible poker faces, and I'm worried they'll spill the beans. I will tell them eventually because they're my best friends, but I need my sister right now.

There's a long pause where I think Anna has hung up. 'Sorry, you *what*?'

Shaking my hand out, I twist the bottom of my hair through my fingers, trying to give my hand a more productive thing to do than ruin my cuticles. 'I might have... *accidentally* kissed Garrick.'

'Like you tripped and fell into his lips?' The laughter in her voice is unmistakable.

'Anna, this is serious. I messed up.' My voice cracks a little at the end. I'm not sure what I'm admitting I messed up – the show or my well-laid plan of avoiding troublesome heart problems.

'OK, start from the top.'

I tell her how Garrick and I have been getting closer and how it's been different than I thought. We can share things we don't usually divulge, and he tells me things I've never heard him say to any of the girls he's supposedly dating. That it's been nice to let someone in.

'Your silence is scaring me,' I say when she doesn't speak after I finish.

'I hate to break this to you, Rip, but it sounds like you might be in love.'

I scoff, getting up from the bed and peeking out the frost-covered window into the parking lot. My heart drops when I don't spot Garrick waiting in the tree. 'Anna, don't be ridiculous. I am not in love with Garrick Walton.'

'All right, fine. Maybe not *love* love, but heavy like, and that path leads straight to the heart.'

'Anna, I called to have you help me, not spout propaganda about the heart.' I put the phone on speaker while I get dressed.

'Sorry, but it is what it is.' There's a loud squeal in the background, and I know this as Molly's noise when she's making trouble.

I pull on my leggings and sweater. 'Ugh. I have to go, but thank you for the unhelpful advice.'

'I love you.'

'Love you too,' I say, shoving my phone into my pocket and heading toward the one person I really want to see and should totally avoid.

Today is another on-screen date. We're ramping up for the last push before the holiday, and everyone is determined to get all the shots we need so we can enjoy the break. As I pass the crew, I walk on eggshells, waiting for someone to pounce on me for my clandestine morning activities. But no one calls me out for kissing the star, so Garrick must have kept quiet.

Not that I thought he'd say anything, but sometimes you never know what will come out of that boy's mouth.

'You all right?' Nathan asks when I get to Glacier Peaks. 'You look like crap.'

The date is what the Waltons call a ride-off. It is a simple concept: you ride the roller coaster until you can't ride it any more. The last one standing wins. The team thought it would make a great segment. Personally, I think it will be a nightmare, especially when the girls start throwing up everywhere. No one liked that comment, but I'm a realist.

I pull my ponytail tighter. 'I didn't sleep much.' Not a lie. When I see the girls come dressed to the nines, my stomach somersaults. It's a roller-coaster day. I thought we'd get baggy sweatshirts and top knots, not cute peacoats and blowouts.

I didn't go to more trouble than brushing my hair with my fingers and topping my outfit with my puffer jacket. I've been wearing it most of the time. It is easy and efficient – and warm. But now that I see these girls all styled super cute to impress, I feel self-conscious.

What does Garrick think of me compared to them? Ugh, why do I care? *Stop caring!*

Garrick smiles at me when he walks in, but then he smiles at everyone. Is the one he flashed my way more intimate than the others? Does it mean more? I wish my brain would stop. But I've spent seventeen years with it and know that's not how it works.

As the date goes on, Garrick is his usual, charming self. No different than he's been every other day. It's like this morning never happened.

Maybe I'm feeling more than he is. I'm being so dumb for letting myself think that Garrick Walton, who has all these outstanding girls to pick from, would choose me. Or choose anyone. We've had that convo. We both agreed love is crap. So why won't my heart get with the program?

Riya takes the win, and I'm not surprised – she even beats Garrick. She is the most adventurous. The other day, in an interview, she said her goal was to climb Mount Everest before she was twenty-five. I wonder if that's something she planned with her clandestine boyfriend. Because she won, she gets a one-on-one date. It's the last one before the double elimination tomorrow, so all the girls were clamoring for it. The contestants are ushered off to do post-date interviews and probably eat something bland based on how green some look. And yes, two of them threw up – so gross.

Garrick comes up to me after the contestants are gone and the crew is breaking down the cameras. My heart ticks up several annoying beats as he approaches. My body is aching to kiss him again for a quick reminder of what it felt like when we were alone.

'So, I was thinking . . .'

I ready myself when Garrick starts a sentence like this.

'What if we do Santa the knight? And Santa could have on some of my knight armor. Like the hat could be part of my helmet? What do you think?'

Oh, so nothing about our clandestine kiss? OK, cool. 'Absolutely not. That doesn't even make any sense.'

He flops down on the stool beside me. 'You don't think Santa was around delivering presents during the medieval ages?'

'I think the armor would way down the sleigh.' *Don't look at his lips, don't look at his lips.* I try, and I fail.

He drums his finger against my hand, which is lying on my leg. And those butterflies are zooming around again. It's not that I've never been kissed before. I have, and they were fine. Nothing I was ready to write home about, but they were nice enough. It's just when they were done I didn't think about them further. That kiss from Garrick feels imprinted on my skin.

'Hmm. That is a good point, Juliet. This is why we make a good team.'

Ugh. Why does he have to look so cute? Before, I could write these feelings off as just a hot guy making me flustered, but now that I know him, the real him, I can't do that.

30

RIPLEY

'Hey,' Imogen says, poking her head into the break room. 'What are you doing tonight?'

I glance down at the homework I was supposed to be working on but have not been paying attention to. The contestants had dinner in here a little bit ago, all of them gushing over their experiences with their knight in shining armor, while Garrick finished his date with Riya. The chatter had been all consuming, which is why said homework has not been touched.

'I'm not sure. Why?'

Imogen runs a hand through her red hair, bright green earrings sparkling in the fluorescent lights. 'So, I have an extra set of tickets because my friend Divya and her boyfriend were supposed to come with me, but she had to cancel. And I was wondering if you would like to go with me? You and Garrick?'

I frown, confused by her spitfire words. 'Come with you where?'

'Oh, ha, sorry. It's a Christmas train. They do this whole like *Polar Express* vibe – desserts, hot chocolate, no Tom Hanks though. It's supposed to be really fun, and I would hate for the tickets to go to waste.'

I shove my hands under my legs to stop from biting my nails – my cuticles need a break after today. 'Did you already ask Garrick?' I mean, I want to go. But I don't know if it's the best idea. And what if it's super awkward after our kiss this morning? Garrick was his usual self when we briefly chatted earlier, but that was with the safety net of the show.

'I did. He was thrilled. He loves a good theme. But he said he wouldn't go if you didn't want to. So, the ball is in your court.'

I could imagine his face when Imogen suggested it, those bright-blue eyes lighting up like a Christmas tree. But I appreciate that he's leaving the ultimate decision to me.

'Yeah, I guess it could be fun. I don't do a lot of Christmassy things usually.'

Imogen does a little cheer in the air. 'Great! You might want to dress warm, cos *baby, it's cold outside*!'

By the time we get to the train station, it's already dark. It's just as magical as promised, with crackling lanterns and realistic steam train sounds, along with festive music. Written on the side of the train with accents of blue and gold is *Polar Express*. The staff's classic uniforms are pressed long jackets and blue hats trimmed in red and green.

We get on board and are seated in a section in the back. The cushions are deep twilight blue with rich mahogany wood tables, and spray around the windows makes them look snow-covered along the edges.

Garrick flips open the menu. 'OK, I am having one of everything. It's included right?' He turns to Tristian.

'Yep,' Tristian says. 'But please don't. I don't want you hurling all over this interior.'

Garrick scoffs. 'Tristian, you know I don't get sick. I'm basically ninety per cent sugar.'

I laugh, more at ease than I thought I would be – but Garrick wouldn't have it any other way. He'll go above and beyond to make sure everyone is comfortable. I look over the menu and the different drink and dessert options. This feels like a real double date. Snuggling together, Tristan and Imogen are the epitome of what Beeloved is trying to present to the world. If only we had captured their love story for audiences, I'm sure the public would have eaten it up.

Garrick leans into me and whispers conspiratorially, 'Maybe we can split the desserts? That way we can try one of everything. For market research purposes, *obviously*. I need to see what the competition is up to.'

'That is a very well thought-out plan, Mr Walton.'

'Oh, Juliet, be still my heart when you speak to me like that.' He kisses me on my cheek and everything I'd been worried about after this morning melts away.

I try to hide my flushed cheeks by holding up the menu.

The waiter takes our orders, not surprised when we ask for everything. It's such a common request that they have a cute little tiered tray they bring things out on. The desserts are crafted into marvelous winter- and Christmas-themed displays. The hot chocolate is served in a silver pitcher with delicate white tea cups.

'OK, favorite present ever?' Imogen asks, dipping her cookie into the hot chocolate.

'Easy.' Tristian leans back, his mannerisms reminding me so much of Garrick I finally start to see the twin resemblance. 'When I was ten, I got a world globe.'

Imogen beams, tugging him closer. 'Of *course*, that's your all-time favorite gift. I love that.' She kisses him on the cheek, leaving a chocolatey lip mark when she pulls away.

'Let me guess.' Tristian wipes it off with a napkin, a tiny smile accenting his blush. 'Yours was a Winthrop doll you slept with every night and carried around until it fell to pieces, and you were devastated.'

Her lips quirk up. 'Actually, it was a Kendrick the Kind figurine, and I still have it on my shelf.' There's a challenge in her eyes, and Tristian looks more than ready to conquer.

'What a coincidence,' Garrick chimes in. 'That was also the best gift I ever got too. Wait – no, it was actually the year I got strep throat and stayed home basically the whole month of December.'

I frown. 'How was getting sick your best gift?'

He uses his spoon to draw a reindeer in his strawberry sauce. 'Because my brothers had to go to school, and I got to stay with Mom. We watched Christmas movies and never got out of our PJs.'

Tears prickle my eyes, and I focus on my desserts so he doesn't see. After all this time, I shouldn't be surprised Garrick would choose something like that.

'That was the year you made me share a room with Aldrich for three weeks straight because you insisted that, to heal and not infect me, you needed to be *alone*.' Tristian air quotes the last word.

Garrick shrugs. 'I know, I'm such a good brother, protecting you from certain death.' He nudges me in the shoulder. 'What about you, Juliet? You finished creating that numbered list in your head with your ranking of best to worst gifts?'

I blush. 'I wasn't doing that.'

I was so doing that.

'Don't mind them, Ripley, we're all ears. But please let it be something better than a viral infection. No offense, Garrick.' Imogen cringes.

If we're ranking a list of gifts, logically, my car should be at the top. It's certainly the most valuable. But bribery feels like it disqualifies it from the running.

I do know what my best gift was, but I'm afraid it'll sound dumb to them. But when I look at Garrick's waiting smile, I forget about being embarrassed. 'I got a super-detailed planner last year from my mom.'

'Do tell me more.' Garrick rests his chin in his hands, leaning on the table. 'Dated or undated? Did it come with stickers?' It could sound like he's making fun of me, but his expression is genuine. 'Wait, please tell me it came with a matching pen set?'

'Unfortunately not, I'm afraid.'

Something mischievous sparks in his eyes. 'That is a very helpful nugget of info to have. Thank you, Juliet.'

'Oh, Tristian, that reminds me, what are your thoughts on matching Christmas PJs? And remember, there is only one correct answer ...' Imogen claps her hands, chatting to him about their upcoming holiday plans.

Garrick brushes a lock of hair behind my ear, then whispers, 'Want to know my other favorite gift?'

'What?' I turn, lips brushing his cheek.

'Beeloved.'

'The app?' I study his face, trying to figure out what joke he's going to make, but then, like always, Garrick Walton surprises me.

'No, the company, because they brought you to me.'

I bite my smile back. 'So cheesy.'

He leans in and his lips brush mine. 'Cheese is one of my favorite foods.'

It's so easy for us to fall back into this when we're together. I always thought being with someone was nothing but tedious work until it broke you into submission. But not with Garrick. It's the simplest thing in the world.

Garrick holds up his fork. 'Here, try this one.'

I take a bite of the peppermint cake. 'Oh, wow, that's delicious.' I cover my mouth as I chew the soft, chocolatey sponge.

'This is the best by far though.' Garrick reaches over to grab some ice cream, but he knocks into his teacup, spilling hot chocolate all over the white tablecloth. 'Crap.' He jumps up, using a few napkins to wipe it. 'Hold on. I'll get some more towels.'

As he's walking toward the waiter, a girl stops him with a shy smile. 'Are you Garrick from the Beeloved reality show?'

Garrick's eyes flash to me, then quickly glance away. He hesitates only briefly before donning that screen-worthy smile. 'Yeah, I am, as a matter of fact.'

'Oh my gosh, I'm loving the show so much.' The girl's face lights up. 'My friends and I cannot wait to see how it plays out. Are you on a date now?'

As she tries to peek at our table, I realize how scandalizing this situation is about to become. Imogen must catch on at that exact moment because she grabs my hand and stands, quickly blocking me from the fan's eyeline.

'We need to use the restroom,' she says to no one in particular.

'I don't think there's one on here,' Tristian says.

'We're making a covert escape,' Imogen hisses, then leads me through the back door into a different train car. This is the observation deck, according to the map at the train station. It's empty at the moment while people are still eating.

'Thank you,' I say, my heart racing so fast that I'm afraid it's about to leap out of my body. 'I don't know what I was thinking.' I collapse into a wooden chair, resting my face in my hands. I spent extra time getting ready for tonight. Applying the make-up Ellie gave me – which felt sort of wrong, but it's all I had – and now I'm ruining it. 'If somebody sees Garrick and I together, they will know the show is a scam. How could I screw up so badly?'

For the first time, Imogen's face doesn't hold its usual sunshine. 'Are you kidding? This is all *my* fault. I tend not to think things through, and I really should've known this was a bad idea. The optics of it for viewers of the show. I just wanted to go on a double date. I thought it would be nice for Tristian and Garrick.'

'No, it was my responsibility, and I made the choice. If I screw this up, I don't know what I'm going to do. I know how much Fairytale Gardens and Beeloved need this to work.' I wrap my arms around my stomach.

Imogen leans against the frosted window. 'Trust me, I know how that feels. I basically nose-dived FTG into oblivion last summer.'

'Oh, right.' I don't know how to respond to that. I know what happened from various sources, and I read the article myself because I wanted to be fully informed about the scandal before we got into business with them.

'All I'm saying –' Imogen takes a seat next to me – 'is I know it feels like we have the weight of it all on our shoulders, and maybe we do, but in my totally biased opinion, having a Walton by your side kinda makes it all worthwhile.'

I shake my head. 'I don't have a Walton.'

Imogen raises an eyebrow, looking through the glass to where Garrick has escaped from the fan and is cleaning up the table. 'Hmm, seems like you do to me.'

'Is this where the real party is?' Garrick slides open the door, stepping into the observation car a few minutes later.

'I think my work here is done.' Imogen stands, dusting invisible dirt off her hands before she heads back to Tristian.

'You OK?' Garrick takes Imogen's empty spot beside me.

I release a long breath. 'We could have got caught.'

'By Gina?' Garrick points a thumb over his shoulder. 'Nah, she's cool.'

'Already on a first-name basis, huh? You really do make friends fast.' I try to keep it light, but my stomach is still in knots.

'I have lots of friends, but I only have one Juliet.'

Stupid, stupid, heart, stop doing that excitable puppy thing when he looks at me.

'Still ...'

'Still.' He slings an arm over my shoulder and pulls me into him. 'Let's watch the world go by for a night and forget about all that, OK?'

'We're stuck on this train. So, I guess we don't really have a choice.'

His body shakes with laughter against my cheek. 'Always looking on that bright side.'

The Twelve Days of Christmas Cookies Countdown
23 December
Day 11
Lemon and Blueberry Chewy Cookies

Servings: 18 cookies

INGREDIENTS:
Cookies
- 225g unsalted butter
- 300g plain flour
- 1 teaspoon cornstarch
- 1 teaspoon baking powder
- ¼ teaspoon baking soda
- ½ teaspoon salt
- 300g granulated sugar
- 3 small or medium lemons (or 2 large lemons), zested
- 1 large egg, room temperature
- 1 large egg yolk, room temperature
- 1 teaspoon vanilla extract
- 100g fresh blueberries

Lemon glaze
- 50g icing sugar
- 2 tablespoons lemon juice

INSTRUCTIONS:

1. Preheat the oven to 375°F (190°C). Line a large baking sheet with baking paper.
2. In a small bowl, melt the butter and cool in the fridge for around 10 minutes.
3. In another bowl, whisk together the flour, cornstarch, baking powder, baking soda and salt until well combined.
4. In a large mixing bowl, whisk the sugar and lemon zest together. Whisk in the cooled melted butter until well combined. Whisk in the egg, egg yolk and vanilla extract until smooth and well combined.
5. Stir the dry ingredients into the wet until just combined. Gently stir in the fresh blueberries until combined.
6. Using a medium cookie scoop (or 2 tablespoons of mixture), scoop the cookie dough into balls and place on to the lined baking sheet about 3 inches apart.
7. Bake at 375°F (190°C) for 10–12 minutes or until the edges of the cookies are set and are a light golden brown.
8. Make lemon glaze by mixing icing sugar and lemon juice together until dissolved. Drizzle over warm cookies.
9. Cool the chewy lemon blueberry cookies on the baking sheet for 3-4 minutes. Transfer to a cooling rack to cool completely.

31

GARRICK

'Does it have to be two girls?' I ask Ms Ripley again as they fit me for my mic. I shift uncomfortably in my knight's leathers. The Beeloved pin I wear, along with the sash for the show, makes me feel a little pompous, but at least I only have to wear it during eliminations.

'Now is a little late for this discussion,' she responds, not looking up as she sends off emails on her phone. I glance around, searching for Juliet, but she's off with the girls getting them ready for the shoot.

'I did bring this up last week.' I feel bad sending two girls home right before the holidays. I'm the guy who dresses up as Santa and hands out presents, not bus tickets to So-long-farewell-ville. But the producers thought a double elimination would add much-needed tension until the show returns after Christmas. I can't disagree with the logic – I love a good shock ending. But being the one creating it is a whole other thing.

'Garrick, we've already set the schedule, so there's no use going on about it now.' I hear a little of Juliet in that tone, but it's a lot less fun coming from her mom.

I clear my throat, focusing on breathing as the lights heat the room above the Royal Fare. Today's the 23rd, and the park is open during the day, which it usually isn't, so we're limited on shooting areas. Still, it's for the best. FTG wanted to get that holiday tourism while we still can.

Which means everything this morning is rushed. Before I know it, the elimination is done – it's easier when there are only six girls. I send home Sofia and Riya. They were both super cool, and I enjoyed hanging out with them, but like all the others I didn't feel like I was losing a love match. I'm sure Riya's boyfriend will be happy to have her home.

It used to be so easy to put on an act, so much so it didn't even feel like that. But ever since the kiss with Juliet ... It's hard not to search for her, which is bad when I'm supposed to be staring at the girls in front of me and not the one behind the camera.

With a quick costume change and a few added festive balloons, the room is transformed into a goodbye party as the girls go home for the holidays. The cameras catch my short chats with each of them. I offer plenty of cutesy one-liners they can add to the episode that will air tonight, like 'I hope Santa treats you well' and 'Don't get frostbite building those snowmen'.

I hug the girls goodbye, and they get a shot of me waving from the castle balcony as the coach heads away. I actually don't see them leave, and when I'm waving, it's to the kids riding Ice Shards, but with the magic of editing the audience will never know.

I don't know where Juliet got off to after the date. But

I have to head to the park for Knight School. I cannot wait for the break coming up. These last few days have been non-stop.

The camera crew is packing up and I say my goodbyes as I walk toward the costume department to get suited. Our new additions to the FTG family have been a lot of fun. I enjoy all the hustle and bustle of people. Makes me feel alive.

'Hey, Raul,' I say to one of the kitchen employees headed out as I'm going in. 'Are you working today? I bet the kids are going crazy with Christmas just two days away.'

He gives me a tight smile. 'Yeah, getting in as many hours as possible before we close for the rest of the year. It's been tight with the holidays, so I'm hoping maybe I could talk to you or the boss?'

'Oh, about?' My palms start to sweat, and there's a churning in my gut. I almost forgot we were going to have to fire someone. I've been so busy doing all the other stuff, but now it's coming back into focus.

'I was wondering, if we keep up the catering, you think I might be able to get a raise? I've been here two years now. And I love FTG, but a little extra cash would be nice.'

I rub the back of my neck, swallowing hard. 'I know, man, you do a great job. I'll see if I can put in a good word for you.' The lie tastes like bitter ash on my tongue, but what am I supposed to say? *Sorry, you actually might be fired instead.* It's Christmas, for heaven's sake.

'Thanks, Garrick. I really appreciate it.' He heads out a little lighter with the prospect of a raise on the horizon. But I feel like I'm being weighed down by all the responsibility I never asked for.

When I get to Knight School, Ivor, Aldrich and Tristian are already there.

'Did you get Dad a present?' Ivor asks.

I glance over to Tristian. He raises his eyebrows. 'Why are you looking at me?'

'Because we're twins, dude. We always go in on gifts together. We're a package deal.' Hot air clouds around my face as I breathe out. I need to get on stage and start some fighting, so I don't freeze my bits off.

'I asked you three months ago if you had any ideas of what to get Dad and if you wanted to go in on a present. You never said. So, I just went ahead and got something for him.' Tristian pulls at his leathers, adjusting the sword shining in its sheath.

'And you can put my name on it.' I grab my sword and give it a shine before we head out.

'What? Too busy with all of your ladies to worry about Christmas?' Aldrich elbows me in the ribs.

'Yeah, and I'm carrying this park's entire future on my back. That should give me some leeway.' It's a joke. *But is it?* If this blows up in our faces, I will be responsible. An image of Juliet flashes before my eyes. Her soft lips against mine.

The fighting helps me loosen up. When I have the sword in my hand, the world falls away and I'm the most me I ever feel – even if I am pretending to be a knight in shining armor. Well, leather.

After Knight School, I head toward the front of the castle for my meet-and-greet by the tree. I'm supposed to use the backstage routes, but I like to wave at the guests as I walk around the park.

'Garrick!' Two high-pitched voices yell as I exit the tunnel under the castle.

My foot misses a step and I stumble, catching myself with the ease of a fencer quick on their toes. I've had my real name yelled at me in the park before, but I sense this is different. I put a hand up to block the winter sun shining in my eyes. Two girls around my age stand to my left with Beeloved show T-shirts. I didn't know they were selling these – maybe the girls made them themselves. I appreciate the initiative.

'Good day, ladies. I'm afraid you have me mistaken for some other handsome fellow.' I smile and give a hearty bow. 'I shall keep word out that you're searching for him.'

The girls giggle as I try to maneuver around them, but they block my way. Fortune favors the bold, I suppose. 'Who are you going to pick?' the shorter of the two asks.

'Sorry, again, you have the wrong knight.' This isn't the first time someone in the park has recognized me from the show. That was sort of the whole point of it, to get FTG promo. But these two are the most persistent.

'I really hope it's Arianna. You two have the best chemistry,' says the taller girl.

My insides squeeze. I knew people would be invested in my choice; that's the trick of these types of shows, but it's different when they say it to your face.

'I do hope you have a lovely day and that this Garrick and Arianna find happiness.' I salute before quickly darting past them.

'I told you he'd pick her.' Their squeals follow me to the Christmas tree.

A cold sweat ices my skin as the winter wind glides across me, sending chills down my spine. Arianna is a good choice, probably the one most people think I will choose since we have the most in common. But the only face I can't get out of my mind is the one the camera has never seen and the audience isn't rooting for.

32

RIPLEY

The break room is quiet now that everyone has left for the holiday. It smells like bleach and lemon wood shine. The harsh fluorescent lights hurt my eyes as I stare at the picture on my phone, my thumb hesitating as I debate exiting Instagram, but I can't do it. It's a picture of my dad, his new wife and their nine-month-old baby, who I've never met – my little brother. I bite the nail of my free hand, a weird rushing filling my ears. They're on vacation in Hawaii. One neither Anna nor I was invited to.

Not that I would have been able to go with the filming, but still. It would have been nice to be asked, at least.

'What are you still doing here?' I glance up to see Garrick leaning against the doorframe to the break room. 'Don't you have some stockings to hang by the chimney with care?' His hair is messy, cheeks red from scrubbing off his stage make-up.

I look at the time and see it's just past eight. I came here after we finished shooting, and I've been working on school stuff, so I didn't realize it was so late. Also, that explains the ache in my stomach – I'm starving. It has nothing to do with the pictures I was looking at.

'I don't have a chimney, so no decking the halls.' I place my phone on the table, ignoring the sting left in my chest, and focus on a more enjoyable sight. Although I've seen him most of the day, we didn't get a chance to talk, with everything going on both with Beeloved and FTG's final push before Christmas.

Garrick is dressed casually in gray joggers, a white T-shirt and a zip-up teddy bear brown fuzzy jacket. 'My halls have been decked for a month.' He lingers near the door, and my body twitches, trying to stay in my chair when all I want to do is kiss him again. To make the world disappear for just a moment.

I'm a thinker, a doer, a to-do-lister, but when I'm with Garrick those things melt away and my brain has a chance to breathe for the first time in forever. I didn't know how much I needed that. I'm like the person who didn't realize how thirsty they were until the first sip of water, then they can't get enough. Which would probably result in them drinking too much liquid and throwing up – sounds about right for the end of this metaphor about Garrick.

'We don't really do Christmas,' I admit, picking at a chip in the table.

'Seriously? Not even a Charlie Brown tree?' His shocked face stays put until he slides into the chair next to me, then it switches to a tinge of sadness in his eyes.

I glance around the break room filled with holiday cheer – a paper Christmas tree on the wall with everyone's name and what they want for Christmas. There is a real tree too, glittering in the corner with sparkly lights. It's nice. Maybe that's why I chose to study here and not in the apartment. Mom is working on the next episode in her makeshift office, so I didn't want to be alone.

'We used to do Christmas before my parents divorced, but then Mom got too busy, and my dad was off making a new family.' I bite my cheek, eyes darting up to his, waiting to see the pity. It's there, but it doesn't make me feel pathetic; it makes me feel seen.

He slides his hand over mine. It's warm and comforting. 'I'm sorry, Juliet. Holidays are tough when everyone's not together.'

God, I feel like a jerk. 'Garrick, I-I shouldn't be complaining. I'm sorry.'

He squeezes my hand. 'Hey, don't do that. Just because your pain is different doesn't mean it isn't there. We're both miserable, just in different ways.' He cracks a small smile, which I mimic.

'What a cheerful bunch we are.'

He leans forward, brushing hair behind my ear. That ache in my stomach is now a thousand butterflies. 'I don't know. I'm feeling pretty cheerful right about now.' He doesn't break eye contact, and it makes my chest warm. My logical side tells me to turn away – to get up and leave before this turns into something more.

But boy, oh boy, do I want the more.

My mouth is full of cotton balls, the single word getting stuck. 'Garrick?'

'Juliet?' My name on his lips vibrates across my skin.

'Kiss me?' It's a question we know the correct answer to – no.

But we both say yes.

He leans in, lips brushing mine in the barest of kisses, and it's everything I've been playing in my mind the last two days. It's better. It's worse. Because I know I'll never get enough. I forget about the world outside the room – forget my parents, who never have enough time for me. Garrick and I are all that exists.

The kiss is interrupted too soon when someone clears their throat by the door. We spring apart to see Desiree standing there, arms crossed, a wicked smile on her face. 'Well, well, well, what do we have here?'

'It's not –' I start.

'– what it looks like,' Garrick finishes.

I'm mortified. My cheeks are scarlet from the embarrassment seeping through me. What the heck was I thinking?

'It looks like we have a new entry into the competition.' Brett steps past Desiree and into the room.

'I thought you all left?' Garrick deflects.

Desiree shrugs. 'I'm waiting for my parents to come get me. But this isn't about me.' She looks us over, and then turns to Brett. 'What are we going to do about this?'

Brett shakes his head with an exaggerated sigh, like he's not freaking loving this. 'I don't think the public would like to know that Garrick Walton, of Fairytale Gardens fame, is actually just a cheater. And that the daughter of the Beeloved founder is responsible for the sabotage.'

'That's not fair,' I say. My heart pounding against my rib cage feels like it's trying to make a run for it. Could there be any two worse people to have walked in right now? 'It was . . .' *What was it? What do I want it to be?*

'What do you want?' Garrick asks, cool as a freaking cucumber.

'Look,' Desiree answers. 'I don't really care that you two are making out. But I might be alone in that.'

'It'll be your word against ours,' I counter.

'Not exactly. Show them, Brett.'

Brett holds up his phone and there's a photo of Garrick and I in his apartment from the night we made the cooking video. I have my hand on his chest while I un-mic him; he's gazing at me with a soft smile. Desiree must have taken it when she came over with Nathan.

Crap. That doesn't look good.

'I'd hate for this photo to find its way to the media.' Brett puts the phone back into his pocket. 'Along with the story of how Juliet Ripley has been orchestrating this to take down her mother's company out of jealousy.'

My mouth falls open in shock at the utter audacity of this man. 'That's a blatant lie. I thought you wanted to work with Beeloved. Why would you try to destroy it?'

'I'm an enterprising guy. I saw an opportunity.'

Desiree places a hand on his arm to make him stop talking. 'We don't want to get anyone in trouble, but we need some assurances to make it worth our while to stay quiet. So, why don't we make a deal? I'll keep your dirty little secret, if you give me more airtime on the show.'

'Seriously?' My eyes narrow in disbelief. She's already one of the girls with the most screen time.

She pulls on the sleeves of her pink sweater. 'Yeah, I need the exposure for my acting career.'

Of course. But whatever, I need to fix this. 'OK, fine.' My heart is still raging, but at least the start of a plan makes my synapses stop firing in overdrive. 'Brett, what do you want?'

Garrick holds up his hand. 'Are you extorting us?'

'I think it's more like blackmail,' I say, trying to keep the panic out of my voice. This is so freaking bad. I already got warned about being too close to Garrick, and then I go and make out with him in a public space. What has happened to my brain? I'm usually way smarter than this. Risk aversion is my number one ally.

Brett taps his chin like he's got to think really hard about not being a total jerk and making up a story to sell to the highest bidder. 'You have to put in a good word for me to Ms Ripley. Tell her how invaluable I've been to this whole thing.'

I clench my fists so tight my nails dig into my skin. 'All right.'

Desiree and Brett share an infuriating smile of victory. 'So, we have a deal?'

I glance at Garrick. He licks his lips, and my stomach flips. *Ripley, chill.*

'We do,' I relent because we don't have a choice.

Satisfied with their Grinch act, they leave happy.

'Well, that went unexpectedly.' Garrick chuckles. Way too chill for my liking.

I shove my phone into my bag, collecting my things from the table as I stand, knee banging into it with a burst of pain. 'We're extremely lucky those two can be bought.'

'But they were.' He hands me my computer. 'It's all good.' His lack of concern is frustrating.

'We can't do that again.' I shoulder my heavy backpack, trying not to look at him directly. My knees are already weak; I don't know if I can stand on solid ground if I do.

'That's what you said last time.' He cracks that stupid, handsome smile.

I straighten my back, holding my chin high in defiance. 'Well, this time I mean it.'

As much as I wish I did, I absolutely do not mean it.

The Twelve Days of Christmas Cookies Countdown
24 December
Day 12
Tiramisu Cookies

Servings: 12 cookies

INGREDIENTS:
Cookies
- 110g butter
- 100g granulated sugar
- 100g dark brown sugar
- 1 egg
- 1 teaspoon vanilla extract
- 230g plain flour
- ½ teaspoon baking powder
- ½ teaspoon baking soda
- 1 tablespoon instant coffee or espresso powder
- ½ teaspoon salt

Mascarpone cream
- 180g mascarpone cheese
- 1 teaspoon vanilla extract
- 90g icing sugar
- 20g agave or honey
- 120g double cream
- 1 tablespoon cocoa powder for dusting

INSTRUCTIONS:
Cookies

1. Melt the butter in the microwave. Don't let it bubble, so you don't lose any liquid in the butter. Pour the melted butter into a big mixing bowl and let it cool to room temperature in the fridge for around 20 minutes.
2. Once the butter has reached room temperature, add the granulated sugar and brown sugar and with spatula or electric beater whisk it together for a minute.
3. Add the egg and vanilla extract and mix until combined.
4. In a separate bowl, stir together flour, baking powder, baking soda, instant coffee powder and salt. Add the dry ingredients to the wet mixture and mix with a spatula until just combined.
5. Using a 2-tablespoon cookie scoop, scoop out 12 cookies and roll into balls. Then place them on trays lined with baking paper (6 per tray). Place the prepared cookies in the fridge to set for 1 hour.
6. Preheat the oven at 350°F (180°C) and bake one tray at a time for 10-11 minutes.
7. Once baked, let them cool on the baking trays for 3 minutes before placing on a wire rack to cool completely.

Mascarpone cream
1. In a medium bowl with an electric mixer, whip together all of the ingredients until the mixture reaches stiff peaks and it holds its shape. If making ahead of serving, place in the fridge, covered by cling film, until ready to assemble.
2. When ready to serve, add the cream to a piping bag fitted with a piping tip. Pipe the mascarpone cream on top of the cookies in a swirl, starting from the middle and moving outwards. Add a tablespoon of cocoa to a fine-mesh sieve and finish the cookies with a dusting of cocoa powder.

33

GARRICK

Juliet said they didn't do Christmas, but I wanted to surprise her. After some persuading, Nathan told me she was at her sister's house and gave me the address when I promised I wouldn't do anything weird.

It's Christmas Eve and I have a family dinner scheduled in two hours, but I decide to make a quick trip.

I knock on a door to a brick house that's not decorated for Christmas other than a single wreath. I've got my Santa hat and pants on and the jacket for my knight costume. Does it look ridiculous? Yes, but I wanted to prove to Juliet that I could be a knight in shining Santa. I shift uncomfortably as I wait for a response, suddenly questioning my life choices up to this point.

Juliet answers the door and looks *shocked* – and I want to say perhaps *happy* – to see me?

'Merry Christmas Eve. *Ho, ho, ho.* I come bearing gifts.' I hold up the red sack I have in my hand.

Juliet examines my outfit, cracking a smile. And my heart sings the loudest and happiest carol it knows. 'I knew the knight Santa costume would be ridiculous.'

'You know you love it. So, can I come in?' I hesitate now that I'm here. I didn't think this through. What if she's got something else going on?

She tugs at her hair. 'Sure.'

It's a modest two-story house with a family room, living room and dining room all in an open concept. The cabin-like wood walls are accented with deep-blue furniture that looks super comfy and is covered in toys. I wave to Ms Ripley typing on her laptop at the dining table, and Juliet's sister, Anna, in the kitchen. A tiny human sits in a chair at the kitchen island and can only be her niece, Molly.

Anna raises an eyebrow at me wordlessly, making me nervous in a way only the Ripley women seem able to do.

'I'm Garrick,' I say. 'Sorry to drop in on you and the festive celebration.' Not that I would say this out loud, but there seems to be no festive or celebration in sight – not even the smell of Christmas roast or spiced beverages of your choosing. I'm not here to knock how one celebrates, but based on what Juliet told me, I think she'd want something.

I scan the house for any signs of Christmas and only spot the slim tree near the front window. 'Let me guess, you decorated the Christmas tree?' I say to Juliet, shifting the bag in my hand, which is suddenly sweaty. My hand, not the bag, although if I hold it any longer, the bag will be too.

'How could you tell?' The cream fuzzy sweater she's wearing accents her pink cheeks, and I find my heart flaring with warmth the longer I look at her.

I clear my throat. 'It's very organized.' All around the tree are rows of red and green baubles, with gold ribbon running in the alternate rows. Except for the very bottom, which is a mixture of soft animal ornaments hung in wild formations, probably with the assistance of Molly. 'You should see our Christmas tree. I just slap anything up until I can't fit any more.'

'Sounds about right.' She laughs, eyes dropping to my hands. 'What's in the bag?'

'Well, I *am* Santa, so I couldn't arrive without gifts. I brought one for your niece.' I scratch the back of my head. 'And you.'

'Me?' Her eyes widen in shock. 'Oh ... I didn't know we were exchanging gifts.'

I hurry to soothe her worry because I can see her analytical brain spinning. 'You don't have to get me anything, Juliet. I like giving gifts. That's enough for me.'

She looks at me but doesn't say anything.

'What?'

She shakes her head, expression softening. 'You just keep surprising me, Walton.'

'Stick around, I'm full of them.' I reach into my bag and pull out the present wrapped in pink paper covered in castles. 'Molly, looks like Santa dropped off your gift at my house.' I hold it so she can see.

Her eyes light up and a grin breaks across her face. She's off the stool and running to me before I can get another word out.

'Molly,' Anna scolds. 'What do we say?'

'Pleasethankyou.' It all comes out in one jumble.

'Happy to help the big guy out.' I hand her the present, and she rips it from my hands, tearing off the paper. Inside is a replica of the Carpathia castle with several figures of the key characters.

'It's cute,' Juliet says. 'Is that what you got me?'

'No, I didn't think you'd like what I could get in the gift shop at FTG.' I wink. I pull out a black-and-gold Christmas bag with burgundy tissue paper.

She takes it with the utmost care and I could kiss her right then and there if we were alone. Placing the bag on the coffee table, she withdraws a red glass jar with a wooden lid. The glass is rippled and vintage with bubbles and imperfections.

'I heard you and Melika talking about how you liked vintage glass – and your apartment smells like a 7-Eleven, so I thought you could use a candle,' I quickly explain. I am so off my game right now, but with her, I almost don't care.

'Balsam and cranberry,' she reads, opening the lid to smell it. '*Omg*, that's amazing. It's like being in the woods with a pie.'

'That's exactly what I said. Look at the bottom.'

Her eyes narrow, and that little skeptical smile I adore peeks out. Flipping it over, she reads the label. '*Romeo and Juliet Candle Company*. How did you find this?' she says through a laugh.

'A lot of Googling.' My voice drops when I ask, 'Do you love it? C'mon, Juliet, you don't have to pretend.'

'By saying I love the candle, that does not mean you can keep up your Juliet game.'

I lean in. 'Oh, it so does. There's one more thing.' She rifles in the bottom and pulls out a set of multicolored fineliners. 'For your planner. Since it didn't come with any.'

Holding them to her chest like they're precious treasures, she says, 'One can never have enough pens.'

My phone keeps buzzing, and I know I have to get to dinner soon, but I don't want to leave. 'Do you all want to come to Christmas Eve dinner at my place?' I look up to Ms Ripley. 'Unless you have other arrangements.'

The three of them exchange looks in a silent conversation.

'We wouldn't want to impose,' Ms Ripley says, studying Juliet and me. Juliet takes a small step away from me and I try not to let it bother me. I know why she's doing it. After the whole warning about hanging out with each other, I shouldn't even be here. But I couldn't *not* come. It's Christmas, I get a pass.

'It's seriously nothing. We always make *way* too much food. Like I have a whole Twelve Days of Cookies thing going on. It's either eat it with us tonight, or I'm bringing Juliet a doggy bag tomorrow.'

Ms Ripley nods.

'Great!' I say too excitedly and try to tone it down, which makes my voice drop too many octaves to seem chill. 'We'll see you in an hour.'

Juliet has never been to my house, despite it being within the FTG grounds. I know she already has a sense of me and my family, but I wanted to make sure the first impression she got of us out of the fairytale land was good.

This means I turned on all the Christmas yard lights and made Tristian help me drag some old ones down from the attic for good measure.

'This is overkill, don't you think?' Tristian says after I plug in the last string of lights. 'You're probably going to start a fire.'

'*We're* probably going to start a fire. You helped.' Moment of truth. I hit the button on my phone to turn them on. The yard explodes in a blaze of – color. Of course, I didn't start a fire. 'Perfect.' I rub my hands together for warmth.

'Great. I'm going in before I freeze any important parts off.' Tristian trudges inside, kicking off his boots at the door.

I admire my handiwork for a second longer before following him into the warmth of the house.

'Hey, Dad,' I say when I spot him in the hallway. He's looking at the family picture hung on the wall.

'It was nice of you to invite the Ripleys over.'

'No biggie. It seemed like the right thing to do.' I just want everything to be perfect for Juliet. It broke my heart when she said she doesn't get a real Christmas. Dad runs a hand over Mom's face in their wedding picture like I see him do every time he passes it. 'Was it worth it?'

He looks at me with a puzzled expression. 'Was what worth it?'

'Falling in love with Mom. Like if you knew how it was going to end, would you still do it all over?'

Wrinkles crinkle around his eyes. 'Of course,' he says without hesitation. 'Not only did I get you boys, but I got to have so many wonderful years with the love of my life.'

'But it sucked when it ended. It broke you.'

He squeezes my shoulder. 'We break in all kinds of ways over the course of our lives, but that shouldn't stop us from living. Besides, love doesn't end just because the person isn't here any more. We hold that feeling inside forever.'

Pearl of wisdom dropped, Dad heads back to work on dinner.

'Are you going to stand at the window all night?' Bradley, my nephew, slides into the hallway. 'I want to play.' He's wearing a matching ugly orange Christmas sweater to mine. It's got snowmen in various forms of construction circling the torso.

I glance down at him. 'Just give me a few more minutes, pal. I'm waiting for a special guest.'

'A girl?' He shoves his feet into my oversized black Santa boots.

'How did you know that?' The kid's pretty smart, but that's a stretch.

'Daddy said it was a girl. Is she your girlfriend?'

My heart spikes in my chest. I lick my lips, releasing my hold on the blinds. 'She's my friend, and she's a girl.' *Would Juliet even want to be my girlfriend?* That's not even an idea I should be entertaining, but now it's dug itself in and I can't shake it.

'Garrick,' Ivor warns, as Bradley goes yelling through the hallway: 'Uncle G's girl that is a friend is almost here.'

'Ivor, can we not? It's Christmas. I just wanted the Ripleys to experience some holiday cheer.' I don't meet his eyes as we walk back to the living room.

'You sure that's all it is?' He pulls me to a stop before we reach everyone.

'Of course. You told me not to risk FTG's reputation. So, I'm not.'

I'm not. *Not really.* Unless Desiree and Brett decide to rat us out, but as long as they get what they want, I don't see them telling on us.

When I hear a car door slam ten minutes later, I jump up from the sofa, leaping over the back to shorten my time to the door. My brothers yell insults at me as I knock over their game board, but I don't bother to respond. I skid to a halt at the threshold, not wanting to open the door immediately and make them think I was waiting.

I'm trying to play it cooler than that.

Juliet gets out of the passenger seat, and I watch her face light up with the Christmas lights, a smirk on those lips I can't stop thinking about.

'Grinch!' Molly yells, eyes wide with delight, pointing at the blow-up in the front yard. I grin. *Mission accomplished.*

'You came!' I answer the door after the bell stops chiming. Chill or not, I couldn't leave them waiting in the bitter cold.

'You did invite us,' Juliet says, shifting from side to side at the looks Anna and her mom are giving us.

'Don't just leave them standing there,' Tristian calls from the living room.

'Crap, sorry. Come in.' I move out of the way, and they shuffle inside, passing their coats to me in a heavy lump. I hang them on the rack next to the window with all our old handprint Christmas cards around them.

'It smells amazing,' Juliet says, handing me her earmuffs.

All I can smell is her peach shampoo, making me think of Christmas at the beach.

But when I place her things with the rest, I catch a whiff of cinnamon and pine cones from the living room, with hints of roasting carrots, turkey and sage from the kitchen.

Bradley slides between my legs, nearly knocking me over in his rush. 'Want to play Santa's workshop?' he asks Molly.

'Yes! I'll be Santa.' Molly strides ahead, having no idea where she's going but moving with purpose like this is her place. She is definitely a Ripley.

'My nephew, Bradley,' I say to Anna, whose eyes follow Molly disappearing into the other room. 'Dinner will be ready soon, but we have some small bits you can nibble on beforehand.' I shove my hands into my pockets, aware of how small this entryway is with everyone still standing there.

'Nibble?' Juliet chuckles.

'Oh, Juliet, I'm all about the nibbles.' My cheeks tinge pink as I realize that might sound super weird. 'Nibbling food, I mean, obviously.'

Stop talking, Garrick.

Ms Ripley's keen gaze has been taking in the house, but she must suddenly remember she has food in her hands. 'I brought a salad.' She holds out the plastic container with a nearby grocery store label.

'Too kind, Ms Ripley. We can put it in here.' I lead them through the dining room and sit it on the table as we pass by. The tablescape is in beautiful silver and blue colors. These are the most classy decorations I have put up. They were Mom's, passed down from her mom and so on. We only use them on special occasions.

My throat goes thick with tears as I picture her in the room making sure all the places are done just right. I imagine what she would say about Juliet. I know she'd love her.

'He's cute,' Anna whispers to Juliet, and it's just the distraction I need.

I dip my chin, smiling to myself. At least I know I won her sister over. Juliet is a tougher nut to crack.

'Ms Ripley,' Dad says when we get to the kitchen. 'Ripley, and this must be your other daughter, Anna.'

Ms Ripley studies him behind her glasses. 'Someone's done their research.'

Dad is wearing an apron with a reindeer on the front, and it's far more whimsical than he'd usually choose – weird, considering he owns a theme park.

'I never go into business any more unless I know what the other person is about.'

I clap my hands together, diffusing what was about to be a very awkward moment. I'm pretty sure we were all thinking about the embezzlement fraud from last summer. 'Let's not talk about business on Christmas.' I turn to Juliet. 'Help me take these charcuterie boards through, will you, please?'

Juliet and Anna go with me to the living room, leaving Ms Ripley and Dad to chat in the kitchen. Whatever that convo is, I don't want to be a part of it.

'What's Mom going to do in the kitchen?' Anna asks Juliet.

'Get lost, probably,' she responds.

Tristian, Ivor, Aldrich, James, Molly and Bradley sit in the living room.

'Juliet, you know the others, but the handsome man next to Ivor is his husband, James. Everyone, this is Anna, Juliet's sister, and it seems like you've met Molly.' Molly and Bradley are playing with an intricate Santa's workshop set-up that Aldrich is helping them with. 'Let's dig in before we die of starvation as Dad finishes cooking.'

I lean in and whisper to Juliet as everyone chows down, 'I'm glad you came.'

'Me too.' She smiles at me, and I swear she can see my heart melt.

34

RIPLEY

I don't know why, but I assumed Christmas dinner with the Waltons would be peaceful, and formal, with elegant china and weighted silverware, accompanied by beautiful candles adorning the table. Probably because I thought of them as the royal family.

But I was wrong.

When an entire family is filled with boys, elegant isn't the first word I'd use to describe it. It's a free-for-all, everyone grabbing food like they didn't just eat a whole tray of meat and cheese half an hour ago. Even Barth, who, to his credit, is the most reserved of the bunch, still doesn't live up to the king's facade I placed on him. They're just a regular family, missing a huge piece: a picture of their mother hangs by the table, watching down on her boys.

If I don't eat soon, all the food will be gone. I load my plate with greens, potatoes, ham and stuffing. The spread is delicious, and Garrick takes most of the credit. In a very humblebrag way. When we first arrived, I worried what my being here might imply, but everyone has been more than welcoming — including Ivor. He might have told us off for being too close, but he doesn't seem to mind that we invaded their family dinner.

'So, is it everything you wanted?' Garrick whispers to me over the ruckus of chatting and laughing – even Mom. We may have never had a big family Christmas like this, but it seems like she's into it. Anna's face is glowing as she chats with James and Ivor about raising kids the same age, while Molly and Bradley make mountains from their mash and peas.

I look around the table, taking in the lights sparkling on the garlands hung around the room and the snowflakes cut out of white paper and strung up with red twine. 'Yeah, I guess it kind of is.' I reach for his hand under the table, squeezing it. 'Thank you. You didn't have to invite us over. But I'm glad you did.'

'Juliet, Santa doesn't need to bring me anything else now that you said that.' Then he adds, 'But if he wants to wrap me up that new video game I've been asking for – I'm not gonna complain.'

I knock my shoulder into Garrick and stay there a moment longer than needed, our eyes locking. Anna clears her throat, and I turn away from Garrick before I do something idiotic.

'Gather round, gather round,' Garrick yells to the group after we've cleared the plates, bellies full.

We all take a seat in the living room, huddling on to couches and chairs, or pillows on the floor.

'Will my lovely assistant please come here?' Garrick has donned his Santa hat once again.

All of us look at each other, not knowing who he's speaking to.

'Pst, Juliet, that's you.' Garrick holds out a hand to help me off the floor. I frown at him, wondering what shenanigans he's about to drag me into. He passes me a stack of fabric. 'Everyone needs to put on these blindfolds first.'

Tristian scoffs. 'Yeah, no. The last place I want to be is in a blindfold around you. I still remember the bow and arrow accident from when we were seven and you busted out two of my teeth.'

I, too, am dubious, so I haven't moved. As the fire crackles behind Garrick, and the Christmas lights sparkle, I feel like I'm living in a story.

'Guys, really? You don't trust *me*?'

There's a chorus of *no*'s around the room.

'Juliet?' He stares at me with that stupid, irresistible puppy-dog face. I hold his gaze for the space of a few breaths. Truly, he hasn't done anything to make me distrust him.

I start passing around the blindfolds as my answer.

'Despite the lack of confidence from my *family*, I'm still going to reward you all with a Christmas Guessing Extravaganza.' Garrick places a large tray, covered in a silver dome he must have acquired from the Royal Fare, on the coffee table. 'There are several rounds, which include guessing songs, treats, smells, touch and much more. The person with the most correct guesses wins.'

This must not be the first time Garrick has done a similar game because they all jump right into competitive mood.

'And the winner gets?' Aldrich asks.

'Garrick's Twelve Days of Christmas Cookies Countdown treats!' Garrick grins. 'And year-long bragging rights.'

For the next hour, we participate in the festive game and I let myself fantasize about what it might be like to be Garrick Walton's girlfriend.

Christmas morning is better than I expected. Molly makes everything better. Her pure joy and excitement at seeing what Santa left her under the tree is contagious. Anna, Mom and I sit on the sofa, hot chocolates in hand, and watch her rip open the presents, even the ones that aren't hers. But weirdly, I don't mind when she opens my gifts for me. It feels so absurdly normal – like this is what a regular family would do – that I'm having an out-of-body experience. Anna doesn't even seem bothered that her husband is away on business. I know I'm not. I didn't want to sit in a room with him and pretend, for Anna and Molly's sake, that he isn't a jerk.

It takes until the presents are open and the breakfast is eaten for Mom to mention work. I'm pretty sure that's a record. 'I need to review the schedule for next week and add my notes,' she says, picking up the remains of Molly's rampage, as said little monster sits on the ground playing with her new dolls. The castle Garrick gave her is the center of the storyline she's creating.

'On Christmas? Come on, Mom, I'm sure it can wait.' Anna's feet are submerged in the foot massage bath I gave her. Her pregnant feet are always swollen, so I thought it was perfect. I might need to try it myself just to be sure.

Mom shakes her head. 'I wish. But this production schedule is so tight, it can't. Juliet?'

I've been flipping through the new book Anna gave me. I like to read the end first. It drives her mad, but I hate not knowing. However, I got distracted by a new message on my phone.

> **Garrick**
> Merry Christmas – hope Santa didn't disappoint

> **Garrick**
> By Santa, I mean me. I'm exhausted from my deliveries last night

> **Ripley**
> Must be the armor

> **Ripley**
> Merry Christmas

'What?' I look up, cheeks flushing.

'Will you stay here with Anna, or do you want to come home with me?' She's already pulling on her coat, keys in hand. Mom never likes to waste time.

'I'll stay here.' But actually, I know somewhere else I'd like to go.

First, I have to stop by Melika's house. I need to raid her

vintage storage for a present. But when I knock on the door, her family insists I have something to eat, and with the delicious smells, I can't say no. After I'm so full I could burst, I find an item hidden in the back that I think will work.

'Should I ask what this is all about?' Melika says as she hands me gift wrap for it.

'No. But I'll fill you in later. You're the best. Love you.' I hug her before dashing off, my heart pounding like I'm running a marathon. I like to know the outcome of things before I jump in. It makes it easier to navigate. But right now, I'm plunging headfirst and hoping there is something – or *someone* – to catch my fall.

Garrick mentioned his family always had Christmas lunch at the Royal Fare, so I wander in the back, trying to keep out of sight. As much fun as I had last night, I don't want to impose on their family traditions any more than I have to. But I had to see Garrick.

> **Ripley**
> Can you meet me in front of the castle?

> **Garrick**
> ?? omw

I rub my hands together, blowing into my gloves to keep warm. Luckily, my pink cheeks can be attributed to the cold and not the embarrassment I feel by being all sentimental.

This so isn't me, but the tug in my gut to see Garrick was so intense I thought I might burst if I didn't satisfy it.

'Hey,' Garrick says, startling me when he slips outside. 'Why don't you come in? It's warmer.' He's wearing a new green-and-blue beanie.

I swallow hard, trying not to swoon as his smile ticks up in the soft way I've only seen him do for me. 'I don't want to impose.'

'Juliet, you are never an imposition,' he says quietly, and my body is suddenly not so cold.

'I just wanted to give you this.' I pull his present out of my pocket. 'It's not much, but I thought you'd like it.'

His eyes light up as he reaches for it. Our fingers touching sends sparks down my skin. 'You didn't need to get me something.'

'I wanted to.' It feels like someone turned up the dial on all my senses. The day feels brighter despite the gray clouds, and the sound of the wind in the trees is extra loud.

He opens the package with such care, taking his time with every piece of tape. Not at all how I thought Garrick would open a present. Inside is a gold coin with a knight on it.

'I'm not sure where it's from, but Melika got it at an antique store, and I know you love being a knight, so I thought you could have a piece with you everywhere. Lighter than armor.'

He laughs softly, the noise warming the air. 'It's perfect.' He looks up at me, those blue eyes swimming with an emotion I haven't seen often. 'Thank you, Juliet.'

'You're welcome.' I look around, trying to calm my erratic heart. 'So, I'll let you get back to lunch.'

'Don't leave. Let's go walk the park.' He extends his hand, and I can't say no.

We reach a bench near the giant Christmas tree, and Garrick turns on the lights. We sit in comfortable silence for a while. Then the snow starts. Small flakes at first until they turn into giant ones.

'I always love snow on Christmas,' I say. 'No matter how the day went, if I see snow, I'm at least happy for that single moment.'

'I hope you were happy for more than that today.' Garrick flips the coin between his fingers as snow catches on his hair and eyelashes.

'I was.' I didn't have much hope for today, so maybe the low expectations helped.

Garrick brushes snow off my nose, leaning in. 'Hi.'

'Hi.' I swallow hard. We both look around the park to see if we are alone this time.

We are.

Blame the snow or the holiday spirit, but right now, all I want for Christmas is him.

We kiss under the Christmas tree lights with the fresh, powdery snow falling around us. And as much as I can try to deny it, I'm falling for Garrick Walton.

35

GARRICK

Fairytale Gardens is closed now and won't open again until the summer season. We have a few events lined up. Not as many as I would like, but more than we had before the show started. We landed a pretty massive wedding in February – Dad was pleased with that one. So, I guess it's doing something.

We've returned from Christmas break, and while I enjoyed having my time off – I finally got to play some video games and sleep past seven – I'm excited to be back, but it's probably not for the right reasons.

All right, it's a thousand per cent not for the right reasons.

My wandering thoughts, which really should have stayed in place in the back of my brain, won't stop. And those thoughts all have one name: Juliet Ripley. I haven't seen her since Christmas, two days ago, but we've been messaging non-stop. It's a good thing I could sleep in because we were up until three the other day. Juliet fell asleep for some of it, but I can easily carry a conversation alone.

Knowing I will see her again today has me buzzing with nervous energy. My foot taps to the beat of nothing in particular as Pierre finishes my hair and make-up for the shoot. It'll be nice only to have the show to worry about and not my knightly duties too.

The group date today is all about the new year. We're stuck in this weird time warp of a week. It always comes between Christmas and New Year. The park is still decorated like Christmas, but a bit of the holiday spirit has worn off. So, like many other people, we will put all our hopes and dreams into the upcoming year.

We're due for a heavy storm tonight, and there will be lots of wet weather. Which is why we're on a time crunch to get everything filmed in case Mother Nature drowns us out. So, it's full speed ahead until the final next week.

Dang. It's kind of shocking it's almost over. It feels like just yesterday that Juliet showed up and offered me the job.

Speaking of.

'Hey,' Juliet says, pushing herself off the wall when I exit the main office into the outside air, heavy with pre-storm gray clouds. I can't help the way my face lights up when I see her, warmth spreading across my body when she returns it, blue eyes sparkling with what I hope is excitement to see me.

'Hey, yourself. Were you waiting for me? Missed me that much?' I stumble on the last words, my thrumming heart reminding me I genuinely want her to say yes because I missed her like crazy.

Juliet does this half-shrug that pulls at my strings, yanking me toward her. 'Maybe I did.' The way her voice lifts in the hopeful peak, I'm ready to throw caution to the wind and drive off to who knows where with her.

My hand reaches for hers without thinking, our fingers wrapping together in an electric shockwave you can't replicate. I want to pull her in for a kiss, but she releases our touch too quickly. We are not alone, and we've already got caught once.

'Ready for your *date*?' The drop-off at the word date feels like we were both doused in ice water.

'Juliet, I ...' I don't get to finish as a PA scoops me up and we're off to meet with the girls.

Just like this is the first time I've seen Juliet, it's been twice as long since I've seen the contestants, but I don't feel any particular way about it. I'm happy they all look healthy and rested from the break, but the urge to wrap any of them up in my arms isn't there.

'Hi.' Desiree is the first to greet me when we arrive, throwing her arms around me. 'We still have a deal?' she whispers in my ear.

My smile is tight when I pull away. 'Glad to see the holidays haven't softened that killer edge.' I flick my tongue over my teeth. 'We're good.'

The other greetings from Zoya, Arianna and Ellie are much tamer. They offer their excitement to be back and ready to get things going again. They all say they missed me, and I genuinely can't tell if it's an act or not. I hope my facade is as convincing.

I clap my hands and slide on the knightly grin. 'All right. So, because the new year is just around the corner, I thought it would be fun –' the producers thought it would be fun – 'to make sure we've all got the right moves to show off at a New Year's celebration. So, let's see what kind of dancers we've got.'

A professional choreographer is here to teach us some classic dance styles. We're performing on the castle stage, which was probably a better idea in theory than execution since it starts to rain about twenty minutes in.

'OK, cut!' Hassan calls and the blasting music goes silent. 'Let's move into the Royal Fare and finish this out. We can do the vision boards after.'

The second activity is cutting out magazine clippings to create our visions for the new year. Crafting a vision for the future is about the last thing I'm interested in doing.

I watch Ms Ripley speaking quickly to Juliet before Juliet dashes toward the parking lot. Instead of following everyone inside like I'm supposed to, I head for Juliet.

As I'm jogging through the ever-increasing rain to meet up with her, I have a sudden realization. It smacks me in the face as hard as the gale-force winds shuttering the buildings. Maybe this whole reality show is working but with the wrong person.

I really like Juliet. Like, *like* like her. Seeing her again only made that even more prevalent. Sure, I didn't want that. I was adamant, as was she, that true love didn't exist. And OK, maybe we both know that it *does* exist, but we understand that it sucks, and you should leave it alone.

But somewhere along the way, I started to realize that it might, in very rare cases, not be so bad. Who knows, maybe I'm one of the lucky chumps who gets to have it.

Tristian got it, and he is my twin – maybe it's in our DNA.

'Juliet!' I yell as she's getting into her mom's SUV.

'What?' she says, halfway into the driver's side, the rain drenching her hair. 'I'm getting soaked.'

'Then get in.' I yank open the car door and take the passenger seat. 'Ooh, seat warmers.'

She slides into her seat but doesn't start the car. 'You're supposed to be dancing.'

I push the button to start the car. 'I'd much rather go wherever you're headed.'

'That's not how it works. You're in the middle of a date.' Sleety rain covers the windows, blocking us from the world.

'Not with the person I want to be with.' I brush a strand of wet hair from her cheeks, the sweetest shade of pink blossoming on them. She stares back at me, speechless. 'Juliet, lost for words – I don't think I've ever seen it.' My body is warm, skin tingling as she moves her hand over mine.

She smiles. 'They'll come looking for you, and then we'll both be screwed.'

'Then we'd better hurry and do whatever you're supposed to do. *Really*, Juliet, you shouldn't slack on your duties.' I up the heat on the warmer. 'Oh, yeah, I could get used to this.'

She quickly pulls out of the driveway. 'OK, let's make it fast.'

We stop at the craft store and pick up a few missing items.

'Pick a hand,' I say to Juliet as I hold my arms behind my back. The aisles are barren, not restocked since the Christmas pandemonium.

'We need to get back. Where have you been?' A basket nestles into the crook of her elbow, stuffed with various crafting items.

'Getting you something. Pick a hand.' I love watching the emotions play across her face now that she's let me past her defenses.

She's debating if we have time for this, but gives in. 'Right.'

I produce a bouquet of fake roses. 'For you, Milady.'

'Thank you. Now, left.' She always needs all the answers.

In the other hand, I'm holding a plastic crown. I slide it on her head. 'I thought it was time you joined the fairytale.'

She takes the roses, smelling them. 'Mmm, plastic and dust, my two favorite scents.' A beautiful pink flushes her cheeks. 'But you know I'm not really into fairytales.'

I scoff. 'I thought it was theme parks? Now you're not into knights either? Are you trying to wound me, Juliet?'

Removing the crown, she inspects it carefully. 'Well, I am into this one knight.'

I scoot closer, placing a hand on her waist. 'Do tell me more. Is he handsome?'

'He seems to think so.' She tries to keep a stoic face while staring at me, but her sweet smile bursts through.

'You don't agree?' I lift her chin.

'I do, but don't tell him. We don't need it going to his head.'

I kiss her on the nose, before lightly touching her lips. 'It'll be our little secret.'

She sighs. 'Garrick, we need to get back to filming.'

Resting my forehead against hers, I sigh too. 'C'mon, Juliet, can't we wait a little longer?'

Offering a quick peck on my cheek, she steps away, giving me all the answer I need. Duty calls, and neither of us can afford to play hooky.

We get most of the items into the car without ruining them in the downpour. I offer to drive us back as the weather worsens. We don't have far to go, but even the short drive is becoming deadly.

'I got to pull over,' I say. The rain/sleet becomes so hard that I can't even see the headlights on the road. I thought it was winter. Beautiful snow is my jam, not torrential downpours.

'We have to get back.' She squints to look out the window. 'You don't think you can make it?'

'Not unless you want us to both get killed on the way there.' My chest tightens at the idea of my brothers and Dad having to bury another body. I slam on the brakes harder than I should in the rain, pulling us to the side. She looks like I may have given her whiplash.

'Sorry. Are you OK?' I reach for her hand gripping the seat. She releases it and takes mine.

It takes a minute, but she nods. 'Yeah, a little rattled, but I'll be fine.' I brush hair from her eyes, and she leans into my hand. 'So, what now?'

'I know a few ways we can kill some time.' I give her a wry smile. The rain isn't so bad when we're in a stable position.

'Garrick.'

'Juliet.'

'You got me caught in the rain, and now you want to make out with me. Could you be any more cliche?' She sounds annoyed, but she's laughing.

'I literally play a knight in shining armor. I am a walking cliche.' I link our fingers, holding on to her for warmth as the temperature drops around us with the car turned off.

'If you would have asked me that a few weeks ago, I would've said one hundred per cent. But I don't think you're as 2D as you pretend to be. You've got a lot of layers when you let someone see them.'

I turn her hand over, studying them like I'm memorizing my lines. 'Not many someones get to.'

'Then I consider myself lucky.'

'I think I'm the lucky one. Did I tell you about my idea for the fencing camp?' I haven't shared this brainchild with too many people. I didn't want to get my hopes up if it never came to be, but I feel like sharing my dreams with Juliet.

'No, but I want to hear all about it.' I know that look of determination. She's already got a mental notepad open, ready to take down all my ideas and create a spreadsheet and action plan for me later.

Leaning over, I kiss her. I know it's wrong. And I know I'm supposed to be finding my dream girl in the batch that she picked out for me. But I can't help it. Just like Romeo, I'm falling for Juliet.

36

RIPLEY

We're soaking wet by the time we get back to the apartments. And it's way later than it should've been. With the early winter nights and the still-pounding rain – but less sleet, so Garrick felt safe driving back – it's already dark outside. They scrapped the date, at least according to the texts Mom sent me. Also, we're both in major trouble. Somehow, me more, for apparently *kidnapping* the star. In Nathan's words.

Luckily, with the storm, we could just make the excuse that our phones weren't working. Plus, it's not like we could risk our lives to drive back just for a dating app reality show. Which, I hate to break to everyone, is not working. At least, if the way Garrick was kissing me is any indication.

'We're so screwed,' I tell Garrick when he parks the car.

'Nah. I'll make sure if anyone is screwed here, it's me. You were just doing what you were told. I'm the renegade.' He reaches for my hand, interlocking our fingers.

'No one can argue that. But ...' I pull away, my hand cold in the absence. 'We need to be careful.'

'Did you see my driving? The picture of careful.'

'Not what I meant. We already messed up with Desiree and

Brett. We can't let anyone else catch us.' I bite my lip, and he reaches for my face before stopping.

'So, you mean like me kissing away that frown of yours would be a no-go?' He's got one eyebrow raised, and I almost ditch my whole train of thought, but then I notice Brett exiting the break room.

'Yes. Like that. Now go.' I wave at the door, grabbing Mom's keys from him. 'Apologize like never before.'

He reaches for the handle but pauses, twisting back and kissing me quickly. The brief touch sends my heart pounding again. 'Last one.' He grins before jumping out of the car and running toward his apartment.

I don't want to go to my apartment if Mom's there – I'll have to answer eventually, but that's not right now. I head to Melika's apartment instead. When I get there, Nathan is also inside, but her roommate, Imogen, isn't. She's probably with Tristian. Those two are so sweet it made my teeth hurt at first. I swear I was going to get a cavity just looking at them. But now I sort of get it. There's something about those Walton boys.

'You look like a drowned cat,' Melika says when she opens the door.

I shake off my wet jacket, hanging it on a hook near the door. 'Thank you, you're so kind. I've barely got to talk to you guys at all today, and this is the welcome I get?'

'You're right,' Nathan says, grabbing my arm and leading me to the couch. 'How was our star knight? Did you two enjoy playing hooky?'

Plopping on to the couch, I pull a pillow up on to my lap. 'I don't know what you're talking about. I was running an errand for my mom and got stuck in the storm.' My cheeks flame red, and I know I'm not fooling anyone, even if they weren't my friends.

They both just stare at me. I sigh, leaning my head on the couch dramatically. 'Ugh, fine. He's ... I don't know ... a good kisser?'

'I would love more details on that,' Melika says, sitting on the back of the couch, legs draped over me. 'And I will get them. But I'm more worried about what will happen if somebody finds out. Kahoa and I haven't even been out in public yet, just in case someone recognizes her.'

'Well, someone did already when we were making out before Christmas. Desiree and Brett.'

'What?' they say in unison.

I rub my forehead with my pointer finger and thumb. 'It's fine. I think. She said she wouldn't tell if I gave her more airtime, and I've already arranged that. And Brett just wanted a good word put in with my mom.' I did manage to utter a strangled compliment about him earlier today. But I'll need to try a little harder to make it believable.

'And now you just need to stop kissing,' Nathan says.

'Easier said than done.' I toss my arms over my head. 'Why are you looking at me like that?' I glance between them and their knowing gazes.

Melika smiles. 'It's just nice, is all.'

'What is?' I frown.

'Well, that smile you were sporting and the rosy cheeks.' Melika bops my nose. 'Love looks good on you.'

My frown deepens. 'Ew, no, that's not – we aren't ...'

'The fact that you can't finish that sentence tells me everything I need to know.' Nathan draws a heart in the air.

'I don't love Garrick Walton.' Which is true – I don't – really. But I, maybe, might have a teeny, tiny, microscopic seed in my heart that could, if left to grow, become something someone – *not me* – might call love.

The thought should send me running for the nearest hill, but, like any fool, I think I might want to try it.

Mom reads me the riot act for letting Garrick in the car, but I don't get in too much trouble since Garrick took all the blame on himself, and I was supposed to leave. We're three weeks into filming, and we've all learned by now it's impossible to get Garrick to do anything he doesn't want to.

Unfortunately, to play it cool, Garrick and I keep our distance that evening and I don't see him until the next morning when we have a foggy castle-side elimination in the snow. Snow is great at Christmas, but now that the dust has settled on the mistletoe and Father Christmas is back at the North Pole, snow is just an immense, cold pain in the butt.

Zoya goes home and we're down to three. An episode airs tonight, which means the crew is busy getting the final cut done with the elimination, and we have the rest of the day off. We're on a tight schedule this week, so Garrick was forced to do a last-minute date yesterday with Ellie just to get more footage for the episode after our outing ruined the planned event.

'What if we got away?' Garrick says as we sit in the treehouse fort, the late morning sun warming the frosted air. We're nestled together in a makeshift pile of blankets on the bottom level because I refused to go to the upper floors. I didn't want to die. Even with the safety hazard above us, it's kind of cozy.

'Go away where? We're seventeen.' I lay against his chest, his gloved fingers stroking my hair.

'I know. I just meant somewhere that there aren't a bunch of cameras.' His warm breath clouds in front of us.

I don't know what Garrick and I are. We haven't had that conversation. But every time he's near, the butterflies zoom around and I enjoy how it feels.

Who am I?

It doesn't matter because Garrick signed a contract, and even if it wasn't for that, we need to finish the show. It's beneficial to both of us, as much as it hurts to watch.

'We can't go anywhere. Not yet,' I add when he sighs dramatically. 'But who knows what the new year will bring. We do go to the same school.'

'Bold of you to assume I attend class.'

'I mean, I don't think I've seen you there.' I grin, looking up at him.

'If I'd seen you before, I never would have said yes to this reality show.' He cups my cheek.

'Even if I asked really nicely?' I copy his signature puppy-dog face.

'Honestly, Juliet, I'd do almost anything if you asked.'

'OK, but serious question.' I lean my head back to see his face better.

'Not my favorite way to start a sentence, but I'll allow it.'

'What do you want to do after high school? I know you go to class.' Mom got his school records and did background on him before we started filming to make sure he was suitable for the role. 'So, what's the plan?'

He gives an exaggerated shiver. 'Even you can't make the word *plan* sound good. I don't know.' He scratches at his pant leg. 'What do you want to do?'

'I want to become a lawyer. But not a criminal defense lawyer or an ambulance chaser. Someone who can actually do some good.' Defending the little guy seems like an excellent way to spend a life. Also, they have to be very organized, and I got that down. If only I could learn to control my flushing cheeks, I'd be unstoppable.

He nods, dimple popping. 'Yeah, that tracks.'

'So,' I elbow him in the rib softly, 'where does future Garrick reside?'

He waves to FTG peeking out from behind the trees. 'Right here. This is my home, has been for my whole life. I don't plan on going anywhere else.' His voice hitches at the end and my lips dip into a frown.

Before, I wouldn't have pushed him to tell me more, but now that we're kissing on a regular basis, I want to know more. Because my heart yearns to learn everything I can about him.

'Why the sad note?' A sharp pain cuts through my abdomen, and I press my hand into my stomach to make it stop. I only had a handful of cereal for breakfast, and my body is revolting, but I don't want to get up just yet.

He licks his lips, chest rising and falling behind me. 'FTG isn't as stable as it used to be. If we don't keep building up funds, I'm not sure how long it can keep going. I've never wanted to be anything other than the knight in shining armor. But when I started working in the kitchen, I realized that could also be cool to do – like my mom.' He clears his throat, and I squeeze his hand as he powers through. 'So, that's my plan. Keep Fairytale Gardens running until I'm an old man and I become a ghost wandering the park.'

'Sounds like you got a plan to me.'

'Huh, yeah, I guess I do. You know, FTG could probably use a lawyer on staff. You could stick around and maybe I'd finally get you on a roller coaster.'

I bark out a laugh, scaring some birds in a nearby tree. 'Sorry, Walton, never going to happen.'

'Never's a long time, Juliet. But don't worry, I got all the time in the world for you.' He leans down and kisses my nose before moving to my lips, making me forget all my problems.

37

RIPLEY

There's a vibration under my chin, and I roll over to my other side to make it stop. I've been tossing and turning all night and only managed to get into a fragile sleep. I crack my eyes open despite my desire to keep them closed for another twelve hours. The bright sun blazes through my closed curtains, meaning it's been up for some time – unlike me. I scramble, searching for my phone in the tangled sheets where I abandoned it sometime in the wee hours.

When I finally locate it under my pillow, the time blinks nine a.m. I vaguely recall my alarm blaring at seven, but I must have hit it off instead of snoozing. I jump out of bed, pain radiating through my core as I grab clothes and head to the bathroom.

I hate being late because it makes me feel rushed, adding to the anxiety already there from the tardiness. This shoot is so nearly over – I only have a few more days left, and I wanted to end them on a high note. Probably to help assuage my guilt about the whole Garrick thing.

I don't have time to shower, so I quickly spray dry shampoo in my hair while brushing my teeth. Actually, first I spray the shampoo on my toothbrush and have to clean it off, then start again. How anyone can manage this sort of chaos on a daily basis is beyond me.

My stomach cramps and I try to remember the last time I ate. I went to dinner yesterday, but nothing spoke to me, so I only had a small plate of chicken and mashed potatoes. But I didn't even finish it. Spitting out my toothpaste, I dribble a bunch down my shirt.

'Freaking perfect.' I rip off the tee and grab another one from my drawer. I twist my hair into a low ponytail before sliding into my boots. I put on my puffer jacket as I take the stairs down to the parking lot two at a time ... regretting it immediately as I stumble forward, slamming my arm into the railing. Pain shoots through my body so strong I nearly just collapse right there and hope that someone finds me. If this is how my morning is starting, I do not foresee the rest of the day going any better.

I take a second to regain what little composure I can muster, forcing three deep breaths out before I start walking again, hoping my inner turmoil isn't written all across my face.

I don't know how all the noise out here didn't wake me up. The crew is turning the parking lot into a relay race. This date will have different stations where the girls and Garrick compete to finish various challenges. It has something to do with *new year, new you*. Blah, blah, whatever. I don't subscribe to any of that. But apparently a lot of people are fitness-oriented – can't relate.

'You're late,' a production assistant scolds me. 'You were supposed to help set up the hay jumps.'

I cannot wait to no longer have a bunch of kiss-asses telling me what to do every five minutes. I am more than capable of coordinating my own time schedule. Except for today – but that is a one-off I won't let happen again.

I press my hand into my stomach, attempting to keep the annoyance out of my response. 'I know, sorry.' The set-up is nearly complete. 'What can I do?' I attempt an eager smile, but a grimace is all I manage to muster.

He stares at me for a beat, frowning deeply, before he points in Melika's direction. She is helping Imogen set up the zip line. 'Just see if they need you.' I don't miss the unsaid *because I don't*.

I walk over, eyeing Imogen on an unsteady ladder. Each time she reaches further than her body, it wobbles. 'Is this safe? Both the ladder and the zip line.' I burrow my chin into my coat to shake the chill.

'Sure,' Imogen says, brushing red curls from her face, making said ladder totter. 'I watched a ten-minute video on how to do this. It'll be fine. But that's why we have the mats underneath them in case they fall.'

'I think Ripley was more worried about the rope snapping and the people falling off.' Melika gives me a once-over, silently asking if I'm OK. I nod back. 'Don't worry, we made sure it wasn't too high. All they are going to bruise if they fall is some pride.'

I bite my lip. 'Does my mom know I overslept?' Not that she would think that immediately. Oversleeping is not something I'm known for. But after that whole 'stuck in the rain with Garrick' thing, I'm worried she might assume we made another run for it.

'Don't worry, girl. I covered for you – told her you went out early to get some supplies. She seemed to buy it.'

'You're the best.' I look around but don't see Garrick. He's probably getting ready for the date. My stomach rolls thinking about him being on-screen with the girls, participating in cute dates. One, because I want it to be me. And two, because I feel terrible leading the girls and audience on. I know I said this thing was fake to begin with, and it definitely is. But now that I am actively participating in its fakeness, it feels so much worse.

'Are you OK?' Nathan asks when we meet him at the start of the relay race once they've finished setting up the stations and are working on the last-minute lighting and camera angles.

My hands are shoved into my pockets. I can't seem to get warm, even though today isn't as cold as the other days – chills run over me every few minutes. 'Yeah, I'm fine. I just didn't get anything to eat this morning because I overslept.'

'We can run to the break room real quick and get some.' Nathan loops his arm around mine.

I shake my head, leaning against his shoulder to keep myself upright. 'No, thank you.'

I know I haven't eaten, but I'm not hungry. My head feels fuzzy and sharp pains keep invading my stomach. Which I know means I probably should eat. *It likely has nothing to do with the guilt I am suppressing about the whole Garrick thing*, I think sarcastically. If this reality show and Mom's app fail because of me, I will never forgive myself.

Mom comes out with Garrick twenty minutes later, and the cameras are hot and ready to roll. The girls arrive dressed in T-shirts they designed with their names on them. It looks super cute. I look like I haven't slept or eaten properly in twenty-four hours.

I make sure Mom notices I'm there, and she doesn't make any comment about me being late, so she must've bought Melika's excuse. I stick around as the relay starts, but as time passes, and they have to keep stopping and resetting because of noise problems, my head starts to swim.

It's nearing noon, and I know they will be setting up lunch soon, so I use that as my excuse to get out of the crowd for a minute.

'I'm going to check on lunch,' I say to no one in particular, but mainly to Nathan and Melika. The FTG staff handles all the meals, but I enter the main office and stop by the break room to see the spread. It's sandwiches and chips, with some fruit and veg. I debate grabbing a banana – it would probably do me some good – but even the benign fruit does little to entice me. I'm hungry – I think – or I'm just programmed to know the times I should be eating, so my body is giving a programmed response. Whatever the case, I don't venture further into the break room, and it takes more strength than it should to push off the wall I've been leaning on.

Making my trip inside last longer, I head to the bathroom. Once in there, I lean over the sink, taking three deep breaths. I press my hand into my stomach as the pain shoots up the center of my abdomen. The aches I've been feeling all day are getting more intense and the random jolts of stabbing are increasing in frequency.

I need to get back to the shoot before Mom notices I'm

missing. I run cool water over my hands, splashing my face before I head out of the bathroom.

Only a few more hours, and then I can crash on the couch and sleep off this weird funk.

I stay near the back of the filming, not feeling up to walking to Melika and Nathan. The short span looks like miles. Garrick spots me, jumping over a haystack and giving me a huge grin. I try to return it, but then the earth starts to spin, the light dimming into a narrow tunnel. I attempt to grab on to the nearest thing, yanking a light down as I fumble to stay upright. Everything goes fuzzy, the noise muffled as the world goes black right before I hit the ground.

38

GARRICK

I'm killing it on my times in this relay, my legs burning as I jump over the hay bale. Catching sight of Juliet, my chest swells with warmth. I flash her a grin, trying to decide when we can sneak out to Tyrone's to get some alone time. The weather is warmer today, almost like spring. Maybe we can have a picnic – I wouldn't mind impressing Juliet with my outstanding snack-packing skills. That feels like something she'd be very into – all that organization.

I'm mid-leap over the final hurdle when a clatter behind the camera steals everyone's attention. I catch sight of a pale Juliet as she wobbles on unsteady legs before collapsing to the ground.

The hay scratches and burns the back of my legs as I land on it hard, not clearing the mound. But I barely notice. Ripping over the relay obstacles and past the sidelines, I push through the crew before I think most people realize what happened.

'Juliet!' I skid to the ground, my knees banging into the cold asphalt. Everything is numb except her limp body in my arms. '*Juliet!* Help!' I yell to the people behind me, heart thudding in my chest as I stare at them with wild eyes. There is an EMT on set, and they're over within seconds.

Someone is pulling me away – I think it's Ivor, but I'm thrashing against them to get back to her.

'What's going on?' Ms Ripley parts the crowd. 'Oh my god, Juliet.'

Minutes pass but they feel like hours ... an eternity.

'Let's get her to the ER.' I think it's the EMT talking, but all the faces swim together in my vision. All except Juliet's. She looks so helpless on the ground, so unlike the person I know she is. Her usually pink cheeks are pale, her lips equally drained of color.

Oh god, she looks ...

I barely register what's being said. The world buzzes as my skin tingles with a familiar sensation. The pain topped with fear and nausea – the same thing I had when my mom got sick. Bile burns my throat and I swallow in my dry mouth to keep it at bay. I force myself to remain here in this moment – for Juliet – and not check out like my default setting is screaming at me to do.

'I need to go with her,' I say as they carry Juliet to the ambulance, her limp frame freaking me out. *Please wake up, Juliet, please, god, wake up.*

'She'll be OK.' It's Ivor beside me.

I turn to him. My tongue feels like rubber. 'I need to be there.' Cold sweat glistens on my skin and the warm day is suddenly icy.

He doesn't wait for more. 'My car's out front.' He places a hand on the back of my neck and steers me away without a word. I have no idea what everyone is doing – if they're wondering what the hell is wrong with me, because I keep my gaze on the ambulance. Even after it's gone, my eyes don't leave the space.

We get to the hospital in record time. Ivor isn't one to speed, but he must have done. Not that I noticed. My mind is laser-focused on Juliet – and the burning in my chest when I think about all the things that could be wrong.

Pain radiates over my ribs, my chest tightens as we walk into the ER. 'My ... uh, friend Juliet Ripley was brought here by ambulance. I need to see her,' I say to the woman at the check-in counter.

She glances at her computer. 'I see she's here, but I'm afraid that's all I can tell you. You're welcome to wait in the lobby and see if you can get the relative with her to give you more information.' Her voice is kind, face sympathetic, but I feel none of it.

'Look,' I lean on the counter, trying to pull out my best charming smile. It hurts my face to do it, so I'm not sure how successful this will be, but I have to give it a go. 'I understand you have rules, but I *really* need to see her. OK? So, please push that button and let us back?'

'I understand your concern for your friend, but rules are rules.'

My blood pulses in my ears, and I think I've left my body. I don't know who's controlling it now, but he's pissed. 'Concern? Of course I'm concerned. That's why I need to get back there. Now!' I don't realize I'm yelling until Ivor puts his hand on my shoulder. The firm grip brings me back to reality.

'Garrick, she's in good hands. We'll stay here and be ready the moment we can see her.' When I don't look at him, he adds more softly, 'OK?'

The world is taking on a gray haze. The colors melt away in

this hospital waiting room as the reality of my location sets in. I haven't been to a hospital since my mom died.

People come here, and they don't come back.

I squeeze my hands into fists at my side, trying to even my breaths. *What if she doesn't make it?* What the heck was I thinking letting myself do this again? I can't watch someone else die. I told myself – I made a pact with my brain – that I wouldn't get into this situation. I didn't want love. I didn't want to be close to someone just for it to end like this again.

'Come on.' Ivor leads me to a faded set of chairs to wait. I slump forward with my head in my hands, leaning against my knees. 'She'll be OK.'

I want Ivor to be right. And a large part of me knows that he is. This situation isn't at all the same as with Mom. But what if it is? Juliet might appear healthy, but you never know. The body can so easily conceal and betray you, sneaking up when you least expect it.

I should have kept my heart locked up tight. Love has no place in it. I was supposed to protect myself from this. If Ripley and I had never got involved, I wouldn't be sitting in a room that smells of disinfectant with other forlorn people, waiting for news that will – *could* – *might* – change my life forever. And not in a good way. What was I thinking?

I wasn't, but I need to now.

My phone buzzes in my pocket and I take it out, seeing a dozen texts from Tristian and Aldrich and a few missed calls from Dad. I hadn't even noticed it was going off in my pocket non-stop. The screen shines in my face and then goes dark. I tap the screen again with all the intention of responding, but

I can't make my fingers move. Dark overtakes the device, and the messages left for me go unanswered.

What would I even say to them? I don't know any more than I did when they carried Ripley away.

No one comes to Garrick for the heavy news. I'm not the guy people expect to hear bad things from. I hide it all away. That's what I did with Mom. I closed my eyes, buried my head in the sand and ignored the wails of anguish around me. It was crappy of me, I see that now. My brothers were all hurting, but I didn't know what to do. I still don't.

Time passes as we sit there, then Ms Ripley comes out to see us. Ivor must have texted her to say that we were there.

I stand quickly, shoving my hands into my pockets. 'Is she OK?'

Ms Ripley is exhausted, but doesn't look like she's seen death. 'It's appendicitis. It hasn't burst, but it's severely infected. They're prepping to get her into surgery soon.'

I glance at my watch – it's nearly midnight. 'Can I maybe see her?'

She shakes her head. 'I'm afraid not. But you're welcome to stay in the surgery waiting room with me and we can see her after.'

A hospital waiting room is the last place I want to spend the night, but I can't leave until I know Ripley is OK. 'I'm staying, but you can go,' I tell Ivor.

'Not happening, G. I'm with you as long as you need me.'

I give him a tight smile, thankful to have him. Ripley is having surgery. An easy one, they say, but my heart still weighs heavy in my chest as we wait to see what happens.

39

RIPLEY

Waking up from surgery is a weird experience. The whole last twelve hours or so have been a blur. I remember coming to in the ambulance, two EMTs and Mom huddled around me and a bunch of wires. It was loud, and they were talking like I wasn't there. It felt like watching it happen from the other side of a TV screen. That human on the stretcher couldn't possibly be me. But it was. The pain in my stomach reminded me it was very much my body that was in distress.

I tried to tell them I was fine – at least fine enough that I wanted out of this cramped ambulance. But they wouldn't listen. Despite my arguing, I guess it was a good thing they ignored the girl who just collapsed in the middle of filming a reality show since I ended up having an emergency appendectomy. I suppose most of those are emergencies, so it seems redundant, but that's what the doctors said I needed.

Conceptually, I know I was in the ER for hours, but with the pain meds being pumped through my IV, I don't recall most of it, other than the moments between doses when the sharp stabs in my lower right side would rear their ugly head again. Mom was there, though. It was nice, in a way, to be the sole focus of her attention for a sliver of time.

In the recovery room, after surgery, all I want is a drink of water. I bother the nurse incessantly until she gives it to me, so I have to wait a little longer before they wheel me up through the darkened hospital. The rest of the world is still asleep at two a.m. When I get to my new room, I promptly fall asleep, thanks to exhaustion and more meds. The sleep is interrupted by the blood pressure cuff and nurses checking on me.

At some point, I'm conscious again, the pre-dawn light scattering through the window allowing me for the first time to see I'm not alone. Mom is asleep on the sofa against the wall and Garrick is curled in a chair next to the bed. I have a vague memory of seeing him after surgery. But it's all glimpses and shards of a broken mirror. I sort of thought I made him up in a fever dream.

'Hey,' he says, voice rough from sleep when he spots me staring at him.

'Hey.' My words are equally textured, but some of that is due to the oxygen tube they had down my windpipe. 'I didn't –' I clear my throat, trying again. I attempt to move and get a jolt of pain in response. I cringe, lips pressing tight.

'You don't need to talk.'

'It's OK,' I say softly, not to wake Mom. 'You've been here the whole time.' It's not a question because I know the answer.

He rubs a hand across his face, leaning against his elbows. 'When you collapsed – Juliet, I was so worried.' His voice breaks, and he stops himself.

I find my eyes stinging with tears. 'I'm sorry.'

Deep lines and a frown distort his face. 'Shh, hey, no, don't be sorry. You have nothing to apologize for. I'm just happy it was something they could fix.' He gazes past me like he's looking at the ghost of someone else.

The room smells like fresh sheets and cleaning supplies. I swirl my tongue around my mouth, trying to cure the dryness so I can speak. It doesn't do anything, but I fill the silence all the same. 'Did they finish the date?'

'That's your first question?' The usual mirth in his voice is missing. Even in the dark, I can see the weariness behind those usually lively eyes – fatigue from more than just lack of sleep.

I try to shrug, but the little movement hurts too bad. I close my eyes, pain etching my face. 'The show must go on, as they say.'

When he doesn't respond, I open my eyes to see him worrying his bottom lip. He's always a bit fidgety, but it's on overdrive.

'Are *you* OK?' I say cautiously.

He sighs deeply, and I don't love where the movement takes him, out of his chair and toward the door. Looking at it for a beat too long, like it's an escape hatch, before he returns his gaze to me. He stops at the side of my bed, crouching so we're eye level. My heart thuds in my chest. Any moment, the machines attached to me are going to catch up to what my body is already reacting to. That primal sense that danger is coming.

40

GARRICK

'Ripley, I ...' I feel myself distancing us by using that name. 'I'm happy you're OK. *Really*.' There's no life in my voice as I force my words to come out.

'Why do you need to emphasize *really*?' Her guard is slamming up, eyes darting back and forth, trying to read me.

'Ripley, let's not.' I look just past her ear, so I don't have to meet her stare. I can't. I'm protecting us both.

'Let's, Garrick. Why do you need to emphasize *really*?' The shake in her voice could be attributed to the post-surgery recovery, but I know that's not it. I feel the same quiver in my own throat.

I cringe like I'm the one that just went under the knife. 'I – we can talk when you get home.' Whatever's been going on between us these last few weeks needs to end, but I'm not going to do that in a freaking hospital room.

'No, I want you to talk now.' A hospital bed is a place of rest and healing, not whatever this conversation is turning into, but Ripley is not one to just let things go.

'Ripley...' Pain radiates in my gut and I wonder for half a second if appendicitis is contagious.

'Come on, Garrick.' A harshness seeps into her already rough tone. I deserve that. 'I know you're never at a loss for words, so don't go all silent on me now.'

Glancing over to where Ms Ripley is still asleep, I sigh heavily. 'You're recovering from surgery. Get some rest and we can talk when you get home.'

Ripley is logical above all else – she'll understand that us breaking things off now is for the best, to keep us from getting hurt. It's just the current location might make it hard to think rationally.

The crushing weight of the sentence we both know is coming dawns on her pale features. 'You're breaking up with me?'

She said it first, *good*, maybe it won't hurt as much if she sees the truth herself. She didn't want this anyway – neither of us did. So how come the end of whatever this is feels like it might crush me from the inside out?

I open and close my mouth a few times, choking on the heaviness in the air. 'We weren't really official.'

Lie, lie, lie. We were everything. But when you make something your whole world, the loss of it is endless.

'Sure, yeah.' She blinks up at the ceiling.

My eyes sting with tears. Good thing she can't see them in the dark. 'Ripley, I didn't want to do this now.'

She doesn't look at me. It cuts deep into my skin, my nerves burning and then numbing. I just want to make it better. But I can't, not right now. She'll see, eventually, that this was my way of saving her.

She brushes moisture from her cheek. 'Well, now it's done, so you don't need to say it again.'

My hands ache as I squeeze them into fists to keep from reaching for her. *I'm sorry, I take it back* – the words scream in my brain, banging against my teeth to be let out. I taste blood as I bite my tongue.

I just didn't realize how deep I'd let myself fall under the spell of infatuation – love, someone else might say – but in that moment she was lying on the ground I saw with total clarity how much of my heart I'd given to Ripley, and I knew I had to get out while I still could.

Images plagued me, bombarding my brain as I sat and watched her sleep. It was like seeing Mom lying there all over again. I couldn't separate the two, as much as I wanted to. Even though I knew they would have vastly different outcomes, all I could think was how wrecked I'd be if something happened to Juliet. We barely got to know each other, and it was already ripping me up inside. Imagine if I let it go any further.

I couldn't do it.

It's better for both of us to end things now. Give it time, and we will see that it is the right thing to do.

'I ...' I start, not knowing where I'm going to go. The words lodge in my esophagus. But she said exactly what I was thinking, so clearly she must be feeling the same thing.

She turns away. 'Just go, Garrick.'

My feet squeak on the linoleum as I stand, hesitating briefly. I reach for her, wanting one last time to feel her touch. But instead I walk out the door without another word.

A nefarious beast has made my stomach its home. I want to vomit as it goes on a rampage when I leave the hospital in the wee dawn hours. Ivor went home after we knew Ripley was OK. He said I could call him to pick me up when I wanted to get back to FTG. But after what I've done, I can't look at him. I don't even want to look at myself.

But were Ripley and I even together? We never said anything about being a couple, so could we actually break up? That's what I attempt to convince myself of as I walk home in weather that turns icy and wet the closer I get to FTG. I try to come up with an excuse that doesn't mean I am a complete jerk who broke up with a girl in her hospital room. But no matter how I twist it, that's precisely what I did. The guilt eating away at my insides won't let me off the hook.

I move like a ghost through the back lot, somehow finding my way to the main building to get ready for today's shoot. Tristian stares at the side of my face from the chair next to me in hair and make-up. Pierre is expertly covering up dark half-moons to hide that I haven't been to bed. This is not the first time he's had to make me look less like the undead, so he's used to it. But Pierre and Tristian keep exchanging knowing glances in the mirror, and it's pissing me off.

'What?' I snap when they do it for the tenth time. Barking out in anger is so unlike me, they both flinch. Instinct surges to make a joke, crack a smile to lessen the obvious tension. But I can't muster any of it.

Then Tristian clears his throat. 'Are you OK, G?'

'I'm fine,' I say way too quickly to be convincing.

'I know that everything with Ripley must have been ... a lot.'

I dig my knuckles into my jeans, rubbing up and down my leg. 'She's going to be fine. The doctors said she did great.' I repeat the words the nurse told me in a monotone voice. I worry if I put too much emotion into the sentences, I won't be able to hide that I'm breaking inside. I can't explain it to Tristian because I can't even explain it to myself. Like, am I upset because I know I hurt Ripley, even if it was the right thing? Or am I devastated that I just wasted a chance at something I might have loved?

Tristian's face, so unlike mine yet exactly the same, looks pinched as he frowns. 'I'm glad to hear it, man, really. Still, if you need me to talk to Dad and get the show postponed –'

'No.' I stand so fast that Pierre drops the make-up on the floor. 'Sorry,' I mumble, leaning down to pick it up for him. I straighten, placing the items carefully on the counter. 'The show must go on. Let's just get it over with.'

'If you're sure.'

When this started, I didn't think I was going to find a girl I wanted to date, but then I did – and it was wonderful, and it sucked and made me want to throw up all at the same time. I just want to go to my room and put my headphones on so I can be lost in a video game where I don't have to think about any of this again.

'How is she?' Nathan stops me when I get outside on my way to set.

'What?' I blink at him.

'Ripley? I called her this morning, but she didn't answer. Just sent a text saying she's healing but tired.'

'Oh, yeah, no, she's good. I mean – the pain meds are helping, I'm sure.'

Nathan's shoulders relax, and he nods. 'OK, good. I'm glad you were there with her at least.'

Nausea rolls through me, bile burning my throat. 'I have to get to –' I don't finish the sentence before walking away. Apparently, Ripley hasn't told them about our break-up. I don't want to say it out loud again, but I can't just stand there and lie to her friends' faces.

Today is the seventh elimination. Without Ripley here, it's bizarre. I'm used to looking behind the camera and seeing her doing a terrible job hiding her emotions about this whole thing. Everyone on set seems genuinely invested in this true love match. So, I could never express how I really felt. But when I saw Ripley, it was like someone was on my team.

The episode tonight will be a skinny one since we didn't get to finish the date yesterday – at least I didn't. They managed to string the scenes together when I was there and mix in the girls finishing it. I want to say I don't care, but I know that FTG needs this to work. It's the only reason I'm here right now, when it would've been much easier to give up.

Before I eliminate the last girl leading up to the final, we film one quick scene. It's the extra airtime Ripley promised Desiree. I almost tell Desiree that she doesn't have leverage any more because Ripley and I aren't going to be found kissing in the break room, but I do what I'm usually terrible at and keep my mouth shut.

Desiree clasps my hand in a vice grip that is supposed to be reassuring. 'I just want to say –' she lets a crack seep into her words as the camera pushes in on her face – 'whatever happens today, I've had the best time getting to know you. And just know that you've changed my life in the most extraordinary way possible.' She flings her arms around me, and we embrace in a hug that feels like it will suffocate me.

The chat goes on a little longer to fill in that empty space from yesterday, then it's off to send a girl home. We made sure this elimination was a shocker. That's why Arianna is eliminated. Most people thought we'd be perfect together, but that makes the final more exciting.

Desiree and Ellie are the last two standing, and it's anyone's guess who I'll pick as my Beeloved.

I wish I could say the elimination was the last thing required of me today, but sadly it's not. We've got a New Year's Eve date later tonight.

I know Ripley is only one person, but without her everything feels unsettled. I'm trying my best to look like I don't care. But I don't know how well it's coming off.

'Great job,' Hassan says. Guess I am faking it just fine. 'We're getting fab social media traction for the upcoming grand finale. People are sooo hyped. Way to go.' No one else seems at all bothered by Ripley's absence. Other than Ms Ripley, who didn't come in to work today.

'Yeah,' Brett says from the edge of the Jousting Horses. 'You seemed way more focused today. Whatever's been distracting you must have finally gone away.'

It's like a thousand bees are buzzing in my ears. An odd

sensation of fire ripping through my veins surges through me. 'You know, *Brett*, if you weren't such a –'

'Garrick!' Aldrich comes out of nowhere and hooks an arm around my neck, spinning me away from my target. 'Dad needs to see you.'

'I have something I need to handle first.' I try to yank away from him, but somehow, my little brother got surprisingly strong in the last month.

'Nope, you don't,' he whispers, tugging me toward the back lot.

'Dude, what the heck? I was just trying to have a conversation with Brett about politeness.'

'That is so not what your face said you were going to do.' He lets go of me when everyone is out of sight and we duck past the golden apple tree and enter backstage.

I brush a hand over my face. 'No, you're right. It's been a day.'

'I could tell, and I hate to add to it, but Dad really did need to see you.' He offers a sympathetic grimace.

'Thanks.'

A year ago, I may have thought Dad wanting a chat was a bad thing, but I think it might be OK.

'Garrick, come on in.' Dad smiles as I head into his office.

Seems promising enough. 'What's up?' I shove my hands into my pockets, grinding my jaw in case the bad news comes to run me over.

'I just wanted to inform you how well the show has done for the promo of Fairytale Gardens. We have had record pre-sales for next season, and we've already surpassed any year we've had since opening. You were right, son. This was a good idea. As of now, we can put the layoffs on hold. We *might* even be able to do the fencing camp you suggested.'

A heaviness I've felt on my chest since I saw Ripley collapse lightens, my breath finally coming in fully. Even in my funky mood, the praise shocks my system. I rub the back of my neck, not sure what to say. 'Uh, thanks, Dad. I'm glad it worked out.'

And I am glad. I wanted to help the park. And I've done just that. So, as long as I don't manage to screw it up in the next episode, everything should be good. But somehow it doesn't have the satisfying feeling I was hoping for.

41

RIPLEY

Sleep comes in fitful bursts, never allowing me to fully rest. I give up eventually. A beat of silence, then another, so long in the dark space filled only by the glow of my buzzing hospital machines. Any minute now, they're going to alert the staff of my broken heart, the beats dipping lower until there's nothing left.

Stupid, stupid heart.

Breathing is impossible. The weight of gravity is too much to bear in my fragile state. I stare at the drop ceiling, holding back my useless tears. The burning in my chest is from more than the slices in my stomach where they pulled out an organ. It feels like something else is being ripped out.

I knew better. God, I knew love only ever hurts you. The ones you think might love and be with you forever just up and leave at the slightest inconvenience. Garrick told me himself that love was a fraud, and I agreed. Why, why, why couldn't my heart remember that? My place was behind the camera. I should have stayed in my lane. Instead, I jumped headfirst into oblivion and I let myself get hit by a truck.

Mom stirs in her makeshift bed but doesn't wake. If she does, at least I can pretend the crying is from the surgery.

When the nurse comes in a few minutes later and asks if I need more pain meds, I tell her yes, because the silent crying has taken its toll on my already broken body. She changes the date on the whiteboard hung on the wall – 31 December.

Happy New Year's Eve to me.

Having an appendectomy is about as fun as it is easy to spell. I get out late in the afternoon on the 31st, having spent just over twenty-four hours in the hospital. Luckily, I had a laparoscopy procedure because my appendix hadn't fully burst. If I had, I would've been in the hospital for a few days. As depressing as it sounds, I kind of wish that I was still there. While I only had my thoughts and a TV with limited cable options, at least there were things to distract me, like a nurse coming in to check on me and the beeps of the hospital machine.

Everyone was focused on my recovery and me being able enough to go home. There were checklists and timetables to fill in – my favorite pastime. I could almost, *almost*, forget about the fairytale theme park in the distance and the knight who broke my heart. When I first woke up groggy mid-morning, I thought I'd dreamt it all. Some nightmare induced by the anesthesia and pain meds. But then I saw the empty chair and the Garrick-shaped hole that was left. It wasn't a nightmare – or it was, but the real flesh-and-blood kind.

'Are you buckled in all right?' Mom keeps glancing at me from the driver's side as I lean back in my seat, arm slung over my eyes to block the sun. My crappy night's sleep is making my vision sensitive to the light.

'Yes, you checked four times before we drove away from the hospital.' I should be annoyed with the helicopter parenting, but it's actually sweet. Mom hasn't left my side since I returned from surgery. This is more attention than I've ever received, and it was oddly nice despite the circumstances – not that I want to replicate this experience.

'Just checking. I'm sorry about the bumpy roads,' she adds as we go over a particularly aggressive pothole.

I cringe, pain spasming across my jaw as I grind my teeth.

'Remind me when we get home to contact the city. Honestly, I don't know what I'm paying taxes for if even the roads near the hospital are torn up.' Her exasperated tone covers the worry pretty well. But I saw the look on her face when I came to in the ambulance, the way she bit her thumbnail as we waited for test results – she was scared. Mom is always so sure of herself it was disconcerting to see this other side.

'Thanks, Mom. For taking care of me.' I squeeze her hand. 'Sorry for ruining the show.'

'Juliet, you have nothing to apologize for. I'm just so glad there was an EMT there. I don't know what I would do if something happened to you. I love you, Juliet. I know I probably don't say it nearly enough, but you girls are my world.'

A lump fills my throat. 'I love you too, Mom.'

By the time I'm shuttled from the car, hunched over because standing straight sends a burning through my incisions, and deposit myself on the couch with the fluffiest blanket Mom could find, I'm exhausted. I don't want to do anything other than study the backs of my eyelids. I couldn't care less that it's New Year's Eve.

I manage a quick video call with Melika and Nathan as proof of life. But I'm not up for much more than that. After I've been fed and watered, given my tablet and several books to choose from, Mom's back to work mode. She didn't go to the set today, so she needs to catch up on the footage and preview the episode post for the day. But she insists on staying in the house in case I develop sepsis or need ice cream.

Since Mom is now preoccupied, Anna comes over to take care of me, bringing a large bag of french fries and chocolate chip cookies. Shockingly, her husband is actually home for a change, and he's watching Molly. Anna doesn't seem that bothered that Mike isn't here. In fact, she seems glad that he's someplace else. Once again, love bites the big one.

Anna gives me a card Molly made with crayons and construction paper, telling me to *get well soon*. Or at least I assume that's what it's supposed to say. It's hard to tell past the stickers and glitter.

This year, it will be an old-school New Year's Eve with Anna and me. We watch the countdown clock out of New York. Not that New Year's is ever a major thing for me, but I'm pretty sure I won't make it till midnight. It hurts to move and talk; depending on the angle, even breathing makes me wince. The bandage around my abdomen keeps me from seeing the extent of the scar. Supposedly, it won't be bad. I'll have to do some research on scar treatment when I'm feeling less like a living corpse.

Resting my head on the mountain of pillows, I let the whims of consciousness take me where they desire, which is annoyingly to FTG and the Beeloved show. I know there was another elimination earlier today – I got updates on the set from Melika and Nathan before I told them I didn't want them any more. Every letter was another stab to my already tender chest. I didn't have the heart to tell them that Garrick and I broke up. Or maybe I just didn't want to see the words made forever permanent in text.

Can I even call it breaking up when we weren't officially together? We were just two people kissing, and now we aren't any more.

That's a lie. It was more than just kissing. I opened myself up to another person in a way I've only been able to do with my closest friends. Letting him see my heart, with all its imperfections – and him doing the same.

I'm glad I can use the excuse of being post-surgery so I don't have to go to the New Year's Eve party my friends have been telling me about for weeks. I'm content with Anna sleeping on the couch, and me drifting in and out as my pain medication kicks in.

Of course, Melika and Nathan said they would come join me, but I didn't want to ruin their New Year's Eve. I know they would've been right at my side, snacks in hand, if I asked. And I love that about them. But I'm not up for company right now.

There's no post-surgery treat that can fix the wound left from the knight who stole my heart and then threw it away. But I can only blame him so far. We both stated from the beginning that we didn't believe in true love – that relationships only end in heartache. We were so smart. How did we both end up in this place?

'Is it time for more meds?' Anna says, rubbing hair from her face. 'Are you in pain?'

I blink, feeling wetness on my eyelashes, tears having escaped the prison I thought I had secured them in. 'No.'

Anna's lips twist as she snuggles down into the blanket with me. 'It's the prince, isn't it?'

I don't bother correcting that he's a knight. 'How did you know?'

'Well, for one, from what I've seen of him, I bet he would've been here with about a dozen party games to keep you entertained. And two, I know that look of heartbreak in your eyes well.'

The tears I tried so hard not to cry, because they would mean I fell for love like all the other chumps out there, come flowing out. 'I'm so stupid. I knew better. I shouldn't have let this happen.'

'Oh, Rip.' Anna pulls me into a hug, careful of my stitches. 'Love is a sneaky bastard. You don't have a choice in the matter – as much as we like to pretend. I always knew when you fell, you were going to fall hard. Because that's what you do. You aren't a halfway kind of person. You put all you have into everything.'

'I hate it.' I don't bother to wipe away the wetness coating my pillow. 'It feels like it'll never go away.'

She pauses for a minute, staring at the fireworks on the TV. 'Sometimes it doesn't. But the heartache can be a reminder.'

'Of?'

'Of how good it can feel. What's the saying? *It's better to have loved and lost than never to have loved at all.*'

I didn't love Garrick Walton. Maybe I could have, given enough time. But right now, I wish I had never known what these emotions felt like. Because the shell of it, the broken, jagged pieces left behind, are bitter in my mouth. The saying should be, 'It's better to live in ignorant bliss than to be left with this feeling for the rest of your life.'

But ignorance was never my way. I have to know everything down to the finest detail. My brain is full of all the knowledge I've gathered over the years. And the pain of this will be etched in my skin until the end of my days.

42

GARRICK

'This is a dumb idea,' I say, trudging behind my three brothers as we walk the lengths of Pirate Adventure. The ride lights are on, the soundtrack at a low hum for ambience but not to overpower our conversation.

'No, it's not,' Ivor says from up ahead, leading the charge to the whispers of a sea shanty. It was his idea to do this. I guess he thought since it's New Year's Day it's a time for new beginnings and putting the past behind us. I'm all for the forgetting part; I've plenty of things I'd liked scrubbed from my brain.

Aldrich slows his pace to match mine. 'Yeah. Besides, I want to see it.'

The *it* in question is the time capsule we buried when Aldrich was five. He wasn't allowed to wander among the water canals in this ride like we were at the ripe old age of seven. Technically, we weren't supposed to either, but it was Ivor's idea, and he promised not to tell Mom and Dad.

I can't remember what I put in there. Something to do with fencing, maybe? I was in full-blown obsession mode. I know I debated for days about the right thing to pick.

'I thought we said we'd open it fifteen years later. We still have five more to go.' I don't know why I'm dragging my feet. Looking at my presents early is a time-honored tradition in Garrickland, but this feels like the last piece of the person I was before Mom died. Before everything changed and we all had to become new people.

The kids who buried this still had their whole family and no reason to believe that would ever change. The naivety of youth I wish I still had. I clamp my jaw shut, molars grinding together.

The water moves along slowly, no boats aboard it today as we walk past the pirates singing their shanties and the fires burning from their raiding. The familiar scent of smoke brings me back to the days spent pretending we were real pirates. We spent whole days here in the off-season. Sometimes, we'd even sneak in when guests were on the boats and try to scare them. Actually, that might be the origin of the ghost stories.

Tristian glances back at me, offering a smile. He can always read my mind – twin powers and all. I used to wish we were identical because I wanted to switch places and play tricks on people. But knowing Tristian, he'd probably be too honest to let us get away with it.

We drew a map to remember where we buried it, but scale and distance weren't exactly top priority. I was more worried about getting the coloring of the gold and jewels just right. We hit our shovels into the ground in the area we know it has to be – the tiny fake island scene with sand and animatronic crabs. It felt bigger when we were kids. Now, the four of us barely fit on it. It takes a few tries, but we manage to hit the payload.

'It's smaller than I remember,' Ivor says, heaving the treasure box from the sandpit. Not much effort is required for the small shoebox we covered in construction paper and treasures draw in crayon.

I lean down, brushing off the sand. 'Last chance to change your minds.'

Ivor places his hand on my shoulder. 'Time to move forward, Garrick.' A heavier weight penetrates those words.

The bottom of the box is fragile. The edges of the cardboard have worn soft over time. Even though there's no movement on this fake beach set – the ride boats only glide by the scene – I feel like I'm swaying. Ivor holds the box with care, rubbing his hand over the top one last time before opening the lid on its hinge.

Inside are pieces of yellowed notebook paper, where we scribbled down dreams for our future. Tristian and I were seven, so our dreams consisted of big things – BIG in capital letters. Mine is a picture of me as a world champion fencer – complete with a whole neck of gold medals. I remember taking so much time to draw this, even though I can't recall what else I put in the box. The memory of me scrapping and restarting every time I messed up is as fresh as if it were yesterday.

Tristian's shows him among ruins in a castle with the Eiffel Tower and the Leaning Tower of Pisa in the background. I guess no one told him that Italy and France are different countries. Ivor's picture is a bit more straightforward. It's him with a family. Both the one he already had – three brothers and a mom and dad. Plus, the one he wished to have when he grew up, with several kids and a partner standing next to him.

'Let's get to the good stuff,' Aldrich says after we've removed the pictures. 'I want to see if there's any real treasure. Because you guys are terrible artists. Guess I'm the only one who got that gene passed down.' I shove him with my shoulder, and he grabs my arm so he doesn't topple off the island into the water. My picture isn't going to hang in any museums, but it's not nearly as bad as Tristian's or Ivor's.

'All right, calm down.' Ivor pulls his item from the box. It's a silver participation statue from the spelling bee he did in sixth grade.

'That's what you put in here?' Aldrich frowns, clearly losing interest by the minute.

Ivor scratches his beard. 'Yeah, because I didn't win. I didn't want to have a trophy around that showed that I was just mediocre.' He brushes dust off the plastic person on top holding a letter 'A'. 'You know what, now I'm kind of proud of it. I'd always been a performer, we all have. But I was scared to go up and spell in front of everyone. And I'm proud that I did, even if I sucked and got out first.'

I remember Ivor struggling with spelling as a kid, but I never thought about how it might've affected him.

Tristian takes his treasure out next. It's an old leather journal with a collection of stamps from around the world.

'You guys put really boring stuff in there.' Aldrich fakes an exaggerated yawn. 'I thought we were going to find actual cool things.'

'Beauty is in the eye of the beholder,' I say. I remember Tristian used to collect stamps from everywhere. Not just other countries but states, too. He would put them in order of importance based on where he wanted to visit. I guess he's always had aspirations to go further than the walls of FTG.

Tristian's lips curve into a smile as he flicks through the colorful pages. When we get home, I'll probably see these pinned to his corkboard in his room. I hope someday he does get to all those places and brings me back souvenirs from each one.

'Looks like you're last.' Ivor passes the box to me.

My hands shake, and I don't know why I've got this churning in my stomach. When I reach into the box, my finger brushes a cool gold coin. My hand freezes as I go for the tarnished currency. 'No way,' I whisper.

'Finally, someone put some actual treasure in here.' Aldrich grabs for it, but I push him away.

Running my thumb over the metal, I clear the grime away. Embossed into the surface is a knight. I toss the box into Tristian's hands and reach into my pocket.

I withdraw the coin that Ripley gave me for Christmas. It's an exact match. I knew when she gave it to me I felt something, but I couldn't remember why it seemed so familiar. Now I do. I found the same one once when I was with Tristian, looking for stamps.

'You already have one?' Tristian peeks over my shoulder.

A sudden lump builds in my throat, and I have to clear it several times before I can get the words out. 'Ripley gave it to me for Christmas. Said it reminded her of me.'

I stare at the two, both aged in different ways. Mine from being hidden away in a box for ten years, but who knows what adventures this other guy had.

'So, Ripley, huh?' Tristian finally says after a few minutes have elapsed. 'Anything more you'd like to tell us about that situation?' His voice rises a few octaves, like he already knows the answer.

Ivor's hand is on my shoulder. 'Come on, Garrick, you know we're not dumb.'

'I don't actually know that.' The automatic, witty response leaves my lips. I sigh, clenching both coins in one hand as I rub my face with the other. Pressure builds in my chest as I stare at the fake cave walls. 'I don't know.'

What is there to say?

'Well, we can get out of the way the obvious,' Tristian says. 'You like her. But ever since yesterday, you've been off. So I'm guessing something happened?'

'Which means you've been a sulky, moody jerk,' Aldrich pipes up, then adds quickly, 'No offense.'

'We broke up. I guess. I don't know.' I kick the toe of my shoe into the soft sand. 'I didn't think I wanted what Ripley and I had, or *would* have had if we'd kept going. Seemed easier to stop while we were ahead.'

It was definitely not easier to stop, but it might be in the long run. This momentary gut-wrenching pain will vanish and I'll be better off for it.

'You can't keep doing that,' Ivor says. 'I know that when Mom died we all coped in our own way. It was easier to pretend that you didn't want to get close to anyone because it would just end in the pain that Dad had. But let me tell you, having James was the best possible thing I could ever have had to get me through it. And I know, as much as it sucks, we're going to have more times in the future that aren't going to be the best. And I would hate for you to do that without someone by your side.'

'Aren't I going to have you three losers?'

'Of course you are. But sometimes you need a different kind of love.'

I lick my lips, nibbling on the skin. 'When I saw Ripley taken away in the ambulance, it was like Mom all over again. It brought back every terrible feeling from that time and I panicked.' Rubbing at the center of my chest doesn't cut the ache. 'I couldn't deal and I made a rash decision.'

'We all do that, sometimes,' Ivor says. 'Doesn't mean you can't fix it.'

Fixing it might not be enough to stop all the collateral damage. 'This reality show was supposed to find me love. If I pick somebody who isn't even on the show, what's that gonna do for FTG?'

I can see the wheels turning in Tristian's head. 'The show is about true love, right? Just like the FTG story. So, maybe the audience would like to see that true love can find you, no matter where you are.'

I scrunch my face. 'Dude, you're so sappy now.'

Aldrich snickers beside me.

'But I really messed up with Ripley. You should've seen her face.' My chest aches when I picture it. 'There's no way she'll forgive me. And besides, she said she doesn't believe in love, and I definitely reaffirmed to her that it hurts.'

She's way smarter than I am, so she may not be willing to give it another try.

But I'm not going to let that stop me.

43

GARRICK

Today's our last day of filming and the moment I'm supposed to make my final choice. I never thought I'd be madly in love with the person I'm going to choose. So I'm not shocked that's precisely the situation I find myself in. But I did think I would at least *like* the girl. I know this is a dating show for teens, and there's no proposal at the end – thank god – but the audience is supposed to think we matched. That's the whole point of the Beeloved app and the reason this wild scenario came into being.

Don't get me wrong, the two girls left are great. Even though Desiree is clearly over-the-top and tried to blackmail me, she's good at heart. Ellie is above and beyond the fan favorite going into the final. Still, we're better suited to making content together than in an actual relationship, which she's agreed with me in private. Despite no contractual agreement needing to be made at the end of this, I still feel bad picking someone I don't want a romantic relationship with. Even if we are all on the same page about this story's ending – it feels like I'm lying to the world.

I didn't think I wanted a romantic relationship with anyone. Not until I met Juliet.

Since unearthing our time capsule yesterday, I've been theorizing how I can win her back – thinking through all those grand gestures made at the end of romcoms to show you've learned your lesson. Honestly, Juliet would hate it, which is why I want to do it. Just to see that little annoyed line between her brows when she's pretending she doesn't actually love it.

But I was a jerk. I wouldn't blame her if she didn't want to see me again – no matter the size of my apology.

Filming is due to start in about an hour, and I am supposed to be getting ready, but I've got more important things to worry about. I snuck over to my house to get some breakfast, hoping that would keep me from running into anyone from production, but as I took the far-side walkway round the back of the apartments, I bumped into – not the *worst* people I could run into, but high up there.

'Hey, guys.' I offer a wave to Nathan and Melika, the weak morning sun keeping us in shadow on this side of the building. My bright smile drops the instant I see their icy expressions. 'Right, can I explain?' A flush creeps up the back of my neck, making the tips of my ears burn, which are thankfully covered by my hat.

Nathan crosses his arms, jaw tight. My excitable roommate is gone, replaced by a stone-cold statue. 'I don't think there's anything to say.'

'You were an ass to our best friend,' Melika adds, to my already heavy shame. Giving me a disgusted shake of their heads, they turn, walking away.

'Wait,' I call, shoes scuffing on the cement as I dart to

get ahead of them. I hold my hands up in surrender. 'That accusation is true. I admit. But I want to fix it.'

They share a skeptical look.

'I know Juliet probably hates me right now, and as the loyal friends that you are, you despise me by association. Which is also fair enough. I don't think too highly of myself right now either.' I'm talking at a million miles an hour, misty air puffing between us as I get out my logic before they bolt. 'But I have a plan – well, not a *plan* plan, but I'm working on it. So, if I'm going to win back Juliet, I could use your help.'

Melika clears her throat. 'Well, when that *plan plan* becomes something worth talking about, you know where to find us.'

That went about as smoothly as it could have gone. When I decide what plan to execute, having them help on the Juliet side of things will be handy. I jog back to my apartment and lock myself in my room. The clock ticking down to when I'm due on camera again is like a bomb ready to explode.

'Garrick, you need to get out here,' Tristian calls to me from the living room thirty minutes later. 'You're supposed to be getting ready for the final elimination.'

Time's up.

'I know.' But I don't move. I need a little bit longer to work through my plan. I pulled a Ripley and made a list of all the possible things I could do to win her back. Maybe I'll just give her this. I know how much she loves a checklist, and it would be a lot easier than implementing my rather elaborate plans – but go big or go home, right? I want to make this something she'll remember forever. I don't know if I'll ever be able to block out the memory of abandoning her in that hospital room, but I'm going to try.

Tristian stands from the couch when I come out of my room. 'Finally. Ready to go?'

'No.' I drop my list on the dining-room table. I squeeze my hands into fists, shaking out the nervous energy as they dangle at my side. 'First, I need your help coming up with an idea for a grand gesture to win back Juliet. So, sit and relax as I dazzle and amaze with my impressive suggestions.'

'Great.' He pinches the bridge of his nose.

I glance at my phone. 'Only, give me two seconds before I do it.' We stand in silence, Tristian trying to read my mind, until there's a knock on the door a minute later. I swing it open – a burst of frigid air pouring in as Tyrone walks inside.

'All right, I'm here for operation *Romeo and Juliet*.' His knitted green scarf almost hides his wide grin. 'What do I need to do?' Everyone needs a friend like Tyrone: minimal questions and maximum effort.

I sit Tristian and Tyrone on the couch and flip open my notebook. I got it for the start of school, but I've never cracked the spine. Today, however, feels like the perfect time to break it in.

My heart beats erratically, and I roll my shoulders to focus my attention. 'As you know, I need to win back Juliet. I was a jerk – we don't need to go into it. So, now I need to find a way to tell her how I feel. I want it to be big, top-level romantic. Here's what I got.' I tap my finger against the paper as I read the bullet points.

'Number one: rent a helicopter and fly a banner across the sky, saying *SORRY, I MESSED UP.*' I pause to gauge their faces for a reaction. Both are playing hardball because I don't get much. It can't be that my idea sucks – because it's incredible.

'Sounds expensive,' Tristian says. 'Did you look into the logistics of these ideas?'

'Tristian, please,' I scoff. 'You obviously know I didn't.'

'And since it's January, who knows if it will be stormy. Could ruin the whole thing,' Tyrone adds. 'But I like the direction this is taking. What's next?'

'Two: I get Jin to bake a massive cake – I'm talking twenty, thirty layers with heaps of buttercream frosting and decorations. Then I jump out of it holding an "I'm sorry" sign.' I decide to keep going and get all the ideas out before they have time to rain on my parade. 'Three: I get people at the football, baseball or basketball game – whatever, the sport isn't important – to paint themselves with the letters spelling out "Forgive me, Juliet". Then have it broadcast on a jumbo screen. Four is an old-school method. I get a speaker and hold it up to her window, playing that song that speaks to how much I miss her and can't possibly go on without her. TBD on the song choice.' I point to Tyrone. 'I'm assuming you can help with that.'

He nods slowly but doesn't commit.

I'm halfway through my list and I'm not seeing the reaction I was hoping for, which doesn't bode well for how Juliet will react. I press the notebook into my chest and glare at them. 'Will you two just spill what you're thinking?'

Tristian rubs the side of his face, glancing at Tyrone before he speaks. 'I don't know, G, it just seems like it's too much. Why don't you just tell her how you feel and that you were a complete idiot for letting her go?'

I furrow my brow. 'Weren't you the one who had a grand gesture, at an *airport* of all places, from Imogen?'

There's that stupid, goofy grin on his face again whenever I mention Imogen. It tugs at my gut because I want that with Juliet. 'Yeah, but it wasn't the grand gesture that made me forgive her. It was her finally being honest with me and me with her.'

I ignore my lovestruck brother, who probably has good advice, and turn to Tyrone. 'Any more comments from the peanut gallery?'

He leans forward, resting his elbows on his knees. 'Well, if I'm picking from *your* ideas, I have to say I'm partial to the giant cake. But if I'm allowed to go off the page, I think I have a better idea.'

I match his cheeky grin.

44

RIPLEY

It's finale filming day. I should be excited, and I am, but just so it can all be done and over with. Garrick will pick his 'perfect match', and Mom will be ready to launch her new dating app, with unprecedented hype for her company and a very happy investor. It all worked out exactly how I planned it. So, why do I want to throw up?

I could blame my healing scar and the pain medication, but I know that's not it.

Garrick's choice won't be real. I know this. He knows this. I'm pretty sure everyone on set knows this – the girls included. But it doesn't make the dread in my stomach disappear. He didn't want me. I was too much or too little. Either way, we ended like all love stories do that aren't written for a fairytale – unhappily, in one way or another.

Melika and Nathan are here, trying to cheer me up. They arrive with snacks and an oversized floral arrangement complete with balloon animals. Mom let them leave set early to help nurse me back to health. So, they're no good in the gossip department. Logically, pretending the reality show doesn't exist and moving on with my life might be the better strategy.

But my brain will only rest when it has all the available data. Whether that data is gut-wrenching or not, my brain doesn't care.

I send Mom a string of texts throughout the day, trying to get her to tell me who he chose. Once I know, I can close this terrible chapter in the book of my life and move on to more important things.

However, Mom gives me nothing but radio silence – other than to ask if I took my meds and drank enough water. She said if I wanted to know the show's outcome, I'd have to attend the finale party with everyone else. I don't know what I did to deserve this cruel and unusual punishment.

'No way.' I lean back on the couch. 'I'm recovering. I doubt the doctor would want me partying.'

Melika perches on the arm of the sofa. 'One, your definition of a party and the doctor's are probably not the same.'

'Yeah, my grandma stays on the dance floor longer than you,' Nathan adds, organizing my snacks on the coffee table.

I pinch the bridge of my nose, my eyes tired from looking at my phone all day, waiting for some news. 'Your grandma was an amateur tango champion!'

Nathan grins. 'She was. That woman knows how to bring a dance floor to its knees.'

'So, yeah. Still not going.' They stare me down, so I continue. 'And even if I was considering it – which I am not – I have nothing to wear. None of my dresses will work with the surgery bandage.'

It's not like I was planning to show up dressed to the nines just to prove to Garrick what he's missing. He saw me lying in the hospital bed post-surgery. That's not exactly an image I can override any time soon, no matter how sparkly the gown.

Melika stands, going back to the front door. 'I knew you'd say that,' she calls from the other room. 'So I got you covered.' She returns carrying a garment bag.

'What's that?' I ask, even though it's pretty clear. But perhaps she just brought me a fluffy robe I can burrow myself into while we watch a comfort show on repeat . . .

Her face lights up in the way only fashion can make it do. 'Some of my favorite vintage finds. These dresses will all work with your bandage. I made sure.'

'She did.' Nathan nods. 'She made me try them on with a bandage as a test.'

'I call them Post-op Chic. Now move, we got a ball to get to.'

'Finale live-watch party, and it's tomorrow,' I correct.

'Same dif.' She grabs my arm to help me stand. 'Come on, I have to check if they need alteration anywhere.'

'Melika, I don't even know if I'm going.' I dip my chin, biting my lip to stop crying again. I've been doing it way too much the last few days for my liking.

Nathan takes my other arm. 'At least try them on.'

I sigh, knowing that even my barely stitched wound isn't going to stop them. I appreciate they're trying – really. But I don't know if the party is the right place for me. The idea of seeing Garrick again so soon makes my chest ache. I probably won't be able to avoid him forever since we go to the same school. But since our gym class has ended, and I rarely saw him at school before that, my odds are pretty great I can go the rest of my life Garrick-free. That thought just makes my heart hurt more.

Ugh. Stupid feelings.

'I'm not going to look good in anything,' I argue as Melika and Nathan drag me into my bedroom. I don't know when she rolled a rack in here, but she unzips the bag and hangs the dresses with a dramatic flurry. 'Plus, is a gown really the vibe for this? I thought it was more just a cocktail hour.'

'One can never be overdressed.' Melika is too busy grabbing gowns off the rack and handing them to Nathan to pay me much mind. 'If you want to show that knight that you're doing just fine without his trifling self, then you must dress to kill.'

I spilled my guts to them yesterday about what happened with Garrick. It feels more real now that I've said it out loud. I hate to picture what it was like when they ran into him on set.

I do appreciate the venom in her voice regarding Garrick, but the thing is, I don't hate Garrick as much as I wish I could. I get why he did what he did, and maybe given enough time I would've done it to him. He would've been the one left at home sulking – even though it's kind of hard to imagine Garrick sulking.

I collapse on my bed and hold my hands over my stomach protectively. The pain pills are doing their job, but it still hurts when I move too much. The last forty-eight hours have mostly been me moving from one soft surface to another. I've slept more than I have probably in my entire life.

But these two are not willing to let me rest.

Nathan takes my hand and guides me back to standing. I groan impatiently. 'I know, I know,' he coos. 'But if you don't humor us, we'll never go away. Like a bad smell.'

'You both smell amazing, and you know it.'

'I know, I really do.' Nathan smiles. 'Now, try this one first.'

They help me get into a deep-purple gown with a star constellation pattern across the velvet fabric. The dress has an empire waist, so it's loose around where my bandages are. You can't even tell that they're there.

'I feel like I should be in Bridgerton.' I spin in front of the full-length mirror on the back of my door.

'Be still my heart. If only.' Melika stares at me in the reflection of the glass. 'What do you think?'

I run my hands over the soft fabric. 'It's pretty, obviously. I didn't expect you to pick anything that wasn't. But I'm still not going.'

She takes my hand and leads me back toward the other dresses. 'Then it's not the right dress. I want to put you in an outfit so killer that you know you just have to show off.'

We try a short, light-blue cocktail dress that looks like it would've been perfect in the 1980s but is not my style. Next, there's a nude one with lots of gauzy fabric that makes me feel like I should be in the Fairytale Gardens story, dancing among the princes and princesses I've seen splashed across the theme park merch.

I was never one of those girls who wanted to be the fairytale princess. Or if I was, it was so long ago I've forgotten. But trying on these gowns, even with my scratchy bandage, my heart flutters as I imagine what it must be like to grow up with this as your everyday life, like the Waltons.

We're getting down to the last of the dresses, the rack looking slimmer with each selection being nixed. But one keeps catching my eye. It is a deep emerald green.

Melika gives me a sly smile. 'Don't worry, I saved the best for last.'

The underlayer of the dress is green silk, with hand-sewn lace over the top. The high neckline goes up halfway on my throat, while sheer lace panels cover the long sleeves that are tight around the wrist, billowing out on the arm. It's not tight-fitting per se, but it hugs the bust and drapes out from there in a gentle flow to the bottom. It looks a little 1960s or 70s in shape, but with an elegant classic feel in the fabric – the perfect juxtaposition of styles. Melika knows I love it.

A warm flush covers my body as butterflies zoom around my stomach when I imagine walking into the party wearing this. There's absolutely no way I can leave this dress hidden in my house for only me to see.

I sigh, knowing that they won. 'Well, I guess we're going to a ball.'

45

GARRICK

Gold, white and blue balloons strung up all over the place bombard me when I walk into the watch party. An archway is erected at the entrance, and I feel like I'm going to prom. All I need is a corsage. The Beeloved logo hangs high above the large screen that will air the finale as it goes live on YouTube.

I wasn't expecting so many people to show up, but the modest event room at the hotel is jam-packed. None of the contestants are here, though. That makes me breathe slightly easier.

I keep my hands shoved into my suit pants pockets, holding my head high and my smile bright. I'm excited and I'm also ready to throw up. The nonstop churning in my stomach since last night when I implemented my plan – or at least the beginnings of it – has decided to stay. It's early evening, and I haven't eaten more than a handful of nuts and a protein shake Ivor forced me to drink this morning.

'How does my hair look?' I smooth out the back that keeps popping out. I've never had an issue, but today, of all days, it would be just as unruly as I am.

'Here, let me try.' Aldrich spits on his hand and tries to wet it down.

I expertly dodge him. 'Gross, dude. The last thing I want is to smell like your breath as I attempt to win back my dream girl.'

'Are you ready for this?' Tristian says next to me, Imogen hooked on his arm.

Imogen answers before I can. 'I am so ready for this. I mean, nothing will top *my* romantic gesture. But this is going to be spectacular. I'll make sure to get a good video for the socials.'

'Well, at least I didn't have to commit a scandal beforehand,' I joke. It makes me slightly less shaky.

'Night's still young.' She winks before pulling Tristian away.

Tristian quickly adds before he's out of earshot, 'You got this, G. If not, I'll swing the car around back and be your getaway driver.'

I throw him a fist bump. 'Thanks, T.'

'If this goes right,' Tyrone says, fixing his bow tie. His plaid green-and-red suit is putting my navy one to shame. 'I'd like you to give me the credit in the epilogue, OK?'

My typical witty response slides into place, but I am too nervous to formulate the sentence. So, I go with a simple nod.

'She's going to forgive you, G. She has to.' Tyrone gives me a pep talk before heading in the same direction as Tristian to take their seats to watch the finale.

I grab a water from the snack table, trying to dislodge the lump in my throat. I nearly drop the bottle with my sweaty palms.

'You look so grown up.' Aunt Maria gathers me into a hug. I try to keep my sweat from ruining her silk dress. 'I swear it was just yesterday you and Tristian were swaddled in my arms. The perfect little cherub cheeks – so pinchable.'

I blush as she releases the embrace sooner than I'd like. 'Some would argue I still have those rosy cheeks.'

Aunt Maria smiles, pinching them gently. 'Best of luck tonight, Garrick. I should have known you'd have a final trick up your sleeve.'

'That's why I'm your favorite.' I wink.

She shakes her head, lips pressed together to hide her grin. 'You certainly are my favorite troublemaker.' With one last hug, she leaves me and sits with the rest of the family.

'Can we get a selfie?' someone says behind me. I turn to see a few girls my age in evening gowns, with pins that say 'Be My Beeloved'. I'm used to people asking for selfies, but it's usually the knight they're seeking, not Garrick Walton.

'Uh, yeah, of course.' I don't know how the crowd will react when they see what I have in store ... When they realize they aren't going to get the storybook ending they thought. I squeeze in to get a picture. They giggle and run off, and I am left smiling at the people shuffling in as the clock ticks closer to the start.

I tug at the collar of my dress shirt, the buttons trying to strangle me. I'm wearing a suit for the first time since Mom's funeral – not the same one; I threw that away – but a nice navy blue one with knight head cufflinks and a tie clip that Ms Ripley gifted me. I yank at my sleeves, readjusting myself for the hundredth time.

'Here,' Dad says, motioning toward me. 'Let me fix your tie. It looks like you did it with your eyes closed.'

'Aldrich did it,' I say, not paying attention. I'm too busy trying to see if Juliet showed up. She could be hiding in the crowd, though whenever she's in a room, it's like a beacon calling me – I always find her.

'I'll make sure to check his next.' Dad pulls at the fabric until it's right.

'Thanks, Dad.' I give him a tight smile.

'You did well, my boy. Really. I know we don't always seem like we've got much faith in you, but you have your mother's passion. I see it behind your eyes, just like her. I know when you find the thing that sparks it, you'll be unstoppable.'

I glance up at him, throat thick. 'I wish she was here.'

He smiles softly. 'Me too. But I'm sure she's got the best seat in the house, looking down on us.'

'I'll try not to trip on the finish line.'

'If you do, just make sure you fall over it.' He pats me on the shoulder before walking to his seat.

As the screen lights up with the countdown for the finale, I'm ushered away to stand off to the side, out of sight, behind a backstage curtain. I still haven't spotted Juliet, and I'm worried she might not even show up. Melika and Nathan were supposed to persuade her to come, but she might not if she really hates me.

I stay backstage as the episode starts. Just as the lights dim, I spot her – Juliet, front and center. OK, it's up to me now. Watching myself on the big screen would usually be more pleasurable, but I can't think straight. My hands are sweaty as

I wait for my cue. The noise of the show seems to muffle, and I'm afraid I'll miss the moment I've been waiting for.

But twenty minutes later, we reach the final part of the episode, and on-screen Garrick is about to say who he's picked as his Beeloved when the screen goes black.

All right, Garrick, it's now or never.

46

RIPLEY

The screen cuts off just as Garrick is about to make his pick, and I'm pretty sure the universe is just screwing with me now. Can't it let this torturous moment be over? I guess it did spare me from seeing Garrick in person. I knew they had a ton of people RSVP to attend, but I wasn't expecting the few hundred excited Beeloved fans and press. After a couple of days in a post-surgery haze, the number of attendees is slightly overwhelming, but I'm ecstatic with the response. Mom got what she wanted – at least that makes one of us.

I shift in the fold-out chair, my pain pills only minimally keeping me upright. 'Is someone going to fix it?' I say when Mom doesn't move to correct the blank screen after a few seconds pass. This hiccup is just the kind of thing she'd freak over. She should be out of her seat, instructing every person in this room to get the show back on track. This is the grand finale of her masterpiece.

Yet – crickets.

Mom just shakes her head. 'It's not a problem.'

My eyes narrow. 'Who are you? And what have you done with my real mom?'

She smiles, mischief in her eyes, and now I'm worried because when I look over at Nathan, Anna and Melika for assistance, they're doing the same. Clearly, I missed something. I lick my lips, eyes searching for someone to make sense of this fiasco. The majority of the audience looks just as confused as I do.

Movement up front catches the crowd's attention and I look toward the stage just as Garrick walks on. He's dressed in a dashing navy suit, and I curse the flips my heart does at seeing him again.

No, Ripley, stop.

He taps the top of a microphone, a feedback loop shrieking in response, making us all cringe. 'OK, so I guess this thing is on.' The flash of his smile does not help the heart fluttering I'm experiencing. 'So, you're probably all dying to see who I pick, and rightfully so.'

I glance at the door and wonder if I can sneak past the row of people and leave unnoticed. I might have attempted it if I didn't have a crinkling bandage under my dress and questionable stability. But my stealth mode is not in peak condition at the moment. I should've insisted on an aisle seat. Mom, noticing my fidgeting, squeezes my hand quickly before letting it go.

'The Beeloved team and the whole crew did a fantastic job putting this show and the app together.' Garrick scratches the back of his neck. 'But even with two great girls at the end, I didn't pick either of them.'

Garrick Walton does not get nervous in front of a crowd. That's his preferred spotlight. But he is. And my stomach twists in response. He's also known for going off script, so my nerves are on edge, wondering where this is headed.

'I think the Beeloved app is great. Dating is hard. Love is even harder. And having a safe space to explore is important. So, I have no doubt Beeloved can do exactly all it says. But see, the thing is, I realized I didn't pick Desiree or Ellie because I'd already found my perfect match before this thing started.' Garrick scans the crowd, eyes finding mine, and I'm having trouble breathing.

'Or, more like, my perfect match found me and duped me into starting this whole thing.'

I frown, and the sly, charming smile he offers in response makes butterflies zoom down my limbs, causing a buzz in my ears. Warmth coats my skin and, rationally, I know all eyes are on me, which should freak me out – but right now I can't think of any of them as I look at Garrick.

Perfect match? Is that what he's calling us? I thought we weren't anything.

All I can picture is Anna and Mike. How many times has he apologized for some indiscretion or for never being the supportive partner she deserves? And every time Anna just accepts it and they return to the same pattern over and over. Is that what this is? Garrick apologizes, my stupid heart forgets, and then it starts the vicious circle once more.

'OK, fine,' Garrick continues and I try to pay attention. I need all the information before I can process what's happening. 'I wanted to do this because I didn't think it would work. I was so far off the love train rails I'd never even seen the station. But then Santa went and gave me the greatest gift: someone who thought the same way.'

I can no longer ignore the eyes of the crowd. My cheeks

are tinging pink at the gawking. I will scold Garrick for this unwanted attention later. The audience came for a show, and he's giving them a front-row seat to a live performance. Only Garrick isn't performing; he's as real as I've ever seen him, and that's what's keeping me from getting up and walking out of this room.

Garrick isn't like Mike or any of the husbands Mom's divorced. He'd never just say these things to smooth me over. When he speaks like this, I know he means it. Garrick is all heart, and when he finally gives it to someone, it will be for keeps.

Garrick licks his lips, chin dipping as he formulates his thoughts before seeking me out again. 'Juliet, we both thought love was for chumps, and hey, maybe it is. But I can say with certainty, I'd rather be a chump with you than the smartest guy in the room.'

I laugh despite myself. A logical person might say I'm out of my mind and need to let my brain do the thinking here, not the heart pounding in my chest. But I've let my brain lead me for so long. Thinking, logic and lists were the only way to survive life. However, it seems like I might have been wrong. Love is for chumps, and I stand by it, but we all fall for something along the way. I would very much like it if mine was Garrick Walton.

'So, Juliet, I know I'm no Romeo, but I am a knight, and frankly I think that's a whole lot better. Please say you'll forgive me?' He stumbles on the last sentence, and I see in his eyes that he doesn't know if this display will be enough to win me back.

I make my face blank. 'Garrick, I think we should talk outside.' He did break up with me in a hospital, so it's only fitting that I make him squirm a little in return.

His face drops, and I feel sort of bad. But it's payback for this grand gesture I'm sure he knew I would hate. Which I do, but also, I'm kind of living for this real-life fairytale he's got me starring in.

Still, I want our moment at the end of the story to be only for us.

47

GARRICK

Crap.

I might have misread this situation entirely and royally screwed my chances with Juliet. I knew she wasn't a 'grand display of affection' type of girl, but I thought she'd let me have a pass for the apology. As I follow her outside, the crowd watching us, my mouth goes dry. All the moisture in my body headed to my sweaty palms and forehead. The audience seems enthralled with my declaration to Juliet. There are plenty of heart-eye emojis going around the place – Tyrone was right, love will always win over the masses.

On the other hand, Juliet is not the masses and might think I've lost my grip on reality.

She spins around when we get into the frigid night air. The lights from the windows and lamppost glow brightly. She's holding herself around the middle, still sore, only being a few days out from surgery. 'Garrick,' she says, a huff of frozen breath coming from her warm lips. 'That was . . .' She bites her lip '. . . A lot.'

I offer a half-smile. I still can't read which way her heart is leaning. 'Then I nailed my objective. I wanted –' I start, but she holds up her hand to make me stop.

'Did you really not choose someone?' Her brows pinch together in a deep furrow.

Of course, she'd think about the show first. What if she's thinking I screwed up Beeloved's good press?

I shake my head. 'I couldn't. It wasn't right to do it just for the show when we all knew the only girl I ever wanted was you.' Maybe it's my keen observation skills, but I swear there's a tiny swoon there. 'Going through with it would have been even worse for the optics. Love's all about honesty, I hear. I figured audiences would appreciate it. That *you* might.'

I talked to Ellie and Desiree one-on-one yesterday before we started the elimination to tell them what I had planned. As I guessed, neither of them was too broken up that I wasn't choosing them as my Beeloved. But they still thanked me for being delicate about the situation and hoped I found someone who made me happy. Ellie agreed we could do a collab on her channel with Pierre, and he'd show her the special effects make-up they use on the characters in the park. Desiree actually asked if she could apply to be a princess next summer.

All in all, for them, everything worked out. Let's see if that's true for me and my Juliet.

Juliet bites her thumbnail, frowning. 'I guess fair enough. But this whole situation kind of ruins the premise of the show. The point was the app doing its job.'

Moving closer, I push a strand of hair off her face, my warm hand resting on her flushed cheek. 'Are you kidding? Everyone loves a surprise twist at the end of a story.'

Her brows dip further, and I want to kiss the ache away. 'You left me in a hospital bed and abandoned me when I needed you most.' Tears shine in her eyes.

My chest aches as I see the pain I caused firsthand. 'I know I did. If it helps, I probably hate myself more than you hate me. Even as I sat there breaking your heart, I knew I didn't mean it. But I *really* thought I was saving us both in the long run. Seeing you lying there, all I could think about was my mom and how it destroyed me when she died. Every emotion I've tried to push away since then came flooding back in, and it was like I was drowning.

'Intrusive thoughts kept running through my brain of all the terrible things that could happen to you – or to me. I never *ever* wanted to feel that pain I felt before again. I didn't want you to experience it either. But I realized that *not* having you in my life hurt just as bad. I'm still scared – I'm not ashamed to admit it now – but I'm ready to shake off its control over me and jump headfirst. That is if you are?'

Her eyes still glisten, but I can see the wheels turning behind them. 'Garrick, I decided a long time ago that love wouldn't be in my cards. I was fully prepared to make my way through life without it. I never accounted for another person getting a space in my heart.' She motions between us. 'I . . . I don't know how to do this.'

'Me neither. Clearly.' I place my hand on her cheek. 'We can come up with a pro/con list if that helps ease your analytical brain's worrying. But truthfully, I don't care if the list is only one pro because one is enough for me. There are about a million ways this could fail, but I'd never forgive myself if we didn't at least give it a try. So, I'm willing to give it a go if you are. What do you say, will you be my Beeloved?' I use the cheesy tagline I've been spouting for the whole show, but this is the first time I feel nervous asking it.

I want what I've seen spread across fairytale pages my entire life. That happily-ever-after so many achieve, even if it doesn't last as long as you want – like Mom and Dad. I don't want to miss out on all the good Juliet and I could have together because I'm scared of the ending.

What's the saying? *It's the journey, not the destination.*

She licks her lips, shoulders rising and falling with a heavy breath. 'Yeah. OK,' she huffs, that perfect, elusive smile clearing the clouds away. It might be the dead of winter, but my body has left this place and is doing the limbo in paradise.

'Ever the romantic.' I'm smiling like the fool that I am.

Her cheeks are pink from the cold, or me, giving her the cutest look. I almost lose my breath when I gaze at her. 'Shut up and kiss me.'

'Whatever you say, Juliet.' I pull her in and kiss her like it's going out of style.

EPILOGUE

RIPLEY

Garrick's hand intertwines with mine. 'Are you sure you want to do this?' he says solemnly, trying – and failing – to hide the hint of a smile and the giddiness that makes him unable to stay still as he bounces on the balls of his feet.

The hot sun shines on us, and I squint despite my Fairytale Gardens baseball cap blocking most of the light. I crane my neck to look at the top of the shiny green roller coaster.

Licking my lips, I push my shoulders back until I reach full height. 'Yes, I'm sure. It's time that I go on my first roller coaster.'

It's early summer, and we're done with school for the year. Garrick and I have been going strong since his over-the-top display at the Beeloved party. A few days after, in what I can only explain as a moment of weakness brought on by my love-sick brain, I made him a promise that I'd go on a roller coaster when Fairytale Gardens opened for the summer.

I'm kind of regretting my decision. But I did watch lots of vlogs where people went on this ride, and I think I can handle it.

Today, Garrick is wearing a casual look, in his soft white tee, shorts and black cap. I don't mind the off-duty outfits, but the knight costume will always hold a special place in my heart. 'We could've gone for a smaller coaster to start with,' he says as we get in line. 'Ogre Escape is one of the biggest we have.'

'I know! That's why I chose it. Go big or go home, right?' I offer a shaky smile. No matter how much I've tried to prepare myself for this moment, I still don't like heights or going super fast while strapped to a metal death trap. But all the vlogs assured me it was fun, as did Garrick and everyone else I questioned about the ride experience.

Still, I'm not ruling out mass delusion as the cause of this reaction. I might be dating theme park royalty, but they're still not in the top five destinations I'd choose to spend my time. Unless Garrick is there, then it doesn't matter where we are.

The line moves up, and my hand starts to sweat in Garrick's. 'Don't worry, you can close your eyes,' he whispers. 'I won't tell anyone.'

'My knight in shining armor.' I don't add that closing my eyes might actually make it ten times worse.

He quickly kisses me on the cheek, and my knees go weak. You would think after nearly five months together it would start to wear off – these excitable butterflies zooming around my stomach. But it just gets better every day. Is this how it is supposed to feel? Love? Is that why people do it?

I guess I'm one of the masses now because I am hopelessly, madly in love with Garrick Walton.

Despite the change in programming, by Garrick going entirely off script for the reality show's finale, it was a hit. Everyone loved the ending, and even though it didn't exactly work with the Beeloved app's promise of finding your match, it didn't seem to matter. When it debuted the next day, it was the most downloaded app that week and it's continued to be successful ever since. I guess Mom was right: people love love.

According to Garrick, FTG also experienced a fantastic boost in sales, both with this summer's tickets and the events they hosted earlier this year before the park opened. Plus, he's got his fencing camp up and running – with a waiting list of kids eager to join. Everyone wanted a taste of the magic Garrick displayed on-screen. I knew the stress of Fairytale Gardens' success weighed heavily on him, and now that there is a light at the end of the tunnel, I think he sees all the possibilities the future could bring. He even floated the idea of attending culinary school after graduation to level up FTG's catering game. I won't hold him to it, but it's been nice to see the change in his attitude about the future.

Mom's been doing better since the success of the app. So much so that she's taking up new hobbies – including cooking. Anna, Garrick, Molly, new baby Teddy (born absolutely perfect in every way four months ago) and I have been subject to several new recipes she's learning in her Tuesday class. It's ... interesting. But it has been cool to have Mom home and interacting with us on more than just a business level.

I wish I could say that now that I have experienced love myself I get why Anna and Mike are still together. But I still don't see it. Garrick supports me in any way I need him, and I offer the same in return. We don't have to spend every waking minute together, but we know that if we call the other person, they will drop everything to help. Mike is just never going to give that to Anna. But I guess what I learned is that you can't make someone see something they aren't ready to see. I just hope that Anna realizes how much she's worth and that if Mike wants to keep such an amazing human he'll have to change his ways.

We get to the front of the line, and it's now or never. I stumble a little, my feet stopping me from moving forward despite my brain insisting we can do this.

'Juliet?' Garrick raises an eyebrow. He's back to calling me Juliet. And I don't hate it – I love it, actually. I guess I just needed to find my Romeo.

Ew, gross. I can't believe I just said that. But also even more gross is that it kind of made me swoon.

I shake my head, hair falling slightly out of my ponytail. 'I'm fine. Let's go.' I pull it back into place as we slide into the roller-coaster ride vehicle. It's made to look like you're on a cart pulled by horses as you try to escape the fearsome ogre. They lower the metal safety bar, the restraints locking us in. I give them a little jiggle to make sure they're secure, and they appear to be sturdy.

'Aren't you glad I let you do a safety inspection this morning?' Garrick smiles. I thought he gave everyone this same one, but I now realize that this one is special for me.

'It's called being thorough,' I counter. But mostly Garrick offered it because he knew it would make me feel better. He does little things like this all the time, like helping me create a list when I have to make a decision about colleges, or giving me the pros and cons of where we should go for dinner. I don't think he's into that, but he knows it means a lot to me.

Which is why I find myself on a roller coaster right now. Because I know it means a lot to him. And that's what relationships are about: give and take.

Garrick takes my hand, linking it with his as the ride begins its upward ascent.

'I got you, Juliet. I won't let anything happen to you.'

And as the vehicle reaches its peak, ready to plunge into a thrill ride I'm not sure I'm prepared for, I know that no matter what, I'll always have his hand in mine.

Another happily-ever-after for the storybooks.

Acknowledgments

Christmastime at Fairytale Gardens was so fun to write. Blending the holiday season with the magic of the theme park really made my writer heart happy.

Thank you to everyone who helped bring this series to life. Seeing all the responses to the books has been such a joy. Watching people hold this little book I created in their hands never gets old. To booksellers and reviewers who took the time to review the book or recommend it, thank you for your kind words.

I wouldn't be here without the support of my mom and dad, who constantly build me up and give me the courage to pursue my dreams and celebrate all my successes.

Thank you to my fantastic editor, India Chambers, for being the best cheerleader and partner. It has been the best experience working with you. You made this process so smooth and enjoyable.

My wonderful agent, Jem, thank you for being such a support in this journey, and I'm so grateful to have you on my team.

Once again, Louisa Cannell knocked it out of the park with the cover illustration. It's so perfectly magical and brings the story to life.

Jess Dunne, thank you for all your help in getting this book polished and into the hands of readers with ease. Debs, your copy-editing skills are a magic all their own.

To the whole Penguin team, thank you for all the love for this series.

To the amazing people who helped shape this story from its early beginnings: Anna (for being my constant sounding board), Elizabeth (who always builds me up) and Scarlett (always there to scream in all caps with me).

ABOUT THE AUTHOR

Cara has been a storyteller since a young age when she would spend hours coming up with intricate lives for her Barbies. When she is not lost in her world of stories, she can be found drawing digital art, cooking and binge watching her favourite TV shows for the hundredth time. She lives in Salt Lake City, Utah, but has never been skiing. Cara also writes adult novels under the pen name Vienna James.